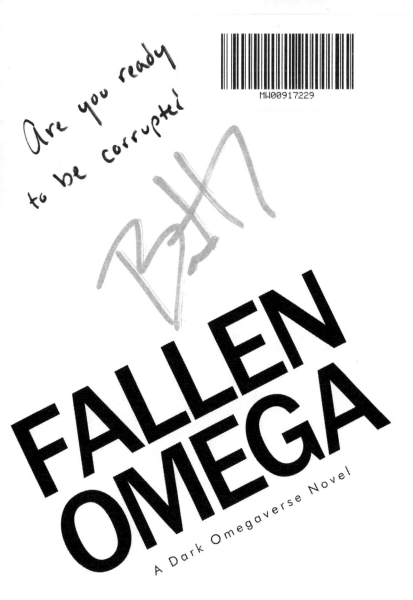

Are you ready to be corrupted!

MW00917229

FALLEN OMEGA

A Dark Omegaverse Novel

BROOKE HARPER

H.A.B. Publications LLC

Illustrated Cover Design: Quirah Casey - Temptations Creations

Interior & Formatting: Jennifer Laslie

Editing & Proofreading: Coby Bettley – 3Crows Author Services LLC

TRIGGER WARNING

This book contains dark themes and highly sensitive topics.

For a full list of triggers, visit Brooke Harper's website:

https://authorbrookeharper.com/fallen-omega/

FALLEN OMEGA

All my life, my dad and I lived as outcasts in Starlight City.

We dodged the council's oppressive laws. But when a sudden accident takes his life, I'm left alone, undocumented, and ultimately screwed.

With my heat coming and no drugs to help me through it, desperation drives me into the hands of the Unholy Trinity. Dante, Knight, and Reaper are three deadly alphas ruling the city's criminal underworld, and they offer me temporary protection—but only *if* I follow their rules:

1. Sing in their club:

2. Obey them without question

And, most importantly...

3. Don't sleep with any of them, no matter what our primal urges say.

Easier said than done.
They might call me Angel, but these dark gods are determined to corrupt me.

And now, with an old enemy and the council after me, I don't have much of a choice.

To save myself, I'm going to have to let myself fall.

To the girlies who swoon over fictional alpha-holes but will cut any man who dares act like one to them in real life.

CHAPTER
ONE

Lizette

The thunder rattles my bones as the rain comes down hard.

It's like the atmosphere knows the maelstrom inside of me. The pain. Frustration. All the crap life's thrown at me.

But apart from Dad's death—nothing is going to fill the giant, gaping hole inside of me—being an omega is the worst.

No one really explains how it rips you apart. How it turns you into a seething slave of hormones and a basic instinct and urge to breed.

I don't want any of that.

Heats turn you into a miserable monster, a ball of pain in desperate need of mating.

It turns me into an animal.

And I've only had *two*.

They were excruciating.

My oncoming heat terrifies me. It's going to be worse than before. I just know it.

The thunder crashes again and lightning flashes bright.

1

The office I'm in is tucked right at the back of the restaurant where I work, where a number of the waiters and back of house staff got into a fight.

Over me.

I sit and stare at the storm, glad it's drowning out the voices and the din of the restaurant.

The thing with my heat is, when Dad was alive, he took care of the worst of it with the drugs he got me. Experimental. Black market. The kind that dampened it all down, the kind that let me function—sort of.

"Lizette?"

My insides clench painfully and a dull ache beats, like the precursor to a stomach bug, but so much worse. I school my features and turn to one of my bosses, Jessa.

"Yes?"

She doesn't sit. I'd say that's not a good sign, but being dragged out of my shift and being told to wait in the office is bad, too. All in all, it's rounding out to be a shit show of an evening.

"Kev asked me to handle this," she says.

She's about forty and nice...nice enough that she gave me an under the table job at an almost fair wage.

"Handle what?"

Jessa sighs. "I'm sorry." She holds out an envelope, and I stare at her. "We're letting you go."

My throat tightens right away. "I work hard. I always cover shifts when you need it, and—"

"You're an omega, Liz," she says, dropping her voice on 'omega' like it's either a dirty word, or something to be revered. I don't know, and I don't care.

My ears start to ring.

"The fight? That was over you. And there are complaints about your scent. It's bad right now, too intoxicating, apparently, and..." She shakes her head, pushing the envelope at me. "I can't afford to lose most of the male staff."

2

"I didn't start it. I don't want—I'm not looking for a mate." The word leaves bitterness coating my tongue.

"We can look the other way a lot, but not if it brings our business down, or worse, the police or Council poking around. You're pretty, you can get another job. Or find your alpha and pack. If you were mated, it wouldn't be so bad. You could come back."

I swallow and stand. Pride wants me to stalk out without the envelope and into the night.

Common sense makes me take it, so I shove it into my jeans pocket, and head for the door.

"Lizette, your coat and bag are outside in the hall. Take the emergency exit."

I don't look back. Shame burns deep as I bundle into the coat and grab my bag. I stalk out the door and into the storm.

The money isn't much, I already know that. It's probably half of what I usually earn. But I need it. Every damn penny.

The rain pelts me as I race into the night.

What I want is to go home, burrow into the nest Dad set up for me so I could get through this hell with more comfort: my third heat.

Some celebration

To me, it's something to be as shunned as we omegas were.

Dad never told me why he chose the life he did, and then he died, stopping me from finding out anything more. Why we were shunned by the Council and the nice packs. He didn't like that life, and me...I don't even remember anything but it being me and him against the world, living on the edges of society, making our life... Just me and him.

Since I was small, he taught me that I'm more than breeding stock, more than animal instinct.

"I miss you, Dad," I whisper, as the sky lights up bright and thunder rumbles. The rain makes it hard to see, and it's really pelting down now.

I duck into a covered doorway for a business that's been closed for years. Instead of heading to the home I'm probably going to lose, I'm journeying into the seedy and dangerous part of town called The Hollows, where anything can be bought on the black market. For a price.

Like the drugs I need, and finally have the lump of money to buy.

"Things are going to be okay." It's a lie I like to tell myself.

I crouch down and pretend to get something from my bag as I count the cash Jessa gave me. I slide the amount for the drugs in my left shoe, and the money that'll make up my rent in the right. Then I straighten and wait for the rain to stop, or at least lessen.

That dull ache inside starts to edge toward pain and an emptiness creeps into my stomach.

Shit. This stupid biological thing in me cost me my job and now it's going to leach sanity if I don't get those drugs.

At least, that's how it felt the previous two times, and now Dad's not here to care for me, and I know this one is going to be so much worse. There's the grief, being alone, the now precarious situation with the roof over my head.

None of it helps. It just weighs me down further.

But I can't stand here feeling sorry for myself. This is the manageable part of heat, where my pheromones might go crazy, *I* might go crazy, but it hasn't yet started, not really.

So, I need to find those drugs before all hell breaks loose.

All I can do is go to the Hollows, the part of the city Dad took me to the last time so I'd know…just in case I had to get there on my own.

My heart hurts.

He was always overly careful like that.

I miss him. It still feels like a part of me has been carved out from my chest.

I start walking, out into the rain, head low, the hood from my sweater up from under my coat, and I keep to the shadows.

4

The cops love this part of town, and it's been etched into me that I need to always be alert, to always stay as invisible as I can.

Otherwise...

Cops work for the Council.

They'll come for me.

I'm an omega, one who's undocumented, a prize. A brood mare.

I shudder and turn left, down a dark alley, past a bar that doesn't have a sign. When I reach the place I'm looking for, I knock six times.

A slat opens.

Whoever it is on the other side doesn't speak.

"I'm Connor Roth's daughter. I need O-blocker. I have money."

The slat shuts.

The door creaks open.

"Come in."

I step inside.

"Crap," I mutter, almost two hours later.

The rain's slowed to a slight drizzle and the storm has passed, but with it comes complications.

For one, it took way longer than it should have to get my drugs through Deckard Price, a friend of Dad's, someone he knew before I was born. He made sure the price was fair.

But even though Deckard's an austere man, one who Dad always told me I can trust, I wonder if the trust only held when Dad was alive.

Dad said I could trust him, if I need to, and right now, I need to.

Loyalty is scarce in the Hollows. Money speaks here and

the Council's reach doesn't extend too deeply into the seedy belly of this place.

I didn't offer Deckard anything like information—not that I know anything—I just grabbed the O-blockers and left.

But now it's after midnight and with the drizzle, it means any pheromones I'm releasing won't be dampened by the rain. I take one of the pills, dry-swallowing it, and wait in the dark for people to pass. Then I start off, taking a circuitous route home.

In my head, I take stock of my situation. It keeps me calm, stops me running, and lets me take note of anyone who might follow. The situation isn't looking good, though. There are no silver linings outside of the O-blockers.

Here, the cars are old and banged up, some stripped clean, and garbage lines the street as grass pokes through the pavement cracks.

Starlight City is a place of contradictions. It's a whimsical name for a dark urban sprawl, the perfect spot to disappear into if heads are kept low. Ever since I was little, when I went with Dad on a delivery run—he never explained what he did and by the time I was old enough to start asking, I was old enough to know not to ask—to the suburbs, I wanted to live there.

The big houses, pristine streets, and voluminous trees. The lawns and gardens and glittering shopping strips and malls. There are places in the city that glitter, too, but those buzz with business men and women.

And the Council.

I have enough money with my sporadic second job of scrubbing floors of businesses that I can pay rent for the next month. And if I sell some things, I'll maybe be able to stretch to next month after that.

But I need to get through this coming heat first.

It could be tomorrow, or in a few days. It's hard to tell when it'll hit since the first time just came onto me, while the second time eked out in little trails of misery until I was in excruciating pain.

The pills take the edge off, dampen me. Some omegas apparently can function like they're a beta or a delta on the blockers. Feel like they're not in heat at all.

Not me.

I'm still in pain, but the drugs make it so I can manage.

The crunch of tires catches my attention.

There's a car, and it's following me. I know because while I don't look, it's no longer background traffic noise but a steady pace that's caught up to me. By staying behind me at the same distance, its pace in sync with mine.

My heart thumps hard.

I'm still in the middle of no man's land, where the gang, the Unholy Trinity, have bars and clubs and probably brothels. I don't go to that part of the Hollows, just the places where I can do business...rather, where my father did business.

I speed up a little.

So does the car.

I slow.

The car slows, too.

White hot fear burns through my blood.

Suddenly there's a hiss of brakes, followed by the slam of two doors. Swallowing down the terror past the tightness in my throat, I turn, just as someone grabs me. I'm slammed into the steel of a body.

"Looky here. A pretty lil' omega by the smell of her, out past curfew."

It's a cop. Big, strong, burly. His friend is wirier, but still strong. All muscle. I know because he has a hold of me and I'm plastered against him.

The one speaking smirks, his ugly face contorted with something akin to hate. I'm not even sure why. I don't know him.

"There's no curfew," I croak out.

"Hear that, Harry? She's a cop now. Says there's no curfew. Is there a curfew?" he asks.

Harry leans down and mutters against my ear, the stench of garlic on his breath. They're betas, so they're just taunting me, probably bored.

I don't want to think of the other possibilities.

"There's our curfew," the one named Harry says, "for all pretty girls who're coming from the Hollows. What were you there for?"

"I was just walking home," I say.

The big one nods. "From where?"

I can't say work. "V-Visiting a friend."

"What did you buy, and where are your papers?" The big cop doesn't wait, just takes my bag and starts pawing through it. He pockets the drugs with a guttural laugh, and then takes the few dollars I keep in there. "No papers, Harry."

"Fuck, Andy, she's like an escaped exotic animal. Maybe there's a reward?"

"Maybe we'll get a raise if we take her in an' hand her over to the Council." He digs out my wallet and shakes it. "Not even a library card."

They both laugh as Harry shoves me at Andy. "What's your name, girly?"

"It's not illegal to walk in Starlight City," I say, trying to stand strong and not piss them off. "I didn't...I didn't bring my papers."

"We'll help you out. What's your name?"

Panic blurs my vision. I'm the world's worst liar. And if I refuse, they'll take me in. I know, I've heard stories. If they take me in, they'll find out. At least this way, I have some kind of chance.

"I-It's Lizette Roth."

They're silent a beat.

"Well, Lizette, seems we're gonna have to arrest you for vagrancy. So—"

"Let her the fuck go."

Their faces change, and they do just as the mysterious voice commands. I spin.

A sleek black car sits there shining, expensive, with its windows tinted. It's the kind of car I wouldn't hear. A motor runs with an almost silent purr.

The window winds down, and I try to see in but whoever it is with the voice that could cause heat in the most literal sex-soaked sense beckons Andy over. "You, here, now."

I have no clue who is speaking, but they've got power and money. Voices murmur and Harry motions at my bag that lies in a puddle, contents spilled. "Just get your shit, bitch."

With a bit-back sigh, I do. I want to ask for my pills, but I don't dare.

As I stand, I stagger. I'm hit by the most intoxicating scent.

Maybe it's the rain and the storm, but it's like the heavy air before a pending storm over an ocean mixed with sex, heady with musk and saltiness. I breathe in deeper. I can't stop myself. The earthiness turns into that petrichor aroma of rain I adore. Fresher and more defined than the rain I ran through.

I'm in love, lust, filled with hunger. I could breathe this scent in endlessly and live out my days.

Naturally, my body wants to move closer, seek it out, and as I look around, all I can do is stare at the black car.

It's him.

The man inside it.

He's the source.

Something's buzzing, annoying me.

"Did you hear me?" snaps Andy. "You can go."

"Can I—"

"Go."

That *go* is dark, commanding in ways I don't understand and it comes from the car. I want to stupidly ask for my pills, but any confidence I have left strips itself from me. I stumble as I obey, taking off down the street.

I don't stop my brisk almost run until I'm breathing wild behind the front door of my apartment. I lean against the door, chest rising fast.

The urge to leave, to obey, seeps away, and I start to reach for the door, to go back and find the man who smelled like my heaven. A man I've never, ever seen.

Only heard.

Only *smelled*.

I drop my hand and weariness overcomes me, and with it, the dull ache returns.

No more pills means a rough time for me when it all starts.

I drag myself to the pile of soft blankets Dad got me and burrow into them. Maybe by tomorrow, it'll pass.

Until then, I need to sleep.

CHAPTER

TWO

Lizette

I stare at the official looking letter again.

Disbelief wars with panic.

The one O-blocker tablet I took helped, but the effects are wearing off and I don't need this. My heat is coming. I don't know when it's going to hit full on, but the loss of the drugs is a punch in my gut.

Maybe I shouldn't have taken the one. Could it make things worse?

My head buzzes, and I force myself to think.

I don't work until tomorrow. It's only a few hours in the afternoon, but after rent, after losing the pills, after losing my other damn job, I'm going to have to try and scrounge together enough money for more.

If I eat only noodles and rice, I should be able to afford the O-blockers. And there are off cuts of vegetables that get sold super cheap, usually for pets, but...

The pills. I need them.

I thought I might wait another day—it's already been two since the storm and the job-loss and the cops and the mystery man, but now...with this...Do I even dare go back to the Hollows?

No, I *have* to.

Maybe I'll go this afternoon. No one's going to expect me to turn up during the day.

"But first, before I open this fucking letter, I need a drink," I say to myself.

There's cheap whiskey and wine. The wine's in a box. Dad was never a big drinker, so to him, it made sense that if he wanted a glass of wine, he wasn't about to waste the majority of a bottle.

I pour some, take a swallow and then set the glass down.

I stare once more at the envelope. My name in print. The embossed logo of the Council.

And their HQ here in Starlight City.

Sliding my finger through the unlicked part of the envelope, I rip it open. A sheet of paper and a photo falls out. A photo?

I pick it up, stare at it, and read the letter.

Numbness spreads.

"Wine is not going to do it."

Nope, not at all. I stomp off and grab the whiskey, open it and take a swallow. The burn takes flesh, it seems, on the way down.

Finally, I sit again and set the bottle down.

And read.

Miss Roth,

It's come to the Council's attention that you are both undocumented and unmatched. We seek to rectify this immediately.

Please find enclosed your future alpha mate, Craig Edmonton, from Hover Valley. The pack leader is a fine and suitable match for you. Please present yourself at our office at 2pm next Monday for omega status registration.

Our number is included should you have any questions.

Regards.

S. Pemberton.

"God, how..." I gulp down air as I look at the photo of Craig Edmonton of Hover Valley, again. "Gross."

I'm not shallow or judgy. But...I'm twenty-one, almost twenty-two. I haven't even started living yet. Dad didn't want me to think about settling down, not until I was older, and met someone. That's how he put it: *meet someone.*

Not matched with a mate.

An alpha.

Just *someone.*

He talked of love.

He wanted me to learn and while college was off the table, I'd been attending classes. Not putting in work, obviously, but attending. Dad's death two months ago put an end to that, and...

Shit, girl, don't cry. Just don't.

My eyes burn and ache, but I'm not sure there are any tears left. The problem with grief is it settles, sits, the ache and pain and sadness get...not boring, but it wears you down until there's nothing. Just ash.

I breathe in and look at the photo again.

This man is a mate, a means to an end. He's got lips like a dead fish, a flattened, misshapen nose. Cruel, hungry eyes, like they don't care about who's taking the photo, only whatever better thing awaits.

And worse? He's gray, balding, and probably about sixty.

He's older than my father.

The man makes my stomach heave.

Who the hell reported me? The cops?

But they had my name, that's it. Those guys were tiny fish, looking to scare me. Maybe even screw me in exchange for them letting me go. Of course, they'd probably have still arrested me, but...

A cold clarity hits.

Not them.

The man with the deep, sexy voice. The commanding voice that somehow made me obey. The man who smelled of salt and dark, rich earth, and the air of a storm. He smelled like rain.

And he drove an expensive car. The cops had rushed to him.

An alpha, I'm thinking, and...oh god. I'm betting he's Council and somehow found me out.

I crush the photo and snatch up my cell, dialing the number on the letter.

A woman answers. "Starlight City Pack Council, how may I help you?"

"There's been a mistake," I say. "I got a letter and a photo and—"

"Just a moment, I'll patch you through to the right department."

Horrible, loud music assaults me, and I'm almost ready to hang up when the music stops and a crisp voice says, "Susan speaking."

"I got a letter, and a photo, and there's been a mistake. I'm not pack material. We're exiled so I can't be eligible for a match."

"What's your name?"

I hesitate, but the clack of a keyboard comes through the line.

"Is this Lizette Roth?" Susan rattles off my address and date of birth. The real one, not the one I've been putting down on job applications. Even cash-in-hand places want some details.

"Yes." I'm gripping my cell so tight it's a wonder it doesn't break.

"First, I'm sorry for the loss of your father," she says, and that old longing I've hidden deep inside me, the one that always wanted a friend, rears up.

It's the worst moment.

This woman isn't my friend and isn't looking to be friends. She's just using her phone voice.

"You see the best in people, Liz," Dad used to say, "but you have to hide it down deep. It's both one of your best and worst attributes."

I'm lonely. My life means one of loneliness. That's all.

I wait.

"But according to our records, your father was the one exiled, not you." Her voice drops. "Actually, we didn't know about you until last night. You have a match now, in Hover Valley."

"I don't want to move two states away." I swallow. "And I don't want—he's old. Don't I get to pick?"

"Hon, you can't be in the world without a chaperone at your age, unclaimed, when you're an omega. And this isn't my decision. It comes from the top. Be here at two on Monday. Actually, make sure your afternoon's cleared because after we register you, there's an orientation, some exams—"

"Exams?"

"Medical." She says this soothingly, as if medical exams make it better. "If you're in heat, call the special number provided in the envelope. We'll reschedule, see if you need to be moved. There are a lot of things in place to protect and help you."

There's a thin card in the envelope that is stuck to the bottom corner. I pull it out, only half listening now as she talks.

I'm still a mess, heart pounding, fear hot and sharp, but I can't do anything and what she's saying is just the whole

Council propaganda spiel. The real things of importance are that they know about me, and I'm not exiled.

I've heard rumors of digital chipping with some omegas, but I don't know if that's true. That's just what Dad had said he'd heard but he didn't tell me his thoughts on it, only to be careful.

But what Susan said about the help, that sounds like making sure they have all the information about me so I'm completely on their records. And...I don't want to be.

She pauses, and I say, "I thought...I thought there were alphas I could, when I wanted, choose from."

"You don't want the wrong man, Hon. Craig is a good pick. Experienced. And you've been put down for a Council sanctioned match," she says. "Even if I wanted to, I couldn't do a thing. Now..."

She keeps talking and I just stare at the card. I've never been to Hover Valley. I don't even know about the packs there. But it's not huge, and he's so old, so mean looking. And he looks like he'd slobber on me.

I don't want my first kiss to be with him.

Hell, I don't want my first, middle, or last *anything* to be with that man.

I put the card with the number down and listen to her finish.

"So, you understand, right? If you can't make it because of your heat, call that number." Her voice drops. "Don't try and run, Hon. The Council will find you."

My hand coils hard. "I wouldn't." But now, that's a shining option to consider.

Hiding is a problem all its own for an omega.

"Good. So take care, bring all the documents you have, and be ready for the interviews and the exams, got me?"

I need to be calm, play the game. "Okay, I'll do all that. Thanks, Susan."

When we hang up, I bury my face in my hands, and shudder out a breath.

My phone buzzes and it's work. My second job.

"Liz?" The gruff voice of Gambon rumbles against my ear. "Sorry, kid. This might come as a shock but we gotta let you go."

"No!"

"Word's out about the Council. And you clean some places where, at night, things might get...complicated."

"I need the money, Mr. Gambon." The panic's back, claws deep. "Please."

"Sorry. My hands are tied. Good luck, kid."

Even though I'm sitting, I crumple. I can't lose my last job. I have a month here as I just paid rent, but when it's up? And I need those pills.

"Oh, Dad," I whisper. "How am I going to do this without you? We didn't even prepare..."

Because he was strong and healthy and the accident—not an accident, my brain whispers—took him suddenly. And now...now I'm scrambling in the mud.

I pour a second drink and then another. Then I pour one more into the wine glass and head into the kitchen to take stock.

There isn't much in there. Emergency canned soup and pasta sauces. Canned tuna. Rice. Pasta. Ramen. A couple of onions and sweet potatoes.

The perishables in the fridge will go first, but if I'm smart, frugal, I can do it. Get through without spending much.

When the heat's over, I—

The Council.

I'm going to have to move. Run. Hide.

I can't work here. Maybe I can find another job somewhere else. Somewhere I can disappear. Somewhere, I think, like Starlight City.

But first, I need to get those damn pills, and if I leave it any longer, it'll be dark out again.

I down the drink, grab my coat, and tie my hair back.

One thing I know for certain: I'm not marrying Craig Edmonton.

"I wouldn't."

The voice is a different deep to the man in the car. This is full of darkness and there's an edge I don't know what to do with, an edge that makes me uneasy.

Then again, strangers always have.

The Hollows are about five blocks over. I turn. He's in the shadows of an abandoned building's doorway, but I can smell him.

He's dark. Like rum, bittersweet chocolate, coffee, a hint of smoke. He's delicious smelling, mysterious, and I can see him being touted as intoxicating, but not to me, not like that man. I can see other omegas, other women losing their shit over this one but the hype is overrated.

Whoever he is, he's an alpha—the darkness seems to hold the same power as the alpha from the car. I can feel it, and it makes me edgy in a way I really don't like.

I don't trust him.

This isn't about attraction or my oncoming heat. It's just him.

I don't like him...

"Wouldn't what?" I ask because I can't help myself.

He moves his head and dark blond glints as some light hits him, and I can see a tall, strong man. Good looking. But he's mostly in the shadows.

"Wouldn't go where you're going. The Hollows. Word's out that the Council's got its eye on you."

I frown. "I don't talk to strangers."

"You're talking to me." A lighter flares, and I glimpse his beauty in that golden flash. Smoke drifts down.

"You talked first."

"So I did. Keep away. I can smell you from here, you know. Delightful. Others might see that as you being available and theirs for the taking."

"They know me—" I stop myself. I've no idea who this is. I never do this. Never talk to strangers. He could be anyone. Council, a degenerate. Dangerous. And yet...it's almost impossible to stop.

"And they know you're now on the radar of the Council. You've got an exiled father, too. Keep away from the Hollows."

Panic nibbles. "Who are you?"

"A ghost, little omega, nothing but a ghost. And watch out for the Unholy Trinity. They're behind this."

Now panic flares bright. "What—"

"All of it, Lizette. All of it. So go home, build a fucking nest like a good little omega. And then...?"

My gut plummets. He knows me. "And then what?"

"*Run.*"

CHAPTER

THREE

Lizette

One pill isn't enough.

I groan, curling up like some kind of addict in withdrawal. I wish for the millionth time that I was just a regular ol' girl. A beta. A gamma. Literally *anyone* else.

On the TV, some terrible movie is playing something I don't have to think about as I burrow deeper into my blanket nest.

Whoever that blond man was...he's just as bad at the one who reported me. The Council guy.

But the thing is, thinking of the man who gave me some convoluted warning doesn't drive me crazy. It doesn't do anything. Except I know he used his alpha command to make me rush home. Just like the Council man used his to warn off the cops.

And land me in trouble.

Oh, hell...

I suck in air. There's something about the Council man

that won't leave me alone. That makes my body thrum and invades dreams.

I can still smell him.

I can conjure him from my memories, dark and hot and pure sex. Even though I didn't see him, I know this. I envision him from his intoxicating scent if I close my eyes and breathe in deep. It twists my insides, makes me ache, and sends painful urges shooting through me. It's like I want to claw my way out of my body and find him and...

And...

I laugh. The sound's so pitiful that I pull the covers over my head.

And what? Sniff him to death? Lick him all over? Jump him?

I push him from my mind and drag my computer under the covers. I go to a discussion forum. It's for omegas, and I scroll through the posts about the mate crap and posts from some of the almost evangelical girls who see their status as a higher calling. Finally, I come to what I need.

How to cope.

There's so much advice, ranging from rubbing cut lemon into your armpits at midnight—like, what? —to going out and getting laid.

I emphatically do not want either of those, and while the word *sex* sets off all kinds of images with a man I've never seen, just smelled and heard, I want that one least of all.

I'm not a machine to make babies.

I'm not.

What's always funny is no one ever suggests over-the-counter pain killers because it's not *that* kind of pain. It's different, an urge that turns into agony if left alone, even with the blockers I felt the last two times. What's going to happen now?

Then I see something about alcohol.

I go through the forum page. There are posts from

hundreds of girls and women talking about how drinks can dull the sensations and urges.

It's preferable to naked moonlight dancing, sex with strangers, and lemon halves in the pit after dark.

"Fuck it. I need a second hot water bottle."

I get up and grab the wine, the whiskey, and a glass. Not that I intend to drink it all at once. I only plan on getting up for bathroom breaks and maybe a meal.

I pour a glass and take a sip, willing it to work.

I might be a little tipsy, but I feel better. Or is that numbness?

I roll up to sitting, ready for another drink, but the bottle and the bladder of the box wine are empty. Pain knifes low through me.

Part of me wants to believe it's all a psychosomatic response. I'm good, and the heat's a few days away. It's just my finding out there's no more booze left that's setting off the pain.

But I don't think so.

The pull in the depths of me, which combines with a painful ache like an itch that's been left too long unattended and needs to be scratched, tells me otherwise.

Heat's coming.

It's instinctual, the knowledge. Beyond pain or aches or misery.

My whole being knows.

The drugs took down the pounding urge, the edges of agony, but for me, they didn't quite manage to wipe it out entirely.

Just like the booze tried to conceal it and... Shit, is my body metabolizing the alcohol faster than it should? Because tipsy isn't where I should be. I should be impending-hungover-tomorrow level of drunk. But I'm not.

The word I'm looking for, I suspect, is *fuck*.

"I miss you, Dad. I..." I take a breath, hugging the hot water bottle to me as I get to my feet. "I need you."

This little threadbare apartment is full of him. Not his things, although they're here, but him. Like his essence has soaked in, like this is safety and home, because of him.

And now...

"How am I going to do this without you?" I hug the water bottle tighter, its contents sloshing in protest. "I don't want to. I...I just want you back. You and me against the world? And I fucked up. They know about me. I didn't exist to the stupid Council until..."

Until that alpha who smelled so unbelievably good pulled up and had me reported.

I'm going to have to run.

As soon as my heat's done, I have to run.

I just don't know where.

The TV chatters on. Bursts of incidental music swell and crash like waves in a maudlin sea. I glance at the screen. Some horrible, sappy romance plays. I scrounge for the remote control and click it off, letting silence settle.

The idea of leaving this place horrifies me. The apartment is so entwined with Dad that it would be like killing him myself.

But I have to.

What is there for me but a mate I've never met? Who I know I don't want.

Maybe if the cruelty hadn't been captured in his eyes, or his lips hadn't looked so fish-like...

Or if he wasn't older than my dad.

As the booze-induced softness dissipates, panic starts to swirl and bubble. I need...I have to go, get more to drink. Get through this heat any way I can and tonight's the last night I can go out, stock up, before I'm hit hard. Tomorrow.

It'll hit me tomorrow.

Swallowing down bile, I shower, dress. Combat boots, a loose floral dress, and Dad's old leather biker jacket. I'm so beside myself I don't even indulge in singing in the shower.

While I haven't sung properly or to anyone but myself since Dad was killed in that car accident, I always sing in the bathroom. It's a ritual, something Dad liked. He always told me it would ring through to wherever he was in the apartment and sounded better than the radio.

Brushing teeth, doing my skincare, getting ready for work, I'd sing in the bathroom.

But not tonight.

I can't. That gnawing inside with sharp, painful edges strangles my voice.

Or maybe it's what I'm about to do.

I shove most of my money into my socks, down deep below the top edge of the ankle high boots. And then I pack a small backpack. I keep it light.

Two pairs of underwear, a bra. Socks. Jeans and a hoodie. Sneakers.

It's light and something I hope won't arouse suspicion if someone comes in. Then I just leave it by the door with black pants and a top on it, like that's what I take to work.

Next, I take important things. Dad's tablet that's has everything I need on it, thumb drives, an external hard drive. Some polaroids of me and Dad. Money, my pitiful jewelry, an address book of his that has numbers, addresses, code names and names for places all over the country.

He always told me that it could be handy if anything happened to him. At the last minute, I take the letter I stuffed back in the envelope with my supposed mate's photo.

My bag's a big bucket bag and it's got a hidden bottom

zipper that I put all those things into. Then I dump makeup, a brush, gum, and a book in the main compartment.

I feel better having packed to run if I decide, or if I need to tonight. And having my important things, treasured things, on me is soothing. The last thing I do is put Dad's old black hat on.

I'm not sure what type it is, but it always makes me think of old school detectives.

With a breath, I add the money I have for emergencies and extra food.

Whatever happens, I won't be here much longer.

And having things on me so I can run in an instant gives me some kind of solid ground to stand on, even if it's false. The bag at home is for the reality.

After I get some booze, I'll go home, wait out the heat, and then run.

But the panic's fluttering hard, threatening to break through and leave me a mess, so I take a breath, spray myself with cloying drug store perfume, and head out into the night.

Someone's following me. Someone's following me. *Someone's following me.*

The mantra won't leave my head as I grip my bag hard. I'm fighting not turning around and bumping into whoever it is. Because there's a compulsion to seek this person out, to run just enough to make it thrilling, and to then get caught.

The wind occasionally washes over me with a smokey scent that's so wild, it almost brings me to my knees. It's up there with the scent of the alpha in the car. Just as compelling as him. As delicious.

I throb. Ache. And I know my thighs are slick.

The smoke on the wind holds hints of rum and roses. Moss

and secrets, naked pagan chases under a big-bellied moon. I want—

"Stop that," I reprimand myself.

I smell an alpha. Another one. That's all.

Someone rushes, bumping into me. The man smells of expensive cologne that assaults my senses, mainly because he bathed in it, and he offers me irritation in a frown. "Don't hog the path!"

He darts off, checking his watch, and my shoulders slump as I force myself to walk.

But the smoke is tinged with a dark note like rum soaked tobacco, and I almost stumble as it rolls over me. So damn close. Danger and sex and blood and need. Rough sensuality. That's the smell.

I whirl around. People are on the streets and cars drive by. Noise the scent blocked out rushes me, and I'm once more in a living, breathing city.

I didn't even notice when that strange blanket came over me. I search the faces of the crowd, men alone, in groups. Women. Couples.

Nothing. No one stirs me and the scent...

It's gone.

This is too busy. Too dangerous. I need...I need a place where people don't follow societal rules. Where I can buy cheap booze, where people keep to themselves.

I'm hoping my vile drug store shield will keep working. I read once that it doesn't stop an omega going crazy over the scent of an alpha, but it can help hide the omega's scent.

It's got to be true, right?

My heat's coming tomorrow, and I need to get something to get me through it. First, I steel myself and head to the place in the Hollows but when I knock and the slat opens, whoever it is slams it shut again and locks it when they see me.

I stand for ten minutes, trying to get them to open, knocking until my knuckles are bruised, but...no one comes.

That blond ghost of a man warned me, but...what am I meant to do? I'll buy booze, yes, but what kind of fool would I be if I didn't try to get the blockers?

I can't stay here. Not tonight. My skin buzzes as I ache, and I'm in the shadowy street. Alone.

No. I'm not alone. I'm being watched.

And as I turn, I catch a knee-buckling whiff of the invisible alpha.

Pagan. Hunter. Killer.

Mine.

I almost stumble back and fall.

Mine? *Mine?* Where did that come from?

It's got to be the heat talking. My body's revving, like it'll take any alpha.

No. It won't.

That disgusting man flashes in my mind. Craig. My betrothed.

Anybody except him.

And I can't stand here all night, either. I turn and walk until I reach the water, the river that runs through Starlight City. There I breathe in the slight salt that comes from the sea beyond and the brackish pools under the boardwalk. It's a nice walk for an ugly part of town and when I reach the Avenues, I turn left, away from the water.

The Avenues sounds fancy, but it's a step up or down or maybe sideways from the Hollows, lots of legit and not so legit places. Streets are old, crooked, and cross each other. They're not on a grid.

But I've heard from snippets of conversations at work that there are clubs and bars where you can have a good time, even buy drugs if you want. And the booze is cheap.

I bet I can find a cheap liquor store here.

I keep walking, going deeper into the Avenues.

I pass a grimy bar and then a tattoo parlor. I turn into another street.

The pink of low-lit neon draws me. The sign says Pandora's Box. I go closer. It's a bar, I think, but not one of those rough ones—upscale, maybe even with more of a club vibe.

That's the other thing about the Avenues. Parts are getting classier, if that's the right word. Sold, bought, and then reimagined.

Maybe this is one of those places.

The sign seems simple, quaint, just the words in fancy script. There's not a naked lady in sight or any kind of advertisement for strippers, topless waitresses, or burlesque.

A nice enough place—nice, for this part of town—where I can find out where a good liquor store is and maybe have a few to take off the growing edge inside me.

I stand outside long enough that a mountain of a man appears in the doorway and eyes me. His hair's long, pulled back, and he's bearded.

Handsome. Virile. I can smell it.

I don't want him, even with my coming heat. Whatever pheromones I pick up from him don't engulf me in need and wild urges. Like what I smell is just a natural thing, something that comes from an attractive and wild man mountain.

I think he's a beta but somewhere in my mind I remember Dad stating love can happen with anyone. That it's only the council who sets rules against it.

But inside my bones, I know another truth.

One I don't want to know.

A truth I want to run from.

I need an alpha.

I need an alpha to help with my heat, to ease the ache, assuage that itch, stop the pain.

Not now, not today. But one day. In the unseen future.

Dad knew this because he never mentioned the *type* of anyone he wanted me to love. Never once said beta or gamma.

He meant, without stating it, an alpha. But one of my choosing.

"Are you coming in or staying out?" the bearded man asks. "Make up your mind."

Someone comes out of the club, and carries with her a whiff of something intoxicating, something I crave. "I'm going in."

"Well then, come on."

He holds open the door and I walk past him.

FOUR

Dante

Fuck.

What the actual fuck's Julien thinking, letting her in here? The omega who slammed me hard in the guts with a feral need to rut and mark as mine even standing outside a fucking car?

I sip my drink calmly. Only the dip in Reaper's gaze to the way my fingers tighten a fraction says he understands my inner state.

Reap always knows.

I flick a glance at him and that scarred, cursed angel of a face is, as always, carved from rock. But I note the slightest lift of the corner of his mouth.

Asshole.

The sultry music of Pandora's beats and winds around us. I need to get downstairs, but...

Fuck.

I didn't know she was here, not until gardenias and sex scent fucking metaphorically bloomed like crazy in Pandora's Box. I smelled the girl—and she *is* a girl, about twenty, maybe twenty-one, if I'm lucky—right before she walked in.

She doesn't just poison and perfume the air with her compelling scent.

It's physically her.

To make matters worse?

She's gorgeous.

Long dark hair, pale skin, a perfect mouth beneath the shadowed brim of a hat. I know she has dark eyes that can burn a soul to the ground.

I swallow. She's in an old leather jacket that's too big, a floral shapeless dress that somehow is beguiling, and Docs or something similar on her feet, with white frilly socks peeking over the edge. Oh, Jesus fucking wept.

She looks like innocence personified. An angel walking this corrupt earth.

The girl's playing dress up and tempting all the fucking fates.

She looks, from head to toe and in the way her essence spreads everywhere, like the titular girl on the club's door.

And just as dangerous.

Julien didn't know. He probably still has no idea what he let in. Fucking betas. He's lucky I value him in the Unholy Trinity. Otherwise, I might be inclined to bathe the floor in fresh blood.

I take a swallow of my whiskey. The place is low-key busy. It's still too early for the big crowd. I've got business to deal with in our offices down below the second level. Fuck, I've even got a meeting in an hour, and yet...

Here I am.

Like I've been welded to the spot.

The girl clutches her bag as she tries and fails not to look like a fresh sacrifice.

She will be, if any low-life alpha gets his hands on her. I don't need trouble in this club.

Some of our other places? Couldn't give a fuck. But this is our HQ, the space that transforms from bar to club, and for the chosen? A speakeasy of fallen class and velvet sleaze on the lower level.

But up here, this early, the club is meant to be trouble free.

The girl's the embodiment of the word *trouble*.

If I can't stop staring, then... Shit.

From her scent, the way it winds tight around my cock, and the way that Reap watches her with his deadly, flat gaze, the one hiding his hunger, I can tell she's about to go into heat.

She's started. Not full on, but close enough. Stronger than the night I stopped the cops. Tomorrow, it'll crash and burn her and send even the most disciplined alpha into a feral tailspin.

Luckily, I'm more than disciplined. As is Reaper. Knight? I'm not so sure. If Reaper is the soul-damaged killer, and I'm the conscienceless criminal, a ruler of Starlight's underworld, then Knight's the twisted heart.

She could wrap him up around her little fucking finger.

Then again, Knight's pretty but as tough as us in his way. We're the parts that click together to form an unstoppable, formidable front.

We're the Unholy Trinity and we rule the world outside of society, outside of the Council.

"Don't make me make you talk, Reap," I say. "It's tiresome."

He utters a small, low growl, and this time I smile. "She's clean."

There's something in the way he says it that catches my attention. I keep my gaze on the girl which isn't hard. Or maybe it's too fucking hard.

Just watching the creature, I have the overwhelming urge to rut. That's what makes it difficult to be around her.

"How?" I ask.

He was given the name Reaper because between us three, he is the most likely to bring death. Of course I know his real name, and he knows mine and Knight's, but the three of us shed our old selves decades ago. We have been reborn as the monsters we are today.

Deadly. Cruel. Powerful.

Reap and I go back years. To times I'd prefer not to remember. Times I refuse to forget. I like to keep those times, the lessons learned, right at the edges.

"I followed her to the Hollows," he grumbles out.

"Did you search her place?" It's too much of a coincidence.

He hands me a photo. The wind's knocked from me as I stare. "Elias Enver?"

Reaper nods.

I can't look away. I haven't thought of this man in twenty years.

Oh. Shit. My hand jerks. "That baby?"

"The name on the mail is Roth. First name—"

"I'm not interested." Even if I was, the moment I find out why she walked in here and if she's a part of something to trap us, her ass is out the door. "Does she live alone?"

"No one else was there."

Maybe this girl is the baby, maybe not. The man who saved both our asses when we were young might be her father, but it doesn't change shit. Just haven't thought about him in forever.

"You think he went back into the fold?" I ask, downing my drink.

Reaper's frown is almost not there and yet it radiates, enough so that the waitress we hired a few weeks earlier, one who wants desperately to bang him, pivots in her path to us and heads to the back of the room.

I make a note to find a place at one of our other establishments for her. Someplace more reputable, I decide, because she lacks the fortitude of a real Trinity girl. She's just a beta, one who'll end up moving on in a few years, and she'll be doing so without a taste of any of us.

Darcy glances at me from where she leans against a wall, chatting up a patron in preparation for a Darcy shakedown. But I don't need her, not yet. I glance in the other waitress's direction and her expression says everything.

Darcy, with her razor cut blond hair and *touch me if you want to die* air, looks slightly smug, like she knows the other girl doesn't fit this particular Trinity establishment.

"No," Reap finally says. "Not Elias. He was like us."

Was. He thinks the man's dead.

"So, she's gone to them?" I ask, rubbing a hand over my unshaven chin.

The girl takes off her hat and slides it into her bag. Not on the bar, but in the bag, like it matters. And I wish she'd left the thing on. Her glow's brighter, more compelling now.

Reaper shifts. "No."

"No, you don't think so, or no, you know?"

"No."

Fucking Reaper...

He doesn't have proof, just what I told him and who was trying to shake her down.

"Want me to talk to the two cops?" he asks.

"Andy and Harry are greedy, pliable assholes we can use. Within parameters," I say, picking up my fresh drink the bartender sets down without me asking. "And if you talk—"

"Words, Dante."

I almost laugh. He uses them sparingly, when he needs to, and when he wants to. But asking Reaper to have a chat is a waste of his real skill sets. Besides, those two will talk, and then tattle.

"Save them," I say.

We have cops on our payroll. These aren't. They'd love to be, but they're Council cops. Council fucking people are weak, they can turn. And no matter if they're Council business people, or Council criminals or Council cops, they take information to the Council.

I'll use them.

Never trust them.

Never take one into the tight web of even the lowest-level Trinity family.

It's not that we live outside the law, it's that we have a code, our own morals.

And trust? Fucking paramount.

"How did you find her place?"

"It was easy. I followed my nose. Her scent is a beacon." Reaper stares at her. "Fucking flowers everywhere."

I'm about to say something when I do the math. He followed her when she left. So, he couldn't go in and be here when she arrived. Not unless...

"Reap, when—"

"She was easy to find."

He searched her out on his own, before tonight.

"She could still be Council," I say.

I heard the cops get her name and sometimes that's all it takes to turn someone because I know where she was coming from. The Hollows.

If she has contacts, then she might have information. The Council doesn't care about those who've slipped through the cracks and ended up there. They care about those who sell certain drugs, identities. Places to disappear to.

She's a young omega.

The Council's gotta be drooling over her.

Because she smells untouched.

I want to touch her.

I need to touch her, mark her, rut her, breed her.

Fuck. No. I don't. I don't want any of that. And the last? Not ever. With anyone.

We're a pack without the norms. There are three alphas. No omega to fuck things up.

We control the dark corners of this city. It's perfect.

So, if she's clean of the Council stench and influence, and unmarked, she can leave here that way. We don't want or need her.

I just want to know why the fuck she walked in through my door when she's about to go into heat.

Whatever she is, her scent is unlike anything I've ever smelled. And Reaper? The way he watches her, like he's preparing to take down his prey, feels the same.

"Her scent is soaked into the bones of her apartment. It surrounds the place." Reaper lifts his eyes from her and glances at Mason, who's one of our bartenders. A beer appears and Reap takes it, gaze settling back on the omega. "She's toxic."

"Toxic?"

"I hunt. Never smelled anything so strong, so alluring." He lifts the bottle and takes a swig. "Toxic."

"The apartment's clean, too?"

He rubs a hand over his haphazardly shaved head. And the move is telling. Though we've only been back in contact a few years, I fucking trust him. Others might not. Knight's on the fence, but Knight's the kind of guy who won't judge until he needs to. He trusts me. That's enough.

And I'm more than aware this dangerous man I'm standing with will fucking gut you without blinking, but he's also loyal. To me. To the Unholy Trinity. To Knight.

"Didn't have long in there."

"But?" I prompt.

"She's not working for the Council," he says. "But she'll be on their radar."

Meaning: young, untouched, omega.

Unregistered or she'd have been knocked up and pushing out some unworthy alpha's fucking spawn by now.

I set my glass down and watch as the girl picks up a drink, her second already. The purse of her lips when she takes a swallow tells me she's not usually a drinker. But already there's a ripple in the energy of the club, the alphas in here picking up her radiating scent. And it makes the air taut, electric. Someone's gonna make a fucking move. Maybe a few.

Darcy catches my eye with a frown. Her mark's no doubt given up whatever information she hit him for—I'll find out later—because he's back with his little crew.

She looks at the fucking omega, and then me and Reaper, like she sees trouble.

I just raise a brow. She does too, and then picks up some glasses and sashays across the room to the door where Julien is, before handing the big mountain of a man a drink.

He squeezes her ass.

The only man known to do that and live.

"There's a difference between working for them and being an unsuspecting plant," I say. "They've done it before."

A few outlier alphas in shady businesses, like us, have been roped in by an omega, and suddenly, they're on the Council's stockpile.

The fucking Council sees it as the natural order, a way of keeping things clean, organized, fair.

It's control, pure and simple, a way to keep everyone under their thumb, their sway.

And I don't like it.

Just like I don't like this coincidence of her walking in here.

"One other thing." Reaper's words send a chill through me.

I wait.

"She spoke to someone. No, he spoke to her. Like a warning."

"What did he say?" I ask.

"I don't know. Wasn't close enough to hear. But body language doesn't lie."

I turn to him.

"I'm pretty fucking sure it was Ghost," Reap finishes.

Fuck.

"That lying, piece of shit prick is back," I mutter, "and sniffing around?"

"First I saw of him in ages."

"I'll make sure our people keep on the lookout." I check my watch. "I need to take care of some things, then I have a meeting."

Reaper's gaze is back on the girl. A muscle in his jaw ticks and there's a vibration of violence around him. He wants her, too. But he wants to do damage.

Not to her. He's fucked in the head, but he doesn't abuse women. But yeah, he wants to cause damage out in the world.

"Let off some of that pent up energy. Talk to some people, get the low down on Council moves."

"Talk?" He takes another sip of beer. Arches a brow.

"Talk."

This time he smiles for real. "No mention of her."

"I want to know what new plans are in place."

"Talk...how?" he asks.

"Your choice."

He looks at me. "Speaking my fucking language now, Dante."

"Send Knight up before you go."

He nods. "Dante?"

"Yeah?"

He sets his bottle down. "Be careful. That omega's fucking trouble."

He's preaching to the choir.

While I wait, I watch her, how she tries to make herself small, the way she orders a third drink. Cheap, below bottom shelf, liquor. That's what she's buying.

She's poor and watching her money. There's a haunted look in her eyes; the pinched aura around her speaks of pain, sadness, fear.

My head says there's something's going on with the girl.

My body's too full of a throbbing need to be bothered to work it out.

Her scent winds around me as I breathe in and my cock throbs. It wants that virgin.

Is she a fucking virgin? She must be. That's why she smells so much sweeter. No one's had her yet. I fucking hate virgins. They piss me off. I like a girl who knows how to please.

The omega turns.

She looks at me and suddenly the bar goes airless. Her gaze wraps around my cock and pulls. It licks against my skin. Whispers in gardenia-scented words.

And I'm hit with the vision of me pushing back the silk of her long dark hair, exposing her throat, and sinking my teeth in, right at her jugular, as I fuck her so hard I knot.

I want to control her, have her under my command, have her give me a blowjob. And fuck me, I want to explore every inch of her as she does every single thing I want, hold every pose, each position.

I want to edge her, fuck her ass. I want to own her in such a way that she can't see straight, that her body answers just to me. I want to bring her beyond regular edging and keep her there, consistently about to come and denying her that pleasure.

Not until I decide to push.

"Dante."

Oh. Fuck. I blink, turn away from her and shift further into the side of the bar, where the darkness pools deep. It leads down to our private sanctum, to the workings of our operations.

"What's that aroma, man?" Knight glances around and it doesn't take him long to zero in on her.

For the first time since the three of us formed the Unholy Trinity, I want to snap another alpha's neck for thinking the same thoughts I'm thinking. That I *know* he's thinking.

"Oh, shit," he says. "It's not even my birthday."

39

I narrow my eyes, and deliberately say his real name. His eyes narrow, too. He hates it when I use his name. "She's not for us. Reaper has the details on her, but our favorite Council cops shook her down the other night, and—"

"Oh, I see now why you were late to the meetup. Holy fuck. Sorry, not sorry, but shit. Look at her."

"Knight. You're not fifteen."

He sighs, rubs his eyes, and the playfulness subsides. It's his schtick. "I'm working on this idea for here, or another club, and—" He stops, the sharpness of his gaze hits me. "You've got that meeting. The info on the guy's on your tablet. Read it first, but he's good to go. I highlighted the parts where, if needs be, we can twist him for more of a safety net." He pivots. "You want me to get her history?"

I almost say yes. If anyone can, it's Knight. He's got the rich, college kid look down. And though he's, what? Early thirties? He looks late twenties or younger, at a glance.

He's a chameleon wrapped in the fuzzy disguise of seeming harmlessness.

Knight's anything but harmless.

He's a true alpha, and he's loyal. Better yet, he's not just our tech guy, it's like he's got a magic touch with it. Me? I can use a tablet, phone, computer. Him? He could take down the government. Give him enough time? Maybe even the Council.

"Keep an eye on her." I look at him. "At a distance."

He puts his tablet on the bar. "I can work and watch, Dante."

"Watch. Operative word."

He salutes and his impulsive ways need to be dampened here.

I lean in. "She's a fucking omega. I'm sure I don't need to tell you. We don't need to be tied down. Beyond that, I don't know if she's trustworthy, so eyes only."

Thing is, it's not just his eyes on her. Men of all kinds have their gazes drawn her way, and my head starts going places.

Dirty, filthy places. If there is a way to bottle up her magic and pour it out on the club, we'd have a goldmine...

"No one else touches her," I amend. "And I mean eyes only with you."

"Heard you the first time, man."

"I'm going to go and prep for the meeting." With that, I head down.

I have time. I could stay, but she's like a glitch, a hook in my brain.

And the things I want to do with her? They keep fucking expanding, getting wilder, hotter. It pisses me off. It fills my head. Worse, it kicks my denial kink into gear.

I want to have her in front of me, her on display, me edging her and not giving in for either of us, stretching the moment out until it's almost too much. And then slamming into her.

Yeah, it fucking pisses me off.

If she's a Council trap to hook the Unholy Trinity, it's not going to work.

We don't give in to their bullshit. Or any of their little traps they've put out over the years.

But fuck, if this girl has been sent here...

I'll destroy her.

FIVE

Lizette

The man in black is back.

He looks like the very devil himself, just walking the earth. Compelling and hot like the kingdom he rules. Like he'll drag a girl all the way down into those fiery depths with him.

When he looked at me twenty minutes earlier, a vacuum opened, sucking everything out except me and him, and tendrils of spice and salt, soft earth and the clean and wild scent of a storm.

I shut down, didn't look, just concentrated on my drink. But now he's back, and I swear that evocative scent is stronger. I can't keep the thoughts at bay.

My heart constricts.

It's him.

From the car.

My insides start a slow melt, but he's not the alpha to answer to my heat problems. No.

He's the one who reported me to the Council.

It takes everything, and I mean everything, to stop me

going over and slapping him.

But I don't think you slap a man like him.

Also, I've never slapped someone in my life.

I want to provoke him. Almost as much as I want to run and hide.

He burns into me. This time, I can't stop looking. His eyes, which might be blue, seem to see into souls. They're the eyes of a ruler, a leader, a man who takes everything he wants and leaves nothing behind, not even hearts.

I throb low. It's hot, that throb. Thrills rise with each beat. And my thighs, if I rubbed them, would be wet with desire, right at the juncture.

This...this is something I've never in my life experienced. And even if Dad was around, there's no way I could talk to him about this.

I try to look away, but I can't. The alpha's hunger is mesmerizing.

It sets it off in me, too. A deep, craving hunger.

And it doesn't help that he's gorgeous in a hard, dark way. The beard growing in should look unkempt, but it doesn't— same with the black hair in serious need of some scissors.

It should diminish the wanting, not make him more compelling.

Not make him like some ancient, pagan god. The devil in his natural habitat.

And the one he's talking to?

Oh, he's beautiful. Caramel curls and a dimple in his left cheek. The pretty one has an easy, cocky smile, and when he looks at me, I'm blindsided.

Utterly beautiful, yes, but the kind of approachable I think I might like. Yet he seems like a man in control, with eyes that say *I see you. I understand.*

Then my gaze goes back to the devil incarnate, the man in black.

He'd been alone when I first took note of him, but before...

I'd actively been avoiding looking over, like another presence had been there, one that wanted to devour.

The one, I realize, I smelled earlier on the street. The ghostly smoke on the wind.

I didn't see anyone then. Or when I arrived in this bar.

Then again, I wasn't looking.

I know, I *know* I should have looked—really looked—when I walked in, for possible danger, but the thing is, this place soothes the soul with its mix of scents and sounds and press of bodies.

When I breathe in, there's the scent of the devil man along with the elements of the unseen one. I search, but I don't see him. I can only smell the rum-soaked tobacco, roses, and wild chases.

Then there's a soft and seductive scent with lavender and leather. Something sweet.

There are three of them.

Three different alphas in the same room.

If I merged them, layered them, it would be almost too intoxicating, the kind of combination that would tumble me down, scramble my mind, make my blood rush and slick flow.

"Stop it," I admonish myself.

The one with the caramel curls is sweet leather and lavender. All things nice and dirty.

I suck in more air, as the man in black gives me a cold, hard look that rakes down my spine, then leaves for the second time.

I turn and stare down into my drink, the noise of the bar coming over me, like it receded when I looked over there.

Pressing hot fingers into even hotter cheeks, I whisper, "Have your drinks, find a store to get a bottle, and then go home."

"A pretty girl like you shouldn't be alone."

I almost jump a mile.

The musk and funk of warm and woody oud and oakmoss

suddenly overwhelms me like I've found myself in a damp forest cave. It makes me both want to scramble away and rub against the owner of the scent.

A wave of fear rolls through me.

The man's nice enough looking, but he's a different alpha and he's zeroed in on me.

In my state, my base instinct, the thing that has no right to rule me, starts to surge.

I down my drink, letting the burn of the booze cut through the surge. "I'm not looking for someone, but thank you," I say.

He laughs. "I'm Jake. And I'm not here to pick you up."

"Oh, good."

My nerves are spinning, prickling.

"Do you mind?" Jake points to the seat next to me and sits.

I shrug, deliberately borderline rude. "It's not my bar."

"Figured that." He leans close.

I swallow down the tiny sigh of relief that his scent, while it still pushes at me, doesn't bring about any of that rush of need.

Heat. Because now all he seems to do is overwhelm me with his cologne.

"I'm really sorry, Jake," I say, turning my empty glass. "But I'm not in the mood for company."

He motions to the bartender. "Beer for me, and a Manhattan for the lady."

My ears burn. I don't know what a Manhattan is, but I'm guessing some sort of cocktail, and I should turn the drink down, I know that, but I can't. I'm too broke to do that. Any other evening, I would but tonight...

I need all the dampeners I can.

"And it's nonsense," Jake says to me, his hand resting on the bar near mine. "People say they don't want company, but they just don't want to bother people, and I'm not bothered. Besides, you're not going to completely crush a man who just got dumped by his date, are you?"

I look at him. "You did?"

He smiles. "Yeah. I know. His problem, right?"

He's gay? It floods me with relief because what better foil for me against the world right now than an alpha who isn't into women.

"I'm Liz," I say.

Jake sweeps up my hand, kissing it. "Pleased to meet you."

"I'm sorry you got stood up."

"His loss, my gain. Now I have some pretty company to protect against the troublesome alphas." And he winks. Then he adds, "Do you have to be at work tomorrow?"

"No. I...I'm between jobs." What's that phrase I heard? "I'm fun-employed."

He laughs. "Better than working in real estate. Starlight City's got some great spots but also some hard sells. Don't let me bore you."

When the drink arrives, he hands me his phone and asks me to put in my number—because he might know of a job in his office—which I do.

Not my number, though. I put in one that's a pizza place Dad and I used to order from. The man might be harmless, but I'm not that naïve. I'm not going to give him personal information not even if I'm dragged to another state to pair with an old pack alpha.

Besides, rule number one, never give out our number.

The pizza place knows me, and they knew Dad. They don't mind getting the odd call and they'd never pass my details on.

I hand him the phone and he calls the number. "Now you've got mine."

"I left my cell at home," I tell him as he looks at my bag.

"I don't mind. I've got something better. You. Here."

And he laughs again.

I sip my drink and it's good. By the third sip, my mind is nice and fuzzy and the conversation flows.

But soon my head starts to spin and my stomach turns.

The walls close in and Jake's concerned face shifts in and out of focus.

"Liz, are you alright?"

"What?" My tongue's thick, too big for my mouth and I try to stand, but I stagger and have to grab hold of Jake.

My heart's beating fast and my thoughts jumble and slide until I can't make words form properly.

Is this part of being in heat without the drugs?

Panic claws at me, and I can't breathe. He takes my arm and helps me up, and he drags me across the room. Things get darker and then a door thumps and cool, fresh air washes over me. I stagger back, hitting something solid.

"What...?"

"It's okay, baby," Jake says, gathering me to him. "I've got you."

I cling, and he rubs my back and the booming beat of his heart is against my ear. And my thigh's warm, he's rubbing that too, sliding his hand up and around.

"Wh-What are you doing?"

He takes his hand from my back and kicks out one of my feet. I pitch sideways, grabbing him as Jake pushes me into the wall. "Helping you, baby, making you feel good. You don't want that nasty, nasty pain by denying your nature. You're made to fuck an alpha. I'm made to fuck and knot. I bet you're wet, releasing slick everywhere for me."

His words flow through me with a weird base pleasure. And need beats hard even as revulsion thrums inside me at the same time.

"No..."

He laughs. "Yes."

His fingers push up at my panties, and a wild throb races through me. He groans low, grabbing my face and plundering my mouth in a wet, sloppy kiss. His fingers rub my panties.

I wrench my head away and start pushing him. "I don't want to."

"Slower? We can take it slow. You're sweet, baby, so fucking sweet. And I'll protect you."

He's still rubbing my pussy, over my panties and my heart's wild in the wrong ways. Panic fights the sluggishness, the darkness that keeps sweeping in. I push at him and try to run.

Jake pulls his hand from my covered pussy and clamps down on my thigh, making me cry out.

He kisses me softly and it's all saliva, all tongue. I start to make strange sounds, sobbing like a wounded animal.

This is my first kiss.

I don't want to kiss this man. I don't want him touching me. But even as I try to fight him, I sink into the darkness, and he starts to stroke my thigh.

"Out here will do. Open those legs, baby."

He pushes and my foot skitters wide. I feel a breeze across my core. Then his hand's there, cupping me.

"No, no, stop, please," I cry. "I don't...I don't want you, please, *please stop*."

Jake punches me and stars explode. The pain's a momentary relief from the storm inside, and my head hits the wall, sending another burst of agony through me.

The world pulsates, and I can taste coppery wetness in my mouth.

He hauls me against him, teeth grazing my skin.

"Don't." The word pushes free. My lips are numb, the syllable thick in the air like it both belongs to me and doesn't.

He tries to bite me this time, mouth open, and coming for my throat.

It takes strength I never knew I had to move my leaden limbs, to lift my hand to hit him.

But the strike's weak. It bounces off him.

He laughs. "I was going to claim you, then take you, but I think I'll have my fill first. A taste."

"No." I move my head, hitting his with mine.

Now he grabs me by the throat, slamming me into the wall. His eyes glitter as he starts to shift and move. Shadow to light. In focus and out.

"Yes, bitch." Jake starts to ease up the fabric of my panties. "I think I'll just keep going. I want that cunt."

Suddenly the panties snap back into place, and he's gone. Something hits bricks on the other side of the alley.

"I think," says a sonorous voice, "you should listen to the lady. She said no."

Jake snarls. "Who's going to stop me?"

I breathe hard and look up the veil lifting a little. It's the man with the caramel curls.

He grins, the dimple flashing, and my insides flare up into life. I throb with real need and desire.

"I am," he says.

And then his fist smashes into Jake's face.

I try to say something, but just a note of a wordless song breaks free before everything goes black.

SIX

Knight

Gardenias sweeten the fetid air. The smell spurs me on in beating the living shit out of the lowlife who was about to rape this girl.

She's out, but she's in heat so her metabolism's working overtime. Let her heal. Let her rest. Whatever.

The note of song from her, pure beauty and infinite sadness fuels me. And just maybe stops me from killing the rapey fuck.

But the rage still burns.

Right now? The rage is fire in my veins as I slam my fist into the alpha's face.

He's muscular, big. I'm taller but he probably outweighs me.

It's not a fair fucking fight.

I'm going to demolish him.

The guy laughs as he staggers to his feet. He swings at me and he connects. The pain blossoms. I grin.

Not because of the girl. This shitbag deserves to suffer,

deserves to be forced to eat his own dick and balls for touching her, for drugging her.

I want him to understand who the fucking Unholy Trinity is.

"Pretty boy, go back inside. The girl's mine." He wipes blood from his mouth, hands coiling into fists as he sniffs the air. "Alpha to alpha, I'm superior. And I got to her first. All that fucking soft skin, and so pretty with her naivety. She should hang a sign saying *virgin in heat, fuck me and own me now*."

I nod. I don't even look at her. Dirtbag has a point. She is all kinds of soft, pretty, but he's not getting her.

Dante didn't ask me to get involved. Actually, it was the opposite.

He told me to watch her.

Which I did. Right up until I didn't. Until now.

"Here's the deal," I say. "You go, and never come back to any Unholy Trinity establishment again."

"You work in this shit hole? They hired you?"

I just smile. "Counting to three."

"Before what?"

"I kill you." I pause. "Better yet, I'll make you *wish* I killed you."

The guy laughs, "Oh, I am going to love this."

"Man, so am I. One."

He rushes me.

"Two."

I step aside as he takes a swing.

"Three." I wait.

The moron turns and lunges. I grab him by the hand, bending his fingers back and slamming him into the wall, face first.

"See, you might think you can take me, dickwad, but you thought wrong. We don't rape or drug girls here. And the thing is, I'm a helluva lot more dangerous than you give me credit for. A wild fucking card. One who knows the score. I could kill you right now with my bare hands. Or with the knife in my pocket."

I twist his fingers again, the noise from the club growing louder. I don't look at the door. It'll be Julien. His girl, Darcy, probably sent him, since he was at the front door.

"The agony you're feeling? It can get a lot worse." I bend his finger, breaking one, and he screams. "And I could continue. Finding and breaking all the small bones, maybe tearing off one of your balls."

I get closer to him. "One of my friends is a psycho. I've learned a lot from Reaper in the art of torture. How to kill slow."

"Please!"

"Not fun pleading, is it?" I ask. "See, I might look like one of those guys with a cushy job and a mommy and daddy who paid my way into school or wherever the fuck the rich dicks go these days, but I'm not. I'm very far from it."

"Please..."

It's music to my ears.

"Maybe I'll do it quick and break the hyoid bone in your throat." I pause, take a breath because I'm teetering on the verge of killing him. "I could cut to the chase, slice your throat, and let you bleed out. Or, if I'm feeling kind, I can use the knife, severe your brain stem and—"

"Knight."

I close my eyes, swallow, and take a breath. Then I snap another finger, before turning the screaming asshole and sucker punching him.

Then I look up at the door. "Yeah, Julien?"

"Need help?"

Ah, fuck. I know I'm not doing any of that to our wanna-be rapist and resident slime ball. I'm not actually like Reaper. I'll kill in defense, but I'm talking straight up fun and games murder. That's Reaper's territory, not mine.

I'm deadly in other ways. I can kill someone just by

sticking a knife in their heart. Or I can destroy them by taking the world from them and hit them where it hurts.

Wallet. Reputation. Standing. Livelihood.

I can empty the first, turn the rest into dust.

"Take this trash out," I say. "He's not welcome here anymore."

Julien's gaze touches on the now groaning girl. "Did he...?"

"No. Get whatever he gave her because it worked fast, and I'd like a look. His details, too."

Julien nods, steps out into the back alley where we keep the garbage and Reaper sometimes comes to smoke. There's another door at the end. Julien hefts the guy up and over his shoulder like he's nothing, and heads out.

He'll work him over, get the details, and have him dumped somewhere, either near an emergency room or just in a park. I'm betting on the latter.

Julien might be muscle, but he's smart, loyal, and knows exactly when to do what needs to be done.

Like how he waited until I inflicted pain on the guy, but stopped me doing something stupid.

I drag another breath in and past the stench of garbage is the sweet complexity, the rich sensuality of gardenias.

This girl's a garden of forbidden desires.

Turning, I crouch down, smoothing her hair from her face, and my heart lurches. It's electric, touching her skin. She's like satin and her hair silk.

She's stunning. A mix of angel and siren.

But the plump, naturally red lips aren't what causes that hard lurch. It's not her beauty, or even that cocksucker's vile scent clinging to her.

It's her swollen lip, the spot of blood, and the black and purple bruise that's bloomed.

"Are you okay?" I ask.

She tries to push at me, but I capture her hands, as she slurs, "No, no, please—"

"He's gone."

Her pretty, dark eyes dart around, unfocused. "I don't...I don't know...what happened."

I'm not sure if she's asking or announcing, but I just stroke a finger over those soft lips, even though she winces, and I say, "He drugged you. Did...did he touch you?"

This time her eyes snap to mine in focus, and there's rage there. "He tried."

"I should have killed him." I sigh. "Just a figure of speech."

Honestly, I'm not sure if either of us mean it, and I'm still touching her. It's only when she leans into me, I realize what I'm doing.

Trying to wipe the asshole's scent from her.

I drop my hand to her chin and gently turn her face, looking at her neck. He didn't manage to mark her. And while I know that already, there's something, an urge, that makes me check.

"Would you have killed him?" she asks.

I let her go and sit back. Then I settle on an answer. "I'm part owner here, so piling up bodies where I work isn't on the agenda."

Shit. She riles so many things in my blood. I know what I look like. I know what I like. I want her as mine, and it's not just the fact she's almost in heat.

I want her. To own her, call her my good girl, praise her in just the right way, until I find the sweet spot that makes her both squirm and pant in exquisite agony and need.

I want to tuck her up, look after her, have her call me Daddy.

There's no weird and fucked up thing to it. I just like the way Daddy Doms can be soft or hard in discipline, control, gifts...

Somehow, I drag my mind back. "You know you shouldn't be out."

"I just...I couldn't be at home."

"Why?" She's not a party girl, and she's not looking to get laid, looking to scratch the itch for a rut to help her through.

If she wanted that there'd be a hundred better places for a girl like her. And if she wanted it, she'd wait until the heat hit.

If she wanted that, an omega who looked like her could get it. Anywhere.

And she'd have taken what was on offer. She wouldn't have fought back.

There's a part of me that stirs, the old earnest part, the purely OG name part from back when I was idealistic—when I thought the world operated in a different way. Before someone fucked up my ticket out of hell, and bad decisions met more bad decisions. It took Dante saving my ass from prison and showed me how to shape this world...that part thinks she's like me. Like us, I guess.

Even Reaper.

Someone who doesn't want the normal shackles of the life the Council decides. Someone who's more than the sum of her parts.

Yeah, and also someone who I want to claim as mine because the longer we sit here, the less I can smell the other alpha tainting her.

"Feeling better?" I ask.

She nods, rubs her lip gingerly. "Yeah, my head's clearing."

"Good." I stand and offer her my hand. "I'll make sure you get home."

I'm a little hazy on whether watching her meant keeping her at the club, but she should be somewhere safe, and that's home. Darcy can do it. Even Julien and—

Oh. Fuck.

She puts her hand in mine and everything lights up.

"I'm Lizette," she whispers.

"Knight."

"Like the opposite of day? Night?"

"No, like your knight in shining armor." I grin.

55

"It fits."

I help her up and we're both breathing hard. Our hands electrify where they touch and it's like her scent's in me, turning my blood into a firestorm.

"I..." Suddenly, she's in my arms, her mouth on mine.

She tastes of heaven, sweet and delicious, the rarest thing, and I'm instantly hard.

I curl a hand in her hair, pull back her head. Her eyes are liquid desire, her pulse throbbing, and I'm overcome with the desire to wipe his scent from her, imprint her with mine.

Lizette kisses me again, a fevered kiss, and I don't care that she's not skilled. She's perfection and her fingers are in my curls, her sweet, soft body pushing into me.

She rubs herself on my hard-on, like she needs to come, like she's going for broke in a fever pitch and I lift my head. "Liz—"

"Shut up." Her voice is low, feral, a melodious note that catches hold of my cock. She claws at my clothes and I take her mouth in a slow, hot kiss, one that has her panting into me.

I look at her. "My way. My rules."

With that, I turn us and slam her into the wall. She wraps one leg around me, rubbing on my jeans, and I swear to fuck I feel how wet she is, her slick, and with it her perfumed skin blooms brighter, headier.

What really drives me insane is the snap to attention in her gaze when I told her it's my way.

She's a natural fucking good girl.

"You wanna please me?" I slide a hand soft along her thigh.

Lizette moans, offering her throat to me as she lifts her hips, her cunt covered in soft cotton rubbing along my cock.

"Yes, I want to. I need to."

I can't fuck her. I know that. But a taste, a feel, just a little more won't hurt.

Plundering her mouth in a claiming kiss, our tongues meet and dance as she surges against me.

It's like two halves exploding and fusing. I skate my fingers higher.

"Please," she whispers, voice fever-thick, "touch me..."

Something short circuits in me.

"Be a good little girl," I murmur. "A sweet little girl, one who wants to please her Daddy."

"I'm good..." She's panting, her lips on me, tongue sliding against me, making my brain start to shut down, my defenses and good intentions melt down into nothing.

"Beg me to touch you," I whisper as I come up for air.

"Please, please touch me, I need it. I need you in me. Make this ache go away."

"You want me to make you better?" I bend and bite one of her nipples through her dress.

Oh, fuck, her tits are sweet, high, nipples hard.

"I want you to make me better, please, please. Please, Knight, save me."

What I want is for her to call me Daddy. I'll take Sir in a pinch but with someone this hot, this potent, I don't really care. She's begging and Daddy's in a generous mood.

Daddy's out of his fucking mind.

I stroke my hand higher.

"Like this?" I ask.

She breathes out, pushing her pussy into me. "Yes... Please...I've been so good..."

Lizette's never done this before, sunk into the submissive nature of hers, it's strikingly clear, and it's a fucking gift to sample it, get the first taste.

"Let's see how good you are," I mutter.

I pull her panties aside and sink my fingers into her hot tightness. Her slick lets me get two fingers in her immediately and she clamps tight, convulsing, an orgasm ripping through her. I kiss her hard, taking what's mine, and I bite where the dickwad hit her.

Then I start to kiss and suck down her throat, needing to feel the heat and the beat of her blood through her pulse.

I'm not going to bite her deep. I'm not going to mark her, just suck that sweet spot.

Her moan fills me as she starts to push up. I find her clit with my thumb and make her come again and all it does is make her writhe more, beg for more.

I don't think I've ever been this hard in my life. Never been in something so tight and perfect in my life, either. She's pliable, too, her body molding around my fingers, squeezing.

I want nothing more than to bury myself to the hilt inside her, claim her, bite so hard that the salty-coppery taste on my tongue is from my mark and—

"What the literal fuck?"

I still, even as she shatters on my fingers yet again.

Dante's hand lands on my shoulder, a biting, bruising grip that's like a bucket of water on me.

"What the fuck do you think you're doing, Knight? And tell me why I shouldn't fucking kill you? Right now?"

CHAPTER
SEVEN

Dante

I t's a cacophony of fury and something darker, far more savage in my fucking veins. "I said, what the fuck do you think you're doing, Knight?"

I drag him off her, his fingers wet with her slick, the scent of her so fucking strong, so fucking good, I almost suck his fingers.

Screw that.

I want to throw her down in the dirt and rut her, knot, fucking fill her with my seed.

She's basically in heat at this point and that's what's driving me crazy.

The girl has sunk down to the ground, and I think she's humming because there's the sweetest, softest sound as she folds around herself.

Yeah, she's in full fucking heat and spinning out all kinds of signals an alpha finds hard to reject.

I get it. I get why Knight did what he did. My instincts are saying I want her, too.

It's not happening.

I glare. "Basic fucking rule, Knight. Don't fuck when they're in heat. Don't even touch. Find someone else. What the hell is wrong with you?"

"Bite me, Dante." He's turned, face to the ground as he snarls.

Then he glances at me, eyes glittering.

Knight wipes his mouth like he's trying to erase the evidence, but I smell them both in the air, almost like a song, like she's got a power to make me pick up on him like I do her.

He goes to rise, but I put a booted foot on his chest. "I wouldn't."

Lifting it, I turn to her. I need to check her over, make sure she's okay, that our fucked up Romeo hasn't gone and done something he shouldn't. As in made an irreversible mistake.

Once I see she's fine, I can get rid of her. Last thing we need is a little omega sniffing around.

I know her name, but I don't want to use it. "Are you okay, girl?"

Her head's down, and she keeps it there.

"Look at me."

The girl's head lolls, her hair falling over her face, but I don't miss the bruised mouth as she looks up. Fuck. I turn.

"What the fuck? Did you fucking hit her?"

Knight surges up, comes at me, and I down him with a punch.

"Fuck!" he snarls and rubs his jaw.

When he starts to get up again, I say, "Stay down."

I use my alpha voice, and he doesn't move for about five seconds, enough to get his shit together.

"You asshole," Knight says, one of his hands grabbing at the ground as he half sits up.

His hair's wild, the curls tangled both from my punch and her fingers.

A sharp, hot pain lances through me. But I don't move, blocking her from him.

"Move, Dante."

"Speak to me like that again, and I'll make you wish for death."

We glare at each other and then he lowers his gaze. We both know I'm not killing him.

Maybe I'll rough him up some more, but killing him? Nah.

Especially not over a fucking girl.

"I didn't hurt her. That prick sitting with her at the bar?" he says. "He did."

I lean down over him. "Whatever they want to do, let them do it. She got fucking drunk. She clearly came here looking to scratch her little omega itch." I lower my voice. "She might be a Council plant."

"She isn't."

"You know this how? You're somehow plugged into the net with your brain power?"

"No, you ass," he says. "The dude drugged her and tried to rape her. I stopped him."

I stare at Knight.

The guy's young, wild, and sometimes he lets his unruliness out along with the chip on his shoulder. But he's good. He fits. He's not a raping asshole. He's got a hero complex, so he's not even a "coercing a girl" kind of guy.

Shit, he doesn't have to be.

They fall all over themselves for him, over all of us, I guess, but the pussy he's offered, he usually takes. And a lot of that's young, early twenties pussy. The pussy attached to ideals and dreams, and melts like hot butter for him.

So, for him to be all over a drugged girl, even one who... yeah, okay, was getting off on him like sex had just been invented, is out of character.

Just like the whole evening.

Which makes me wonder if Reaper's wrong and she's got something to hide.

I'll put this idiot on it. But first… "Get inside and send out Julien and Darcy. And open the basement door. Then get me everything on Lizette Roth."

He opens his mouth, then shakes his head like he thinks better of speaking back. Knight gets to his feet and hightails it out of there.

I sigh, turning to the girl.

Her dress is hiked high and in the moonlight, her thighs catch a silvery gleam from her wetness. And…fuck. Her panties are twisted so pretty, wet pink petals show.

I'm not fucking touching her.

No way.

But I do use her name.

"Lizette?" I tug down her dress. "We're going to put you up for the night, let you sleep it off."

"I don't…" Her voice is slurred and irritation and anger knife through me again.

Fucking Knight. He could have just kept his mouth and hands to himself. Drugged, drunk—

"I don't want to stay here," she says, those mesmerizing eyes on me.

And they're stunning, just like her.

Except, though they're melting darkness, promising a night of sin, they're also full of sadness, lust, longing, innocence and loneliness.

I take a deep breath. "Look—"

"I'm tired and I hurt."

"Everything good, boss?" Julien's at the door, taking in the scenario before him.

I turn, right as Knight sidles back into the scene, hand at his mouth, gaze stormy and wearing a frown.

"Yeah," I say. "We need to get her down to the private level."

Next to him, Darcy casts dark looks, first at me and then she settles on the culprit for this particular scenario. Culprit, savior, it weirdly works out to be the same thing.

She wants to say something, that's clear, but even she knows her place—mostly.

All Darcy does is lean a hip against the wall, the music low, sultry around her as it seeps out.

"Can you do that, Darcy?" I press.

She tucks one of the long white-blonde locks behind her ear, on the side that isn't buzz cut. And just raises a brow. "Maybe Knight should."

"Maybe you need to learn your place," Knight says.

Julien swings a look at his girl, then to me. "What do you need, boss?"

"I think," Darcy says, "we defuse this. Knight and Julien go open the door, and I stay here with you."

This is Darcy through and through. Utterly tough as nails and not above challenging us. It's totally unacceptable gamma behavior.

Then again, it's probably why we work.

"Do it." I nod at Julien.

Knight's scowl is something I feel burn deep into my flesh, but I ignore it. Just like I ignore the fact he was meant to unlock the fucking door earlier. All I do is flash him a look.

"I'll get digging," Knight mutters.

The two leave and Darcy helps Lizette up. "C'mon, kid, get it together."

She runs a hand over Lizette, and I shove my hands in the pockets of my suit pants, turning away so they have a modicum of privacy. Voices murmur and I tune them out.

"She's fine, but she's already started her heat. You're right, she should stay until morning. Or, let's face it, until it's over. She needs a safe space to ride it out."

I don't want Lizette to stay, I don't want her here period, but I keep the thought to myself.

"What was the kid thinking?" Darcy mutters.

"He wasn't." I don't point out that Darcy is younger than Knight. Shit, she's probably only a handful of years older than Lizette. I pause, kicking at a rogue stone, trying not to breathe in Lizette's scent. "And he's your alpha, too. You don't talk about him or any of us that way."

"Yes. Sir."

My mouth twitches but I fight the smile. "One night, then we take her home in the a.m. Full-service delivery with a warning to stay the fuck away."

I turn back to her, and she gives me a mock salute. "Julien and I will get to it before dawn breaks."

"Thanks."

Further down the alley, there's a clang and another door opens. It's well-oiled, and bolted from the inside. The route is for clandestine and highly illegal meetups, and for us to come and go when we don't want anyone who might be watching to see us go. Julien pokes his head out.

And I head for the main door. "Put her in the suite, and then lock the door and get back to your posts. I'll be down when I'm ready."

By tomorrow, this is going to be nothing more than a nightmare ready to be forgotten.

Precautions. A new moon. Another fucking night. Life on the cutting edge of society. Take your fucking pick. But with everything going well from this vantage point, where I like to keep an eye on things—the club on the floor below isn't open tonight, thank fuck—I take her bag from the bartender and go to my office.

Knight's door is closed, which makes me roll my eyes to the ceiling.

I get it. She's phenomenal in her scent. And he's young enough to make mistakes.

Or, considering he's actually early thirties, he's lucky to have us to guide him from making the mistakes an alpha's dick might get them into.

Until now.

I stare at her bag. Cheap leather. Old. Well-used from the worn creases and the softness. Yet I'm loath to open it up and I don't know why.

Maybe it's the hat that sits in there. It is clear the thing's beyond personal to her. I don't want to tie myself anymore to the situation than I am—than *we* are. Right now, we have a girl who's in heat, one who stirs the blood, and one who's in no state to go home by herself tonight.

Or maybe it's just her and everything she represents.

Innocent or complicit, I do know she's been untouched. As untouched as a girl can be before Knight finger fucked her.

I suck in a breath.

Reaper's poking into things, and between him and Knight, we'll get a good picture of her. But banning her from coming near our places should be enough.

Girls like her will be mated within the year.

Something claws into me, deep.

"Get it together," I say as I empty her bag.

Hat, makeup, wallet. Odds and ends that I assume women carry with them.

But it's got a heavy base that most wouldn't think twice about.

Except smuggling small things is part of our business and secret compartments are a must.

A bag this cheap should be light now it's empty. Even taking in the base.

I feel around inside. It takes a little longer than I'd like to find the hidden zipper, which tells me this is a custom piece, made to appear cheap, and made to smuggle. I undo it and take out the contents.

A tablet I can't open without a thumb or fingerprint. An old-fashioned, worn book full of names, numbers. The writing's basically chicken scratches in notes and dates jotted down like little reminders from over the years.

Chicken scratches, that is, until I reach the names and numbers. They're written legibly.

Important?

Next are polaroids of Lizette and her dad. And he really does look like the man who saved my ass, along with Reaper's, almost twenty years ago.

There's money, wrapped in a band. Not crisp and new, but old, like it's been painstakingly saved.

It's a piteously low amount.

There's an external hard drive I set aside, and some jewelry. Simple, old and not expensive. I won't say cheap because the simplicity brings it class, but there aren't any expensive stones.

I pull out one more thing.

A letter.

From the Council.

I unfold the contents from the envelope, scanning my gaze across the note.

"Ah, fuck."

"Here." I don't bother knocking.

Knight spins in his chair, cockiness back in place. The kind of cocky that always makes me suspicious. Because it's the cocky he pulls out when he might have done something he shouldn't have.

"I've gotta door, Dante. Right there. You can knock. And

everything."

I shove the hard drive and tablet at him, then settle back against the wall and fold my arms. "See what you can find on those."

"Aye, aye, captain."

"Cut the bullshit, Knight." I eye him carefully. "We both know you fucked up."

He swallows and nods. "That tasty morsel is hard to resist. Especially when she rubs her cunt on you, kisses you, and demands you touch her."

"Well, glad to hear she's a villain and you're the innocent one in this scenario."

He plugs in the hard drive then looks at me. "I didn't say I was innocent. I said she's hard to resist when she's begging."

"And you're meant to be better than that. A girl like her is worse than jailbait. Fuck, she's Council bait."

"She's clean."

I straighten. "You found something?"

"No, and that's the point."

I pull the letter from my pocket and hand it to him. Knight frowns. "He's like a million years old."

"That's what you focus on?"

He waves the paper. "It's a standard fucking letter, man."

Frustration rolls over me. "You say she's clean. How?"

"Clean as in no real history. She's not registered." He meets my gaze. "The Council catches the ones who try to live outside their rules. That's what the letter is."

"The girl's trouble."

"Oh, she's trouble, all right," Darcy says behind me. "Dante, come with me."

I follow her and she takes me into the room with the girl who's curled up, eyes closed, a blanket over her. There's an empty glass next to her, and I'm willing to bet Darcy gave her something to sleep.

"Yeah, we have a *temporary* problem," I reply.

"She's out until dawn. But look." Darcy flips her hair from the girl's throat and I see it—the indent of teeth. A binding mark.

Fury hits, searing me.

"Oh, fuck me." I stalk out of the room. Darcy follows hard behind me.

I put my hands flat on the wall and force myself to breathe into calm.

"Dante?"

"Yeah?"

"I locked the door. Here." Darcy holds out the key and I take it, pocketing it.

"Go back to work. I'll handle this."

I return to Knight's quarters.

He's completely fucking still. And he's staring at the computer screen in front of him.

"Just family photos on the hard drive. Cracked the tablet's password, but it's all up and up. No secret contents, and—"

"Knight." I say his name softly.

He nods slowly, my deadly note more than registering with him.

"What the fuck did you do? I'm going to assume it was you."

"What do you mean, Dante?"

I take a breath. "Jesus. You knew," I say, "we couldn't have an omega here. It's dangerous. To us. She's a virgin. How could you be so stupid?"

"It might take a while to go through everything again, and—"

I grab Knight, hauling him up, and into the wall. "Got something to say? If so, I suggest you do it now."

The slide of his gaze gives him away, even as he says, "No."

"Bullshit."

"Dante—"

68

"Congratulations," I say. "The omega isn't going anywhere. Do you know why?"

"I might." Knight pulls free. "Fuck."

"I hope not. I hope to hell you didn't manage to somehow fuck her, too."

"Dante, listen."

"You bit her. Marked her. Know what that means? She's not going anywhere until we can work out what the fuck to do."

CHAPTER EIGHT

Reaper

I don't like to think about the past. It's pointless. Mine is full of murder. Pain. Destruction.

And Dante.

He knows me. Understands. Trusts. Never mistakes a thing about me or my intentions. Better, he knows my skills, my loyalty. My ways.

Others, like Knight, who tried to talk about the past when we first met, think I'm stupid. Because I'm not a talker. But that's their problem. Not mine.

I thrive on being underestimated. It opens doors. Makes a man my size with my face slide into invisibility.

Like now.

Whoever's following me is reckless. As his carelessness grows, it blooms into confidence and the bolder he gets.

Because he thinks I haven't noticed his presence.

Male. Not female.

Females don't underestimate in the same way.

Maybe it's their size, I don't know. Don't care. They're more cautious because they have to be.

I continue to hunt the hunter. Draw him out.

The buildings on the street, past the small apartment complex where the girl lives, cast black shadows in the yellow spotlights of streetlamps. It would be easy to disappear into that ink, slide around a building's side, or down an alley, but I don't want to lose them. Not yet.

There's a labyrinth of streets, houses, stores, offices, and apartments coming up. There in the jumble are restaurants and empty places. More people, a better chance to see my hunter, slip the tether I'm allowing to tie us together, and either turn the tables or disappear.

I need to get in her place. I want to get my hands on my follower, but out here, doing that's too dangerous. It will garner attention, even this late at night.

Not like I care about attention. Not like I give a fuck about the law.

But when I put hands on this would-be hunter, I want to be able to do it unseen. So I can extract information.

I picked him up about ten minutes after leaving Pandora's which means someone was either watching the place, or looking for me.

Anyone who looks for me and wants to live knows not to follow. Approach without an attempt at subterfuge.

I move at a good pace, slowing at restaurants, pausing at menus to look in the wavey reflection.

At the third place, I think I see him. Average height, jeans. Black hoodie, baseball cap. I move on. Fifth place confirms it.

Same guy.

I hate amateurs.

At least I know it isn't Ghost. Though it would take me longer to pinpoint him.

I correct my thoughts. Clearing out all the noise that's in my head.

Tonight, it's not Ghost physically, but it could be someone he sent.

I mark that down silently. Though Ghost would hopefully send someone with more skill.

Fucking Ghost. Nemesis, betrayer. Someone I don't under *or* overestimate.

Dante should have let me kill him when I had the chance.

But he has kernels of real humanity in him, hidden deep. And Ghost had been Dante's partner and close friend. Our partner. Not my close friend. I never trusted him. So...Ghost lives.

I pretend to peruse the latest menu once more. My stalker remains, hanging back, cap low, standing just at the curb.

I go inside.

The looks I get as I walk are things I'm used to.

People see the scars. My height. The tattoos on my neck. If they're brave or stupid, they see the flatness of my stare, the fact that I'm devoid of warmth, a heart.

Emotion was beaten out of me as a child.

I take a seat in the back. Order coffee and whatever the third thing on the menu is. And I put the cash down. It's habit. Something I never question. The kind of move a man who might want to turn invisible will do.

The waitress isn't sure whether to try and eye fuck me or not. But she takes a closer look. Sees the scars. My stare. And she pulls back into herself.

The coffee, when it comes, is hot and that's all it has going for it.

My stalker is inside now, sitting at the counter so he can watch me in the mirror behind it.

Hazel eyes, brown hair, because he takes his cap off to smooth a hand over his hair.

He's new at this.

I'm not celebrating. Facts are facts. He's new so he could be a pain in my ass and follow me when I leave, causing me to make my move before I'm ready, or he'll get scared and scamper off.

Timing is everything.

I want this easy. No chase.

When I have half my coffee—a good amount of time to wait, my meal should be coming soon—I get up and go to the counter, bumping the guy, lifting his wallet in the process. I ask the girl behind the counter two things.

"I need to make a call. How long until my meal?"

"Another ten minutes," she says, sounding all levels of nervous.

"And the bathrooms?"

She points to the back. "Past the kitchen."

I smile, nod, and put the wallet back without being noticed.

Then I head out, just to the outside of the place, and I pull out my cigarettes, lighting one up and pretending to make a call. As I cross to the tree opposite the restaurant, I memorize his ID.

David Finch. Forty-two. He lives in one of the nicer suburbs, but not the nicest. He's just across the water, so he may have lived there before gentrification hit.

I smoke, slide my phone away, and enjoy about half of the cigarette. Then I stub it out.

When I go in, I make a beeline to the bathrooms, dropping David's ID right below his chair.

I don't go all the way to the back, but I look for an exit. There's an emergency one but it's hooked to the alarms.

Instead, I turn left and cut through the kitchen and out into the alley, where I scale the fence separating this building and the one facing the street beyond.

I take the long, circuitous route back to the girl's place and there I wait in the shadows, unmoving, until the outside light goes off.

Fucking cheap landlords. So many across this part of Starlight City do weird shit like this to save money. They turn off the external lights, making it unsafe for tenants and a gift to people like me.

I'm good at being still, being at one with where I am. Disappearing in plain sight.

Even with a face like mine.

One scarred.

The face of a hardened criminal.

I've heard the word psycho thrown in my direction before.

Maybe I am. I haven't examined it too closely. I'm exactly who and what I need to be.

And that particular word makes most keep away from me.

This suits me fine.

Apart from Dante and even Knight...Julien and his woman, Darcy, who understand me, I don't like people.

The women I fuck? Let's say it's not about forming a bond or a relationship.

It's down in the dirt, primal play, the hunt stripped back to animalistic urges, rutting on a different scale—and never with an omega.

Most of them are bred and raised to mate and breed with an alpha themselves. They want it.

So, I keep away from them. I stick to the others, the outlier gammas and deltas. Even the betas, and the occasional alpha female.

I don't take part in the chase with them often because there aren't many who want to be chased.

Slowly, I let my gaze take in the surroundings. A couple walk past, holding hands, weaving slightly, soft giggles on the breeze.

They pass.

Then...nothing.

When I deem the area's stalker-free, I walk down the side of the building, into the dark.

There's no fence between this building and the next, only dumpsters. No lights.

I veer right and go to the back entrance of her building.

It's old and it takes no work at all to get it open. Besides, I've picked the lock before.

Her apartment's the same. Even with her flimsy locks on and inside, it's nothing for me.

I go from room to room, making sure I'm alone, then I lower the blinds, flick on my flashlight I tucked into my jeans, and examine the back bedroom blind.

Just like I thought.

Black out blinds that fit perfectly.

I go around, turn on a lamp, and search the room.

Her father's, I'm betting. Pristine like he left and didn't come back. But I know that didn't happen.

If he's Elias Enver and not some guy who looks like him, then there's no way he would walk out on his kid. I remember the baby he had.

An alpha taking off with the kid rather than have her stolen from him.

At the time that didn't hit me, the significance and sacrilege of such an act.

I was more in awe that he wanted a baby so much, how he was willing to help us and blow up his life.

He's dead.

I know it in my bones.

Next is her room, pretty without being girly, but still feminine. The clothes are dresses and jeans and T-shirts, hoodies and sweaters. Flat shoes. All of them from thrift stores. All of them to be worn for practicality and not to catch a man.

Then again, a girl who smells so fucking good wouldn't need to catch anyone.

There's nothing in her room.

Except...

My breath catches.

A small leaflet, and I'm betting there's a worn one somewhere on her person or in her bag, from a city funeral.

She did it. On her own.

I can see her, standing there at the no-nonsense marker after the burial, trying not to cry.

I shove most of them back in the drawer, there's only four, so I'm thinking if it is Elias going by Connor Roth, then others from the Hollows would have come.

He was the type of man, even way back when, who'd befriend half the Hollows.

Folding the one I took on the photo printed on the front, I call Dante, setting it on speaker.

"What?"

Okay, he's extra snarly. Something's happened. I don't ask. I'm sure he'll tell me or I'll find out when the time comes. It doesn't bother me.

What does bother me is what I tell Dante. "Someone's been through her place already. Amateur."

There's a backpack, and I pull it to me, going down on my haunches to go through it. Clothes, not much. But I recognize it for what it is. A runaway's prep kit.

Dante and I made plenty of those over the years. And ran plenty of times without a fucking thing.

But that's what it is.

"She got a letter from the fucking Council," he says. "They're marrying her off to some schlep in Hover Valley. He's old."

"Name?"

I repack the bag. She'll have money somewhere else, papers someplace on her. And the fact Dante has a letter addressed to her backs that up.

But no way a girl like her is a seasoned runner. At least, I amend, on her own.

Her father, though, if he was Elias Enver...knew how to run.

"Craig Edmonton," Dante says, still sounding all the circles of hell pissed off.

"Haven't heard of him."

"Knight's looking into him."

Knight? The way Dante says it, the name is like a dirty word. He's pissed at the fucking guy. "She's not Council, as I said," I finish.

It's an easy tell if someone is. Closets of appropriate clothes, files sometimes if it's a sensitive thing where paper is better over computers. Or a work computer.

None of those things here.

Just some empty booze bottles, an attempt at a nest and not much else.

"So do you think she's being used by them?"

"Against us?" I ask.

It's an interesting theory, but it's not one I've thought about. Now I am.

"Not sure yet. The Edmonton alpha could be some way to send her our direction. Pretty little thing, untouched, in heat. She's a time bomb."

"They've tried before."

Yes, they have. And have met with no success.

We've spawned a criminal empire. Dante carved up a place for us to gain control, and the Unholy Trinity are not to be messed with.

Unless we're taken by a Council approved little omega.

Or one of us is.

We haven't shared. Not the three of us.

Dante and I have. He likes control. And he likes free play. I want the hunt, blood, bones, elemental sex.

It makes an interesting dynamic when we throw a willing woman into the mix.

I take my mind from the image and back to the right thought track.

"Yeah, I know," I say. "But if we take a Council omega, which they mainly are, then they'll think they have control."

They will. The Council's reach is deep and once a mating with one of theirs happens...

I'm a little fuzzy on the details, but it's got to do with registration. We're not registered and it pisses them off.

But... "I don't see any sign she's registered."

"She's not," Dante bites out. "Yet. But she's meant to be."

"So, we ban her."

"It's not going to be that easy."

I wait for the bomb to explode.

He growls, then says, "Fucking Knight marked her."

My blood runs cold, but now it turns to ice. "But he didn't rut?"

"No."

"I'll be back soon."

"Good, because we need to work this out."

I finish my search, and then I turn off the lights, and let myself out, glad to be out of there, glad to breathe fresh air that doesn't hold intoxication.

I take the long way back and find David Finch looking at the apartment. He's talking to someone on the phone. "I fucking lost him, okay?"

Then, "Yeah, I hear you. But she isn't home."

When he hangs up, I follow him.

Idiot's heading to the Hollows.

He's easy—boring—to trail. And I manage to get ahead of him. Then I step from the shadows.

My adrenaline surges. I love this part.

"Looking for me?" I bark out.

The man takes one massive step back.

I'm on him so fast. In the next second, I drag him into the alley and have him face down, knee on his neck.

"I think you and I need a talk. And be honest. Or I'll snap your neck."

When I get back, Dante eyes the blood on my tattooed wrist.

"Not mine."

I like to wear a little of a kill's blood. Just for a few hours. If I can.

"Sick fuck."

I don't smile. "Dante. We've got a problem."

"Another one?" he asks.

"Yes."

"Shit."

CHAPTER
NINE

Lizette

My head pounds and every piece of me is tied tight into balls of misery.

Inside, I hurt.

Everything's beyond fuzzy and for a moment, I can't remember anything. Apart from feeling good at one point, like better than I've ever felt before. Orgasmic, and the way he moved his fingers in and out of me—

"Oh. Oh my god!"

The man, he...he... Shame burns hot in my cheeks. My body ticks into throbbing life for him, even as he repulsed me.

What was his name? John? James? Jake.

I shudder at the thought.

I didn't want him, but my physiological urges went crazy. And then a beautiful godling with caramel curls and dimples and too much sex appeal saved me.

Jake didn't penetrate me. The golden-haired godling did, with his fingers. And he showed me a taste of divinity.

You threw yourself on him. Begged him...

Now my body throbs hard with remembered pleasure.

There's a sore spot that aches oh, so good, on my throat, and I touch it. Waves of muted desire spread.

"Where...did I—" I frown, looking around. I'm on a feathery soft bed, the kind of thing I want to burrow into, deep. The room is neutral, calming, low light, and...no windows.

A knell booms in my blood, making my heart lurch. "Why are there no windows?" I whisper.

I drag myself up, ignoring the pain wrapping around me, and make my way to the door, looking around. There's another door, just one, that's open and my reflection passes in a mirror in that room as I do. An ensuite?

When I reach the door, I try the handle, but it's locked.

Using all my strength as panic batters me, I shake it. Then I start banging my fist.

"Hey, hey, let me out! Is anyone there?"

A key scrapes in the lock, and I fist my hands, wishing I'd grabbed something as a weapon, and ready myself for a full charge.

The door hits me, knocking me backwards.

A gorgeous, edgy blonde amazon stands there. "It opens inward. Be a good little omega and get back on the bed."

She holds a tray laden with bowls and some juice in her hands, and I take a step forward.

Her narrow-eyed look stops me in my tracks. "Kid, you can rush me, but there's no way out. You'd have to get through three alphas who are mean as shit, and yes, that includes the one who marked you. If you manage to do the impossible, you'll still have to get through Julien, my man."

She steps in, uses her ass to slam the door shut, and nods at the bed.

There's also a bag slung over her shoulder, and I dart my gaze around, looking for mine.

"Where's my bag? My father's hat?" The other things I hid are important but the hat...it's priceless to me.

"Chill." She nods to the bed again when I step forward. "Julien? Giant man who let you in? You're small, no way you'd even get a step past him, so sit the fuck down."

I do, resentment heating my skin.

She sets the tray down. Then the bag. She reaches in and throws me a hot water bottle. I hug it.

"I hear there's a lot of pain associated with heat."

I frown. "You're not an omega? Are you an alpha?" To me, she's the epitome of an alpha female, but she laughs.

"Gamma."

"Oh." I swallow.

Dad really never took me through the ins and outs of all of the hierarchy breakdown. I just know I'm an omega and that's why we had to stay off grid.

"Oh, Jesus. Your face. You're a fucking little babe in the woods."

She pulls a small bottle of pills out. And she shakes out two. "We don't have any O-blocker, but these'll knock you out in about twenty minutes. So eat, get comfy and lie down."

"Am I a prisoner?" I push the words through stiff lips.

She shrugs. "Kid, I don't make the rules for the Unholy Trinity. That's going to be Dante, Reaper, and your boy Knight."

With that, she turns and starts for the door.

"I'm Lizette." I don't know why I blurt it out, but when her sharp eyes pierce through me, I instantly regret the choice.

"We're not bonding, okay? There are extra blankets in the closet."

"I'm in Pandora's Box?"

"You're in the beating heart of the Unholy Trinity. Take your pills or not, I don't care."

"The Unholy Trinity?"

The blonde goddess rolls her eyes. "You're not so innocent, really?"

A savage heat rushes my veins and I clutch the hot water

bottle with one hand and smooth my dress on my thigh with the other. "Of course I've heard of them."

The woman folds her arms. I have vague flashes of her. Blurry photographs in my mind at the bar waiting tables. Touching my cheek, brushing my hair from my throat. And questions I know I answered but the words from both her and me are lost in a swirl.

She can be soft when she wants to.

Right now, she's annoyed she's here with me. And that makes two of us.

"Everyone's heard of them," I say. "They're outlaws. They live outside of society."

As I speak, my tone is slightly snotty. I'm aware of the idiocy of my words.

Worse, I'm aware of the hypocrisy.

Dad and I, we didn't commit crimes, not in the way the Unholy Trinity does—with their gambling and illegal goods running, bars and clubs open past city and state law decrees.

Hell, I've heard it all. Murder, prostitution, shake downs, loan sharking.

And living in a way that's uncomfortable, when you look at it, like we do—did...outside Council reach.

"I'm guessing your life," the woman says, "is in some ways similar to ours." Then she sighs. "I'm not your enemy, but I'm not your friend."

"So why did you kidnap me?"

She points at her chest in the tight top. It's not low cut, but it's tight, like leather that's been painted on her skin. And if anyone has the body for the second skin look, it's this woman.

"Me?" the blonde says, "I didn't do anything."

"Then—"

"For the record, no one kidnapped you. Dante deemed it wise not to let you out to get yourself mated and marked by some low life. Which you were very much on your way to doing when Knight stepped in."

I grimace.

"Girl, you're in heat. The beginning stage before the main event, but you're gonna have to ride it out here. At least until the worst is over. Unless you want us to turn you out right now."

The blonde comes in close and puts her hands on her thighs, leaning in. She's all sleek muscle, lithe, like a huntress, and I almost draw back.

Except she isn't trying to attack me.

"And judging by the way you look, the way you're shaking and clutching that bottle, I don't think you're gonna make it far. So take your pills, eat, drink, get extra blankets if you need them. I'll check on you in the morning."

"So, I can leave if I want?"

"Now, that's not very civic minded of us, is it?"

And with the final word, she leaves. The click of the deadbolt lock tells me my answer instead.

"Which means," I say to no one, "I'm a damn prisoner."

I try to think of what Dad would do. But the thing is, Dad was the wily one. He wouldn't get into this situation. He wouldn't have panicked.

I have vague memories of the places we've lived when we were on the run. Sometimes we'd leave in the middle of the night, and since I was so little, I only have bright images that fade, but I always remember that it was important I stay quiet. Do what he said. And act like all was normal when things were in freefall.

Dad didn't panic, and he told me he picked Starlight City because it's big. Here, we blended.

Until he died and left me.

Then everything fell apart.

I hug the water bottle tighter, trying to draw the heat into me.

For a few moments, I give in to the self-pity that wants to crush me into a puddle and I squeeze my eyes tight.

"Get it together," I mutter. "You got yourself into this, you can get yourself out."

Steeling myself, I push up to my feet and drop the water bottle. As I clench my jaw, I look around, opening drawers. I find a remote control and, even though I heard the key turn both times in the low-tech door, I press a button.

Sound blares and I whirl. A screen has come to life, a TV, one made to take on the same image as the wall's paint when off, making it almost invisible.

"Shit."

I turn it off, and press the other buttons, but now I don't switch the TV on, nothing else happens. So, I drop the remote control on the bed. I continue my search. There aren't any windows, no secret doors or Narnia or the outside world.

But I'm not ready to concede defeat. Ignoring the agony that's a dull whine in me, I go into the bathroom, feeling the walls either side of the door for the light. I hit it.

There's a vent, but no windows in here, either.

Defeated, I try one last thing.

The door. Just in case.

But the door's very much locked.

A wave hits and I stagger as misery and pain crash over me. The itch for relief, something that ebbs and flows, never leaves me.

Instead, I go to the bed and sit, taking small sips from the bowl of soup that smells of chicken and noodles and the kind of medicine that helps a little.

Then I take a bite of the sandwich. Egg and lettuce. It's on thick whole grain and I whimper.

Because this is the kind of meal Dad made for me the second time I went into heat. And I know he'd want me to eat, to gather strength, calm, before I decide to do anything.

But the pills?

I stare at them and then I sweep them up and throw them, something I'm sure is a mistake. But no, I'm not taking them.

I'm not letting these people, this Unholy Trinity, keep me out of it.

When it comes down to face to face, I want—no, I need—to be alert.

A wave of pain hits me, and my stomach tries to eat itself at the same time, like I don't know which way's up.

But I eat, and I drink, and when I start to feel a little woozy, like the edge has been taken off, I switch on the TV, turn the sound low.

Then I climb into the bed, dragging the hot water bottle with me, and close my eyes.

Blackness claims me.

I don't know how long I was out, but I come awake fast.

My senses are tangled, and I can smell rain in the air, and earthy something. It's hot, salty, and it makes me think of sex.

This time there's pain, but desire flares up, taking me hard.

The TV is still off and I realize the scent isn't something my sleep or drug addled mind made up—I think the food was drugged—because I'm not alone.

Someone's in the room with me. Dark and dangerous and so compellingly male, so overwhelmingly familiar.

I know who it is before I look.

It's the man from the car, when the cops ripped my life apart. When *he* ripped it apart by turning me in.

The tall devil in black.

I throb deep inside.

Not from pain.

But the kind of desire I've never felt or imagined. The only thing close is the other one, Knight, but my desire for him was different. This feels...

This feels like crushing domination.

Worse, I want to be crushed, dominated. Made his.

I want this man to rut in me.

I turn. Look at him.

It's a mistake.

He's even worse up close.

Because like this, I'm his willing sacrifice, and what I thought was desire was nothing at all.

He's pure combustion.

The man—I'm positive he's the one the woman called Dante. He's an alpha, yes, but it's DNA, bone, and soul deep in him. The man leans against the wall, arms folded, eyes half mast, and one leg resting on the wall behind him.

He's in black. Head to foot.

The devil.

My destruction.

The most potent man I think I've ever seen.

I breathe in, and I'm consumed by him.

And even though I'm in bed, my legs shake as I sit up.

"Oh, good," he says in a dark and sonorous voice edged in sex, "you're awake."

CHAPTER

TEN

Dante

This is one of the most fucking foolhardy things I've ever done. Coming down here. *Shit*. The girl gives off scent like crazy, and it's hard to fucking think straight.

I'm still mad as fuck at Knight, but I'm beginning to understand the little prick. Because I'm both lying and telling Lizette the truth.

I'm glad because I need to question her.

But honestly, I wish to fuck she still was out for the count. Better yet, I wish she wasn't here.

She's too...disturbing.

The girl's gorgeous with her sweetness of innocence that makes one soft and available and the last one's exactly what I don't want. I can't release her, either. Not yet. Not until her fucking heat's done and not until we get down to the ground about why she turned up at the club, of all places.

The mark...is something we need to work on, something that's going to decide the extent of her freedom after her heat. But I do know if we let her go, she'll be under close watch.

"Y-You must be Dante."

"Did you come looking for the Trinity? That it? Figured your heat made you so fucking alluring we'd be yours to... what? Manipulate? Have us hand you information for the Council?"

She recoils, and I try to take shallow sips of air, to not breathe in her aroma. But it's almost impossible because she's everywhere, coating my skin, sliding down into me, wrapping around my fucking cock. There's a whisper to grab her by the hair and flip her so I can take her hard and deep and long while she's on her knees and her ass is in the air.

That scent makes me want to mold her hot, wet cunt to my dick. I want to fill her with my seed. I want to take her in the hardest, longest, most mindless and satisfying rutting the world's ever seen.

Never in my fucking misguided life have I ever wanted to do that. Just take her. No games. No fun denial torture. Just straight down and dirty fucking. The animalistic kind.

I meet her dark melting gaze, and from here I can see the mark Knight left.

She didn't bite him. They didn't rut.

Thank fuck.

All he did was be the lucky bastard to slide his fingers into her pussy.

Christ, he's lucky I didn't take his head off his shoulders when I caught him licking at his fingers later. Much later. Which meant he'd sucked her slick from them already and he still wanted seconds or thirds, or let's face it, probably fifths.

Because her scent clung to him.

I breathe out heavily, keeping my gaze guarded, cold, unreadable. It's taking everything I have not to claim her. Everything I have to keep the erection at bay.

His mark should lessen her appeal to me.

It doesn't.

A part of me wonders if his mark heightened her allure,

but that's not how things work. But who knows. We're not exactly a pack that follows the 'rules.'

Lizette frowns, and though I know she hurts, and her eyes are getting fever-bright and pupils so wide the expression is a siren's call of an invitation to smash myself against her rocks, I don't give in. I don't move.

"I asked you a question," I say. "I expect an answer."

"You think I want...this?" She throws back the covers and swings her feet over the side of the bed and runs a hand in the air along her body. "To be this? Feel this? Be reduced to fodder to basically be sold as a baby making machine?"

"That's your choice. I don't give a fuck. You do what you want. And as far from here as we can get you."

Her eyes flash. "It's easy, isn't it, for you? Why did you do it?"

"Do what?" I ask.

"Turn me into the Council?"

I don't reply immediately. My first instinct is to believe in her innocence, that she's not a trap. But it's fucking lust whispering to me, not common sense.

Common sense says flatly it's one hell of a coincidence she turned up here. And I'm not sure how what Reaper found out fits in with her, but it does. Has to.

They were following her.

"Who's Jake?" I ask.

Her expression turns mulish, and she shifts, half stands but her legs wobble and she sits, dress riding higher.

There are fading purple bruises to match the ones on her face and they tell me Knight was right. The fucker, Jake, tried to rape her. She's just lucky he didn't. And that he didn't mark her, claim her, own her, tie her to him.

Or maybe she's his honey pot for us? Who the fuck knows except for her, a dead man, and the missing Jake.

"Who the fuck is he?" I press.

"He told me he was gay." She doesn't look at me, but her

cheeks tell the story of her shame as they turn red. The decent part of me, that small part, wants to tell her it's not her fault.

I don't.

"He got me a drink and—"

"You gave him your number. Why?"

Her head snaps up. "Because he asked for it. And I didn't give him mine. I put in the number of a pizza place I know. I'm not a total idiot."

"Debatable."

"I guess that makes you a dumbass who likes kidnapping girls."

"No one kidnapped anyone, and Darcy's been looking after you, right?"

"Darcy?" She frowns. "The blonde Valkyrie?"

It's a pretty fucking apt description of Darcy. She could go anywhere, be anything, until she chose a pack, as long as she stayed within her own group to mate with. But with us, she has a special kind of freedom, one that doesn't pin her down. One that allows her the forbidden—her relationship with Julien.

"She's a gamma. They aren't ever submissive to omegas."

"I didn't ask her to be. I didn't ask for any of this, I just..." Lizette swallows, glances down, then meets my gaze again.

Innocent. The word rushes through me.

"Just thought you'd wander in Pandora while in heat."

"Almost in heat," she snaps. "I—"

She stops, shakes her head.

I don't push that line of questioning yet, but I will.

Her too-big dress has slipped off one shoulder, showing the black strap of her bra, her unsullied skin. I wonder what it would be like to tease her, leave her a quivering mess under the order not to come.

It's about now, when I'm looking at a woman, usually a beta, or delta, I'd have her ready to do my bidding. Or, if I'm feeling like something rough and tumble and edged in danger, a gamma fighting me.

Reaper likes to play with gammas. He likes the challenge, the fight, the hunt. If he's in the mood he'll go for a beta, or occasionally a delta.

Now, Knight's a delta and beta guy. His particular taste in play is that he wants a sub. Gammas don't tend to want that.

The one thing we keep away from?

Fucking omegas.

I can have her flavor in others. Maybe not her particular scent and the way it curls in deep, but she's weak, made to want to breed, and breeding is the last fucking thing on our agenda. Especially mine.

I don't think she's weak of mind, but she'll have that omega subservience, the kind I've seen so many times in the females the Council mates with an approved alpha and his pack. Simply because they're an omega.

And also I've seen them with the alpha pack that's dirty and off the grid, the omega either bred or used. Some of them okay with it because that's their role.

I digress.

She's able to get into my blood because she's in heat, and it's worse now. Because before she was on that edge or just starting.

It's full blown now, and her pheromones are thick and irresistible.

"You what?" I ask.

Her mouth clamps shut, and she shakes her head again.

"Nothing," she finally mutters.

I put my foot down then raise the other. No way I'm moving from this wall or taking a step in her direction. Not right now. Not with that fucking mark on her. But I need what she knows.

Yeah, I'm being a masochistic ass by being in here, soaking her up. I could have sent in Julien who's immune. The guy's loyal, smart, happy in his relationship with Darcy. Fuck, I could send her back in, too.

She's exactly the same.

But...

And there is a motherfucking *but*.

I need to be the person questioning her.

Need and want all mesh together in this room. Yeah, there's want, but I also know I can't trust Knight in here, not with her in heat, not with his mark on her.

And Reaper's liable to scare the shit out of her. He can be... not the gentlest, but good at extracting information. He might be able to twist his depraved instincts into something slightly more benign, but he'll scare her.

The reason I need to be the one is I'm the one who first saw her.

She recognizes me. My scent. My voice. On a base level, she recognizes me. Her lust strokes against my skin but I think I'm the one who can get her to talk.

If she has anything to talk about.

If she's being manipulated, I'll find that out, too.

Plus, I don't want anyone else in here with her. Fuck that.

"Nothing?" I ask. "Nothing gets you fucking jack, you know it, right?"

"I'm not in any position to bargain. I'm your prisoner." She fists her hands, notes her hiked up skirt and rubs it down her thighs to cover up. She doesn't uncurl her fists. "Prisoner. One you drugged and tried to double drug. In a locked, windowless room with the threat that even if I get out, I won't be able to get past you or your minions."

"Not a threat. The truth. And my minions aren't what you should worry about. My pack members are."

"Knight?" The way she says it is a sharp twist in the heart. "I thought... Is he a delta?"

"There's a reason we're called the Unholy Trinity. Our pack has three alpha leaders."

She studies me for a moment. "And you're the top dog leader of the alpha pack, that it?"

"We're equal."

"What's the saying? Some are more equal than others?"

I nod slowly. "If you're trying to stroke my ego, it's not going to work, little omega."

"You're the Council. I don't want to stroke anything to do with them."

The bitterness, fear, and hate are real. The fear's new, because it fits with someone who's been out of their sight up until now. The letter...maybe it's all real. But still, I look for cracks, for where her attempts at creating a truth don't line up.

"I've got nothing to do with the fucking Council." I offer a small, nasty smile. "Three alphas. No omega. Outside the fucking law. What do *you* have to do with the Council?"

She stands, a grimace of pain marring her face. But she raises her chin. Looks me dead in the eye.

I ignore the lack of respect deep inside. Why? Not sure. She intrigues me.

"Nothing. You turned me in. That's how they found me," she says.

"Your little cop friends did. I stopped them from arresting you." I rake my gaze over her. "An act I'm starting to regret."

"Dick."

"Not my name and I do have one."

"You turned me in. And now—"

"Craig Edmonton?"

She recoils.

"Of course," Lizette snaps, "you went through my things. Read the letter."

"How did you manage to keep out of their reach now you're in heat. It started, what? A year ago?"

"This city's full of jobs where you don't need registration."

I smirk. "I'm aware."

It's the only type of person we employ. The girls who work

the lower level and some of our other places, the men who bring in the stolen goods, deal in contraband—women, too— not one of those are registered, or they're shunned. And some, according to Council records, are dead.

"Then—"

"Craig?"

She shudders this time. "Some old alpha the Council wants me to mate with."

"You'd be queen of the pack."

"He has mean eyes," she says. "Cold. It'd be a loveless match."

I scoff. Love? Is she really that naive?

"I thought...I thought I was shunned, but I'm not and now they expect me there next week."

I nod. She can't go. They can't see the mark. "Will you go?"

"I... It's not your business."

It makes sense how she thought she was shunned, especially since they were off grid. Somehow Roth showed up on their systems when the idiotic cops handed over her name.

Our connection with the cops on something like this need to be handled right, and I'd personally prefer not to involve them. It's not worth them getting caught. And if they turn...

"I'm not interested. Curious." I shrug. "But what you do next with this Craig is up to you, Lizette."

"Can I go?"

"You're in fucking heat. Do you want me to spell out what might happen to you?" I say.

"Can I go?"

"No."

Her father's dead, and she's protecting him. Or herself.

But the way she put that hat away and the photos...not to mention the little leaflet of the pauper's funeral tells me it's all about him. In death, she doesn't want to give up anything that might seem like betrayal.

I go along the lines of things in my head. Every place I stop has a thousand possible outcomes or motivations.

Life isn't cut and dried. It's not simple. People do things that are muddied. Her love of her father might be pure, but her motivation might not be. His might not have been, either.

Fuck, he might not even have been the Elias Enver I knew.

Which brings me back to how an unregistered little omega managed to be stopped by idiotic cops who both didn't know what she was.

And— "Here's one thing. When those cops grabbed you and I fucking *rescued* you, why didn't you have fake papers? You have to have them. Anyone off grid or shunned has them. Because there are things that come up, things you need them for, even shitty housing wants something. You know there's a curfew so—"

"Because I don't *have* any." Her burst of words makes me stop, and I unfold my arms, running a hand through my too long hair before I fold them again.

I wait.

Silence stretches, and she finally says, "I didn't need them. I didn't have a reason for them until...until recently."

"What happened?"

"Not your business," she says, her voice catching. "Not anyone's business."

I change direction, toward the man, David, who Reaper killed for reasons I understand. He also said the book she has contains nothing but the names and info of old rebels and nobodies. His area of expertise, not mine.

"Who's David Finch to you?" I ask.

She frowns. "Who?"

"He was outside your apartment last night. A friend of your Jake's?"

"He's not—" She stops. Glares. "I don't know either man. I didn't do anything wrong." Then she looks down, takes half a step toward me before changing her mind and stopping. She finally looks at me. "At least not intentionally. The only stupid thing wrong I did was make a bad judgment call and go out for some drinks to take the edge off the heat. Because you...you motherfucker, it *hurts*."

The raw edge of her voice slices into me but I ignore it.

"Okay. Then tell me this."

"Tell you what?"

I give her a cold, blank look, one she steps back from.

And what I really want to do is stride over and throw her down, and fuck her so senseless she's utterly mine.

She's fucking witchcraft. She makes me want to do all the things I don't. Corrupt her sweetness.

But I just keep that stark expression in place and stay where I am. Pressed into the fucking wall. Like a special kind of coward.

One who won't risk trusting himself.

Coward? Or is that man who knows what, exactly, he's capable of doing and is hanging on by a fraying thread to keep this side of control?

I'll send someone for O-blockers. The best on the market. But first...

"Who's Elias Enver?"

She goes still, but the expression is real. "I heard the name, but I haven't met him."

"But," I say, "you have. Question is how the fuck did the Council know Elias Enver was Connor Roth? Your father."

ELEVEN

Lizette

"What?"

My voice cracks and the world with it. For a brief moment, the pain inside me is dwarfed by the agony caused by his words.

I don't even know why it hurts. The lies Dad might have told me? The implacable truth of what he's saying rings through me.

I stagger, but Dante makes no move to help, makes no move at all, just shows me his hateful, cold, impassive face. I grab at the bed then sink down, dragging the now cool water bottle to my lap and digging my fingers into the purple silicon, the water sloshing as I do.

It soothes a little, that sound, the feel against my fingers. But it's a lie, a fallacy.

The pain is rocking through me. Both agonies now. Inside my body and inside my heart. And I squeeze my eyes shut to stop the burn and blur of tears. I'm definitely not going to cry in front of this demon.

I swallow. Hard. Over the hot lump that makes it hard to breathe.

Dad lied through omission all the time. I knew it. He had to lie. His past had been locked and bolted away, along with the truth about whoever my mother was. That she died is the only thing I know for certain. And to stop the Council from taking me, my father ran with me.

But dad was Connor. Connor Roth. Like I'm Lizette Roth. If he had another name, he'd have trusted me with it.

Right?

Right?

Elias Enver. The name's known. A murmur and whisper. Passing conversation with peers of Dad's. Just in earshot of me I'd hear it. But—and it's a big *but*—they all called Dad Roth or Con. Or Connor.

If it's true, it makes my life a lie. A joke. It makes me wonder what I don't know.

I stare down at the water bottle.

"My father... Dad's name was Connor Roth. He was shunned. We both were. Apparently now I'm not."

"You know his real name."

"It isn't." I push it out. And I know it's a lie. It makes sense. And the grown-up part of me even understands it. But right now, the little girl who's still crying for her dad is hurting over this. "I've heard that name. But everyone called him Con or Connor."

Dante sighs, irritated. He doesn't like me, I can tell. My body might want him like I crave him, and we haven't even really touched, but I don't like him right back.

"Elias Enver's a wanted man," he says. "He wasn't shunned. He was on the run. Which you know."

"I don't...I don't know anything. If you have a problem with him, it's too late. He's dead." A tear escapes, and I smack it away.

"Doesn't change the fucking fact you wandered in here

and fucked the status quo. Fucked the equilibrium and probably would have fucked the pretty, curly haired asshole, too. Jesus, you already got him to mark you."

Panic slams into me and my hand flies to my throat. The place that hurts and feels so good. I press into it. Feel the shape by the sensations.

Bite mark.

Oh, holy hell.

"I didn't ask for this," I say.

"You were humping him."

"I'm not the only one involved," I snap. "And I was drugged."

Dante doesn't comment, but the set to his mouth spikes my blood pressure.

"I'm not some kind of femme fatale," I say.

"No, you're definitely not."

"Ass."

"Here's the deal. You're in heat. So, you're staying here, with us." His gaze drops to the hot water bottle. "I'll have another sent in. And some sourced omega blockers. That's why you were in the Hollows that night?"

I nod, my chest tight. "How long will I be a prisoner?"

"Not a prisoner."

"Unwanted guest," I say, pushing the words out through gritted teeth. "How long?"

"Until I say so."

Fury breaks free, burning like acid. I throw the water bottle at him, but he just looks irritated as he easily catches it. "Saves me the trip closer to you," he mutters.

"You say that like you don't want to come closer."

"I don't."

"You're a bastard."

"And?" His gaze flickers over me. "You can like this arrangement or not. You're here until I change it."

"You don't want to come closer," I snap. "I don't want you *anywhere* near me. Who the hell do you think you are to take me prisoner—sorry, make me your unwanted guest—until you say so? Just because I came into your shitty establishment? What gives you the right to act this way?"

The corners of his mouth turn upward in a cruel little smile, and it makes my insides swoop and lust burst forth. I'm sick in the head and I know it. The other one, Knight...he was nice to me.

This one?

I'm sick with lusting for him. It's my heat. That's all this is —the heat puts hormones into overdrive.

"I'm one of the fucking alphas of the Unholy Trinity. I can do whatever the fuck I want."

"Including kidnapping."

"If I wanted to, yes. As it is, you're a guest. Unwanted, but a guest. Consider it protection for what happened with that dick bag, Jake, on our premises."

"Then just take it on the record," I say, "that I don't want to be here."

"Great, because I don't want you here either. I don't need to babysit a fucking little drunk of an omega who's recklessly trying to get herself a mate by hitting up bars. Or did you choose this one in the hope that you'd get one of us? Maybe this Jake actually helped you?"

"What?" I recoil from his words and grip the edge of the bed where I sit, every part of me hurting, vibrating with tension while he just stands there; relaxed, uncaring, hating me.

I didn't do anything to him. At all.

"It happens, Lizette. Girls come in, Council plants or girls looking for what they think is going to be an exciting ride with one or all three of us. Those girls try to trap us. Fuck, omega men, too. Never works."

"What? The boys aren't pretty enough for you?"

He doesn't do anything but shrug. "The boys are not any of our type. It'd probably be easier. But then again, we don't want those fucking girls, either. None of us wants to change our way of life. We're a trinity, not a nursery. We trade in illicit goods, underground bars and clubs. Not Council fucking life. And we're not splitting up. Go be a drunk elsewhere next time."

"I'm not a drunk. I barely drink."

Dante just laughs. "The empty bottles in your apartment suggest otherwise."

I stare at him.

"Yeah," he says, "we searched it. Reaper did."

My head's starting to spin. It's not that sense of betrayal. It's him, my body, it's the fact I want to launch myself at him, lick him all over, and offer myself to him like a willing sacrifice.

It's almost enough of a shocking thought to drag me back from the edge, but it's the heat, and the fact that this might be the first time I'm plunging in without drugs.

Bad enough I only had one O-blocker. The booze helped. And, like it or not, the drugged food did too. But all that's faded.

And for the first time, I'm left with the real force of being in heat. My thighs are wet, and I'm hot, feverish, my clothes are both too much and not enough. I start to clench at the material of my skirt, hiking it up to mid-thigh.

"I'm not a drunk. I'm in heat and I don't...I don't know why you hate me. Why you're repulsed by me."

"Fuck." He rubs a hand over his eyes. "I think we're done talking. Darcy will be in with some drugs, something to knock you out until we can get the blockers."

"I don't want drugs," I snarl.

"You drank a shit ton of booze. That's a drug. So are the O-blockers you went to the Hollows to buy." The nasty smile appears again, and I want to run my fingers over his shadow of a beard, his lips, dip in.

I want to run my fingers over him, rub my slick over his mouth. I want to grind into him, drown in his heat, his touch, let him do what I know he can: stop the pain and make me feel good.

"If you don't want me, Knight does."

I rise.

"Oh, fuck." He points the hot water bottle at me. "Stay the fuck down on the bed."

"No."

I cross to him, and the closer I get, the more that intoxicating scent of secret places, earth, salt, and rain. All of it comes together and whispers sex to me.

The closer I get, the more soothed I am. And, at the same time, inexplicably, more feverish. I stop right in front of him and look up.

Everything spins in me.

Oh, this man is handsome, hard edged, dark souled and I can't help but want to drop down and offer myself to this god-like creature, have him make me his slave. Do with me what he wants.

"Back the fuck off."

It's a warning, a challenge, a taunt, and to my fever and heat fueled brain, a come on.

I put my hand on his chest.

Electricity sparks through me, lighting me up.

He's hot. Beyond hot. Fire itself. From hell. From the heavens. From all the secret places.

I'm fused to him in a way that doesn't involve the physical self. And the slight parting of his lips, flare of his nostrils, they tell me he feels it too.

"I just need...I need..." I rise on my bare toes to kiss him, one hand reaching for his cock.

Suddenly, I'm slammed hard against the wall, wrists in a tight grip above my head.

The world spins, and when it stops, when I can breathe, all I can taste and feel and smell is him. I whimper.

"Listen up, little omega, and listen good, because I'm only fucking saying this once." His gaze drops to my mouth and the hunger in it makes a liar of the harshness in his tone. The rejection.

"You want me," I whisper.

"No. This is heat. Omega. Alpha. Fucking nature and base animalistic needs we feed into because that's all society can be bothered to cling to. Because it's easy to control people when you set up rigid rules and ways. I don't want you. My body might, but fuck that."

"Fuck *me*."

"We don't need groupies like you hanging around, squeezing out our kids, tying us to a life we don't want," he murmurs. "The norms and restrictions and all that fucking bullshit the Council pushes on people."

"I'm not a groupie," I say.

"Then don't fucking act like one."

He comes in close, his mouth a whisper from mine.

"Please..."

His lips come closer still and every single part of me zeroes into him, into the kiss that's going to happen.

"Please what?" His free hand comes up to take my throat, closing around it, and stopping me from moving forward, into the kiss he's refusing me.

His hand vibrates, both hands do, with the effort of holding himself back.

I shouldn't know that.

But I do.

I feel his effort pulsate from him into me. Like telepathy. Like wishful thinking.

"Take you? Fuck you, knot in you? Kiss you?" His breath paints my lips in a warmth I want to curl into. "Not happening, Lizette. Not here, not with us, but you do prove one thing. You're in heat now, and you can't be out there alone. You'll be eaten alive."

"But—"

"I'll send in Darcy with something to knock you out. And a fresh hot water bottle. You're going to lose your appetite, and probably not want to drink. I'm not up on the ins and outs. I don't have nor have I ever had an omega, but clearly, I know more than you. Elias didn't teach you better?"

"My dad got me blockers. And I just..."

"Started. Your second one? Third? Fourth?" He meets my gaze, and I try to move into him but I'm pinned and my hips connect with his.

He grinds into me and sparks ignite inside me. I shudder from the sweep of euphoria. I want him inside me. I want Knight. I want the other one. I want them all.

I should be shocked, a part of my brain whispers. But I'm not. The thoughts fall through me. So many random and hot thoughts. Naked. Sweat. Cocks. Men in me. I'm drowning because this one is denying me what I want.

Oh, God, why—

"You're experiencing it unaided. So, we're going to aid you. Not with a knot though, so don't even go there. And when you're through this—"

"You'll send me home."

"We'll continue the conversation," he says. "We need to get that damn mark removed."

My head spins trying to keep up with him. I don't want to talk. I want to fuck.

"Then home," I say, almost delirious. "No sex. At least, not between us."

His eyes narrow, and he steps back, letting me go. My legs give way and I slide down the wall.

"You'll stay here until you're through it, and then we'll talk. Basically, you're here until I say differently."

"Please..."

"Oh, one more thing. Touch me again, and I'll make sure you'll fucking regret it."

With that, he walks out, the door locking behind him.

CHAPTER
TWELVE

Knight

I twirl in my chair and put my feet down so I stop, facing the demon himself, Dante.

I look at his grim, brooding face. Does he kill with his bare hands? He's given orders, sure. Gotten himself in the thick of it and shot a few pricks who deserved it. But bare hands? As in straight up murder? A murderer of male beauty?

Yeah. Not sure about that one.

Me, being the male beauty in question, is bothered and then some.

"Are you still mad?" I ask.

Dante raises a brow. "Fuck, Knight, I don't know. Hey, Reap, you think I'm still fucking furious at this asshat?"

Freaking hell, but Reaper moves like death itself. Cold and silent. One minute I'm in my suite, and I'm aware that Dante walks in. Just, but I was aware.

Reaper? Not there and then boom, present. No awareness. Nothing. That psychopath is on a different plane of existence.

He'd also kill me in a blink, then not lose a second's thought about me. Or anyone.

Except, perhaps, Dante.

The man with the scarred face, who's a bonafide pussy magnet in all the ways a magnet works, eyes me. Reaper then moves about the office. "Yes."

I breathe out, tap out a tattoo on the arm of my chair. "She's been in there for three days. I can't really smell her anymore."

"That's a lie." Dante glances at the three computer screens, and then at the laptop that has something else on it. "She's got a potent scent and for some reason, we can all still smell her."

"It's not my fault." I shrug. "That's not how bites work."

"You had to fucking do it, didn't you?" Dante asks.

"Hey, I didn't fuck her or knot her." I smirk. "That's worth something."

"A stay of execution."

I shoot the filthiest look I can at Reaper for the comment. He's joking. Is he joking? Does the man joke? Fuck.

"It'll wear off. Right?" I look from one of them to the other, and they exchange a look of their own. "What?"

Like, yeah, I'm younger than them, and way prettier than them, but I'm not a child. I'm thirty-two. Not five.

I'm not telling them I got Darcy to bring Liz a super-soft blanket for her heat. Just like I'm not mentioning how I feel both bad and not bad I bit her. I waver on that.

What I do know is I can almost feel her, and every now and then a twinge hits me, like a sliver of her heat somehow infiltrates me.

"Did you get something on her and the Council?" Dante asks.

"Not really." I turn, pick up the laptop and hand it to him as Reaper slides deeper into the office in my suite, gaze on one of the bigger screens. "It looks like they don't have much. Only that her father was shunned—and they have him listed as Connor Roth. She's unregistered and has an interview scheduled this coming week. She's twenty-one and they want to mate her with some dick named Craig Edmonton who's about a thousand. He's an alpha of a small pack of no consequence."

"So nothing we didn't know already." Dante frowns. "Why give her to them, to him?"

"Wrong question," says Reaper quietly. There's a cigarette behind one ear.

I almost tell him not to smoke, but if he's going to, he will, so I leave it. Reaper's a definite "choose your battles" kind of guy.

"Maybe," Dante says. "But I know how the Council operates. She'll be considered a prime cut of meat. A gift for a bigger outfit, one that's either got an alpha ready to move on and start his own pack, or where he's poised to take over. Fuck, I'm shocked they don't have a mating war for her."

"Mating war?" I look at him with a frown, uneasiness spreading through me.

"Where they do their version of speed dating, only to see who matches with her in soulmate terms." Dante taps on the keyboard of the laptop.

Reaper's got a book in his hand. I didn't even notice him picking it up. He doesn't glance up from the page. "Or they match her to the highest bidder."

I cough. "Bidder?"

"Where people put in money to gain a better standing with the Council," Dante says. "Keep up. You should know this."

"I wasn't interested in any of this bullshit. I wanted to go to college and make a shit ton of money in some skyscraper that glitters and rains cash in a big, expensive city. Pack living wasn't exactly front and center conversation in my home. I'm an anomaly."

Thing is, I'm putting my best, cocky, asshole foot forward here. I have to. Dante's the kind of alpha that makes most alphas wish they were betas. And Reaper is... well, he's something else.

I'm up there when I need to be, but I prefer my place behind the scenes.

I just want them to know. As the new kid on the block. These two...they go way back. We're past the new alpha in the pack bullshit, but my head still plays that game.

Because I know if I were with any other alphas, they wouldn't *be* alphas. I'd be at the top.

The three of us are meant to be equal. And we are. It's just good old Dante's right there. At the peak of our triangle.

"I know. I know." I hook an ankle up to the opposite knee and resist the urge to play with the dark denim edge of my jeans. "I fucked up. And I know the basics, but I didn't study Advanced Council Studies. The bite's going to reverse. I didn't—"

"Bites," Reaper says, "are used to track, to control, and to bind."

There's a grimness about him right now that's got zilch to do with the reaper part of his name. Or maybe it does. He's hard to read, even for me.

The man isn't a talker and when he does, he's often just blunt. At first, I took it as him not being as smart as me because I'm fucking smart. I'm up there. So's Dante, in a different sense.

But that aura of people misreading him is something I suspect he cultivates. Or allows others to cultivate for him.

They underestimate him.

Once.

The time I did, he could have killed me, snapped my neck. He didn't. Instead, he taught me to kill, fight, defend, hurt. And he told me I never had to use the skills as killing isn't in my blood, not like him or like Dante. But now I know how, and that's important.

Even, he said, if I never utilize it.

Biggest fucking speech he ever gave me.

That moment changed our dynamic, and I went from the new kid to full on accepted. By him. And me accepting him.

Dante? Never an issue. He saved my ass, saw my potential, made me a partner when he could have just claimed the top job in our outfit and lives.

Which, I guess, is why I feel his displeasure like a fucking brand being held against my skin. I owe him, in a way.

"Yeah," I say to them both, "but..." I turn my chair and clear one of the screens to type on my keyboard. "See? I didn't mate with her and she didn't mark me. She'll be fine. She's out of heat, she's not bonded, not truly. And we can use it to track her when we let her go. At least until the bite fades."

"If it fades." Dante slides the laptop on the desk next to me. "We might have to look into getting it reversed. Somehow."

"What—"

"He means, Knight, her scent's potent. To us. You bit her and marked her, and since we're a pack, we can feel the pull."

Fuck, another long speech from Reaper. Maybe I'm unconscious and this is a dream.

"If we can track her through it, others can track us through her," he continues. "He's saying if it's a soulmate kind of bullshit situation, or to put it another fucking way, if your pheromones are a particular and rare match, and you've gone and taken us along for the ride in pheromone matched hell, she can be used."

"I've told you and Reaper's told you, she's clean." I frown. She's clean, a good girl, a good person. It's as bright as day, that fact.

Liz just oozes sweetness and innocence. And goodness.

"And she sings," I say. "I heard her."

Dante stares like I've lost my mind.

"She does." Reaper shrugs, turns a page of the book. "I heard her walking by her room."

"What the fuck?" Dante rubs a hand over his closely trimmed beard. And eyes both of us with evil intent.

"It shows she's innoc—"

"If we have to have her around, we could use her. We have a stage," Reaper says, cutting me off.

"And if we need to bring people to us, then she might be the drawing card," I add. I don't particularly want to do that, but earning keep or sent away are the only current options.

If I was Liz, I'd choose the stage.

"I vote for Reap's idea," I say.

"Why not utilize her talents while she's here?" Reaper turns another page.

"Yeah, and it's better than her being a prisoner." I shrug. "If we want to know who might be interested in her, what's wrong with offering a little honey from the pot?"

"Honey from the pot?" Dante looks disgusted. "And I'm not keeping her as a prisoner. The moment we know what's up and that mark's gone, I want *her* gone. In the meantime, I'll *think* about having her sing."

In Dante-language, that means no.

I turn to Reaper, looking for some kind of back up. "She'd bring in a crowd. Her looks can pack the house alone. Add in her singing and the money... It'll rush in."

"Fuck, Knight." Dante huffs.

"Because she's clean, you mean. And pretty." Reaper doesn't look up from the book.

Well yeah. "Also, her father was shunned by the Council, but she wasn't. His death brought about her coming to their attention. To the point where they rushed to find her a match. It's a bit weird, if you ask me. So it stands that they have something..."

As I say this, I start to falter.

It isn't about sweetness and innocence or a new omega falling into the Council's clutches at the right time. It's something else. Something I'm not seeing.

"What is it, Knight?" Dante asks.

"The timing's all really convenient, isn't it? Dead father, discovered omega, a mate in the wings... an ancient mate at that. Also, if the Council knew about her father, then why not just take her?" I frown. "Unless there's a bylaw that states a shunned societal member's offspring out of reach until the parent dies or they go into heat."

"I don't think so," says Dante. "If there is, it's so arcane and buried that someone might fight them on it."

"Just like I doubt there's a clause about pairing her off immediately to an old dude," I snort.

"Even if there was something like that, which there isn't, people would fight. Relatives for one." Dante crosses his arms.

"No one fights the Council," I say. "You're talking court? No one takes them to court."

"He's not talking court." Reaper's face is shadowed. "He means a different fight."

"That's what I mean," I say. "There's something off."

"No shit." Dante shakes his head. "But maybe you're right. They wouldn't be seen dead in court, and I don't think the council wants to actively fight us over a girl who doesn't want to be handed over to someone she didn't pick."

"So, she stays?" I ask.

"There's a difference between stay and hold." Dante's mind is clearly ticking. "We can't hold her here forever. Not against her will."

"She could work for us." I repeat, looking at them both. "Sing."

"Even if she doesn't want to?" Reaper says.

Though the thought crossed my mind. "She will. I think it'll be worth it for us. I can charm her." I smile.

"You've done enough damage, Knight." Dante narrows his eyes at me. "Next you'll say you should fucking bond with her."

I don't want to bond, but fuck, she tasted sweet, and I do want to go there again. When she's safe.

Which is now.

It's been three days. Her heat's done. Apparently, she's sleeping, according to Darcy, who's the only one that's been in there. The only one with a key.

Fuck.

And fuck again. Y'know, just for good measure.

And I think I just like her. She's refreshing, and I...oh, hell. I want to get to know her. Just in a simple no agenda way.

I'm pathetic.

"We need to do something," I say. "She's got her meeting to register—"

"Darcy's going to call, pretend to be Lizette and tell them she's in heat." Dante rubs a hand over his chin. "In all honesty, I don't think we should let her go. Or sing. Or be seen, really."

"A prisoner isn't a good idea either, man." I glare at him. "C'mon."

Reaper meets my gaze. Then he looks over to Dante. "Plan A's good. And we can shift it into a plan B."

"What the fuck's plan A?" I ask. "And plan B? How many plans do you have?"

I fucking know Dante's playing with me when he says, "Plan A is...we let her go."

"No." I point at him. "You're going to somehow make her come back."

"This part of the conversation is over, Knight," Dante says. "We have a plan. We let her go. If she comes back on her own because she realizes here is safer than out there, then we'll see about your plans."

"You want to find out if she heads off to the Council." I pull up the old dude she's meant to mate with on my screen. "I don't think so. Look at this guy."

Fuck, that old man is one ugly guy. And callous. The

cruelty's dark and glints in his eyes. To me, he looks like a weak man who's alpha by proxy.

What did Reaper say?

"What's plan B?" I turn to him. "And what did you mean, wrong question?"

"She's beautiful, very young, and she smells untouched. That's worth a lot. There are all kinds of black market deals when it comes to untouched and pretty omegas. Maybe the Council's not above that. So, why is she being shipped to an insignificant and unheard of pack in Hover Valley instead? What's their worth to the Council?" Reaper closes the book, but doesn't put it down. "What do they have? What is the strategic place they hold, or what is it they're sitting on in terms of wealth for the Council?"

Wow, we're breaking Reaper milestones by the second here. Another speech.

It's smashed all the records I know about. Which, to be fair, is the one I keep in my head.

"Hover Valley's nice, but it's a getaway for the rich. A couple of insignificant packs, and Edmonton's the most mundane of all. He's not rich."

"Not talking money."

"Then what?" I ask Reaper.

"Not sure." With that, he leaves. With my book.

"What do you think, Dante?" I ask him.

"I'm fucking thinking you got us in this, you get us out."

I nod. "And apart from magic?"

His expression's dark. "I think maybe we look into who's in his pack, and any connections with the Council. When Reaper talks, it's worth it to fucking listen." He taps a hand on the wall as he starts to turn to go. "And keep an eye on that Jake person if you can. And Ghost."

✝

Hours later, I crack my neck, mind wandering back to the meeting.

And Ghost.

The name fucking haunts me, and I don't even know him. He was before my time. All I know is, he and Dante used to be close. He betrayed Dante and now he's the enemy. I won't say he's the only one, but he's up there near that prime spot.

I work for a few more hours and when I'm done, with lots of nothing's, maybe's, and could be's in all the areas Dante asked me to look at. I don't know if we're near any kind of answer.

Except both Dante and Reaper are right. Something's up.

I just don't know what.

Upstairs, on the club floor, I get a glass of red wine. There's a girl catering to the patrons, scantily clad, a beta who's fucking more than hot, one I've had call me Sir before. I don't have them play at calling me Daddy if they work here, but she's so fucking pretty. The perfect good girl. Blonde and blue eyed, full of trust and a natural sub who's a freak in bed.

I prefer that dynamic to straight up Sub and Master. I like the softness, the ability to indulge in praise kink. I like to shower a girl in gifts, or turn stern in a loving way.

Not that I love any of them.

It's a game.

Role play.

I like it because I'm not the idea of a Daddy Dom. It turns shit on its head. And it gets me all sorts of women who want to play. My favorites are the older women. Having them crumble down into trusting me with everything is a power trip that's orgasmic on its own.

Lizette was...unexpected.

She fits it, but it's her, not a game, and I don't tend to play with actual innocents.

I stop eyeing Cora as she gives a lap dance in the corner to her customer. It's not forbidden, it's not required. We just draw the line at the guys touching. Or fucking our girls.

When the burlesque dancer comes on, I go back down to our private floor.

Something's moving low through my blood.

Like a hunger, a need, a disturbance in my own personal equilibrium.

It's not until I find myself, glass in hand, outside the door where a sweet and seductive spell flavored with rich and complex gardenias seep through.

Fuck.

Darcy left the key in the lock.

Double fuck.

"Move away, dude," I tell myself.

Instead, like it's totally autonomous from me, my hand turns that key, then the handle, and I push the door open.

I close it just as a boot sails close to my head, hitting the wood with a thump.

"You."

Well, she's definitely not in heat now. Her hair's damp and she's got on...I don't know what the fuck she has on. It's too tight, too short and it looks fucking spectacular. Shit. My body pulses in response to her.

More than it should.

It is because I fucking marked her? I have no idea. I haven't marked anyone before. I edge around, sipping the wine.

"You ruined my life," she says, all snarl and claw.

"On the bright side, we helped you and kept you safe through your heat."

Her gaze slams into me. "I'm stuck here!"

To my horror, she gives a gulp and then she covers her face with her hands, dropping to the bed. Her shoulders shake.

Is she fucking crying?

Shit, she's fucking crying.

"Hey...hey..." I down my wine and set the glass on the

dresser as I pass. Then I go to her and I kneel. I stroke hand over her damp hair. "It's okay."

"No, it isn't." She looks at me, cheeks a little damp, but the tears are gone. "I just want the world to be normal again. I don't want to be here, and I don't want to marry that horrible old man."

"I get it." I almost say I'm not sure a wedding's involved, that it's about claiming and mating which is far more binding than a wedding, but I decide not to. "But right now you're here."

"Where I don't want to be. No one wants to be a prisoner or a guest who isn't allowed to leave." The bitterness bites the air. Then her lip trembles. "I miss my dad."

"It's going to be alright." I shift closer and so does she and suddenly all I can think or breathe is her.

She's clutching my shoulders, pulling me in, and I do the same until she tumbles down on to me and our mouths fuse in a slow, deep kiss.

It's carnal and sweet. Sex and romance. And connection.

It's a fucking drug, and it starts to morph into more, into wild licking heat. And I start to tug at her top as she pulls at my T-shirt. I want that spot again, just to suck, it's so heady that spot on her throat, the perfect taste and—

"Jesus F., Knight," Darcy snaps from the door.

I push Lizette away from me as she scrambles free. We're both breathing heavily, and she won't look at me. I get it. I'm one of Darcy's pack alphas, and I sure as fuck don't want to look at her.

Woman's got a stare of disapproval that could fall a fucking army.

I scramble up. "I was—"

"Dante sent me to get you. And tell you to get out. Now."

I do and slide past her and her tray of food. The door slams.

I'm halfway to my room when I'm grabbed by Dante, who slams me into the wall. "Do you have a death wish?"

"No."

"Then we have work to do. And if you step out again, I'll hand you to Reaper."

Fuck.

THIRTEEN

Lizette

"Look," Darcy, the blonde goddess, says, dumping the tray on the bed. "I get it. I do."

She so doesn't. It's in her tone.

"They're hot, but don't give your kind a bad name by humping legs just because they're alphas. It's not cool."

Warmth flares. My energy banks are almost at full again, and I want to put the whole incident down as vulnerable because I gave in to a few tears. But it wasn't that.

I wanted him.

The shame's heavy and hot and cloying. "I just want to go home, Darcy."

Her gaze shifts to me. Then she nods. "Fuck, do you have to look so woebegone? They're a good outfit. And the pack's tight. I'm allowed to be with who I want when this vile society wouldn't allow it. But they do. Dante, Knight, Reaper."

Reaper? The one I haven't met. The one I've smelled. Dark and wild sex, he chases me in my dreams, a shadow with teeth and rough hands. Of incomparable softness and violence.

120

That's what I've dreamt in all my feverish and pain filled dreams. "He's one of the alphas?"

She doesn't answer.

I sigh. "And your man, why...?"

"He's a beta, I'm a gamma, and we should never touch in the society the Council set up."

"My father hated their rules and restrictions, too."

"And where's he?"

I steel myself. "Dead. An accident. I...I'm still dealing."

Darcy nods. "How are the clothes?"

"Too tight? Too not me. I prefer my own stuff." I stop, swallow, drag out my manners as I pick up a water bottle and take a drink. "But I'm very grateful for something clean."

She isn't my friend and my longing for a cure for loneliness must be making her uncomfortable. It does for me. I'm way too aware of my own pathetic ways.

"I just..." I search for the words. "I'm ready to go home."

Darcy moves about the room, collecting the towels I used for my shower. There's a pile of basic cotton panties that give me rushes of panic and unease, because they tell me I'm not going anywhere.

As do the clothes that are folded. I'm not sure they're hers. They're all clean, though. And they fit. A little too well. I'm not overly tall, but I'm not in Darcy's league of fit and built.

And unease slides cold in my bones at those.

I meant it when I said I want to go home.

But it's also a place I can't stay. Even if I lie to the Council about when I'm going into heat, it'll just buy me a handful of days.

"You know, Lizette, if you were smart, instead of plotting on how to get out of here, you could make this work."

I shake my head, push the tray away and draw my legs up. "I don't want to be mated to someone. I don't want to be owned by an alpha, let alone three." Then I frown. "How does that work here, exactly?"

Darcy laughs and collects the wine glass Knight set down. "Oh, hell, girl, they don't do that. These guys live outside of Council run society so they don't have to mate and have kids. Pups. Whatever the popular term is these days. They don't want any of it. They don't want an omega."

"So, if I'm smart, I should go."

"No, honey, if you're smart, you'd find a way to stay which doesn't include sex to become a part of the pack. A free omega. Under their protection. *That's* smart."

It sounds like a prisoner by a different name.

At least if I get out of here, I get to go home. For a few hours or a night. I'm not ready to just let go of Dad without that small goodbye.

"If I don't want to be smart?"

She shrugs. "I'm not privy to their plans or thoughts on you. But...I'd make up my mind. Fast."

When she goes, I let my mind trail over what she said, follow the paths. But I know deep down this is the same as being forced to be some old alpha's mate. A prisoner's a prisoner, no matter what it's called.

I eat slowly, deliberately. What I want to do is cram the food in, fast. But I take it slow to let my body get used to it after those few days of not eating—my last meal was the soup and sandwich, the last thing I could eat before the heat took me down its twisted rabbit hole.

When I'm done, I stand, feeling stronger, more centered. Calmer.

Last time I checked for a way to escape, I was half mindless. This time... This time I'm awake. I'm over my heat and recovered.

I want out.

Who could blame me, anyway? I search the room, checking behind the large painting of some beach at sunset— a weirdly generic and benign thing for the Unholy Trinity to have in their underground lair.

They don't want me to stay, surely, not after what I did.

I look around, under and behind everything for a secret control panel or something that'll open up and let me go free. Surely they're the types to have secret tunnels so they can escape in a moment's notice.

There are no CCTV cameras, no telltale little hidden nanny cams in the lamps or on the TV. With a breath held tight and burning in my lungs, I go to the door.

I try the handle. It rattles but the stupid thing's locked.

A small cry breaks free.

Christ, still stuck here, under lock and key. I mean, I remember Darcy pointing out I couldn't leave even if I escaped the room, so why lock the door?

What? Am I going to walk in on them all having some kind of pack orgy?

I place a shaking hand to my mouth. My knowledge of packs is very sketchy. Dad told me bare bone basics, but we kept to the outsiders, the shunned, those who weren't registered.

The Unholy Trinity can't want me here, they can't. Not after I tried to hump two of them. Those memories swing into the front of my brain under bright lights randomly now I'm back to normal.

Those memories fueled fantasies when I was out of my mind with my heat. And even with the O-blockers they gave me, I still had fevered dreams.

Of course, then there was the kiss.

Not long ago with that delicious and gorgeous Knight.

I smile, a little dreamy with the happy feeling wafting through my limbs. Knight's the perfect name. He saved me, gave me untold pleasure I'd never even thought could happen, and he kisses like a dream. He really is a knight.

"Woah." I slam on the thought breaks. What am I doing? My first kiss and orgasm when on the cusp of heat and I think I'm crushing hard.

Dimples and curling hair and a mouth made for pleasure and sin isn't worth shit when Mr. Dimples is one of my captors. Nothing more and everything less.

There's nothing to read in here, and I don't want to watch TV. The news depresses me and stupid shows and movies really aren't going to hold my attention.

"And why do they care about who Dad is?" I close my eyes. "Was."

The name, Elias Enver, still sticks in my throat. The thread of betrayal winding tight around me when that horrible, hot and dangerous Dante treated me like dirt, dismissed me as a nuisance and a drunk, asked about him is still there. Even if Elias was Dad's real name—and I'm more than aware it makes perfect sense why Dad didn't tell me or that he had a different name to the one I grew up with—why was Dante interested?

The questions threaten to add to the frustration and anger in me and crush me into the floor. I make myself breathe.

"Dad would tell you to leave all that behind for later. He'd tell you to deal with your current problem. This room."

I'm locked in here. No way out, except through the door.

If I can get out of the room, I'll have a better chance of planning my next move.

I'm not strong, but I'm smart.

Maybe I can talk to them, convince them. After all, they clearly don't want the Council or the cops here, looking for me. They've got my letter; they know I'm due for an appointment any day now.

So.

First move is to get out of this room.

My ultimate goal is to get out of this damn club. Pandora's Box is right.

"Concentrate."

When I've accomplished the first move, I can work out how to make my goal happen.

So, I start to bang on the door. "I demand to speak to the alphas. Someone let me out!"

Julien, the beta, is larger than I remember.

But the big bouncer beta man doesn't really speak. His long, dark brown hair is in a ponytail that makes him inexplicably more manly. Maybe it's because I'm pretty sure his muscles have muscles and he sports a beard. But he's got to be about six foot seven.

I see why Darcy is with him.

To me, he's a giant. And when Darcy handed me to him, he even made her look short, and I'm pretty sure she's around six foot herself.

Maybe that's what they do here. Breed giants so they can take over the world.

I follow him up a flight of stairs where a soft thumping grows into music and low lights. As we go, I keep an eye out for an escape, but I don't see any. Only the hall we came down, a room that looked like a fancy living room with its own bar.

No windows.

We come to a stop at an open door that leads to an entire club room that's about as big as the one above, but more opulent, the bar expensive looking. And that's all I see as Julien steps in front of me.

"Wait here."

He goes in and I follow. I could run, but the only way is back down the stairs to my prison room and I'm not backtracking. Dante's lounging against the bar watching a stage where a scantily clad woman dances.

Dante knows I'm here. I sense the vibration that connects us as it runs through him.

And Knight's around, too. He looks over and heat streaks

through me as his eyes burn with intent. His soft smile makes my knees weak.

Dante still doesn't look at me. He moves, though, heading to the stage as he waves the woman to him. She jumps down, eager, no doubt, to be in his energy. I hate her automatically.

"God, what's wrong with me?" I mutter under my breath.

Julien comes back. "Not good at following orders, are you?"

"Usually. But there's just something about being locked up, y'know?"

"The other choice was you on the streets, or you at their mercy. Three alphas, Lizette. Not good. Darcy was right. Be smart." But there's no unkindness in his tone, only a hit of gruff that I think is him.

He leaves and suddenly Knight's there. He smiles at me, leaning against the wall, blocking my view. "You keep being a bad girl, Liz." He runs a finger down along my cheek then drops to my lips.

It's butterfly light. A flirt. And my stomach flips and sighs.

"I want to go home, Knight," I whisper.

"Yeah, but you have to behave."

I frown. "Behaving is hard. I want to go up there and... punch him. You too, actually." I smack his hand away and try not to think about how good he smells, how much I want another of those melting and addictive kisses from him.

"You're a naughty, naughty girl, tempting me." He leans in, mouth grazing my ear, and I shiver as heat and longing shoot through me. "I could get into trouble for this. He's mad as hell."

"So am I." It doesn't help that I basically pant out the words.

But he doesn't kiss me or touch me. Knight straightens, and the charmer—I think it might be part of his actual DNA—is still there, but it's dialed down.

"Being mad won't help. He's a hard bastard, but he'll—"

"Don't you say he'll take care of me. I don't need that. I don't deserve to be locked up," I say.

A smile drifts over his mouth. "Depends on how you're locked up, and by whom."

His meaning hits me and my face burns like fire.

"I'm trying to get you out, but we need to make sure you're safe once you're gone, Liz. Stay calm, and be a real good girl for Daddy—for me, I mean." His eyes glitter as he shrugs.

He's so not sorry.

"Be good for all of us and things will hopefully pan out." Then he sighs and steps back. "I'll take you to Dante."

I follow him across the bar to where Dante's sprawled in a chair, talking to the woman. She's leaning forward, ass out, fantastic boobs basically in his face and falling out of her top.

It's a position that's completely unnecessary as he talks to her. Honestly, she's the worst.

All he does is nod to her before the girl flashes me a glare and flounces away.

Then Dante motions to the spot she vacated.

I go and stand in front of him, the lights aimed at the stage hitting me. I can see him clearly, but I'm lit up. And I hate and lust after him even more.

"You have five minutes," he says. "So make it fucking count."

FOURTEEN

Dante

L izette doesn't answer immediately.

"Cat got your tongue?"

Her eyes narrow, but there's misery, too, and anger. "No, I'm trying not to rip into you."

Man, this little omega has balls.

"If you think you can, go right ahead, but it's not going to get you very far."

She looks past me, over at Knight, who, if he's smart, has taken himself to the bar. Better yet, out of the fucking club room.

Actually, scratch that. It's better if he's here. His presence just might keep me from jumping her bones.

The bartender who's in early stocktaking certainly won't help. He's one of our pack members. He knows his place.

So does Knight, unfortunately, and his place is on the same level as me.

But yeah, better if he's in the vicinity.

I flick my gaze up at her. "Your boyfriend over there isn't coming to your rescue this time."

"He's not my boyfriend."

Fuck, she's gorgeous, so fucking pretty it could hurt a heart if I had one.

It's bad enough her scent's compatible, and somehow, through the bite, I think fucking Knights temporarily bonded her to us three. We're a gang, if you want to call it that, but we are still a pack, and a pack with three alphas means the connection felt by one is felt by us all.

I didn't know it could do that.

Then again, there aren't many packs out there with more than one alpha.

In the corner near the stage, Sienna is hovering. She's got girls that she's auditioned and is going to then run them by me.

Unfortunately, it's me who makes the final decision. Knight would probably audition them in his bed because they'll work here, not become pack members. There's a difference and Knight, for all his pretty boy looks and easy smiles, is a shark when it comes to using the gray area to his advantage.

And Reaper?

I'd love to make him do this. He'd probably lose his mind.

Lizette sucks the corner of her lower lip into her mouth, then releases it. The bruise has healed a lot. But it's still there which means the fucker hit her hard. It's now green and yellow.

Her omega metabolism will have it gone in a day or so. She's lucky, I guess, that she went into heat right when he hit her.

He's lucky I wasn't the one who followed. Or Reaper.

Although judging by her face, what Knight told me, I'm not sure who would have been worse—me or Reaper. Reap's a cold-blooded killer who borders line of psychopathic. But he kills without compunction.

If I do it, it's either in the line of whatever thing's gone wrong, or it's personal. This? I'd have been a sadistic cunt.

Then again, would Reap have taken his time, applied the art of torture?

The bruises are enough to send him back to our childhoods, to take out buried hurts on the asshole would-be rapist. He doesn't like the weak, old, young, and very innocent getting hurt. I might be the only living being who knows that about him.

I'm not saying it's a softness in him. More a way to assuage what happened to him.

Lizette's trying not to glare. "Don't flatter yourself. I don't want you either. Any of you."

"Bold words to a big, bad criminal alpha."

Lizette sniffs. "I've met worse."

She's aiming for indifference, but something catches and her vulnerability shows. I'm betting she's fucking thinking of the asshole who tried to take advantage of her.

I change my mind then and there about Knight. He's got heart. He's not a natural killer. He's suited to run diabolical things using his tech skills. He's suited to digging the kind of dirt that gets hidden in files and behind firewalls and complex passwords. But he's killed. He'll kill again.

The only thing that saved the dickhead, Jake, was her.

Knight wanted to save her more.

And fuck her.

"Reaper?" I ask. "But you haven't met him yet."

"No." She looks around like he might be lurking and there's a sudden energy to her, a lift.

Of course, Lizette has smelled his scent. And she's into it. Like with mine. Like with Knight's.

It's the fucking mark.

"He's worse. Bad to the fucking bone, Lizette. A psychopath, they say. Better keep him on your side."

"It's hard to keep someone on your side when everyone

either wants to fuck me or own me." Her eyes sharpen. "Or reject me."

"Got someone in mind with that rejection?"

"And it's hard," she says, ignoring me, gaze shifting as she plucks at the material on her thighs that's like a second skin, "when I haven't met them."

I nod, glancing at Sierra and motioning to the stage. The music starts and a girl does a routine like the one Sierra did. I keep my gaze on the lithe, big titted girl.

The girl's probably Lizette's age, but she's decades older in experience. And it shows in her boredom, her hardened, jaded expression.

The girl is good.

She won't work out.

I need a mix of experience and sex and seduction wrapped in pliant, and one who's innocent looking.

What I need is Lizette.

Fuck. No. What am I thinking?

I need someone *like* Lizette.

No way would I put a fucking omega on the stage.

Not unless she had scent blockers as well as O-blockers, and she only danced when she wasn't in heat.

I know omegas do this kind of job that way. They're only in heat a few times a year, so they know how to time it all. But I prefer to keep omegas out of our mix.

It's too much like flirting with fate and the Council.

"You've met me," I say.

She makes a small sound. "Yes. And you despise me, find me repulsive."

"Do I?" I actually look away from the stage and catch the naked misery I don't think Lizette knows she's wearing.

The girl shifts and my being's flooded with gardenias, that intoxicating and sumptuous scent that makes my cock start to harden. Fuck.

Repulsive? I had to keep away, be like that, otherwise her virtue would be in shreds and the pack would be in trouble.

If I or any of us rutted her while in heat, while she riled us up into the kind of lust I don't think I've ever felt, then...

I don't finish that thought.

She glances at the stage, pressing her lips together. And I hold up a hand. Sierra scurries over to lead the girl off, and then the next one begins. Lizette looks back at me.

"Guess I can see why. You're surrounded by sex and beauty. No one needs me in the mix." She stops. Swallows. "I don't want to be in the mix. I just meant—"

"I know what you meant, and I'm getting fucking bored. What do you want, Lizette?"

"To leave."

"I'm not finished with you."

She turns a little pale. "You know I need to be at the Council building very soon, so you'll have to let me go."

I offer her a small, hard smile. "You think you're that important, they'll come looking for you?"

"Well, they tracked me down, so yes, maybe they will. Do you want to take that chance?"

Nice move, right there. I'll give her that.

She's angry but she managed to pull reason out of the hat. Because it is reason.

If we hadn't thought of this already.

If the call hadn't gone through today with Darcy pretending to be her.

The appointment's been pushed back.

I watch the latest girl. She's okay. In looks and demeanor, she fits the part. She'll make a great waitress down here. Some of the girls will be topless waitresses at private events, but that's up to them. Whatever... She'll be scantily clad and make money. Not as much as performing on the stage, but money.

And she's what the punters want.

"If I'd known you were that anxious to register and be on

your way to your new handpicked-by-the-fucking-council mate, I'd have driven you myself." I pick up my coffee and take a sip. "We can go now."

"I just want to go home." She drags in a breath, fingers worrying at the too-tight top she's got on.

Dark colors suit her. Tight and body revealing is a honey pot. It's a distraction. A thing to stir desire.

She needs to wear layers. Baggy, long fucking dresses. The baggier the better.

Yeah, and that'll do fucking nothing.

Her appeal is more than tight clothes and curves that caress a man. It's fucking *her*.

God, I'd love to send her far away and forget her, but with the mark, which could lead others right to us...I don't fucking think so.

"Do you know what we saved you from?" I ask.

"Knight saved me." She crosses her arms. "From a bad situation and I'm thankful. But I want to go home."

Broken fucking record.

I'm about to taunt her, rile her, offer her a choice, when I catch movement near the door.

Reaper comes in and goes to the blackest corner of the bar. The bartender stops stocktaking and serves him.

I glance at Lizette, and her gaze is glued to him, cheeks flushed, and her pulse throbbing.

Then she meets my gaze, and it throbs harder, that pulse. "Is that—"

"You're not staying, not your business."

She frowns as her cheeks redden. Fuck, it's hot. I stand, crowding her.

"What do you want from me?" she asks breathlessly.

Oh, so many things...

Do we send her away, stick to plan A and let her go and make it so she has no choice but to choose to come back into our fold—until we can fix the problem with Knight's nibble mark—of her own free will? Yes.

In her mind, it's free will and her choice.

We'll make it so we're her only option.

"Nothing really. I'm busy enough. Shipments, bars and establishments to run." I move a hand through the air. "Clubs. The Council and structured fucking society to tumble. Fortunes and power to take as ours. We're busy men. We're a busy and productive pack. You...you're a pain in the fucking ass. Just rust on the gears, not oil."

"That's a lot of metaphor."

"Think of it as a hobby." I lean in. "So, little omega, are you going to stay and see if we can remove Knight's mark, or do you want to explain it to your geriatric mate-to-be? Those are your choices. Pick one."

"You're a prick."

"So I've heard," I say. "You know going home would be temporary."

"I know."

My phone buzzes on the table, lighting up. It's Knight and the one word, *shipment*, flashes. Fuck. I do have a shit -on to do today, and I forgot about the drugs and booze coming in. Some of it legal, some of it not.

I nod at Sierra and motion for the next girl. Then I text Knight back.

Handle it.

I'll join him when I'm done on the three fronts in this room. The burlesque dancers and strippers, Lizette, and Reaper.

"Then again," I mutter, "I could make you fucking stay and you can't do a thing about it."

"They'll look," she says. "And I'll find a way to get a phone or a way out. Then...I'll report you."

Her triumphant check-mate smile is adorable.

Because I can, because I want to, because I need to, I lean in close to her, lips brushing her soft, sweet-smelling hair, and

I breathe in her skin, that scent, deep into my lungs and blood and bone.

"That outs you, too, sweet Lizette," I say. "And when they find out you're not so pristine..." I trace the mark on her throat, pushing in a little to make her moan. "They'll probably nix the old guy and auction you off to someone far, far worse."

She recoils, staggering. "You disgust me."

Her eyes tell a completely different story.

"Right back at you." I raise a brow. "And that's exactly what they'll do."

I'm not lying.

"I don't care."

"Yeah, you do." I laugh and shake my head. "I'm out of time and this was a fuck-ton longer than five minutes. Go and see Julien. He'll get someone to take you home."

I turn and go over to Reaper.

He's watching the girl on the stage, but he didn't miss a moment of our exchange just then. "Not her."

I stop, look at the dancer. "Her? Why?"

He shrugs. "She's weak. She'll steal and try to blackmail us."

"You know that by looking?" I get a drink from the bartender, Mason.

"Yes." He pulls out his phone and types some things in, then slides it to me. "But I've met her."

I nod and pick up his phone. It's a picture of Craig Edmonton but young.

Wait. No it's not.

It's his son. Who's a weak alpha, but is looking to carve a name. The article doesn't say that, but it's the gist as I scan the gazette from Hover Valley.

"Do you think this is why they really want Lizette?"

"It's interesting." He takes a swallow of his rum. "You're letting her go? Plan A?"

"Yeah. I wanted to wait until tomorrow, but she's antsy.

135

She'll find herself in trouble and come back for our protection. Then we can work at removing the fucking mark"

Reaper nods, taking a sip of his rum. "And when we fix it?"

"Then we release her somewhere to make her own way. Far from Starlight City."

Far from us.

Far from me.

FIFTEEN

Reaper

Technically, I followed her home as Dante requested. I've been here thirty minutes, which is longer than it should take her to arrive by car. I don't mind. It gives me time to check out her place again, inside and out.

Time to look for signs of others doing what I'm doing.

But I'm back out in the front, in the shadows, as the sleek car pulls up.

I'd like to say I don't think anyone's out there, watching her also, but there's an unease that pricks and teases my spine, a sixth sense regarding other, hidden eyes.

Ghost?

He's good enough.

Then again, he's also like me. Good enough to be picked up on, good enough to be invisible.

After all, Ghost isn't just a name he likes to call himself.

He can seemingly drift into places unseen and most ignore the niggle of another presence.

Ghost being here changes things on some level. It means he's working for someone with an interest in her. He's not

137

interested. If he was, he'd make an actual move on her. Not hide and lurk and wait.

The Council is a safe bet.

If it's Ghost.

If anyone's here at all.

The car door opens.

I go still.

Lizette Roth. Earthy and ethereal, the hum, buzz, and heat of blood making her special.

Julien didn't drive. It's another beta. Christopher. He works bodyguard jobs, guard jobs, low rent clandestine deals that have to be done without us. He's even worked behind the bar on occasion and run errands.

He's trusted. I amend that—all the pack's trusted. He does his job well.

The man takes a bag with leafy greens spilling over the top into the building. Lizette follows. He'll check and make sure her apartment is clean.

Smart move of Dante's. Or smart of Dante to listen to Knight. The groceries are a simple, subtle touch that says so much. It opens the door of return. It's care, in the shape of good, clean food.

Yeah, Knight over Dante. Knight had a fucked up life, too. But he had family.

We didn't.

We were just kids of broken-down packs.

We got bounced around, unwanted, and shoved into a pack where we met and had each other's backs. The only reason they tolerated us was the fact we were alphas. And young.

I prefer prison to that kind of pack life. One under the rule of the fucking Council.

Actually, there are times I prefer prison to other things and places.

There are rules, yes. People leave me be in the slammer.

Kill or be killed is a thing in there, but other inmates learned early on I'm the kill kind. Not the be-killed.

I'm tall, scarred, covered in ink, but I'm lithe. They mistake that for weak. Once. It only ever happens once. After all, the dead don't make mistakes.

Prison gave me room to think, breathe. I honed my body and mind. Learned. Some lifers expected me to try and rule or form a pack to take down others. But all I wanted was to be left alone. And it got me respect.

But prison had limitations. No pussy. No real freedom. So, I'd always break out. The two times I got taken back there was for a reason.

This time, they think I'm dead.

But an alpha with a habit of shunning packs needs something.

Maybe it's why, when I found Dante again, I joined his pack.

Fuck, maybe I got sick of escaping from prison. I've no intention of serving a life sentence for murder. They only know about the one. I've killed countless and not lost a moment's sleep over any of them.

Killing in prison tends to erase parole chances.

So, one day I used my skills and disappeared for the final time. I turned invisible; it was that easy.

Now I'm out for good, and I'm more finely tuned, the skin around me harder, my kill set wider.

And I can track and hunt and surveille like no one's business.

I give Ghost a run for his fucking money.

Inside, lights go on. Christopher carries the groceries and then he disappears. Lizette flits from room to room. Someone needs to tell her to pull the fucking blinds. Her father was the one who put them in, otherwise, she'd have pulled them down before turning on one light.

Dante wants to manipulate her, have her come back to us.

Wants her to hand her trust over to us. Fine by me. Things are easier when someone comes in on their own.

Knight's not a fan of the plan.

I don't like him or dislike him. He's family now, but there are times...he looks at me like he thinks I'll slice his throat in his sleep.

He's right.

I would.

If he betrayed me, Dante, or the pack.

However, I don't think he will.

But he also didn't grow up in a pack. Like Lizette. He had beta parents, a normal, shitty upbringing. He's an anomaly, born of betas, but he's an alpha.

This should interest me.

It doesn't.

People are, essentially, people. No matter the differences. It's what they do that makes me kill or leave them alone. It's simple.

The longer I stand, the more I realize something.

It's a good plan.

But Dante's wrong.

He miscalculated because he isn't me. I'm wrong at times, too, but I also like to observe, think. Not talk.

People open up. They give themselves away.

Like Lizette did today.

She's defiant, soft, yes, but defiant, and at the core of her softness is steel. She looked at me like she saw me.

Not the ink. Not the ex-con. Not the psycho. Not the man with the scarred face.

The creature I truly am inside, the one I was before my name change.

And she looked at me with lust.

She's complex. More than I think Knight or Dante see.

It could be because they've been in such close proximity with her. I don't know. I don't care.

I do know he's wrong. There's more to her.

Christopher leaves the building, pulls out his phone and makes a call as he gets in the car, closing the door. He murmured low so I couldn't tell who he spoke to.

Probably Dante.

Still...

The car pulls away, and I look around, but apart from a couple walking down the street who head into the building three doors down from her, there's no one else.

There are pedestrians, cars that drive by, but no one of interest to me.

No...I know Dante is wrong.

He sent her back where she could easily be taken. Too easily, if I wasn't here.

Which changes dynamics.

But even if no one comes for her, and she gets to pack a bag and go, and I implement the scare campaign, it might give her enough push to defy us.

Because she's going to soak up the memories and comfort of that apartment. Take it all in as nourishment for her steel.

I'm going to up the timeline of the campaign and change the rules. I pull my hoodie on.

There's a place I use that no one else knows about. Utilitarian. Away from what she knows, in an abandoned building.

I need to take her out of her comfort zone and leave her there, with her apartment off limits, and she'll come running to us, desperate for some sort of familiarity.

Especially when she learns how we met her father.

I don't bother texting Dante. I make my move.

Now.

Glass shatters as I step into the kitchen, the cup tumbling from her hands and cracking into pieces on the floor.

"Lizette."

Her hand trembles, eyes dilate, and pulse beats faster in her throat as she stares up at me. The air is thick with possibilities. Parts of us recognizing the other. That instinctual reaction no one can hide.

"You...you were at the club. Reaper."

She is stunning. From the flow of dark hair with the hint of wave, to her small frame with a tiny waist, flare of hips, and full tits. Her legs are fucking long, too, and the perfect shape that suggests velvety skin and a welcoming cunt at her apex.

The outfit is too tight.

I like it.

But the thing that catches me is full lips, naturally pinkish red, and those dark brown eyes that hover on black.

Divine and pagan at the same time.

She's a masterpiece in womanhood.

"Pack your things."

She frowns. "I just got here. What do you mean, pack?"

Lizette doesn't ask how I got in. She doesn't move.

I do. The grocery bag hasn't been unpacked, so I take it and put it in the hall with the backpack from the other day, next to the door with the lock I picked.

"What are you doing?"

I move about, purposefully, taking all the things I found which are important to her, and us. They're not the *most* important. Those are in the pack and her leather bag. But I want all information on her and her father gone. The photos, all of it. She won't be getting that in her new digs.

I put them all into a bag I find. It's coming with me.

"Lizette, if you have anything else hidden, get it. And pack clothes. Now."

I don't raise my voice or harden my tone to an order. Instead, I keep it calm and flat and soft.

This tone is easiest. And it scares the shit out of most people.

Anger, fury, hate, lust, jealousy, fear; all of these are easy to ignore when they come at you. And it's also easy to build a defense or a counter attack.

But with cold, calm nothingness, the smooth, implacable wall of reason in its base form? Of an unemotional situation? People obey or exhaust themselves or get themselves dead.

She isn't most people, and I don't think Lizette's scared, which is good. I'm not setting out to scare her, just get her to do what I need.

Obey.

She does. When she's done, she looks around in the living room, at the blinds I pulled down, at the remnants of a life lived.

This, I don't understand. Having roots and a connection to a place that provides shelter. Even people.

I'm loyal to my pack, to Dante and Knight. But if something happened? I'd turn to the next page in the book of my life.

That isn't to say I wouldn't fight, wouldn't go down in a battle for them, would ever betray them. Any of them.

Trust isn't a tool I give out. It's not, to me, a tool. It's a gift, one that must be earned. And when I give it...

I look at her.

Is she pushing these thoughts out in me?

"Where are we going?" she asks. "Why? Your boss? Partner? Dante, he said I could go home."

I nod, slinging the bag I want over my shoulder. I hand her the pack and her bag, and I take the wheelie fucking case of clothes, along with the groceries.

If someone comes at me, I can drop the groceries, get my gun and hurl the clothes—or leave the damn case and grab her if she's in danger.

Lizette breathes out and doesn't move. "I asked you a question. I know you can talk."

She's not afraid of me. She sees me.

The two thoughts drift once more.

"This isn't safe. I'm taking you elsewhere."

Her fingers turn white on the backpack's handle. "Why can't I stay here?"

"Because if you run, whoever else is watching will follow."

"S-Someone else is following me? Other than you?"

I only look at her. "This way."

Lizette sits, crowding in on herself on the sofa in the bare bones basement. She can come and go, if she wishes. It'll take her longer; she might get lost. But considering she's got nowhere to go, no job, this is better.

Isolated.

If I were a different man, I'd feel sorry for her.

But all that's in me is the hunt, the stakeout, the watching.

And, yes, the lust. For her.

I'm not Dante. I don't tie myself up in knots over wanting something I shouldn't. Or think I shouldn't.

The girl's no longer in heat, and if I choose to take her, fuck her, then I will.

I'm not about to. It's just lust on a deep flesh and marrow level. It's earth, blood, and sweat. And it's a rough, hardcore fantasy I'm not bringing to life.

Everything about her is tied up in her toxic aroma, that sweet, sensuous slide through the air.

I amend myself for honesty. I'm not about to fuck her right now. But I know I will. Eventually.

She's too tempting not to.

After we remove the mark.

Or maybe before.

Before will be intriguing, especially if there's an *after* once it's gone. Just to see if it makes a difference in her appeal.

Her taste.

"I'll be back," I say.

She looks up. "You can't just leave me, not until—"

"It's safe. You have your phone. There's WIFI. Password is in the kitchen cutlery drawer. This isn't a high-tech place. So..." I shrug. "I need to go get your things. The rest of them. You remember the way we came?"

Lizette stares up at me, her hands gripping each other, her eyes big, liquid, like prey. "Are you locking me in?"

"Keys are on the coffee table. This is a basement apartment. Studio. The other room's a bathroom. I'll be back."

It doesn't take me long to check to make sure we weren't followed. There's always some kind of sign, and I hid the luggage at one stop, one of the Trinity's hole-in-the-wall bars.

I take a convoluted way out of the grim area in the Wharf district. Once it was busy, but now it's a lot of empty places, warehouses, run-down apartments, and businesses. Not many people are out. Some criminal types, and the beauty with them is that this area tends to be crime free and people keep to themselves.

Whatever they're doing, they don't want to be seen. And no one cares to see them.

I don't speak to the pack members in the bar, or the staff that I know. I check out the clientele, see if anyone doesn't fit. It's all normal.

But still.

I transfer everything to a duffle, put on a cap and head out the back entrance.

Some might call it overkill. I call it covering bases.

I know something's wrong when I reach the building.

Her scent.

There's a whiff, but it's not that strong of an aroma I can taste.

She's fucking gone.

I don't bother checking when I go in and dump her stuff. Instead, I lock the door, and for the first time in a long time, I smile.

Time to hunt.

CHAPTER
SIXTEEN

Lizette

I smell him.

Breath catching in my lungs, the rum and tobacco with hints of roses scent winds down into my cells, regardless.

My heart thumps as fear runs a low buzz, making me shiver.

I didn't run away, but I didn't want to be cooped up. And okay, my first thought was to follow Reaper outside, but he moves like he isn't there at all. Silent, invisible, a creature who can slide between worlds.

I don't know if he's seen me, and I'm not looking around again. Once I thought he was on top of me, his presence pressing into me like a cloying shadow, but when I whipped around?

Nothing.

No one.

So, I slip past an empty warehouse just near the water; the soft lap of waves and whoosh of traffic a few streets over are the only sounds.

I don't like it here, in the gathering dark.

Dirt crunches, and I almost scream out of instinct, but it's me. My foot.

Breath comes harsh as I dart into a half open warehouse door. It's full of old crates and empty shelves. Broken furniture.

Why do abandoned places always have broken furniture?

Concentrate, I tell myself, pulse racing hard.

I don't know why I'm running, hiding, or why I'm panicked.

But it's the kind of fear and panic that has an electric beat to it, and my heart spins.

There's a half-broken table, and I dive behind it, hitting my knees hard.

The door doesn't creek, but light from outside casts a wider stream and then a shadow eats up the middle.

It moves.

I don't.

I don't even breathe.

What if it's not him? What if the danger isn't studded with excitement because Reaper's hunting me, and it's real danger in the form of someone who means me harm?

Reaper can be deadly. I don't have to know him, see him more than once, to understand.

It's in his eyes, stillness, his stance. He's a master, and I'm nothing but a thing to be played with. Stalked.

Hunter. Prey.

Those words turn bright and brand me.

I don't even know why I didn't stop and call out to him. Just like I don't know why he didn't make himself known. Announce his presence.

Because, I think, Reaper likes this. He gets off on it.

Between my thighs, heat rises and turns into a throb of desire. Wetness starts to slick me, wet my panties. I don't think it's actual slick but something like it.

Oh...if I can smell him, he can smell me. And I'm aroused.

Things scrape.

Now footsteps start. Slow. Deliberate.

Getting closer.

Then he stops and nothing, not a sound, until that shadow reappears in the light, and recedes.

I lean back, breathing in gulps, trying to be quiet as I stare up at the high ceiling.

Hell. How do I even know he's hunting? And I'm to run? But I do and I can't explain it. His scent is in the air, beguiling, not enough. Everything inside me flutters into life.

It feels like foreplay, and I want more. I want him to chase me, to hunt me down. I need the rush of adrenaline.

There's a part of me that wants to take off, hard and fast and absolutely mean it, like it's life or death. To experience that kind of chase from him would be...

I swallow.

Insane.

Addictive.

Slowly, I rise, unsure who this new Lizette is. I'm like a whole being, a primal animal, both willing to taunt my predator and needing to run.

I don't recognize myself. Just like I didn't recognize the snarling woman who tried to goad the sinfully hot and hardcore demon, Dante. Or the little submissive who wanted Knight, to please him, to have him punish me for being bad.

Dante would be like winning a prize. The kiss is something that just might be a work of art if he gave it to me. But he doesn't like the weak, the clingy. He hates the girl who walked in and got drugged and felt up out the back of his bar.

I want that kiss.

I want to earn it, win it, do whatever it takes. Be that slinky, sexy woman who could be with him and reap all his rewards.

And Reaper? This is a dance on the wild and dark side. It's blood. It's death. It's pure lust and life.

I want him to chase me. Take me, drag me screaming into whatever he might want to do. I want his teeth on me, I want his mouth.

I'm connected to all of them and it's like I instinctively speak their language, like a part of me rises to each of them and it doesn't make a lick of sense.

They all fascinate me. But with Knight it's comfort. Dante is sparks, fire, hurdles. Reaper is...untold and unexplored highs and lows. He fascinates me.

What the hell am I doing? Waxing lyrical over the alphas of an outlaw pack who kidnapped me and dropped me home with a fuck you very much? All before being yanked to a strange apartment somewhere else?

I don't even know what this is.

What I'm going to do is go back, let myself in the apartment, and pretend I didn't leave.

I move as quietly as I can to the door. I slide out and stand, looking around.

I'm not alone.

It's in my blood and sinew.

I sniff the air and with the slight breeze that's sprung up, I smell the brine of the water, the must of disuse behind me, and the regular city stench the light breeze carries along.

No one's here, at least I don't think they are, so I start to turn back to the building where Reaper put me.

Something makes me stop.

And my breath stops in my throat as my chest tightens.

A man steps from the shadows. Like he's appearing by magic.

The lone street lamp showers him in yellow light as his shorn dark head tilts and he looks at me. I can't see the obsidian eyes, but I feel them piercing into me.

His face is worthy of a painting in a chapel, or my wall as a girl. The light catches the scars and instead of the faint red lines, they seem to glow.

I drink them in. All of his beauty. The slightly curved scar running from his right eye to the corner of his lips. There's one slashing up from his throat's corner near his ear, moving across his lower right cheek to the other side of his chin. A cut over his nose that stops close to the right eye and the left side.

Just one more scar.

A jagged, violent thing starting low and runs up to the middle of the orbital bone, and then continues through his brow to an inch above it.

He watches me impassively. Not angry. Not lustful—no there's lust. It makes his eyes shine dark. A current runs through him, so vibrant it lights me up and I'm about twelve or so feet away, runs through him.

Reaper doesn't move.

All he does is say one word.

"Run."

With a small shriek, I turn and take off, running hard. He's behind me, his scent's all over me, surrounding me as I dart in and out of buildings and over the road.

My body's alive, more alive than it's ever been.

Every time I turn, Reaper isn't there.

I want to see him, get caught, eaten, but it has to be clean. Not a cheat. When he said run, he meant for my life, and the adrenaline pounds as pump my arms.

Run for my life.

Reaper is pacing himself. I can feel it. Thick in the air, clogging my lungs. I turn and yell. An animal howl of sound.

And he's there again. He stops.

This time, his mouth ticks up in a smile, and my knees turn liquid. I could fall.

The smile isn't romantic, or even nice. It's not friendly.

It's harsh, deadly.

The smile of the predator who's got his prey and is playing with it.

My pussy throbs so hard, pleasure surges.

He's so fucking beautiful.

So unbelievably handsome. The fact I don't think he gives a damn about how he might look, how people see him, heightens his appeal.

And yet...

I don't want others to notice. I'm greedy. He's mine already.

Reaper starts towards me, small steps, and I shriek to the heavens again and tear off, up a side street.

He's deadly. Emotionless. On the outside. I want to shatter that. I want...I want to matter. To him.

It makes no sense, and I don't care.

In this very moment, I want to matter.

He breaks my heart.

Not because of the scars on that face that could grace a magazine. No, they add to his beauty.

But he breaks my heart because he's both a monster and an angel fallen low.

Someone hurt him. I'm betting when he was young because it feels like a black and white thing, lacking shades of gray. For him. And that's young.

Love or hate.

Worlds crash. Suns soar.

There's nothing in between.

And it's that kind of pain that shapes a monster over the small child in him, the vulnerable part, to protect.

He's smart. No one could hunt like this and not be. And the intelligence is in his eyes...

I turn again, down another street, not daring to look behind me. I lose precious seconds when I turn, so I just run and weave and duck and hide.

My side starts to hurt with a stitch and my lungs burn. To distract myself, I go back to the puzzle of Reaper.

By child, I don't think he's stunted, more that the concept of child represents an innocence which someone tried to crush out of him, to cut out of him.

I dart behind a fence. My legs are a thousand pounds of weight, and I collapse, looking around.

There's a tiny house wedged in between two grim and dark apartment buildings. It doesn't belong, this weird little house, one that's falling apart but seemingly holding on by sheer strength of defiance. It's clearly abandoned.

To me, it's another lost soul in this city.

A twig snaps. It's his only mistake. Or did he mean to alert me?

My breath rushes out, and I push up in the dark shadow of the fence and take a step, but an arm clamps around me, hauling me against him.

"Good chase. Did you know you smell of gardenias? A garden of Eden."

His voice is dark like him, calm, and I sink into his front. He's hard.

A thrill flares bright inside. Hard, big. For me. Because there's nothing like a virgin thinking she's queen of sex. I rub against him and he growls low, pushing me away and then turning me.

"I'm not going to fuck you, little omega. Because I like rough, elemental sex. You're a fucking sweet virgin and I'm not interested."

"What are you going to do?" And I reach up, trace the line of the scar that ends at the corner of his lip.

Reaper takes my face in his hands and leans in close. He walks me backwards into the darkness of the wall.

My ass hits bricks and his lips hit mine.

The kiss is pure heat and explosives. It's a taking, a claiming. He tastes like cigarettes and rum, almost like he smells. But there's more. He tastes of fire and sex and something so dark it steals a part of my soul.

This is my second real kiss. Second person, I mean. I don't count Jake. Just Knight.

And they couldn't be more different.

Reaper kisses like he moves through life. No compromises, just the dark and the sweet and the smoke. His tongue slides against mine and he sucks mine into his mouth.

My knees give way, and I clutch him as he deepens the kiss in a way I can't fully explain or understand. It's a demand without pressure. Without words.

And I want more. I want to explore his body, touch all those strong, hard muscles. Trace the tattoos. All the scars I know that live on him, all of them with a story I need to hear.

I want to move lower, explore my first cock, touch and stroke and taste.

I just *want*.

He releases my tongue and makes mine dance and duel with his. Air is a commodity I can do without. Then he bites my lip so hard, I taste copper, and I moan, digging my nails into him as I quiver from that bite alone. It goes straight to my pussy, lights up my clit, and I'm on fire in a different realm where pleasure is tied to blood and pain and foreplay promises better things.

The tiny sting fades as he pulls back, hands still on my face, holding me up that way. My blood is on his mouth, smeared a little, and then he licks it up.

That should have been disgusting, shocking. It's not. It's filthy, thrilling and wild.

Elemental.

"Hands and knees."

He releases me, and I almost fall to the soft grass. Before I can scramble up or even to my feet to ask what he's doing, one of my shoes goes sailing and then he pulls down my stretch pants and underwear.

"What? I'm not—"

"I'm not fucking you. But I'm having you. Payment for your life, for releasing you."

His eyes are savage fire as he speaks.

I almost choke on the air. "My— No one's seen me like this. You can't—"

"I am. I'm collecting."

"That kiss. My blood." In the deep throb of my being, I recognize this is a different sort of foreplay. "You licked it up."

"You're delicious. The kiss doesn't count."

He comes down on me, fingers stroking me between the thighs making me hum high. My body singing. And he kisses me again.

Then suddenly he rolls off, pushing my head down so my ass is up.

And then...Oh, God...

He licks me.

His tongue is hot, velvet rough as it goes from my clit up to my ass. He moves, bites my asscheek and then he shoves my leg, moving, doing something under me. Everything's hypersensitive and each touch is exquisite agony. A promise of things he could do.

Then his breath hits my pubic bone, and I moan.

The attack's twofold.

His mouth closes on my clit and he shoves two fingers in me.

I jump with the shock, with the sensations.

I can feel the stretch because he's moved his fingers apart, in and out and then... he sucks and licks and nibbles my clit, moving to just below it and pulling back until I'm seeking him out. And he settles into a hard rhythm with his mouth.

It's insane. I'm on the verge when he upends everything again by shoving a third finger in me.

A high note breaks free as I come. My body shakes, and I'm

leaping, body doing that of its own because my clit is so sensitive, it's pain, too much. I pant.

He doesn't let me go. Reaper starts to finger fuck me hard, borderline brutal, hitting something in me each time that rings out with a pleasure ache and then pure pleasure. But it's not enough, and I push back, rocking into his pistoning fingers, grinding on his sucking, biting, licking mouth.

The orgasm starts again, contracting beats of euphoria as it gets bigger, bigger, and I'm singing. I'm singing.

It's not a song, a chant of need and lust and pleasure.

"More. More. More," I sing. "More, Reaper. More."

It reaches a crescendo, the euphoria, and I come again, but this time I push back on him harder, grinding down like I want to smother him. The crescendo was only small and it builds and builds even as I come, until it explodes that orgasm through me. A galaxy bursting into life.

When I come down, I'm on my back somehow, and he's between my legs, licking everything, and then he kisses me again, his tongue and lips are full of a wild taste of me and him. Finally, he lifts his head.

"That's what you taste like. Decadence. Mine. Next time I chase you I won't be as kind as this time."

A thrill shakes me.

"Time to get you back."

And I think, what the hell have I done?

SEVENTEEN

Reaper

After helping her dress, I take her back to the apartment, and she looks at me, big eyes, like she's caught feelings.

I want to say I shouldn't have devoured her. But it was a hunt, and she's a natural at primal play.

Lizette alone made her part real.

I always play it real. It *is* real for me. But so many women play at it, and they giggle and let me catch them. Depending on my mood and interest level after the chase, I might fuck them. Some will go down on me.

They don't interest me. What gets my fires up is the chase, the hunt, a real one.

And this, from a virgin, was incredible. I wanted to fuck her so hard, take her ass, let her see all of me like her gaze begs.

But I ate her out.

With her, the rules of the play didn't seem to exist.

Could be the mark fucking Knight left on her. I had the sense to keep away from her throat. The rest?

Fuck, she riled me beyond anything before. Shone a light. Made a connection that felt like we knew each other, could see into things.

This is, I decide as I pull out my cigarettes, ignoring the look of disapproval on her face, as the caught feelings morph to confusion, nothing more than false intimacy. A false closeness brought on by similar kinks.

By the bite, the mark, the brand, the bond—whatever you want to call it.

I don't pretend to understand how it all works, how Knight's mark can affect all of us. But I think it does.

There's not a blood bond between us.

Doesn't have to be.

Our pack has three strong alphas who share the top position.

We are the lead alphas. The core pack.

Fuck. I hate the word *pack*.

It's never sat right since I was a kid. Since that fucker tried to kill me after he decided he was bored of using me as his punching bag.

I ended that. By ending his life.

I don't even remember how old I was when I slid the knife he used on me between his ribs as he slept. I remember everything else. Perfect clarity. Waiting for his eyes to open as he woke only to die. I wanted him to see my bloodied face.

My eyes.

The last thing he ever saw.

After, I stared in the mirror. Face black and bloodied, skin split open here and there, the only thing alive staring back was my eyes. Black fire. Pits of hell.

Dante found me. We didn't know each other that well. But he was older; he helped burn the house, and find someone to sew me up.

After that, things blur. Another pack, one of the misfits,

took us as no one wanted to care for the freak kid with the Frankenstein's monster's face.

It suited me fine. They left me alone.

So, why do I feel at home for the first time since finding Dante again?

Maybe I'm caught in her headspace of the hunt's aftermath.

I put the cigarette between my lips.

"Why did I feel like I knew you intimately?" Lizette whispers. Her gaze meets mine. "I still do. Out there, when it was life and death...I knew it wasn't and I was safe, but I was also fleeing for real...out there, it was like I could see into you. Knew you intimately without knowing anything about you. Like the details of your life were on display. The thing that makes you *you*."

I don't say anything. My phone's buzzing in my pocket. Dante. I don't need to look. He can wait.

"I-Is it normal? Or am I seeing things? Making it up so I'm not so..." She shakes her head.

Lonely. The word she isn't saying. Lonely.

The girl who grew up loved. But isolated.

"Not so ridiculous," she says, her words soaked in her lie.

Or maybe it isn't. Maybe it's a compromise, a way to step back from her bleeding honesty.

In my experience, ridiculous and lonely tend to intermix.

Removing the unlit cigarette, I contemplate her words.

"We were rough, dirty, in a game you got caught up in. I like primal play. It's blood, heat, violence. The hunt. That feeling you had of life and death. It's in you, too."

She takes a breath and nods. "Is that why it's like I know you?"

"I'm not sure."

That connection hums in me. Alive. Present.

"Maybe," I say. "We see what we want to see. A reflection of us, a glimpse of something to weave a tale around."

"You didn't feel it?" she asks.

That's too far. "I'm the monster you get to deal with the other monsters. An ex-con. I murder and protect what's mine. But I leave things alone if they leave me alone."

It's not an answer. But it's the best I can give. This isn't like any kind of conversation I've ever had, and I've been forced into therapy. Once.

Her complexity and loneliness make her insightful. And she probably recognizes the parts of me that is human. Experiences that have left marks.

She sees me.

"You can do what you want, but I recommend staying inside. One of us will drop back in to check on you."

Lizette stands and comes up to me, and I smell us on her. The funk and musk and heat and wildness. Sex. Need. All of it. All at once. "Are you running away?"

"When one of us comes by, in a few days, you can probably head home, or get out of here. I would recommend keeping away from the Council. Unless that's the life you want."

"Reaper?"

She puts her hand on my chest, over my heart.

"Go rest, little omega," I say. "Try and sleep."

"Well, at least you didn't apologize."

I drop my gaze back to her face and cup her cheek for a moment. "For what?"

"For what happened?"

"I never apologize over shit like that. It was mutual?" She nods. "It was good."

"I want—"

"Everyone wants." I step back and leave.

Everyone does want. Even me, it seems. Even fucking me.

✝

160

"Did you fuck her?"

I blow out a stream of smoke, rum next to me in the command center of Pandora's.

It's not what it's called. I call it that because, in here, I can watch all corners of each floor. Even the private areas for private parties.

We make sure things don't happen.

This floor is the only place in the club without cameras, where the three of us have suites, and the alley where the fucker tried to rape Lizette.

Her voice that held a perfect pure note, a thrill of orgasmic pleasure ringing through it, is still inside me. It was something almost sacred in the most elemental way.

"No."

Dante's eyes narrow. Knight's curious gaze moves from one of us to the other.

The kid snaps his fingers and points at me. "You touched her. You dark horse."

But behind the jovial tone is something tight. Jagged.

Jealousy.

A sliver of it.

I don't respond. "I moved her and put her in my safe house in the Wharf district."

"A love nest?" Knight asks. Then he glances at Dante. "Why is it all *hands off her* to me but not him?"

"Shut the fuck up, Knight," Dante says, almost absently. "Why?" he says to me.

He walks from the command center to his office, Knight hot on his heels.

I take a drag on my cigarette, pick up the rum, and follow. Once in there, he starts his paperwork. I've no interest in what he's doing. We make money. We grow. I have my place in the dark. The silence. The clean up.

I'm muscle. I'm the deliverer of death, if and when needed.

I'll do whatever, whenever, in the name of protecting this pack.

"Isolation."

My one word hangs in the air, but Dante looks up as Knight stares at his tablet.

"Wharf district?" Dante blows out a breath. "That's a rough fucking area."

"It's remote. People keep to themselves."

"A perfect place," Knight says, not looking up, brown curls falling into his eye, "for him to fuck her."

I cast him a long look. And although he doesn't look at me, he squirms.

Then Dante glances at us both. "Knight, Reap says he didn't. And what's it to you? You're not picking a fucking omega for us. Fuck whoever you want, but get back to working on digging up anything and everything on this pack in Hover Valley, and on that guy, Jake."

"Look into if Ghost is back." My words turn the room into silence.

Knight breaks it. "You really think he is?"

"Yes," I say.

"He would do anything if he thought it'd get back at us or get him ahead." Dante frowns. "Did you see him?"

"Not yet. He's like me." I ignore the snort from Knight. I know what the kid wants. *Her.* That perceived prize of her virginity. Like I told her, I don't fuck virgins. "But I keep getting a sense of someone."

"Look into it more deeply, Knight." Dante leans back in his chair. "Fuck."

"Will do." The kid cuts his eyes at me, but the sharpness bounces off. Then he sighs. "That dude you killed? Fucking creep."

I know. He told me everything.

Right before I killed him.

"What about the other one? Jake?" Dante asks.

Knight's grip on the tablet tightens. "Disappeared. Not sure if Jake's his real name. I've got a Jake Jones, but...I'll play with the security photo, cross reference on facial ID. Maybe it's a different name he goes under. Or he's so protected, he's not online."

"Don't bother. Reap, tell him what you found."

I sigh and take a drag on my cigarette. Then I pull over a shallow dish I think's an ashtray. Not that I care.

"Does it matter?" I ask.

"Maybe." Dante gets up and helps himself to a drink, pouring a whiskey for the wine-drinker, Knight.

He points the bottle my way, but I nod at my glass.

"David Finch informed him that they have a ring of girls. Omegas." Dante takes a deep swallow of his drink. "They pick one out, often finding them on the verge of heat, and then... They fucking use the bite to control. They work girls, push them into sex work, a particular type, where they take them, mark them, and keep on deepening the mark."

"You could have told me this earlier." Knight turns to me.

"If you're thinking, Knight, that you can find information online, you can't. This is low brow, old school, word of mouth and secret fucking handshake shit," Dante says.

"I wanted to find out if anything had gotten through. Or if there was anything else of worth. A different marker." I take a drag.

Knight isn't a happy boy. "I could've searched certain arenas. I could—"

"No. You couldn't." I shake my head. "This isn't a big ring. And it's so illegal that everyone would end up in prison."

And I don't want that. I want to, when the time comes, hunt down every last fuck involved and kill them.

"He's not a fucking threat to us. This Jake stumbled on her, got lucky. Or," Dante says, "got unlucky, and on our radar. He's on the hunt for omegas. Nothing more than a low-end fucking recruiter."

"How do you know?" Knight asks, as the tension in the room gets tense and thick.

"Because we've seen it," I say. Then I add the detail David told me. One that's stuck with me because right place, unwilling girl... "The omegas wear a locked, thick leather collar around their neck."

The tension changes, becomes charged.

They both see what I'm seeing.

A way to play with a seemingly willing girl.

Then Knight's face morphs to disgust as he puts what it is into the scenario. "Holy shit. A chastity belt for the throat? Do they barcode them? Fun and games are one thing, but this..."

"Unwilling fucking girls." Dante's gaze flicks to me. "Not Unholy Trinity business."

"My business now." That's all I say on the matter.

I stub out the cigarette and finish my drink.

As they discuss our issue, I slip out and into the early hours of the night.

Clouds blanket the predawn in gray, and the water's choppy, the brine thick with that brackish scent from the pools of stagnant water remaining under the boardwalk. Even from here, it cloys.

I hunted for information last night. The lowest haunts. Places not owned by us.

It's easy for me to slide into that world.

But the talk was banal, and I think I need to find one of the omegas who got out. People always do. But that's going to take patience, time, an archeologist's brush. Fine by me. I'm a master in the art of patience and teasing off miniscule layers to get to what lies beneath.

I'm also good at murder with extreme violence and fast moves.

I do, however, know what this takes.

So why the fuck am I heading to where I put Lizette? This time is perfect to uncover things.

A movement catches my eye, and I go still.

There she is, her scent like rich and heady perfume on the air, displacing the brackish water, mating with the salt.

She doesn't notice me, though there's a hesitation to her step.

Lizette's hair is back in a ponytail and she has a shapeless dress on and her leather jacket. No hat. Her bag's slung high on her shoulder, and she dips her head and powers on.

I keep back and tail her, then the moment I work out where she's going, I make the shortcuts to get there before her.

This is my world, the streets and their secrets, and I wait by the tree where I watched her before.

Her damn apartment.

A car pulls up and a woman in heels and an expensive suit gets out with a man.

I don't know them. I don't have to.

I know what they are.

They disappear inside and make a hatchet job on the lock. I can see it mangled from here.

Lizette comes into view.

Now she pauses, at the corner, looking around. But like someone who hasn't had to do this herself, she doesn't pay attention to the tree.

She starts to walk down the path as lights here and there come on in windows and the street lamps go off.

When she turns up to her building, I glance at the windows of her place. The blinds are up, lights on, and two silhouettes move to the door. I know the layout now.

So, I move.

Fast.

Silent.

And I take her. Hand clamped on mouth to stop the scream, arm around her waist.

I drag her bag into the shade of the tree, turning her, trying not to let her scent in.

This is the first time I see her fear.

Real fear.

I want to sink my teeth into her throat and bite, then lick the fear and sex up and claim her as my own.

But the fear switches to shock and then anger.

"Council members are in your place right now." I lower my hand and bring my head to hers, our lips a moment apart. "Coming, I think, down the stairs. So, I'm going to kiss you. It's too late to run."

Too late because she's with me.

I can't move unseen with her. People are known to try to avoid looking at public signs of affection. It makes them uncomfortable, so I use that to our advantage.

The kiss is a drink from a forbidden fountain and she opens for me, her tongue seeking mine. I crumble a little, licking and dancing with her tongue. A taunt. A game and then, as the motor roars and fades, I break that kiss.

She's breathing hard.

So am I.

Fuck, my thigh's pressed between hers, and she's hot, damp, I can feel that sweet dampness. My hard on pushes into her and she moves. Rubbing up against me.

This time, when I drop my head, I lick along where Knight bit her, and she shudders out a low moan.

There's fire, and then there's burn your house down. This is veering into the latter.

So I release her and step back.

"What the fuck are you doing?" I ask.

Lizette drops her hands from my shoulders. I didn't even notice her touching me, just that connection to her.

"Are you sure they were Council, Reaper?"

"They looked it."

"If they weren't?" she asks.

"Then they were an unknown and worse than the Council."

Lizette sucks in a breath. "There's worse?"

"Yes." I pause. I want to taste her again. I count to ten, then step back. "Why did you come?"

She frowns. "I...wanted a necklace I thought I had."

"Jewels?"

"Something Dad gave me when I was little. Worthless. Priceless to me." She darts past me and takes a step in the direction of her building.

I grab her arm and drag her back in the shadows. "Don't go in there."

"But—"

"It might now have spy cameras, sensors. What does this necklace look like?"

"It's a tiny heart on a chain. Gold."

She's easy prey. Too easy. Too trusting of the world.

"I'll get it. When it's safe. So go back to where I put you. Now."

She hesitates and then she takes off, back the way she came.

This, I hope, is enough to send her into the arms of the Unholy Trinity.

Then again, I don't operate on hope.

I get my phone to send a text.

Then I start to follow.

EIGHTEEN

Lizette

Fear and arousal skitter along my skin and my nerve endings.

Reaper's following, I know it. But he's not following because he's changed his mind about sex or he's so enamored he wants to kiss me again, lick my throat. Does he even get enamored? He's so quiet on a level that's part of him and he takes everything in.

The kiss wasn't from lust or need.

It was to hide me, shut me up.

And I took it and ran.

I'm no fantasy girl. I'm just me, a sheltered, stupid virgin.

There's a part that wants to lay blame at my own feet for my predicament. And yes, going into Unholy Trinity territory, one of their domains, was stupid. If I'd been alone and going mad with heat, I'd...I'd be in the hands of the Council and shipped to Hover City for my so-called chosen alpha.

No one's to blame. My dad died and the cops took my name. And there's a part of me that wonders since the letter got to me so quickly, if they'd been aware of me since Dad's death.

If I hadn't gone to Pandora's Box, then...

I shudder.

"Hey, Liz."

The rough voice startles me, and I turn to the pizza place where the metal roll gate's half up and light spills out. Ray, who owns it, is outside, apron on, sweeping the walkway.

"Ray, how are you?"

I don't really want to talk, but I'm not rude, and he's not one for idle chitchat. Or maybe he is. Our paths usually cross inside the restaurant when we'd pick up pizza for dinner on occasion. He and Dad were friends.

"Still a damn shame about Con." He shakes his head and tugs on the corner of his salt and pepper handlebar mustache. "Listen, I gotta make a batch of dough and check in the marinara I've been simmering since last night, but...some people have been asking about you, Liz. Well dressed. Oh, and some guy in a cap who said he was your cousin? Told 'em I didn't know you. Figured since you're passing by and I'm doing early morning work before we open for the lunch crowd, I'd tell you."

"Thanks." Cold spreads through me, and I shiver.

"Be careful, okay?"

I nod, and he salutes, then pulls the gate up, and goes in, only to send the gate screaming back down.

His words sit inside me like little jagged shards of glass. Ray didn't tell me when they came by but it had to have been at some point since I stepped foot in Pandora's.

This time, I look behind me, to the sides. I study the shadows of alleys and deep doorways, the heavy branched trees that dot the nature strip before the curb.

I don't see anyone.

Maybe Reaper left.

His scent is on me, so I'm not sure if I can pick him out as the city wakes and fumes, breakfast carts and people who wear either their own aromas or ones from a bottle start to fill the world for another day.

I have a hoodie on under the jacket. It's big, Dad's, and I like it because it's old and worn and a faded black that's now dark gray. I'm not cold. Sure, the early morning's crisp, and there's ice from fear in me, but it'll warm more today. I zip it up and pull the hood over my head.

Better than nothing since I don't have the skills of Reaper in the disappearing arts.

My stomach lurches. Or that man who warned me.

As I scurry back, head down, hands shoved in my pocket, my fingers wrapped around my silent phone, I attempt to distract myself with who the man was. A friend? Not of the Unholy Trinity, but maybe of Dad's and by proxy mine. His advice to keep away is something I should head, mark on my throat or not.

We didn't do it. Knight didn't go into rut. No knot. No release for me to catch, so to speak.

Maybe the man works for the Council. Or maybe—

I bump into someone, and I dart up a startled look at the woman. She's well dressed. Not flashy or anything, but she could work in an office in her pants and blouse and vest.

People, Ray said. To me, people is shorthand for a man and woman, or men and women. He mentioned the man in a cap. Not person. So...

I give up with my convoluted thoughts as the woman speaks. "I'm sorry, I wasn't looking, but now I have you, can you spare a moment?"

My heart both sinks and slows its beat to normal.

The smooth transition into pre-sales speech is familiar and innocuous.

"A moment, but I have to get to work," I say.

I've played the game before. It's part of city living having people approach and try to sell you something. Whether it's a pack recruiter—some do that, usually weird, freaky ones—or people looking to get money from you and everything in between, it's a familiar dance with familiar dialogue.

She throws a curve ball by shoving a photo under my nose.

My heart almost breaks free of its bone prison.

"Have you seen her? She's not in trouble, but I'm so worried..."

It's me.

Oh, fuck. It's me.

Looking up at Dad, smiling, hair free and—

I breathe slowly, carefully. "I'm sorry. I'm new to Starlight City, so I don't really know many people." Average and nondescript is key. Dad drilled that in. Average melts into faceless and into forgettable.

"Have a look." She shakes it under my nose.

I take it, looking because running brings attention. I pretend to study it, but my eyes are blurred with unshed tears as my heart hurts looking at Dad.

Finally, willing my fingers not to shake, I hand it back. "Sorry."

I step past her and keep moving at the same pace, turning off on a street that leads to a lot of stores and businesses. From there, I wait at a closed restaurant, staring into the plate glass window.

It's busier now, but people are moving by, not looking at me or lingering.

Inside, it hurts. I try to hold the aching parts of my heart as I keep going, back to that desolate and bare bones basement studio in the Wharf district. Seeing that photo tore at something. I think because it's one I haven't seen. A candid moment.

And—

Candid.

Someone took that photo. Someone who was watching us. The Council?

171

Each beat of my heart urges me to quicken my pace, to run, but I don't.

I walk, and my spine is ice, prickling like a thousand eyes are on me.

It's in my head.

Not even Reaper is behind me now.

I want...I want those touches. Those kisses. The rough and honest elemental from him. The seduction and satin-wrapped sternness from Knight. The pretty, pretty man with the soft curls and dimples. The one who asked me to call him Daddy.

I liked it. The place of control and domination in a kind form from Knight, who can kiss like an angel with a dark heart. Or a devil with a good one.

And I liked the thrill of the chase, the hardcore finger fucking, and eating me that Reaper did.

Both are iceberg tips with so much more beneath the surface. How can I want to dive in and explore both in equal measures? How can I want a man that tells me I'm a good girl and asks me to call him Daddy, and also want the dark, bloody danger and thrills that the primal chase with Reaper brings?

Those are so different, yet...they both make me feel unbelievably good.

If they do that, what would Dante like, want, desire? How would he take his fill? What pleasures await from him?

The man doesn't like me. Sure, he got hard when he was around me, but that's because I'm marked by another alpha in his pack. And I was in heat.

I deliberately shut the door on them all, and continue to my solitary confinement. It's safer that way.

Reaper doesn't come.

Do the others know I'm here?

All the ways I decided I could see him, into him, understand and know him, start to fray as the doubts build.

Maybe he mirrored back the things I want because of my stupid naivety, my loneliness, and he isolated me.

To kill me.

I make myself keep that in my head.

Because he is a killer.

A person only has to look at him to know that. It's the one real truth that I can be sure of from all the things I saw or thought I saw in him.

I go through my phone. Rearrange my things. I pack, repack.

Finally, with my stomach rumbling, I get something to eat.

It's late afternoon, and I keep looping back to the photo the woman showed me.

Who took it?

And when?

I think about what we wore, and...the photo is about a year old by my estimations. We were laughing about something that happened at my job, something so stupid Dad couldn't stop his mirth and it set me off.

The memory pierces so sharp and bright I can't breathe for a few seconds.

I hug myself and look around at what my life's become: hiding, a prisoner again.

"But that's not true," I whisper. "Reaper gave me keys."

So, what am I meant to do? Every sound outside that filters down here, like when a truck backfired with a boom, I jumped. Some of the time, it's in my imagination, like footsteps that approach.

No one comes.

I try to nap, but I can't. I finally start looking at places I could go. I've still got my money.

Does it matter if I find somewhere? The Council has reach, and if they or the mythical people who might be worse can break into my apartment, can watch me and Dad and take photos and seemingly wait until he died to make a move, is anywhere going to be safe?

I know this city. In the world beyond? I'd have to go somewhere big. Congested. Another city. But that's another set of dangers. And—

It hits me why I repacked.

There's no way I can stay here. It's dangerous. Lonely. I'm a murder waiting to happen at the worst, and a sitting duck for someone to find me and take me to the Council. Or to that alpha I'm supposed to mate with.

I need help.

I take my backpack, and I slip out.

I run.

NINETEEN

Dante

I stare at her, little fucking omega lost.

She stands in the office upstairs, looking like what she is, the girl marked by an alpha and out of options.

That's not strictly true.

There are options. But none she wants.

None we want.

I eye her backpack and the bag at her feet.

It's a little lesson in discomfort, and she presses those soft lips together before releasing them, the move making blood flow to them, making them redder. Her skin slowly flushes as those wide, dark eyes fixate on me.

"Trying to decide if you hate me?" I ask.

Her scent weaves around me, and it pisses me off. Just like it did before Julien interrupted the pre-private event prep we were undertaking in the downstairs club.

Knight's handling it. There's just the approval of the dancers and the vetting of the add-ons for the guestlist. He's got Darcy helping, but he'd prefer to be here—he's more than aware Lizette turned up since he fucking bit her—but I need someone downstairs. And this is more my domain.

Besides, I'm not about to fuck her.

No matter how tempting she is. I have more control than Knight or Reaper.

"I already know that," she says, the fierce tone making me smile slightly.

"Claws in, Lizette. You came to me, remember?"

"What else am I supposed to do?" Her eyes glimmer as her hands clench and release, clench and release, at her sides. "I don't want to go to the Council, or to that pack. I don't want to register."

"You know that's a serious offense."

She tosses her hair back and takes a step toward the desk where I sit. "What is?"

I sit back. "All of it."

Lizette's silent for a long time. Then she says, that mouth twisting, "I guess that makes me one of you."

"An alpha?"

Her eyes narrow. "A criminal."

"Moving up in the world?"

"More like down." Her snap is like a sting against steel. "If it's with you."

I'm not sure if she means just me or her boy, Knight. And, I'm guessing Reaper, who has a destructive edge that women find hard to resist.

But I let it slide.

Instead, I let my gaze travel the length of her, lingering on her breasts. "No one gets a free ride here, girl. Not even you."

"I'm not sleeping with you."

"Good," I say, "because I never said you were. Never said I was interested."

"Of course you aren't." Her bitterness gives her away.

Reaper's off dealing with a troublemaker, and Knight's busy for now, so I have all the time to toy with her.

I want to. She riles me the wrong ways, and I pick up my drink, taking a swallow.

"You'll work. You saw the club downstairs, where the girl's dance?"

She nods and goes to say something, but I shake my head.

"If it's anything other than a yes, don't say it. Because, omega, there are consequences for everything."

She doesn't move, but finally, she nods and I can feel the waves of hot resentment that wash up against my libido, stroking it. I do love a challenge. And a girl in denial about who and what she wants.

Business, however, comes before me giving her a lesson.

"There's a private event tonight downstairs in the club. We get them all the time. This is for a group celebrating some big deal. Normally something like this wouldn't be in Pandora's but one of our more legit places on the edge of civilized society uptown. We know them, we deal with them and they want the thrill of the Avenues.

"But they're a company we deal with, an above-board business who have underworld ties. So it's here. They're spending big."

"I assume there's a point?" she asks.

"Glad you asked." I get up, pick up my drink and round the desk, leaning on the front edge, deliberately crowding her in the medium size office. It might as well be a broom closet for all the space it suddenly seems to have. She gasps but stands her ground.

And I have to begrudgingly give Lizette points for that. Others would back the fuck into the wall.

I'm not hiding who I am.

She knows I'm deadly, carnivorous, and I don't give one fuck for her.

And all Lizette does is raise her chin and meet my gaze.

"We," I say, "are short a girl."

"And that's my problem, how?"

"You need to earn your keep, starting tonight."

She swallows. And I could come from the thoughts that cross her face, at the fact I've got her exactly where I want to. Plan whatever the fuck it is, is in motion.

I can play with her, and she can't do a fucking thing.

"You want me to dance? Fuck someone?"

Something sharp slashes through me. "No. I don't want that. Fuck, I'm not about to throw you out like fresh meat."

"And here I thought that's what I am."

She's got some mouth on her. I stand, walk about her, sipping my drink. "You're both too marked and too fucking naïve to be considered fresh meat. They want the look of it and a girl who knows the score. Not a virginal omega who's marked."

"That isn't my fault."

"Maybe. Maybe not. I wasn't there to see."

"You're an asshole," she breathes.

I deserve the insult. I know I went too far and not far enough. But I let it slide. Instead, I take a sip of my whiskey and lean in, using my free hand to brush her hair from her throat, letting my fingers skim the mark.

She shivers and bites her lip, like she's trying to squash a moan.

"These men are animals, Lizette," I say. "They only want female staff. I need you to earn your fucking keep by dressing in the outfit that's going to be sent to your room, and then get your ass back here."

"What—" She frowns. "I'm not going to do anything until you tell me what I have to do."

"You will."

I hand her my drink and get my phone, sending Darcy a text. Right now, she can wait tables, work her way up to the stage. She'll make a fortune, too.

But not naked.

Knight and Reaper told me she can sing, so... If I lay down

rules, make her do that... Fuck, even if she can barely hold a note, she's money in the fucking bank.

Not to mention that setting down some hardline rules with her is a hotness all on its own.

She wants to know what I'll make her do to earn her keep, but I'm not telling her it's only going to be serving and maybe singing. Not yet. The not knowing's driving her mad, and I like that.

Lizette licks her lips. "Tell me—"

A flick of my eyes stops her words dead in their tracks. I come back at her, take my drink, and set it down, then I move, deliberate, slow, not stopping until Lizette's got no choice but to back off into the door.

She tries to hold ground but she doesn't. Her pupils are dilated, lips slightly parted, and her tits rise and fall unevenly.

Some might mistake this as fear. It isn't. It's pure, unadulterated lust. She's drowning in it. Her scent blooms, giving her away, taunting my senses.

That's the problem with her. Games are dangerous. A double-edged sword.

Lucky for me, unlucky for her, I like those games. I'm a master of control and denial. I can have her so fucking hot, she'll come without me touching her.

Unless, of course, I deny her. Order her not to.

And, I think, I'm going to do just that.

"Baseline rules, Liz. One, you'll be on the floor waiting tables, and then you'll perform, sing, who knows? Two, you obey us without question. And three, you don't fuck near your heat. With anyone. Even your knight in shining armor."

"Not even with you."

I grit my teeth. "Never speak back to me. I'm your boss now."

"You don't want me."

Oh fuck. Despite my warning, her pushing back is hot.

"Maybe I just like the control. Maybe I want to make sure

you keep your fucking scent and baby fatale ways in your fucking panties." I lean in, lips almost brushing her ear. "Maybe I don't want anyone else to touch you."

A small moan, so soft it's like a sigh, breaks free and washes against me, making my cock hard.

"I will not be your slave," she whispers.

"Oh?"

"N-No." She struggles for air. "I came here looking for help. What are the other rules?"

I ignore the last part. "Nothing's for free."

"Knight—Reaper. I...they..."

"They what?" She's just given Reaper away. He didn't fuck her. I'd know, but she wants them both. She's flinging them at me like they'll save her.

Fuck, Knight probably would.

Reaper? He'd watch whatever it was I wanted to do to her. Maybe join in.

And in the end, Knight's loyal to the Unholy Trinity, not a pretty little omega.

But I play with her some more.

"You think they have control over you? Or they'll come to your rescue?"

"I..."

"Tonight, you're going to do what you're told. No man is to touch you. If he does, I'll have him killed. You aren't a dancer, you're just cleaning up, bussing the tables. And then, if you pass, we'll keep you on in exchange for protection. Then I'll let you know if you'll sing naked, or just strip."

"I despise you."

"Do you? I could tell you to drop to your knees and service me, or I could set up a room for you so you can lie on your back and fuck all the men who attend the event."

"Bastard." She turns pale and I... My triumph is tempered with a touch of guilt. That's her power, she makes men protective. She also makes them want to fuck her.

Or maybe it's Knight's bite and how it somehow infiltrates me and Reap.

We're the three alphas of the pack, all equal. The mark is bound to affect the three of us in some way. But I lean right in so she's pinned, and she can feel the heat of me just like I can feel the heat of hers as it infiltrates flesh and bone and marrow, engorges my cock.

"But I won't. As I said, I don't want that. Fuck, I'm not even going to stop you getting it on with Knight, or Reaper, if you can, but you can't do a fucking thing until your trial period's over. A week. One week. And you can't even try and get yourself off."

"I'm not about to do that," she says, voice all melting with heated need.

I close in a little more, my mouth skimming along her throat, not quite touching her, but I can fucking feel her pulse leap, her uptick in temperature. Smell her arousal.

It brings a musky complexity to her scent, so fucking sweet and erotic that it could fell a man.

Christ, no wonder Knight marked her.

She isn't even in heat now and she's as potent as if she was.

Fucking Lizette's dangerous.

My kind of danger, the flame I like to taunt and tease and play in. My mouth hovers right at the mark.

And I blow out breath over it.

Lizette's breath stutters and she arches her throat, the offer so fucking blatant I'm not sure she knows she's doing it.

That move licks my balls.

"No, you're not. You're going to be good and obey me."

"Fuck you."

"You wish. But know, either way, I'm your fucking boss now. Your lord and master." I pause, sniffing her scent as I move up to her ear and plant a hand either side of her. She's quivering, a hum that delights me running through her. "You better not touch yourself. You don't come. And you sure as shit don't let Reaper or Knight fucking touch you."

I stop, rethink that, and lift my head so I can look into her eyes. Her gaze catches and the longing, lust, hate, and anger are a special aphrodisiac for me.

Like a wild creature, she needs to be broken in. Made to see who and what I am to her.

I'm going to be her puppet master, control her, and be in charge of her orgasms. When I decide to let one of the other two fuck her, then that's an implicit yes to her coming.

If she goes to one of them or lets them touch her when I haven't handed out permission...

It's on her.

And punishment's going to be fucking sweet.

The way she looks pulsates in me, and I revel in it, letting it stoke the fires of my pleasure, my own denial and my power.

"Actually, Lizette, let them touch you, but don't fuck them. And, no matter what they do, you can't come. If you do..."

"How will you know?" Her voice is almost breathless.

"I'll fucking know. Consequences, sweet angel."

The sudden nickname for her makes me pause. It rings something true in me.

I rather like it. It suits her.

"I know you hate me," she says. "Don't mock me. Please."

I only smile. "The things I could do to you to turn you on. To make you come so hard you won't be able to walk."

"Dante—"

"I wouldn't kiss you." I drop my gaze to her mouth. "Or, maybe I would because that's the plumpest, most inviting mouth I've seen. Those lips would be perfect wrapped around my dick, you on your knees, begging to be fucked in the throat."

Her little gasp scrapes down my spine.

I'm being crude, but she's the one who likes it. I bet if I put my fingers in her panties, she'd be wet. To make for easy fucking into her passage that's got to be tight.

She likes the dirty, filthy talk.

"I'd start slow, the first time, let the experience of the warm cloudlike softness close around me. Just a little to hold me there, on the brink. Your tongue working the head, over my slit and drinking any precum. There'll be precum. Your mouth demands my cum. You're made to get on those knees and service, offer up your wares. And I think you'll like it, too."

"Lies," Lizette moans.

"Yeah, you'd be desperate to suck me down, let your pretty lips stretch tight. Then I'd grip your hair and fuck your mouth. I'd push in, all the way, hammering into your throat that's so hot and wet and pliable, making you gag until I fucking come. I'm not sure yet if I'd want you to swallow or let my cum trickle down over your chin. To your tits." I put my mouth at her ear. "Fucking hot. You're just a deprived angel begging to be corrupted by me."

She moans again.

"Next," I say, "I'd have you suck my balls while fingering yourself, and then, sweet Lizette, I'd have you spread yourself open for me. Then I'd fucking eat that sweet smelling cunt. Bite you, lick you. Suck. I'd use my fingers the way I'm betting Reaper's done, like I know Knight did, I'd stretch you open. And I'd stretch your ass, too. I don't like waste. And ignoring your ass is fucking waste.

"I'd hook my fingers to stroke your G-spot while also hitting your A-spot in your ass. I'd show you pleasure you'd never dream of. And..." I drop my voice, shift so she can feel my hard on if she brushes against me, and she does in rhythmic little moves. "All the while I'm going to be sucking, biting, licking that clit of yours. I'll build it up, to the point you ache and need release. Fuck, you'll beg for it."

"And then?" she asks, voice slightly ragged.

"Then, right as you think you're going to come, I'll stop

and spin you, bend you over the desk, and plunge my cock, balls-deep, in your cunt. I'll fuck you for a bit, and..." I put my mouth close enough to brush her ear. "This is the good bit. I'll fuck your ass. I'll go back and forth between both holes until we're both aching for release. Just like you want to come now, and, with me sucking your tits through that dress, I know you could. But I'm not doing that. Just like when I fuck you over my desk, I'm not letting you come either. I'll send you away, orgasm so close you can fucking taste it."

Her entire body shakes with need.

"I'll send you away with the order I'm giving you now," I tell her firmly. "You're not to come. Because I'll know. And trust me when I say, you don't want me to punish you."

I step back, open the door, and motion her out. "Be back here in five. I think you know the way to your room."

She looks at me like I slapped her, robbed her, and then she turns, and walks away.

CHAPTER
TWENTY

Lizette

"Should I even ask why you look so fucking forlorn?"

I shoot a look of resentment Dante's way. He's lounging against the bar upstairs, and I'm washing endless glasses from the night before.

"Do you care?"

The impassive expression is all I need to tell me he doesn't as he takes a seat and opens his tablet that has a flip out keyboard.

I've been here a week, and it's been excruciating.

I'm lost in this giant new world, even if it starts and ends with the walls of Pandora's.

He hasn't told me what he expects me to do. He hasn't outlined the rest of his rules for work in exchange for protection.

And I know it's not just this. He told me as much.

It's excruciating and lonely.

Knight is busy. Reaper keeps his distance when he's here. I don't think it's me because he's like that with everyone that I can see. Besides, he's hardly around, which I don't know if it's normal or not.

And why should I?

I don't, when I think about it, know these men, no matter what's happened with them.

But it doesn't stop me from thinking, it doesn't stop me wondering and wanting something intangible.

It's not intangible.

The thing I want is comfort.

When Dante doesn't answer, I say, "What else do you get up to?"

"Criminal things, Lizette. Why? Second guessing our arrangement? Thinking you'll be better off with your mate-to-be?"

His brow lifts as he goes back to the tablet he's typing on, the little keyboard softly clicking.

"Hardly." I try to sound heartless, a brazen, hardened criminal, but I just sound pathetic to my ears.

I catch the half smile that flashes on his mouth. "Well, I'll make sure to come to you next time we pull a heist."

"And here I thought you worked in kidnappings."

Now he looks at me, humor dark and sparking in his eyes. "Oh, we do, but only the girls who come to us and get themselves marked. It's niche."

I glance down at the fluorescent light under the bar turning the edges of the bubbles blue as I dip two more glasses onto the whirring brushes.

"When are you going to trust me?" I ask.

"It isn't about trust."

"Sure. I know you keep Knight from me. And Reaper."

The words hang, and he just stares at me. Then he starts laughing. "Fuck, you're a comedian, too. What other secret talents do you have?" Slamming the glasses down, he goes back to whatever he's doing. "Contrary to what you might think your magic pussy can do, along with my powers to order around the other two alphas in this pack, they're busy."

Dante's definitely the one even his equals bow to. He's got that edge to him, a dynamic. Hell, I bet if there were a god, even he or she would bow to him.

I'm no god, and I don't want to do that, even if the urge to bow to him, to obey him like he ordered, beats in my veins. It's almost overwhelming and it feeds my resentment.

I lick my lips. "But—"

"I issued you a warning. Gave you a rule. Not them. Knight's got a lot going on, and Reaper... It's important."

"A mission?"

Dante doesn't say anything. He doesn't have to.

One night, Reaper came back, blood on him. His face was thunderous clouds and my heart flipped and squeezed because he looked like he gave away a piece of his soul. Or lost it.

Then again, I'm out of my depths. This is a part of the world I'm not used to.

I just... I want that thing I've been missing ever since Dad died. The connection with someone. Deep, without trying to be anything but what it is.

And Knight? I shiver with longing. He's so sweet, and I want those dreamy, bone melting kisses.

I want it all. Any time I'm near any of them a dull throb starts in me, feeding unwanted filth dipped thoughts to my head. I'm not sure if it's better or worse than the loneliness or a different version of the same thing.

I grab another two glasses and wash them. And yes, the dull throb is in me now, sending whispering vibrations along my nerves, because Dante, the man I hate, the devil himself, is sitting near.

Because of Dante and his threat. Promise, whatever it was.

He had me so turned on, I spent my entire first shift in a

throb of need, an ache from not being fulfilled, not finding release.

Similar to now.

"Did you hear me?"

I dip two glasses into the treated water and down on the whirring brushes, rinsing them in the next sink. "I wasn't listening."

"Thinking about fucking someone?"

I press my thighs together. "Why do you care?"

"I don't." He shrugs, that wicked darkness dancing in his eyes. "I'm just making sure you're keeping up your end of the bargain."

There's no bargain, he just told me he'd punish me if I came, broke those first set of rules.

I hate him. Loathe him.

"Like I have a choice," I snap.

His eyes meet mine, sending a shaft of heat through me. "We all have choices, Lizette. I was letting you know we might keep you on the lower floor."

"Why?" I frown.

"Precautions." He reaches down and pulls up a bag, handing it to me. "Got you something."

I wipe my hands on my apron and stare at it.

"It won't bite."

"No, something from you is going to be far worse." But I open it, and almost throw it at him. It's a vibrator.

"For when I let you come." He takes the bag, leaving me with the box that announces what's in it. "Or maybe it's temptation personified; I haven't decided."

The devil gives me a nasty, feral smile that makes my needy insides quiver. Whether I hate him or not, I want him. More and more with every passing minute.

Never in my life could I have imagined wanting three men in different, sexual ways with the same intensity.

I take off my black apron and wrap the toy up in it and put it on the bar.

"What do you say?" he asks.

The words *fuck you* come to mind, but the insult's exactly what I want to do to him so I don't answer. Luckily, I'm saved by the buzz of his phone. He snatches it up and presses the answer icon as he stands.

"Talk," he says as he walks out of the bar area.

Shit. He's trouble. The devil's always trouble. Charming and desirable in ways he shouldn't be.

To slow down my racing thoughts that like to tie themselves in knots, I think about my situation.

I haven't left here. Yet. I know they have a place elsewhere, but I'm never left here alone, and there's even a kitchenette down on the third floor.

They're here at night and there's something both thrilling and comforting about one of the alphas or even all three staying in the building until the sun rises.

Reaper told me they're preparing a place for me at their main residence. But it's safer here for now.

Safer, I'm guessing, and easier for Dante.

When I finish the glasses, I start to wipe the bar and then the tables.

It's not until I turn that I realize I was singing because my voice stops.

Dante stands there again, statue still, staring at me. His eyes are wide in disbelief.

"Oh, fuck me," he breathes. "You sound like an angel. Why didn't you tell me you could sing like that?"

"You said you knew." I shrug. "I didn't think it mattered. Does it? Should I stop?"

"No."

The 'no' sends everything into a flurry. Does he mean it doesn't matter or that he doesn't want me to stop singing? His expression is no help. It reminds me of the blankest look of Reaper's. Except...I think I understand his, the ones I've read. But Dante's?

It's there to turn me away from whatever he is or isn't feeling. So, I can't get a handle on it, and worse, control over my own emotions slips away. It feels as if I'm pinned to the spot, just like I would be with his hand wrapped around my throat, holding me there.

"I'm not that good," I say, suddenly nervous. "Nothing Grammy worthy."

He continues to look at me, the pressure of this endless moment rising, and my stomach flips.

Then it ends as Julien appears and catches his attention. "What?

"I need you, Dante."

He nods, gives me one last look, before crossing to Julien. For a moment, I thought I saw a flash of something, like warmth in his gaze, along with the surprise, but I probably imagined it. And I remind myself not to soften towards him, that I hate him.

I throw myself into work.

I'm about to start setting out candles for tonight when suddenly my senses prick all over. Dante's there, hovering close and staring at me, a frown on his face. "Go downstairs. Now."

"But—"

"Now."

I start for the stairs, disappearing just as voices reach me. He's talking to someone, and I want to stay, listen.

This isn't just nosiness. If it's to do with me in any way, I'd like to know. But I don't hover. There was something in his face, beneath his bored tone.

Almost like a plea... But that's fanciful thinking.

Still, I go into my room. It's not the same one they put me

in for when I was in heat. This is bigger, the bedroom nicer, and there's also a little living room. I stand, at a loss, and decide maybe I could freshen up.

I go to undo my apron, and I freeze.

Oh, good lord, I left it upstairs, wrapped around the vibrator.

I run to the door and pull it open, running into a warm mess of welcoming scents. Lavender, leather, honey, and the heat and strength of a male form wrapped in something snuggly soft.

"Knight," I whisper, looking up at his smiling face and the caramel curls. "I need to—"

"You can't go up there." He walks me into my room and closes the door, snipping the lock behind him.

My heart beats fast.

"Sit." He steps away and motions to the sofa, and I get why he's so damn soft. He's got a throw, and it's big.

"What's going on? Are you..." I have to stop myself.

He looks like a rich college boy with those curls. The soft, welcoming smile's enough to make me want to run to his arms. Before I met these men, before I went into heat, I hadn't thought about sex. Now? It's on my mind all the time. I'm basically a fiend.

"Just stay here." He puts the blanket down. And a part of me sinks.

"First, Dante bosses me around, now you." I don't look at him, even as my fingers itch to touch the super bouncy material of the throw. It's a pretty deep rose, and—

I swallow down the tight, hot lump in my throat. Along with the sting of tears that hits the back of my nose.

"Why am I even here? No one wants me except when I'm in heat, and I can't help that." I look up at his frowning face. "You want to know why I came here instead of running off?"

"Me?"

A small laugh breaks free.

"It seemed smart. I-I figured Dad would want me safe." I look down at the black trousers I'm wearing for my bussing and cleaning. "That's why I came here."

"Dang, you mean you didn't come so you could jump me?"

He's not playing his Daddy-master role. He's flirty, funny, and to my horror, I sob.

An ugly sob that makes me drop my head to my hands in shame.

"Hey, Liz?"

I shake my head and utter a squeak, the only sound I can make. Hell, I'm like some sex-starved idiot, lusting after these men, sobbing because...because...because he hasn't touched me since I got here.

"Liz, please don't cry." Knight leans in, mouth brushing my hairline. "Breaks my heart."

I sob a little louder as I try to get myself under control. "I don't really cry." I try to breathe, try and get my shaky voice back in order. "I know you'll keep me safe, you and Reaper. Dante too. I just wish the loneliness didn't eat at me."

He sighs softly and kisses my forehead again, pulling me in against him. I close my eyes.

This is nothing like Dad, nothing like anything I've experienced.

To me, it's a little like the start of something...romantic, the sort of thing I never had and it only makes me ache more.

He likes me. He wants me. I'm not sure if it's the same thing, but I snuggle in a moment, breathing him in, losing myself.

"Liz?"

I push away. "I'm okay."

"I didn't ask you to move. You feel good."

But I look at him. Those eyes of his are chameleon. Right now, they're like shadows in the woods, muted green-brown, hazel. But when he kissed me, touched me, bit me, a flash of emerald hits. I remember.

Breathing gets hard again. "But you won't touch me."

"I am."

"No, I mean..." I suck in air. Then I shake my head. "Dante said no...no men."

"Dante isn't the boss of me." He takes back his arm and pushes his hair back. "Fuck, he's an ass, but there's more to him. And there's more to feelings, closeness, than sex. I like you. *You*. I like the rest, too, but...I marked you. Shit."

He stands.

"Everything isn't just sex, no matter how much I want you."

Then he picks something up and my heart sinks.

"Oh."

He unwraps the apron. "Oh, indeed. Dante gave it to me, said you left it?"

The tears are gone now. Rage and heat streak through me as I snatch it and throw it.

"No, he gave it to me to taunt me."

"Taunt?"

I nod. "He told me not to jump any of you."

Knight looks at the vibrator then back at me. "And he gave you that?" He pauses. "Well."

That wasn't what he was going to say.

"He's horrible."

"Right now, he's up there dealing with the Council," he finally says. "Dante's a lot of things, but you wouldn't be here if he wasn't going to protect you. We all will."

"The Council found me?" The world shifts.

"The Council are doing their rounds. Why are you so important to them? They don't usually venture into Unholy Trinity territory."

"I'm nothing. No one. I should go." I start looking for my backpack. I spy my case that wasn't there that morning.

"Dante doesn't want me here, and...I wouldn't even mind his nasty little rule. I know he can't possibly force me to not have any orgasms, not really."

"I'm not sure. Dante is... Well, he's insane in a different way than the rest of us." He comes up, brushes a kiss of such tenderness, a kiss full of promises, across my lips that I almost cry. Again. "He can try."

Then he lets me go.

"Knight, I...I'm sorry."

"Don't be. Your life is all upside down. Thing is, I'm betting he's got a fucking hard on for you. And he hates it."

"He does, but not like that. Not out of want and need and lust that's based in any real emotion. And Dante hates it and me."

"But, Liz, he's out there right now fucking doing something dangerous, risking a full-on sanction on us. They won't, because I know how to retaliate, but the Council? They're powerful cowards hiding under the guise of order and civility. Fuck them."

"You sound like my father."

"No, I'm Daddy, not a relative. So just hang out, and I'll get you something to eat." He kisses me again, making my heart surge, and then he's gone.

I go and stroke the softness of the throw. A second one, the other I got during heat, and I don't know where from, but I think now I do. That other one is a dark leaf green.

My heart spins this time and a sweet warmth spreads.

I wrap the throw around me, even though I'm not cold, and it smells both new and like Knight. It smells perfect.

My suitcase catches my gaze, and I cross to it and unzip the top. It's full of everything I left behind, I suspect, as I pull out the sleeve of a top I left.

Reaper. He must have gone back, packed, brought it here. That makes me get a little warmer. I drag it into the bedroom and leave it near the bed, so I can unpack later. I'm about to leave when a glint of metal catches my eye.

Heart beating fast, I go to the side table.

There, on a black piece of material, is my necklace. From the apartment.

Reaper went in and got it.

I really, really want to cry.

TWENTY-ONE

Knight

A fter Lizette's fed and calmed, I take the damned vibrator and leave it in Dante's office before going back to her room.

The door is as I left it. Still closed, but as I reach for the handle, I close my eyes and drop my head against the wood.

Fuck.

How someone as smart as Dante can screw things is beyond me. Sure, he's got his kinks, so do I, so does Reaper, but the sweet thing in that room's innocent. He's torturing her and enjoying it.

Okay, sure, I might have marked her, sunk my teeth into the most delicious thing I've ever had in my mouth. And I tasted her slick. Point is, it's all fucking up there in the land of decadent and divine and he needs to get over it.

No, that's not the point.

Point is that she doesn't deserve his brand of hard-core edging and denial shit. She might like it. Not gonna lie. Liz might like the way she quivers and almost purrs at

Daddy/Dom play, even if I just dip a toe in with my tone, a touch.

But none of that takes anything from the fact she's innocent. A virgin. And he's giving her vibrators?

I head up the stairs, and Dante's at the bar, a well-dressed woman next to him. She's older than me, maybe around Dante's age, gorgeous. And a weak alpha. She's also Council.

Without sparing them a glance, I head to Julien, her gaze on me. She's trying to work out who I am. It's not anything like lust. I know that look, the pheromones it sets off in the air, even if I'm not interested.

And though he's not looking at me, yeah, I can feel the hot lick of anger from Dante.

Fuck him.

Liz is no idiot. She won't come up here. Ask me, and he won't, but he wants to get his dick in her and he hates that. Fucker. But I don't slow, don't speed up, just head on out to the front where Julien is.

Glaring at two men.

"These are?" I ask.

"Council fucks."

I pat Julien's arm and smile at them. It's the benign one that Dante couldn't ever be bothered to put on, if he even has one, and the kind of smile I don't think Reaper possesses. Speaking of...

"Julien?"

He nods, eyes still trained on the men who are standing there, their fear and unease in the air. They don't like this area, or this place, and they definitely don't like Julien. Good.

"Yeah, boss?"

I almost roll my eyes at the title.

"Let the others know we're busy and to push appointments back to further notice."

Julien knows I mean Reaper.

He's meant to be dead. Or in prison. When the wrong sort of law or government comes near any of our places and he's there, he vanishes. But the last thing I need is for him to decide today's the day to walk in through the front door, and, well, I don't feel like organizing a full-on cleaning job and impromptu burial.

I'm talking about the Council dudes, not Reaper.

He'll fucking murder them straight up and Julien will probably offer to hold them down.

As Julien steps out of their sight and hearing to make the call, I go up to them and lean against the wall. We don't use this part of the club often. It's for day shit, and the official entrance that only people like this would come near. They'd also never drop by at night, not in any official capacity.

"Can I get you anything?"

They look at each other. The younger and better dressed one—probably second in command under the weak alpha inside...at least, second in command on their field trip—straightens his tie and says, "I'm Mal. You are?"

"None of your fucking business," I say nicely. "I'm just expecting a shipment of wine, and the rep's very pretty, so... crowds n' all."

Disgust crosses both their faces at the meaning of my mythical, pretty rep.

"So, I just wanted to know how long you were going to interfere with our operations today."

"As long as it takes," says the second in command.

"Okay. Cool."

With that, I step out as Julien goes to step in. "Want me to rough them up?"

"No, just get their cards, and text your girl to dress up and come in. She's a wine rep."

His mouth thins.

"Dude, she's just coming in to hang out," I assure him. "With me. And trust, I'm not touching her. She'd kill me."

Julien's mouth flickers into a small smile. "That's my girl."

Love. It's annoying.

As I walk off, a glimmer of guilt hits. I'm not in love with Liz. I don't really know her yet, no matter how I react to her, no matter that I bit her, and I know I'd do it again.

I'm betting she believes in forever and all that shit that this place and this pack isn't. We work with a different kind of happy. One that isn't her.

Shit.

Well, we're not all bonding with her, that's for sure.

I head behind the bar to get a drink, and I slide the tablet from Dante. "New friend?"

"Don't you have work to do?" he says easily.

I flash an irritated smile.

"Waiting for the wine rep. I guess since you've got company..." I do some quick magic on the tablet so it's just the regular and above-board site on there, complete with wine shipments. I add the rep, Darcy R. And then I make a show of it to him.

Dante glances down and then over at me. He moves the device, closing the tab and making sure a list of fake employee names are up.

"You can handle a wine rep on your own?" He nods at the Council woman, who's still hovering close by. "I'm busy."

"Don't let your date hold you up too much, sir. It's a busy day of restocking the booze."

And I wander off back down to my office and my computers, where I pull up information on these three members of the Council.

It's easy to find them. They're nobodies according to this, middle management. But the woman works in registration.

I make sure I have their names, and where they live, before I do a deep dive into them.

When Darcy comes down, she's in a suit, dressed to

fucking perfection, like the wine reps we deal with at the classier places we own.

"Do we need a shipment?" she asks. "I can make calls."

"So can I."

"Tongue back in head, Knight." But her words are a light tease. She knows I'd never dare.

As hot as she is, as gorgeous as she is, Darcy's not my type.

"Okay, I'll get some work done."

She sets the folder she's carrying down. And with a sigh, I pick it up. "Come on, we'll have a drink..."

The drink's nice and we do discuss the next order of wine.

I flip through the folder and point out a few I'd like. I'm not a fucking idiot. Reckless maybe, on and off the computer, but never an idiot.

Reaper couldn't be fucked about the ins and outs of the pack business. He kills and provides the deadlier muscle and delves into the blackest depths of our crime connections. I'm honestly not sure what lines he won't cross.

But I set up a way to use our legit businesses as a buffer. Like Darcy and the wine. There is a real rep, one who's stepped foot in our classier joints. And they do sell to us here. There's definitely an order to be placed. Sometimes I do it. Other times, Dante, but the person who delivers the order, and organizes visits to the other properties of the Unholy Trinity?

Darcy.

So, on days like today, I can pull that out of the hat, and if it's looked into, it all pans out.

"That's expensive." She shakes her head.

And I top up my wine and high-five myself. "I know. I also need two of me."

"One's enough, Knight," she says with a smile.

"Time with Julien has made you cruel." But I just take a sip of the wine. "Put the order in. The usual for upstairs and some fancier stuff for—"

"You?"

"The speakeasy." I stop, look at the space. "What do you think of classing it up a little? More burlesque, call it the Scotch and Cigar?"

She's too busy filling in the wine order as Mason, our head bartender, comes in.

"For here?" He looks about, setting down a tablet. "Yeah, I like it."

"You're not the boss," Darcy says. "What does Dante say? Reaper?"

"No, I'm one of them." But her jab rolls off me. She likes to poke us. Me more than the other two, probably because I'm not a psychopath, or the one who just might have the veto power to kick someone out. "And numero uno hasn't been asked? Numero...er...two...is never interested."

"Fine, get that ass kicked out," she says, trying not to grin.

There's only been one person kicked out on their ass, and that was Ghost. Another alpha. I take a swallow of my wine and glance at Mason. I check the time. "It's a little early. Couldn't keep away from me?"

I try to squash the uneasy thought he turned up to see Liz.

Not that I'd blame Mason, a delta. Liz's a fucking vision, but y'know, hands off and all that. She's ours. Mine, Reaper's, and whether he wants to admit it or not, Dante's. For as long as we keep her.

I know my thoughts on that, but the other two?

"Got a delivery? Booze?" Mason asks. "And I need to set up upstairs, but Dante's got some Council woman there. Not to mention the fuckwits in the day entrance foyer."

I smile. "Send the delivery guys down, through that door

and not the service one, and if they step on or get too close to a Council asshole...it's—"

"An accident?" Mason asks.

I nod. "Or a business hazard."

"Obviously," the bartender says. "I'll unpack and restock—"

"No," I cut him off. Liz is dancing in my head. "I'll do it. Darcy, take the order into the wine distributor. Mason? When you're done with the booze delivery, take care of this floor...."

"Who's going to unpack and stock?" Mason asks me.

I pick up the tablet—it's open to the delivery slip—and I grin. "I will."

With a little help.

The last bottles are delivered to the correct floor. Dante finished with the meeting and the place is footloose and Council free. I grab the bottle I opened earlier and two regular low-ball glasses, since I figure I need a little celebration for the menial labor of doing the unpacking, counting, checking and delivering.

Liz helped.

I know I'm playing with fire here, but the way her eyes lit up with the happiness of being useful was worth it. Still is.

And she's good.

She's sharp, hardworking, and she helped get the job done in a fraction of the time. She also stayed down in the storage room, seemingly happy with the status quo, and the fact Dante wanted her out of the way.

I like how she's pliant in the right ways, subversive in others. Oh, I don't mean subversive in a sexual manner, but I can see that, too. No, she's able to look at things and subvert the submissive parts in her into staying small and out of the way to learn what she can.

I felt that down in the storeroom. Because the moment she worked out I wasn't about to get on her case with doing the job, she did it better, faster, and different to me.

Is that why she's still there, I wonder. Apart from making herself useful? To stay away from Dante?

I would.

But he's not about to venture out and change his version of hellfire over things.

He's locked up in his office so I don't disturb him. So she doesn't. No doubt he's dissected the entire visit and watched the video feeds of it over and over. No doubt he's going over numbers and surveillance of trouble spots in our other places, like always.

Nothing is going on with those, I know, but I marked the places for him to look at as usual in the files I sent before the Council arrived. We check everything. People are jerks. People are easily bought, so anything suspicious is examined.

Or after this visit here, everything checked out, rechecked and checked again.

And the length of time he's taking, he's got his magnifying glass and fine-toothed comb out.

Normally if something pans out to trouble, Reaper moves in and...

The sweetest melody caresses my ears, making me falter to a stop.

What the living hell is that sound? The voice is a marvel shifting from one song that's sweet and high and pure, to another that has that smoky layer of classy sex over it. I recognize it. One of the girls did a bump and grind to this song the other night.

This version...is better.

Hotter.

Shit. It's doing things, to me, that voice.

When I heard her sing last it was pretty, she was in heat, but this...

"Liz?"

I push open the door.

Her ass moves in time with the song, and she puts bottles on shelves, her voice rich and seductive, and I wish I smoked so I could take a drag.

She suddenly stops and turns. Eyes big, hair damp. "I'm sorry."

"Stop saying you're sorry."

I put the wine and glasses down on a shelf and come at her and take her face in my hands. She's soft and sweet smelling. She melts into me, eyes unfocused, and she sighs. "Knight."

I kiss her, taking my time. This kiss isn't particularly sweet. It's a slow building need and desire. It's shared moments.

"Good girl," I say, lifting my mouth. "You make Daddy very happy when you kiss me like a sweet little angel. Such a good, perfect, girl with the most amazing feeling tits." A tremor runs through her. I go to her ear, sucking on it. "And the most gorgeous cunt. Will you let Daddy touch your sweet pussy?"

She squirms, parts her thighs. "Daddy—Knight, I..."

Shit, what am I doing? Pushing her? It's just she sounded good enough to eat, feels and tastes better, and I think she's into me praising her. She's shuddering, restless, the side of jumpy that comes from too much stimulation.

I let her go, stepping back. "I didn't mean—" I stop, because clearly I did. I meant it. "I should have held back. I know you've got that order from Dante."

"He hates me."

That weird little power game he's playing with her, one that blatantly drips in sex. And she can't see that. She's too close.

I take a breath.

She considers me. "Fuck his order."

"Really?" I raise a brow and lean against a pile of boxes.

Liz blows out a breath. "Yes."

I offer her a dirty, sleazy, bad Daddy Dom smile. "You're going to use that pretty, pretty mouth for such nasty words, baby girl?"

"I'm all grown up," she says.

My cock twitches. I like the little, bratty, bad girl twist. It's so fucking hot, it's adorable because she's more brat than bad. My kind of brat. The one that wants the praise even if it's too much.

"Prove it." I watch to see what she does.

What she does is not disappoint.

Liz comes at me with more determination than anything like a practiced move. And she runs her hand down my chest to my now hard cock.

Her hand squeezes and her eyes widen. "Oh, my, Daddy."

"Yeah, all the better to fuck you with, to really teach you a lesson, Liz."

She rises on her toes and looks up at me. She's almost tall enough to kiss me, so I lower my head and take her mouth in a kiss that makes my cock jerk and my toes curl.

I grab her by the waist as she kisses me back with wild abandon, her tongue playing and teasing mine. And I set her on the boxes, stepping between her thighs.

"Lesson number one...you always, always come for Daddy."

She's in one of her dresses, thank fuck. Clearly, she changed and showered after I left, and she came back to continue working. I like her in dresses.

I flip the skirt and her scent is thick in the air. The gardenias are dipped in sex, and I want to inhale them so they fill my every cell.

Instead, I slide my fingers in her panties. My cock is aching now, in need of her. And she's hot, wet, and touching her is like heaven itself. I push two fingers into her and thumb her clit, determined to make her come as I dip back down to her mouth. And after she comes, I'm burying myself in—

The door bangs open.

"What the fuck do you think you're doing?" Dante snarls.

Right then, she screams as she comes on my fingers.

Fuck.

TWENTY-TWO

Lizette

"I'm not in trouble?"

Humiliation still coats me, head to foot. I can't believe I came in front of Dante.

I can't believe I got off yet again by calling Knight *Daddy*. Oh, I more than get the illicit thing, and how it makes me feel both dirty and his to control. Submissive.

He doesn't even look like a guy who gets off on taking control. But he is. In his way.

That soft edged thing over steel. I like that side, the one that makes me want to sigh and just be.

Just like I like the indulgent Daddy. I want to give over to the regular Knight, too. But it's sexual, colored by lace and silk. And it makes me both fuzzy, painfully hot, and on the edge of too much, as well as just melting inside with lust.

I'm also betting he's a "take all the control man" out in the real world, too.

My cheeks flame hot, and I shift on my seat. I just... I wish the devil hadn't caught me. I wish the dark thrilling knell of his words weren't ringing through my head.

How can I lust after three people?

Even if they *are* the pack alphas. Or—

"Stop thinking about getting your girl rocks off, Angel," Dante says as he motions for me to sit. "That goes for the rest of you."

There's the nickname again—Angel. I haven't confronted him about it or asked him to stop calling me that, but even I can see the dichotomy of the name he's given me and his own.

Reaper slides in through the door to Dante's office, silent, and to those less observant, a creature carved of ice and emotional flatness. But I can see it. The flicker of curiosity. It's like sparks lingering against my skin, a tiny uptick in heat.

I press fingers into my hot cheeks.

"Stop thinking that shit, Angel," Dante murmurs low and my breath hitches. "We can all feel it from you."

Horror and embarrassment streaks through me. I know the mark is affecting us in some way, but they can sense my desire for them through it, too?

Oh, god.

Knight catches my eye as misery threatens to swallow me whole, and he winks, setting off a thrill in me.

"You don't want us thinking about getting our girl's rocks off?" Knight asks. "I don't think I have any." He turns to Reaper. "Do you have any?"

Reaper just gives him a mild look, then glances to the devil in black. "Dante?"

Dante pinches the bridge of his nose. "Just sit. Both of you. All of you, and stop fucking around, Knight."

"Am I in trouble?" I ask again, as I push my hands under my thighs.

I'm still in the dress I changed into, and honestly, even though it's big and shapeless in a comfy way, it's still showing thigh, and I can feel the slide of Knight's fingers as they ride up my inner thighs to my pussy.

208

Dante just raises a brow, like he knows where my thoughts went. Dammit. I need to stop that.

"Am I?" I ask again. Then something horrible comes to me. "Are you making me leave?"

"No. To your last question, Angel."

A shiver passes through me.

Dante finally settles his gaze on me, and it burns deep into my soul. He's definitely the devil, because the sheer brimstone and sexual fire in that look sears my flesh. Brands me.

Oh lord. What if he does make good on those nasty, hot words to me in this room that time? What—

His gaze drops to my mouth.

He knows I'm thinking of his rules, his threat. Or was it seriously a promise?

I know he's thinking of it, too. It glitters, like burning stars.

"The first?" I ask.

"Now that," he says, "is a different conversation."

Reaper's gaze touches me, and I swear it softens a little before he looks at Dante once more.

And Knight...he winks again, this time with a proprietary smile. I try to breathe, but it's hard.

Everything in me is hot, alive, my blood hitting my pulse points hard. And there's one more thing.

Something I can't ignore.

It could be psychosomatic. It could be just because of me and Knight, and my body still tripping on endorphins. It could be the closed space of the office.

Or it just might be them.

Or me.

The mark on my throat throbs. It's working overtime and sending out tendrils of need and want and wicked desire. And I think it's doing that because the three of them are in here with me.

I'm not up with any of the pack knowledge beyond the fact

I'm an omega and go into heat. Just the bare bones. I'm coveted because of what I am. Dad told me I needed to keep away from regular jobs. And to bond with someone for love. Down the line. My choice.

This...This throb isn't something he told me about. I guess I don't blame him because who wants to talk about the ins and outs of sex with their daughter?

But he never mentioned it, and now...now it's like this throb has a direct line to my clit.

All three of them are causing this overtime beat in me.

I don't dare tell them that because what if it's bad? What if it isn't normal?

Worse, what if it makes Dante deem me too problematic?

He already went out on a limb today. Dealt with my problems that arrived in the form of the Council.

"Stop scaring her, Dante. And while you're at it, stop being a prick," Knight says.

"Angel's scaring herself." Dante turns to me again. "What's got you pulling in on yourself?" He pauses. "Well?"

I open my mouth but then I just shake my head, and he sighs. Reaper's gaze shifts to me, and for a moment, I'm caught in the black abyss of his eyes, an abyss that's so alive it steals my breath. And again, I think I see a glimmer of something soft, secret, and just for me.

Or maybe I've lost my mind.

There's that, too.

"I caused trouble." The words are out before I can stop them.

"If you mean getting down and dirty with Rusty Knight here—"

"Hey!"

"—then yeah, you did," Dante says, ignoring Knight. "But if you're talking about the fucking Council? Angel, they're a constant thorn."

I frown. "But you sent me downstairs..."

"Precautions." Dante leans back against his desk, tapping a hand against it. He's all in black, a suit. Jacket's on the back of the chair and the sleeves are cufflinked, and his tie is silk, the vest's got a geometrical pattern, in tiny raised ridges.

It's the outfit of a suave criminal. Of dangerous intent. And it fits him to perfection.

I drag my gaze away and look at my Docs as I try to stabilize myself. Because I'm going haywire.

The three of them pull me in different directions like they're touching, teasing, stimulating me. And it threatens to spin the world off its axis.

"I got the message to keep things on the down low." The low, quiet tones of Reaper soothe in ways I don't understand. It's like he can calm the frightened creature in me. Speaks to the darkness I feel when I get lost. Because it's where he dwells. "Were they after Lizette?"

"Gonna say maybe. Which we need to take as a yes. The woman, Susan, kept it vague as shit. Fine by me. I speak that language." Dante pauses. "But, assuming it's a yes, we need better security."

"Dante?" One word, from Reaper.

"Add more people?" Knight pushes past, his fingers skimming my thigh, drifting over my hand as his gaze hits mine, all warm and sweet syrup I could drink from forever.

It lasts a second but it's mine for a lifetime, that private look and touch.

It lasts a moment, and then he's behind Dante's desk, on his laptop, punching in something. "I can get people, trusted people. Weapons or no weapons?"

"Julien and I are weapons." Reaper pulls out a packet of cigarettes and shakes one out. "I'm fucking lethal."

"I want some scouts, people who can keep an eye on the streets, ears to the ground. And one or two hidden security types. No weapons," Dante says. And I hear the unspoken *yet*. "You and Reaper deal with that."

Knight looks up, frowning. "I don't need—"

"Get Reap's input, Knight." Dante rubs a hand over his beard. "But I mean something more subtle. Cohesive. Julien and Darcy are good, they stay here or on the floor of our home if we go there. Knight, set up a schedule with our other pack members for them to pair up in coming and going. Minimum two people. I know we all do our own thing, but it's time to act more like a pack. Run together in small groups. Get the scheduling sorted."

His gaze touches on me, but it's dark, glittery, and gives me nothing but contemplative heat.

"The real issue is us. We do it too. One of us stays here, we all do. If we decide to go home, we all do. And that brings me to Angel, here."

The bottom falls from my world.

"You're getting rid of me," I breathe.

Irritation flashes on Dante's face. "No, I'm not. And even if I wanted to, I don't think I should. You're important to the Council."

"But...you said..."

He cuts his eyes to me. "I said she kept it vague as shit. She talked of kids looking for adventure, troublemakers and how places like this could fall under the Council's watchful eye. There was a lot of other crap, but when someone comes in with all that? Then they're looking for you. So, Angel, you're stuck with us, and we're stuck with you." His gaze travels over me. "If you're wanted by them, you're useful to us."

Not exactly words of kindness. Then again, Dante never said he was going to offer me that. I nod. "Like a bargaining chip."

The corner of his mouth rises. "Maybe."

Knight's displeasure thickens the room's tension. "Dante—"

"Shut up, Knight," he says.

"Fucking Council," Reaper says. "But if Lizette's important then she should stay with us, where we can protect her, and we need to get to the bottom of why."

"Because I'm an omega?"

All of them look at me and Knight speaks. "No. It's because they're showing interest. More than they would normally, from jumping on you the moment you came to their attention and the mate they found you, to turning up here, where you showed up."

"One's a coincidence, if you believe in them. Two," Reaper says, "isn't."

"In the meantime, Angel no longer works upstairs." Dante crosses his arms. "She just works down on the second floor. There's plenty to do."

I perk a little. I'd love a chance not to be the busser. He hasn't brought up the signing rule so hopefully he's dropped that. I'm not bringing it up. "Can I waitress?"

"They wear skimpier outfits." Dante raises his brows.

"I don't care." I look at him in defiance. "They're just clothes. I'll do it."

Dante pushes off the table. "The patrons often touch the waitstaff. You? No fucking way. We can't let them touch you."

I glare at him. "What if I want them to?"

There's a ripple in the air, and it hackles with anger. I can prick my skin with the sharpness of the spikes.

"No fucking touching." Dante's voice is low and dangerous silk, the kind a man might let brush over skin before wrapping it tight around a woman's neck to choke her into orgasm, or unconsciousness. I swallow. "Or you'll really understand the word trouble."

I don't really want anyone touching me so I just nod.

I amend that. I don't want anyone but *them* touching me.

"I don't want her waitressing," snaps Knight. "Too risky."

"No one gets in without being vetted." Reaper's words are

almost lost by the scrape of his lighter. A curl of smoke hits the air.

"Guess that brings us to the fucking birds and bees talk, kids," Knight says as he looks heavenward. "We need ground rules."

"Rules?" Reaper asks.

Dante nods. "I caught him knuckle deep in her pretty pussy and her coming all over his fingers yet again, so unless we want a permanent bond, or worse, fucking spawn—"

I wince. "Spawn—"

"Unless we want that shit," Dante says, ignoring my sputter. "We need ground rules."

"I don't want children," I snap. "I don't want to be treated like a baby machine. I just want to live and make my own choices."

"This is more for the men, Angel," Dante says. "Because like it or not, babies are up to them and knotting."

"The men." I say it so quietly I don't think anyone hears.

Dante turns to me. "If they knot and you catch, then welcome to fucking Babyland. You give off pheromones like you're fertile enough for a hundred women. You can't control that, Angel. No, the part you can control is if you open or close your soft thighs. That's it. If they lose control..."

He shrugs.

"You're talking as if you're not included in this," Knight says. "Shouldn't the warning be for all of us?"

"I'm not planning on fucking her." Dante glares.

"Your mouth says one thing," Reaper says, "but your body says another."

"So—" I start only to be cut off by Dante.

"And you're not in heat, but Angel," the scarred, earth-bound demon says, "your scent's so potent it's almost irresistible."

"Like you," says Knight. "I think you'd be that way even without your scent."

And I melt for him.

"So, what do I do?" I ask. "If I'm staying, I'm happy to keep house, to work. And if I have to be abstinent—"

"Says the fucking virgin," Dante says.

"I will."

"She's ours," Reaper says. "The mark links us all to her for as long as it lasts and that bite has staying power. As for abstinence?"

"You know it's going to happen, Dante," Knight says. "We all do."

I look at them confused. "But I just said—"

"We can take the risk away, Liz," Knight says.

"Fine," Dante mutters. "I'll get the drugs."

"Drugs?" I look at each of them. "Like the O-blockers?"

"There *are* other drugs. Your father couldn't afford them or didn't know or figured it should be your choice," Dante says. "There are O-blockers and then there are what they call deferrals. It's like O-blockers on steroids. You can't get knocked up."

"Then—"

"According to the Council, they can cause side effects, apparently. But you wouldn't get pregnant," Dante says.

"Anything, I'll do anything to make sure I'm not at the mercy of men. If—If someone was to grab me like that Jake then..." I don't finish. I don't have to.

"Actually..." Dante exchanges a look with the other two. "Let's remove that risk. Wear the mark on show. Enhance it— with make-up—" he says pointedly to Knight. "Make it known that, to all intents and purposes, you're our property."

"No one will dare touch you and since getting into the second floor means we've got their details, it should keep you safe," Knight says. "It's just an added precaution. You have us for your primary protection and it's more than enough."

Nodding, I take a sharp breath, hating the way the arcane sentiment zooms through me like a secret, delicious thrill.

"I'm definitely going to want that better job."

Dante gives me a look that sends dark wanton sparks through me.

"We'll talk."

TWENTY-THREE

Dante

No one's touched her.

In the past fucking week since I got her the damned drugs, no one's touched her.

Instead, we circle around her, sexually charged buzzards, waiting for her to crumble down so we can pick and suck at her bones.

It's not pretty imagery, I decide, but apt.

"Stop wiggling your fucking ass." I glare at what might be one of the finest asses, high and rounded, small but hand sized, fun and perfection.

Lizette twirls to face me, long, dark hair whipping out, and I'm fucking regretting the insistence of her in a ponytail.

"Fuck, I'm old." That fucking ass wiggle slides into my blood, pumping to areas I don't want blood pumped to. Shit. And she looks young like that. Too young. "Not to mention perverted."

Her being only twenty-one makes me a pervert, that's for sure. And—

"Darcy."

The snap of her name fails to make the blonde leap to my side. I glare at her, but she just gives me her *fuck you* look, the one that's pretty much telling me she's on the fucking ball with my mood, and I should handle it myself.

Honestly, I briefly fantasize about tossing her out of the pack, but Darcy's beyond vital.

Still. I am one of the alphas. I'm motherfucking Dante. "Darcy."

With a sigh, she stomps over. "You do know we're down two girls. One's sick and the other's a lazy bitch who, if she doesn't decide who the better place of employment is, will find herself out of a job."

"Fire her ass—"

"I will if I can't sort it tomorrow, big boss man" —she's pushing it— "but..." Darcy, swipes on her tablet. "Emma's good." She goes back to Sierra and the logistics of tonight.

"Lizette," I growl. Because the hot little number's wiggling more. And the worst thing is? I think she's actively trying not to.

What the fuck did I deserve to be landed with a naïve omega?

"What did I do now?" Lizette asks. "Other than having an ass and walking."

"Stop it."

She stomps over to me, tray in hand, and she puts one of her fists on her boy-short clad hip, the halter showing off way too much cleavage and pale belly. "I have to walk, Dante," she says. "It's part of the job."

"Go back to doing the bussing."

"I don't want to do the bussing."

I'd stand, but she makes things hard. I cross my legs and thrum my fingers against the table. My tablet sits there, and I've got work to do but this...I need to fucking deal with her.

Lizette, the angel from either heaven or hell.

"Last time I checked, I'm the fucking boss."

218

Her cheeks flame, and I know she'll be a prize for the men who come here. A prize they can't touch. One they'll beat off about and for some reason, it makes it just as bad. It makes me want to rip them to pieces.

"Three bosses." She holds up three fingers.

"You and I both know this is my pack, Angel. I share the power, yes. I chose wisely." This time. "But when it comes down to the line, my word is the one with the most clout."

She puffs out a breath, gaze sliding to me, dark eyes a wild storm, but then she nods. "How am I going to be a valued member of this pack if I don't help? Isn't that what you're doing?"

No. What I'm doing is fucking torture, that's what I'm doing. Telling her how to move, to get as much money in tips without compromising herself, how to bend—walk—

"You're a guest. Not a trialing pack member."

"Dante, I...what am I going to do out there? After I stop being a guest? There are people after me. If I run, it'll be fine for a while, but when I go into heat? When I run out of drugs?"

She can't stay with us permanently. It'll be too chaotic. And she's such a fucking trouble magnet. The visit from the Council told me that. Fuck, the way they danced around, dragged it out. That woman, Susan, was hoping for a glimpse of her, an excuse to poke deeper.

Pity, I've got some of the best and dirtiest lawyers. Two of which are pack members. They don't interact with us too much in public, but they're loyal beyond a money bond.

Last night, Reaper told me he took someone out who was poking into things and asking questions about a girl who could only be the one trying not to glare at me.

Turn her loose and she's in their clutches. Keep her and we court more and more trouble.

But I put that aside. Consider her.

"Not my problem."

"Yes, it is. You took me."

"Saved you. And if you want to be a member of our criminal pack, then maybe start doing what I fucking say and stop wiggling your ass." I stop, take a breath. "Okay, let's start again. I'm one of your patrons, had a little too much to drink."

I haven't forgotten rule number one, but I'm biding time, especially because she'll have to deal with patrons up there.

I'm not sure I want her that exposed.

That seen.

I leer at her and raise my coffee cup. "I'm also handsy...so, how do you deal?"

"Well—"

This time I stare at her tits and the sweet cleavage that way too much on display. "No. Show me. Action time, Angel. Action."

Later that evening, after Knight's peptalk that honestly made me want to hit him up the side of the head—what the fuck is it about Lizette that makes a wild freak like Knight so fucking gooey like some kind of lovelorn teen? —I leave him to the first shift.

It's on my damned feed on my tablet.

He's got first shift because it's quiet, and I prefer being up here on the public floor where the early deals with the Unholy Trinity are done. I can also keep an eye on the fucking people in here.

I flicker a glance at Julien who's off to the side, watching, waiting. And he comes over.

"Dante?"

"That troublemaker who owes?"

A muscle works in his jaw. He knows who I'm talking about. A gambler who keeps promising payback but keeps going over. He's not affiliated here, but he is at our gambling club in the bowels of the Hollows.

"Not paid?" he asks.

"Owes nearly seven hundred thousand as of this afternoon and hasn't paid back a dime, not since the first time we rolled him."

"The guy should be good for it. Rich as fuck." Julien's eyes narrow, and he rubs a tattooed hand over his big, broad chest.

I lean back. "Rich as fuck is usually just polite speak for douchebag."

"Aww, come on, now, Dante, don't give douchebags such a bad name."

"Gutter dweller?"

Julien's face splits into a smile. "He lives in a condo in the Park."

"Christ, he's not even where we have our home." His daddy lives near where we do when we're not here in our hub. I thought the gambler still lived at home, but...

You learn something every day.

"Not surprising," I mutter. "The Park's for rich poseurs who want to make a statement."

And our complex is an old converted fifteen floor building, landmark, gorgeous, and built like Fort Knox, harder to get into than a spinster sister. We live where the real rich are, and in the heart of the corrupt, the old money, the big names most don't know about.

I like being amongst the enemy and those who despise us. I'm not even sure most of them are aware of who and what we are.

But this guy... He's a nobody, a kid of the rich and powerful, and thinks he's got power himself.

His daddy wouldn't care if he dropped off the face of the planet. The dude's got other kids. Plus a daughter. And this kid is a delta. Daddy likes his alpha son and omega daughter.

Other than driving myself insane watching the wiggle of

Angel's ass, one I doubt she can get rid of, I've been going over some books and diving into the backgrounds of our clients deeper than usual.

"The guy's fucking rich and he thinks he can fuck with us?" I laugh. "Fucker."

"Probably thinks we can't fucking touch him, Dante. Daddy's got clout."

"Daddy's got a lot of clout, but nothing we can't handle. And daddy really doesn't give a shit. Even if he did..." I shrug. "Fuck his daddy."

"Rather not," Julien says.

I look at him. "We don't get busy until later. Can you take care of him?"

He nods. "Reaper care, or mine?"

I contemplate it. "Take Reaper, see how it plays out." He starts to turn when I grab his arm. "After you collect. And take out any cameras first."

"Got it, boss."

When he goes, I watch Angel on the feed, and I watch fucking Knight watching her. Shit, he's got it bad. I want to blame it on the bite, but I'm not entirely sure anymore.

With a sigh, I make the footage small and bring up the research from Reaper.

I frown. It's all legend shit that people don't hold with anymore and it's not like Reaper to give me stuff like this. So, I sideline it for later.

If he gave it to me, it's not for fucking fairytales, that's for sure. He'll have a reason.

He always does.

"Dante?"

I look up as Mason puts a glass in front of me and brandishes a bottle.

"Fuck, yes," I say. He pours, and I thank him, before picking it up and taking a swallow of the caramel-edged whiskey.

I look into the mirror behind the bar, right as a shadow passes over me in the low-lit space.

Reaper's there, right behind me, and that man's more than able to bypass anyone's awareness levels, but for some reason, that shadow, more felt than seen, made me look up.

He's not looking at me. His gaze is riveted down. On the device on the bar. That small corner, where Lizette serves the few customers who are in.

"That wise?"

"Fucked if I know." I wait until he takes a seat, his cigarettes in one hand. Black sweater, jeans. Tattoos adorning at his neck and that fucked up face garnering long glances from a woman a few seats down.

She's seeing a man, one with a marred beauty that makes her think romantic thoughts. The haphazard buzz cut, the quality clothes in black. The tattoos, she's guessing, travel all over him. The blank canvas expression she can paint all sorts of fantasies on.

He doesn't seem to even notice her.

Right until she gets up to come over.

Reaper turns, and though I can't see him, I'm guessing there's death and destruction given in that expression because she recoils. "Not interested," he says.

She scrambles back, and when he turns to me, I get the last vestiges of his look. It's not violent. It's just...empty, endless night and devoid of humanity.

I grew up with him. I know his history. Know what he's been through.

And fucking little Lizette looks at him like he's anything but a living representation of death. She looks at him like she understands him, too. And she looks at him like she looks at Knight. With want, tangled lust and emotion.

And me?

She hates me and wants me, too.

"You were rude to a paying customer, Reap."

223

He frowns. "I was?"

"The woman?"

"Wasn't interested."

He wants to light up which means something's on his mind. He keeps pulling a cigarette half out before pushing it back into the packet. Then, finally, he takes it and places it behind his ear.

"Did you look, Dante?" he presses.

"At the old folk tales?"

He sighs and nods at Mason, who sets down a glass of golden rum for Reap. "Yeah. There's one—"

"I didn't take you for the big bad wolf and witches in the woods kinda guy." I sip my drink.

"Knight's research into a reversal came up with some tales."

"Fuck me, Reaper. We don't go around trading facts and evidence for stories." I glance at the screen just in time to see Lizette sidestep an ass-reaching patron who I want to see parted with his fingers, cock and balls. I make a note to find out who he is and maybe arrange a talking to with a fist, or five.

"You're a real ass when you're unfulfilled and frustrated," Reaper barely looks at me.

"I prefer you strong, silent, and a psychotic killer. Not Mr. Chatty."

Knight would volley insults merrily. Not Reap.

He ignores my words.

"I'm not asking you to believe anything. But fairytales are warnings, or explanations for things people way back didn't understand." He takes a breath, downs his rum and hits the bar with the glass for another.

"There's a story of the Never Ending. A girl born of two alphas, whose families only ever produce alphas and is the most beautiful in the land. On her eighteenth birthday, she's discovered not to be an alpha, but an omega. And her scent's so potent she causes wars, makes alphas fight to the death. Makes even betas want her. She's locked away, but stolen by a renegade alpha. Her powers wreak havoc on his pack and he chooses two other alphas to share the burden—"

"Burden?"

"But it doesn't work. They fight. They end up consulting an oracle who says they must all mark her or kill her to end the line and restore order in the world. But if they mark her, then the three are bound to her for eternity. And no one can touch her. She's safe and theirs."

I stare at him. "Are you saying we should kill her?" Is he saying this is true? It's us?

He continues. "This lot decide to mark her, but they're stopped, then all ejected from society. And die."

"So...happy ending?"

"It's a fairytale. They're always fucking gruesome." He takes a sip. "It's old, and it's one of those obscure ones."

"It's fantasy. This kind of shit is full of the power of three and seven. And oracles and their ilk. What's the point?"

"Point is the bond. The mark dulls her scent to others, but to us, it's the same. She's powerful, and as a pack with three alphas—maybe it wouldn't hurt if we marked her, too."

Now I'm probably gawping at him.

"That's the stupidest thing... Fuck, Reap. The story isn't real."

He takes in breath, checks his phone and then nods. "I know, but I got to thinking about the elements of it. The real bond works in the forever way if she bites us back."

"We don't want that," I say.

He shrugs. "It's an idea."

"You want her to bond with us?"

"If she doesn't bite back, if we prevent her, then it's a strong, *almost* unbreakable bond."

"Fuck, Reaper. The mark's still on her from Knight." I take a gulp of my whiskey. "And you want to add more."

"We have to do it soon, if we do."

I grab his arm. "So what? We tie ourselves to her? We treat fucking Lizette like she's this Never Ending?"

"Listen to me, Dante. If the three of us bite her? It'll really mark her as ours, but without her claiming us, she can still leave."

Suddenly, my head jerks up as I get what he means. "But only if we release her. Once we work out what the fuck the Council is up to."

"And if Ghost's with them now."

If we mark her, it's strong, protects us and her, and also claims her. But there's still the get out of fucking jail card. The claiming isn't complete if we just bite and she doesn't return the favor.

Fucking Reaper, leading me through fairytale land.

"Yeah. Okay, I see it." I take another swallow and shake my head. "Should have led with the bite theory. Are you going with Julien?"

The change in subject doesn't bother Reaper. "There's an illegal, and I mean dirty, dangerous, illegal name in the shipping yard. We'll get him there." He gets up. "Think about it. The mark from all of us."

When he puts his cigarette between his lips and heads out to meet Julien—another bouncer's on the door, here nice and early. I glance at my device.

The club's filling up enough for me to go down to the lower level.

"Out," I say to Knight by way of greeting.

"Fuck you, dude. I'm enjoying the eye candy."

He glances at the stage as one of the girls comes out, but his gaze drifts back to Lizette.

"Enjoy it through my device." I hand him the tablet. "We're swapping places, as planned."

Muttering he goes, Knight leaves and I lean against the bar, watching her, making sure she's following my teachings.

Watching her ass in those too short booty shorts is dangerously easy. The shiny black does all kinds of sweet and filthy things to the shape of her ass. And when she turns, it shows off her thigh gap, the hint of camel toe.

I narrow my eyes as someone drops a napkin and to the fucking bump and grind, she bends to pick it up.

Oh, fuck. I don't think she's wearing panties.

And that's when a man reaches out and slides a hand up between her thighs.

Not just any man.

A dead one.

TWENTY-FOUR

Dante

I haul the man out of his chair and into one of the private rooms where girls can dance for extra cash. The only one who'll be dancing in here is this fuckwit. And he's going to dance off the mortal coil.

"What the fuck," I snarl, wrench his arm up, and back as I slam his face into the wall, "do you think you're doing? Touching my girl?"

"I didn't know!" He screams as I break three fingers and then turn him to punch him in the stomach.

I pull my arm back and land a punch in his face as he doubles over, falling to the ground. I haul him up by his hair.

"Didn't know? Didn't fucking know? Were you missing from school the day they taught fucking manners? You don't touch in here. Ever. And especially not her."

"Everyone touches a little," the guy says, sputtering up blood. "Nothing meant by it. They get tipped big. I tip big!"

I fucking grab his balls and twist, enjoying the inhuman howl. "Nothing meant by it, huh? How about I tip you big?"

"Let me go, please!"

"I'm going to fucking pull you to pieces, feed you to the crows, fucking dance on your bones for touching her. And in such a fucked up way. She isn't yours, get me? She, like everything else in this place, is *mine*, and when you come to my place, you respect my fucking things."

"Dante?"

I shoot a sharp look at Lizette who stands just inside, stock still.

Fuck. I realize the outfit's wrong. On her, it makes her look like she's dressed like a stripper, or an expensive escort. She looks both classy and filthy, cheap and gorgeous. She's a walking fantasy and this guy's going to fucking die for thinking he could even have a taste of her. I'll take his eyes. I'll—

"Boss."

Behind Lizette, Darcy appears and her expression is one of annoyance, snapping me back to my senses.

"What?" I say, not willing to let this go.

"You can't kill him."

"I'm the fucking Unholy Trinity. I can do what the fuck I want."

Her expression doesn't flicker. "For one, he still needs to pay his bill, and it's a hefty one. And two, I think he's learned his lesson."

"I didn't know," the guy starts, but I cut my eyes to him, and he shuts up.

Darcy pushes Lizette out. "Go back to work, kid."

Then she rounds on me as I let the asshole go. He tumbles to the ground and curls in a ball.

"Dante?" She stalks up to me. "He's a good patron."

"I'll get cleaned up," I mutter. "He's not welcome here anymore."

Darcy pulls me close. "I love being part of this pack. You know I do, but either fuck that girl or get rid of her."

"We can't." I pause. "Yet."

"And we can't give our clients a reason for a grudge. I'll handle this." Then she shoves me out the door. "Mr. Albion, you touched the bosses' bitch," she says as I hold the door open a little. "You didn't notice his mark on her throat? It's why her hair is up. She's very much off limits. I'll get someone to take you home and see to your injuries. And well make sure you're taken care of—"

Fuck that. Fury still whipping through me, I stride off. Lizette's at the bar, shoulders hunched as the bartender puts drinks on her tray.

She gives me a stricken look as she goes back to serving.

No one else dares touch her.

Good.

I know I'm being a fucking dickwad, but the man put his hand between her legs. He's fucking lucky Darcy stepped in.

Shame slides down my spine. Not at hitting the jerk, but because it took Darcy for me to see reason. I pride myself on my control, and I lost it in a millisecond because of *her*.

Angel walking in set me off more. Made my blood start to go from boiling into steam.

Shit.

She's fucking dangerous.

The most dangerous thing I've met.

Knight's hot headed. I'm way more reasonable.

Except, apparently, when it comes to her.

I look up as she jerkily walks to the bar once more, and fuck, even like that, the ass has a slight wiggle, an airy bounce unique to her.

And she's definitely not wearing panties.

The shorts are like second skin in some of the lights in here, showing off every damn line and crease of interest on her.

Inside me, things shift, grow restless, and I rise and go to her. "When I said not to wiggle, I didn't mean sex robot walk."

"You're a violent ass, Dante," she says, looking down. "I'm

230

walking. This is how I walk. It's not a crime." She then drags her gaze up, and she goes from subservient with brat energy to furious siren.

Because she is a fucking siren. Men would bash themselves to death on rocks to glimpse that body and face, and her voice when she sings...

The memory grips my cock.

I suck in air. "He touched you, and he should've died."

"But I'm not yours."

"You're ours. As long as you're with us, you're ours."

"Servant or payment?"

"Candy treat, Angel. One with a kick." I lean in. "They're in suits, most of them, and they have money. But don't be fooled. They're feral fucks so don't let them touch you."

"If I want them to?"

My insides twist and something searing hot cuts through my lungs. Somehow, I manage to breathe normally. "Think about that, very carefully."

"Will you add it to my punishment?" Her voice quivers as our own little world wraps tight around us.

I move closer to her, brushing against her, and she makes the kind of sound that fuels erotic dreams. "You want that, don't you? I won't let you come, Angel. Not until you're mindless for it."

"Then I'll let these men touch me."

I look at her, every muscle in me snapping taut. She's all fucking bratty defiance, the smallest of a sheltered litter confronted by hungry wolves with snapping teeth. Smelling blood. And she thinks she can tease. Then pet them.

She's a meal waiting to be devoured.

Tension ticks.

"Angel, do that, they die."

Our gazes lock. Fuse.

And I want her mouth. I want to taste her magic, the

231

sweetness. I want to delve deep. Test us both to the edge of limits and madness and lust.

Fuck that. I'm the hungry wolf with snapping teeth. A beast of nightmares just below the surface. I don't want to kiss her. I want to devour, suck sweet marrow from her bones.

And then I want to burn us both in a pyre of desire, one that's made of pure fucking flame.

When she rises, she'll be changed, morphed, rebuilt into something utterly mine.

"Don't think I mean it?" I say softly. "I do. I'll paint the fucking place with their blood. Brand you with it. And then I'll fucking punish you."

A shiver races through her, and her pupils dilate. Her lips part. She sways, just that tiny dip toward me. "You wouldn't."

"Try me."

She sucks in air and looks at me. "Then I'll let Knight, a- and Reaper touch me. I'll give myself to them."

I let my lips caress her ear, and I'm filled with her, that scent, the heady note of sexual want that infuses it. She's fucking beyond potent. She's deadly. "You're going to do that, anyway. And you'll lose yourself, come. But you know what? With each wave of pleasure, a part of you will think..."

"What?" She sways against me. "How good it is?"

I grin against her, breathing her in so she melds with my molecules. Fuck, her attempt at fight riles in all the right ways.

"A part will think, what's it going to be like with Dante?"

There's a little moan and then she pushes at me. "No, I won't."

But we both know she will. Her breathing gets heady, gives her away.

I laugh. "Get back to work."

The moment I step back, the air clears a little, and she moves away, stops, and turns back.

"Those rooms? I've seen some of the dancers take a man in there. The other waitress, too. What—"

"Private dances, lap dances for money. No touching, but..." I narrow my eyes. "Not for you. Get back to work."

She stomps off, and I pull up the feed when I'm at the bar, taking Pandora's tablet and watching upstairs.

Knight's leaning against the bar, glass of wine, charming the metaphorical pants off five different women. There's at least one pissed off boyfriend who doesn't quite dare to do a thing. I've seen it before.

The little shit's beyond charismatic and charming. Women fucking love him. And they make the mistake of thinking he's harmless.

He isn't. He's a fucking shark who likes to play and dress up in preppy clothing.

Except with his little omega.

There's a side I've never seen she brings out. A realness in him he's never shown other women, even ones he's been totally obsessed with.

It's Liz. Lizette. Angel.

He finishes his wine and gets another, an excuse to look at the feed. He gives me a not-so-subtle finger. Asshole.

Christ. Even Reaper's different with her. He's always him, but with her, he's more himself. The Reaper I knew when he was a kid. A teen. Before we got out and went separate ways.

Thank fuck she doesn't affect me like she does with them. One of us needs a level head.

But maybe there's something to what Reap told me. Not the bullshit tale, but the three of us marking her.

I look around, but she's not there.

Frowning, I wait, but she doesn't reappear. "What the fuck, Angel?"

I glance at the bathrooms. She's probably taken herself there. The moment between us got intense, and she's ridiculously innocent. Fuck, if she's crying, she can do that shit on her own time. We've got customers, and even if I don't like her out there, she's good for business. They like pretty. They like her.

So, I start heading that way to drag her out, but I catch a glimpse of Sierra. She nods her head to the private rooms and holds up four fingers.

For a moment the world stops.

Room four?

What the actual fuck?

Did some man drag her in there?

I don't wait. I stride over, ready to let hell rain down.

Ready to fucking kill.

The door's ajar and the heavy curtains aren't quite shut so I slide in, about to pull them wide, when I hear her speak.

"You can't tell the alphas," she says, sounding young and playing it sexy.

My blood turns ice.

She did this.

She fucking did this. To defy me. To push me. To rile me.

Angel dragged a man in here.

Lizette might think she's in control. That this is innocent. But it's not.

Things happen in private rooms.

Especially to little girls who think they can play with fucking wolves.

I'm betting whatever fucking dead man she has in there's got a boner that could break stone.

And he's planning on using it on her—maybe getting her to jack him off. Use her mouth. Touch her.

His hands. On her sweet fucking body.

That ice melts. Things boil as anger, thick, black and potent, rising from the depths of hell, fill my limbs.

After he dies, I'm killing her.

The guy says something but it's too low to catch. Shit, there's no music. And he's sitting there like the place pulsates with sex-filled music.

The breathing corpse is literally sitting there. Planning on tasting her flesh, fucking her. Having what's off limits to everyone but her alphas.

"And," she adds, "you can't touch."

She says that, but he's not going to listen. No man, not even one living on borrowed time, would. They'd touch, grab, take. Fuck.

That blackness of rage surges into red hot. I need to kill him. Now. I pull back the curtains.

Oh. Fuck me.

"Angel? Get the fuck off that asshole, right now."

She freezes, turns, and stares at me. She's fucking straddling him, those slinky booty shorts that show every fucking line and crease of her rise up in the back showing ass cheek. And his eyes are locked on her pussy lips, outlined in the front.

I don't need to see to know that. I fucking took note out on the floor.

The man's eyes raise, and his hands—that are on her hips, in the middle of sliding down and around, which more that seals his fate—go out to the side.

"I said get the fuck off him, Angel."

The man registers my face. The rage. Who I am.

He almost throws her across the room. She lands hard on her ass on the floor before scrambling up to her feet.

"Out." I don't look at her.

The man rises and takes a step.

I do, too. Towards him, the anger and rage pumping through me instead of blood.

"Not. You."

"D-Dante?" Liz says, voice hesitant.

I don't fucking look at her because I might lose my shit altogether. I'm very, very close.

"Get the fuck out, Angel. Now."

"No."

"Now, or I'm not responsible."

She doesn't leave. I feel the warm, fluttering buzz of her presence, but it isn't enough to stop the storm in me.

I grab the man and slam him against the wall. "What the actual fuck? You know the rules."

He whines, the sound scraping over my senses, rousing them into a wilder frenzy and every cell is dark and out for blood. His.

"Everyone does. They pay—"

I grab his throat, digging my fingers in, not caring that he starts making choking noises. They just fuel me, that terrible fire consuming me, tunneling my vision to him and me and what I'm going to do.

Each time he tries to scream, it's an unholy sound. And it only makes me squeeze harder, more vicious until he loses consciousness.

Lizette's terrified scream rings in my ears, but I ignore her.

I drop the barely breathing man to the floor and kick him hard in the ribs. He rolls, sputtering. Then I bend, grabbing his shirt, and sucker punch him so hard his nose breaks, his lip mashes against teeth and we're both sprayed with blood.

My ears are a roar of my own blood, my heart's beat. It's not like a living heart. It's one of hate, fury. All the vile, unspeakable things are in me now.

And that sound, the *thump thump* is all I have. He's just an open maw, needing to be shut down for good.

He fucking touched her. Had his fucking pants undone, dick at the ready. If I had time, I'd torture the shit out of him, slice his dick off in measurements. Like I'm peeling a fucking carrot.

Then I'd slice and dice parts of him, leaving him alive. Letting him feel every excruciating moment for thinking it's okay to touch what belongs to the fucking Unholy Trinity.

What belongs to me.

If she has that mark on her, she belongs to the pack. To us.

To me.

The rage whipping through me is blinding, consuming. I don't even realize I'm crushing my fingers into his throat again and wrenching it at an angle. I'm pushing so hard, more and more, until something finally snaps free, his neck breaking and his body sagging.

I dump the worthless bag of bones on the ground.

And rise.

I should calm, feel better. But I don't.

Standing, there's an audience behind me now.

Knight. Darcy.

Lizette.

Darcy leaves, muttering.

Knight's pissed off.

And Lizette?

Oh, sweet fucking Lizette.

I'm not finished with her.

The bloodletting, the primal, pagan killing hasn't softened a thing. Something savage now prowls my veins. Ravenous for her. For a punishment. For a feast only Angel can give me.

"Out, Knight." I don't look at him.

I settle my gaze on Lizette.

"My office," I say, my voice a primal rumble. "Now."

TWENTY-FIVE

Lizette

His eyes are blazing darkness. The blue so black it burns me. And I shake. Fear and horror at war within me.

And something else.

Something I can't fathom.

He killed for me. Broke that man's neck.

I'm turned on.

Dante's got me locked to the spot. Like this, he doesn't just look like the devil. He *is* the devil.

And the devil has never been more dangerous, more controlled, with terrible power that pushes at me, filling the room. And he's never, ever been so desirable.

My knees almost buckle, and I clutch at the curtain, falling back, and slamming into the door where Knight shut it.

I'm alone with him and a corpse, and Dante's covered in blood.

One corner of his mouth lifts, and he snarls low.

The sound vibrates through me, sending throbbing tendrils of need down to my sex, making me wet with slick.

He comes right up to me but doesn't touch. Doesn't lay a finger on me.

Somehow, that's worse.

So much worse.

I feel...violated. Roughed up.

Untouched in the worst way.

Like I'm unworthy. And I did it to myself this time.

My eyes burn hot with unshed tears as his glow with the darkest midnight blue fire. And heat surges in me, too.

My clit throbs like it needs something, like it needs him. His touch. His fingers. Mouth.

Like—

"Why the fuck did you take him in here? Got a death wish?"

"No," I whisper, "I just thought..."

"You'd have him killed instead?" Dante laughs, and the dark, jagged sound sinks into me, lacerating as it goes.

"I didn't."

"Yeah, you did. He's dead, Angel." He smiles. Mockingly.

And then he comes close, and through the copper smell of blood, I get a hit of him to my veins. He sniffs, breathing me in, nose and lips skimming just above the surface of my skin, and now it's not just my clit reacting.

It's all of me.

I throb everywhere.

"They're not tipping me out there," I say. "I had to do something."

"No one's tipping you for a fucked up lap dance either."

I'm so angry, I can barely get words out. "Did you say something to them?" I ask.

"Oh, Angel, why the fuck would I talk to assholes about that? Now, get the fuck out and go wait in my office. And consider yourself off waitressing duty."

"But—"

"I don't like insubordination," he says, his tone silky steel threads that whip against my skin with every word. "I do like punishment. So, think about that next time you want to talk back. Get the fuck out and wait. Now."

I clamp my mouth shut, my heart slamming against my ribs, fear making all my extremities ice, and I fumble with the curtain, then the door, and I stumble out into the floor of the bar.

Every eye is glued to me as I try to slow down to get across. But I can't. My chest is tight with the horror of him killing that man, for what? Touching me? It's still swirling in my head.

I don't understand my reactions. Yes, there's horror, and I get that. But the thrill and the need and the way I ache for Dante? That I don't get. My vision waivers, and I almost fall into someone's lap. But a hand grabs me. It's firm but not biting, and I look up.

Darcy.

I can't even speak. She leads me through and into the back and shoves me on a chair in a small office.

Not his office though. This is one where the main staff come and go, where someone can watch everything on a bank of screens.

My breath hitches.

"Dante k-killed him."

"I'm aware," she says, as she leans against the plain desk, and she crosses her arms over her black dress. "What the fuck were you thinking? You dumb bitch."

What was I thinking? "I thought I could make some more tips."

She sighs, straightens, and picks up some whiskey. Then she pours some in two glasses and hands one to me.

"Drink," she says. "You can't be that naïve. The men here will eat you alive, think you're offering yourself for sex. They all think that in those rooms. The trick is to handle it and not upset them. And you, kid, will end up having sex every single time. Whether you want to or not."

"I—"

"Dennis touched you, didn't he?"

I lift the glass with both hands and drink it down, the warmth of the burn doing little to help.

Putting a name to the dead man makes him more real. And...I swallow. "Yes."

"Of course he did. The guy was a total douche. So no one's going to miss him. He's married. Fucking beta asshole, treats his wife terribly. He brags about it, but he spends big, and he has a lot of gamma and delta friends. A few alpha acquaintances. So, I bet he knew what a prize you are." She shakes her head.

"I'm sorry. I didn't mean..." *I didn't mean to get someone killed.*

Even that man, who turned out to be way worse than I thought. But he kept getting bolder, kept telling me how to get closer to him or he wouldn't pay, to show more skin. And he undid his pants and—

I tried my best to ignore that, tried to be cute and sweet and not give him everything he wanted. After all, it was just a dance. Right?

"You're too fucking young to be in here. Dante should know better. The Unholy Trinity have a lot of businesses. A lot of pies. Some of them are legit. So, they should've put you in something like that instead of...shit. Instead of here, in the middle of it."

"The Council wants me."

Her face turns hard. "And put that together with Knight marking you..." She blows out a breath. "I'm sick of this so-called law-abiding society who allow people to order others around due to what they are when they're born. Do you want a life of being a homemaker and baby factory?"

"No."

And I think I hate myself more because this man who was killed fades in my little blossoming moment. Darcy's treating me almost like a friend, and I'm hanging on to it all, hugging it close.

If I could choose a friend, I'd want someone like her. Maybe not quite so scary, but then again, I like that about her. She's smart and fierce, things I want to be, too, and she loves Julien, who's even scarier in size. But he's always been nice to me.

"My dad didn't want that, either. He kept us away from the Council's reach, homeschooled me. I wish you could have met him." I stop. That sounds weird. "I mean, all of you. He was good and respected in the Hollows."

Darcy looks at me and starts laughing. She refills our glasses. "Oh, man, kid. I think I would have. And, I think I like you, too. Anyone who speaks about someone being respected by the Hollows and says it with absolute pride, is a fucking badass in my eyes."

"Dad said the people there were realer than the ones in rich packs and high rises. The working class, the undocumented who keep the city going, the rejected, the shunned, and those who get creative to make ends meet are the real people. Not the council with their stupid rules. And..." I smile. It's shaky, but it's there. "I agree."

"Creative, like criminal activities?"

I nod.

"Well, kid, he sounds like a smart man. And he's right. In the Council's eyes, Julien and I are forbidden. We can never have kids, but do we look like the picket fence type?"

"I think you are if this is your happy pack."

"Lizette...Christ. These guys are going to eat you alive."

I frown. "I'll be okay."

I want to say I'm learning my place in this pack. I want to say it isn't true. But I don't know. Just like I don't know how I can want three different men so much.

And I do want Dante. It doesn't matter how I feel about him, my body wants him. It wants them all.

"Learn your place." She puts her glass down as her phone buzzes. "It'll make life easier." She reads the message on her phone and looks at me. "But a word of advice? They're all dangerous men. Knight's wild and ruthless when he feels like it. Reaper... He doesn't *randomly* kill. I don't think he commits crimes of passion. Except, perhaps the fucker who cut him up. And if I'd been around? I'd have helped." She shrugs. "But if he has to, he'll kill you. That's it. Friend or foe. He's cold blooded, deadly, what some might call a psychopath."

"I call it surviving."

Darcy doesn't speak for a long time. "So would I. Outside of Julien, Dante, and maybe Knight, I've never heard anyone else put it that way, or get him."

"There's more to him."

"A lot more that should be left alone."

I don't miss the warning in her voice.

My heart starts to beat faster.

"Dante?" I ask.

"Don't fall in love."

"With him?" I push out a laugh, even though I know the weird emotional and physiological dynamic with him and me, with all of them, and me, well...I don't think it's in my hands. Not unless I disappear for good.

And I don't know what to do.

I'm scared, curious, turned on, wrapped tight.

"With him. He's handsome, always gorgeously dressed. He can move in all parts of society and look at home. From the deepest parts of the underworld to the highest levels of the privileged and connected." She looks me in the eye. "But he's a volatile bastard. Red hot in his violence and need for revenge. And he's calculated and controlled. When that goes? He's the most dangerous of them all."

I flicker a glance at her. "I'll be alright." How many times do I need to say it before I believe it?

"Just...don't be so vulnerable. Shit. You need to go. And I need to take care of Dante's mess."

Terror rides waves of thrills through me and I don't know which way's up.

"You should go to bed."

"Darcy, I have to meet him," I reply.

"What the fuck are you doing here? Go."

She leaves, and I sit. Not moving. I'm not sure I can.

My heart and brain whisper to run.

My blood and hormones scream to run to him.

It's that bit tacked on the end that's a killer.

I can't face him. He wants to punish.

He killed a man.

Because of me.

With shaking fingers, I top my glass to the brim and take a deep swallow. I cough, sending the burning whiskey up my nose.

For a brief, sweet moment, all I can smell is the booze.

Shit.

I take another swallow.

Then I set the glass down and head out of the room, down the stairs to what feels like my doom.

TWENTY-SIX

Dante

Where the fuck is she?

I left that dead fucker, strode across the floor of the club like I wasn't covered in blood, like I wasn't crazed as I am. I strode past the gaping patrons, the staff who shrank back. Past Darcy and her filthy look as she organized people with equipment I barely glanced at.

They'll go in through the back, down the narrow walkways that connect to the private rooms. It'll be clean and ready, and no one will be able to prove anything more than a physical fight happened in there.

In my room, I wash my face, clean off the blood from my hands. Then I pick a new outfit in harried, angry movements. Another suit in black, just to fuck with her. I hang the suit in the office near the sofa and chairs, and pour a triple whiskey, trying to ignore the fact that my dick is so fucking hard it aches.

Where the actual fuck is she?

I strip my jacket, tie, vest. I pull off the cufflinks, undo the shirt, and pace. Each step is a bite of violent intent.

The wild heat and anger, the unfurled and hungry beast within remains unfed.

The innocent fucking vixen isn't here.

How dare she disobey? How—

If she's with Knight, I just might kill him, too.

I spin my computer and stab the button to bring up the feeds. But he's upstairs. Near the bar, drinking something harder than wine, anger on his face. Right until a very rich older woman comes up to him. One he likes to have every now and then and play Daddy.

Asshole.

But his smile is fake, and he's shaking his head. I'm so sick of him right now with those fucking dimples and curls, and the fact he fucking bit my omega, that I just might kill him, anyway.

A little.

Then there's Reaper. Sure, I've known him forever, but he's—

But a knock sounds on the door. "In. Now."

"Dante?" She pokes her head around the door, and I narrow my eyes.

"Don't make me repeat myself. You're late, so that's a punishment in and of itself. And this? Fucking talking back and standing there? Angel, you're going to be in chains, covered in wax, whipped and tortured with ice for the rest of your fucking life at this rate."

Her eyes widen, and I don't miss the sexual interest that lights up, even as she tries to squash it.

"I like obedience." I crave control. I *am* control. She...she tests it.

But she steps in. And her nipples are hard, poking into the material of her top. Fuck.

I look at her. And then I'm on her, mouth devouring, tasting, licking, and biting. It's like I need her. Like I can't fucking breathe without her.

I push one hand under her shirt, and she's not wearing a bra. Goddamn it. The anger drives itself higher and my vision tunnels down to black and her. I thumb over her nipple and a burst of sweetness hits, flaring and fanning the fires.

I want her. More than I've ever wanted anything in my entire fucking life, and I hate it. I hate *her* for it.

I shove her the fuck from me, and then take a deep swallow of the whiskey to try and rid myself of her taste.

"Dance." I wave a hand at her.

"D-Dante? Y-You just..."

"I know what the fuck I did," I growl. Moving away, putting my phone on my desk, and setting it up. I turn back. "And if you don't dance, you might not fucking survive."

She makes a sound. "You'd kill me?"

"If I fucking touch you right now, I'll take you so hard, I'll do things to you that'll leave you ruined for anyone else." I take another swallow then put the glass down. "Dance."

The savageness is free, lashing at me. And the ravenous monster snaps jaws to taste more of her.

I had a morsel. A taste.

I want more.

But if I keep fucking touching her, I'll hurt her. I'll take her too hard, rough, and wild. I'll chain her up and empty myself in her over and over and whip her if she dares come. In the mood I'm in...fuck safe words, fuck soft hands and gentle ways.

I'm not gentle.

Right now, I don't give a fuck about her innocence. I'll corrupt her, bring her down to Hell with me

Her virginity is neither here nor there, but her innocence? Unleash me on her as savage as I am, as riled by blood and the kill? I'm not sure I can pull back. I'm not even sure I can stop myself from touching her.

I don't know if I'd want to.

But this dark anger and savage need in me demands the taste of denial. Holding off until I can't? It's the sweetest payment ever.

I can't touch her.

I don't think I'll be able to stop.

She's fucking mine.

I look at her. "Do it for me."

"What?"

"Fucking dance, Angel. *Now*."

She shakes her head. "No—"

"Do it for me."

"I'm not—"

"I said do it, Angel. There are rules, remember? Show me a good lap dance." I take her face in my hand and push her into the door. "So fucking help me. Just dance or I'll fuck you here and now so hard you won't be able to walk. I'll fucking rut the shit out of you, Angel. Knot you. And you know you want that, don't you? You're aching for it, slicking up for it."

"Dante, please."

I lick her throat, and I'm close, fucking close to sinking my teeth into her, drawing blood, making her mine in the most elemental way. I shove her away and turn.

"You broke my fucking rules, so you'll learn how to fucking lap dance properly. Who knows?" I narrow my eyes at her. "I might even rent you out."

Thing is, she looks at me, feeding the darkness in me. Because her face, her body, the way she breathes, the way her scent fucking blooms, it tells me she's turned on.

She's fucking waiting to be sullied, destroyed, to be turned into something else, something that I can take down into the depths.

I pull my chair out in front of my desk and sit. "Show me, Angel."

She reels.

"Behind you on my desk is my phone. Press play." I'm not in the mood to explain how it works in the private rooms.

She's not going near one again. Not unless it's with me. And, if I let the other two live, they can join in, too.

Slow, sensuous music fills the room.

"Move your hips, casual, as the music moves through you, Angel."

She does, jerky at first, but when she turns to look at me, I speak again. "Move."

I'm fucking perverse. I know it. Because I want to teach her how to lap dance, how to make money from a man. How to, if she wants, decide how she'll take it further for more money.

Even though there's no scenario that doesn't end up bloodier than the one upstairs if she so much as thinks of setting foot in a private room with a man who's not me. Or Reaper. Or Knight. If I don't murder them, too. I probably won't. But anyone else?

I will tear them into pieces.

I want to bring her down, degrade her, see how far I can go, see how much she likes it.

Punishment without the whips and chains. Or the wax. Then again, there are all kinds of punishments. This is one, and she looks fucking amazing doing my bidding.

"No. Don't look at your mark. Not yet. Don't speak to him, make him wait, sweat, wonder if you forgot him. Stretch it out. Deny him the thing he wants, because he'll want it a whole lot more."

Denial. My language, and she can speak it. I see it as she stills and listens to me, and then she moves, just looking at the wall, touching the covering, and the pull on my senses and dick is real.

I'm not lulled or soothed. If anything, she hooks into a

darker piece of me. There's the rage and there's the desires that drip with blood. I want this. The torture. Her moves that wrap around me like her scent and test my limits.

She's getting into it now, and my hunger grows. Control slips.

As the music moves through her, she rolls her hips, her ass shifts a little, side to side. She pulls her ponytail, loosening it, just a little.

I think she was going to release it and changed her mind, but it gives her a just fucked look and it's mind blowing.

She swirls to the side and her nipples are hard, then she turns back and does something with her top.

Oh fucking hell, she's rolling it up, her back's exposed a little more inch by inch.

"When you're ready, when the moment feels like it's going to break, wait a beat, and then glance over."

My voice is rough and her whole being vibrates in response. The room's filled with us, the scent we make together, that sex thing that's beyond addictive, something I've experienced exactly once before. But not like this.

There's nothing like this. No one like Lizette.

She looks at me, and I almost come, my cock jerking in my trousers.

I groan. "Now, casually come toward me, but don't touch me. Touch the chair, move by, then stop. Look at me once more."

Shit, she does and the need claws at me. I need to touch her. Taste her again. I need to fuck her, rut her.

She's not degraded. She fucking likes it.

"Come to me and move your ass against me," I say. "Then your tits, come in close, breathe my skin, rub that fucking pussy against me."

I shut the fuck up because she slowly comes back like she forgot something, and she trails her fingers over my shoulder, up my throat, through my short beard.

And that touch is liquid electricity, lighting me up and pushing me higher. She rubs her tits down my arm as she bends, turning her ass in my fucking face, and I'm hit by the heady aroma of her. Gardenias and spice and something I'm labelling as *please fuck me now.*

She's way too close for a fucking lap dance, yet she doesn't feel close enough.

She rises and arches and then begins a slow dance, her body moving around me, over me, and we stare at each other. No words are spoken. This is a battle and conversation on a different level.

She makes fucking hot and dirty sex in the air with the music. It's almost a filthy version of making love. Making lust.

She exudes it everywhere, and I'm having a real hard time not taking her in all the ways.

I can feel the thrum of her heart, the heat of her sex, the slick of her desire, and she isn't even touching me.

Until she does.

Lizette straddles me and starts to rock that cunt against me, up and down my aching cock. Her wetness slows her down, gives her shorts a drag that feels both like hell and divine. Her hands come up, and she lowers her top, giving me a front seat view to the most gorgeous tits I've ever seen.

Her nipples are dark red, with a wide areola. And the fucking minx plucks at them and slides a finger in my mouth. I suck it and then she pulls it free to swirl over one nipple and then the other.

Never in my life has my control been so tested. I want her to fuck me. I admit that. And she wants me to take hold of her and have my way with her.

It's a fucked up battle of wills that's soaked in erotic intent.

My Angel is a dark pony. She rubs her bare tits against me and then she puts her hands either side of my face and kisses me.

I explode inside, my control in tatters. I hook a hand in her hair and rock up against her while dragging her over me, and I plunder her mouth hard.

She tastes of whiskey, sex, and need. She's dark and light, innocent and the fallen. She's perfection and addiction, and—Fuck. I. Need. Control.

Breaking the kiss, I pull her head back by her hair as she rocks harder into me, little mewling sounds spilling from her.

I want to bite her throat, but instead I lock on to her nipple, my other hand pushing down into the shorts as I shove three fingers into her. I bite hard on her nipple.

Reward or punishment, I don't know, but she cries out, her cunt spasming on my fingers as I suck on that nipple. I switch to the other tit as I start thrusting roughly into her sweet, hot, tight pussy. She's wet, slick. She's willing, and I rub her clit.

Oh, fuck. Control's out of reach. I'm ready to throw her down on the ground and have my way.

What the living fuck am I doing?

Before I completely lose it, I shove her from me. She falls onto the ground by my feet with a humph, her eyes wide with shock while I'm fighting the urge to suck my fingers.

"You're not giving lap dances." I look down at her, tits out, shorts pulled low on her hips. She looks like she just had sex. And it's an image now burned into my memory. I know I'll be jerking off to this moment in time, this picture of her.

Or—No.

She needs to be punished.

I crave it.

I find and lock on to the one thing that gives me a strand of my control.

"You came."

"I—"

"But now, it's time for punishment, and another fucking lesson, Angel."

"What?"

Standing, I grab her by the arm, lift her up, and push her to the guest sofa at the side of the office. Then, I pull her shorts down and off.

The world's prettiest pussy is spread open before me. Puffy lips, a small patch of trimmed black hair right above her exposed clit. And she's wet. I pull the lips apart, and she struggles.

I grab her hip and look at her. "Do that again, and I'll tie you down. I'll find the biggest dildo and fuck you senseless with it. Both holes." She whimpers, and it's pure want. "Spread those legs and keep them spread."

Dipping my head, I bite the delicate skin of her inner thigh. I dive in, a man starved beyond reason, and it's not a feast, it's carnage. I thrust my tongue in her, shove two fingers in her ass and pump. She squeals and grabs at me, shaking, moaning. Her hips rise.

She loves it.

Angel tries to rub herself into me, to get more, and I pull out, and use my chin to rub and grind into her as I push my other two fingers into her cunt. She's not big, all delicate and soft and unbelievably responsive as she pushes my frenzy higher when I realize I don't have to stretch my fingers wide to have them in both her ass and her cunt.

I thrust as I close my mouth around her clit, sucking hard, thrumming her sensitive nerve bundle with my tongue. Scraping it with my teeth.

She's fluttering. Tiny wingbeats against me as she's on the edge of coming.

So, I bite down, still my fingers and change the tempo.

Over and over, I lead her to the edge and snatch her orgasm away. The power it fills me and makes me invincible. Her personal God. I can do anything. I have the fucking power.

I'm not letting her come. No matter how hot and tight she is, no matter how sweet her juices, and she's beyond fucking sweet. She's glorious. She's goddamn worth killing a hundred men to have one taste. She might even be worth dying for.

I keep going, learning all the little things that make her wild, all the things that make her whimper when I stop. I learn every fucking one and pack them into my arsenal that I'm going to use against her at a later date.

I'm fucking drunk and high on her. She's getting closer and closer, at a faster pace. Each time I bring her to the brink of release, her moan gets more guttural, and she keeps whispering *please*.

Her body's shaking, and I'm pretty fucking sure she's bathing my sofa in her wetness. Just like I might suck that juice out of the material when she's out of here.

She almost comes, and I can feel heat streak hotter in her, her jerk of her hips higher, and she undulates faster, trying to rub one out on me.

I curl my fingers inside her, taunting her G and A spots, and she's slurring.

"I'm...I'm...oh, God—"

I pull out of her, right as she's about to come, and I stand staring down at her.

Those pretty dark eyes flutter open, and it takes a moment but she focuses on me. "No, please, Dante, please."

I smile slow, nasty, evil. "On your fucking knees."

"I want to come."

"Knees." I grab her ponytail, wrapping it about my fingers, tugging hard, her little cry sweet fucking music. "You don't get to come."

She scrambles up, panting, tits out. Fuck, I wish I had my phone in hand to take a photo.

I tug her head to me. "On your fucking knees. On the floor. Now."

I loosen my hold enough to allow her to move, and she sinks to her knees in front of me.

That savage, vicious front moves in. I'm going to play a filthy little game with my control. See if I'll end up fucking her before she can fucking blow me. I give myself fifty-fifty chance. Generously.

"Take my cock out." I look at her.

Hate. Resentment. Lust. A perfect cocktail of an Angel storm.

"I—"

"Do it."

Swallowing, she shakes as she does so. Her eyes widen as she sees the size and heft of me.

"Lick around the head, under the edge."

She comes in, tongue out, and she delicately touches me.

Everything goes haywire and my cock jerks. She moves in a little more, and she starts to lick, taking me into her mouth. She sucks and starts trying to move, her eyes glitter as she looks up at me.

"Take me deep. I want you to fuck your own mouth with my cock, take me all the way down."

I let her move on me, enveloping me in the heat and wetness of her mouth, the sucking moves, and the slide of her tongue. She's hot, alive, and not very good. But every moment is both agony and bliss and the best fucking blowjob I've had. Because fuck, she might not have skill, but that mouth's magic.

Our entwined scents bloom and roll in the air, and I grip her hair as she manages to get me almost all the way in, little choking noises and her fast little swallows at the back of her throat a god's gift of stimulation.

But I need more.

I grab her hair and force her forward on my cock. I push into her throat, fucking her face hard, and then pull back a little, and I snap my fingers and those glorious eyes, tears leaking, full of hate and lust and need, lock with mine.

I stop, and she sucks on my cock. I give her my most

depraved smile, running a finger through the drool on her chin, and I paint her face with it.

Her gaze shifts away as she sucks. And I laugh softly.

"Still hate me, Angel? Even with my cock in your mouth?" I stroke in and out. "Go on, Angel, look up at me and tell me how much you hate me."

She makes a sound, and I start to pound her again as her eyes roll up to mine and she grabs at me, pulling me to her, gobbling me down even though I barely fit.

Filthy fucking little Angel. She likes a good hate mouth fuck.

She gags on my cock and stays there, her uvula working me.

I crack. Come apart. My control is shattered and just the wild ferocity of the need. The hunger is there. I grip her hair down to the scalp, and I start fucking into her mouth, hitting her throat, deeper and deeper each time until its fucking balls to her chin, with a rough, hard beat.

She's still grabbing at me, and I don't even try to hold back. I grab a fist of her hair and hold her in place, slamming in and out like I'm brutally fucking her cunt.

It's too big—the orgasm is there, built to monstrous proportions since the moment I walked into that fucking room upstairs. Since that first guy dared even think about touching her. I slam into her, into her throat, and she's gagging now, drool slicking the way, and she's going at me too.

Power surges through me like nothing else before, and the wild bite of the orgasm's electricity zaps down my spine. My balls rise. I grab her with my other hand too, holding her as it shoots up my cock, and I come so fucking hard that some dribbles out of her mouth. I stagger, dragging her with me, not willing to let her go.

Black stars burst in front of my eyes as the orgasm rips through me.

The waves keep crashing and building, and it's transcendental.

When it ebbs, I pull out, staggering back.

Holy fuck. That...that was like knotting.

I stare at her, and my cock jerks. The ache of desire whispers through me again, but I tuck myself away. It doesn't matter that she's a vision with drool and cum down her chin, her tits. Her thighs glistening, the puffy lips of her cunt slightly spread and red.

I find her shorts and toss them to her.

"Dante?"

"Get. Dressed."

"Dante, please, I...I want to come."

She doesn't move, and I haul her up. "Get dressed and get out. And no, you don't get to come. Punishment, remember? So, you don't come."

"Or?"

I savagely round on her. "Or so fucking help me, I'll chain you up in the dungeon. Get dressed and go to your room."

"Dante, please." She struggles, hopping around as she pulls on the booty shorts.

Her shirt's down, but it's wet from our shared fluids. She looks good and fucked.

"Jesus, dude."

I whirl around at the voice. Knight stands there. Shock, anger, and disgust on his face. That's for me. There's concern, too.

That's all for Lizette.

"What the fuck do you want?" I snarl.

"Showing off your tats?" He nods at my chest. "For the girl, or just because?"

Lizette shoves me, her clothes back on straight. "You're an utter bastard."

I ignore her flung words as she runs off.

Knight shakes his head as I button my shirt. "What the fuck's wrong with you? She's a good person. She's lovely."

"She's a liability."

"And you're a fucking monster."

With that, he takes off after her.

I close my eyes.

He's right.

I'm a fucking monster.

The biggest one of all.

TWENTY-SEVEN

Lizette

I'm numb.

Aching.

Hurting from unfulfilled needs.

Humiliated.

Not from what he did, but from his dismissal.

My eyes are dry and hot. Booty shorts uncomfortable, rubbing places I'm now hyper aware of, places chafed, sensitive, wet. Wanting.

Each breath makes my nipple sing from where he bit and sucked, makes them rub against the material that's now like sandpaper. A thing designed to slough inhibitions until I'm left, bare boned, naked, the real me. Whatever that is.

I press a hand over my stomach. I pass my room and up a short flight of stairs, into the storage room.

My plan, which is genius in its simplicity, is to steal something strong and alcoholic. And then I'll disappear into my room, drink a few glasses until the edges soften, and those new memories fade and sleep comes.

And tomorrow...

I clench my hand.

I'm not going to wallow too deeply. No matter how much I want to. Tonight's for shallow wallowing and licking of wounds.

Tomorrow?

The lines of bottles in front of me offer an escape, however brief, and I need it or else I might do something stupid in the early hours, like run and land smack bang in the middle of whatever danger lies in wait for me outside.

Or worse.

I might return to Dante to take his brutal brand of sex some more.

Better to blur reality in my locked room and plot and plan and rampage, then when morning comes, work out what I'm going to do.

Work out the details, I mean.

Because tonight solidified something.

Staying here isn't an option.

Not long term. If I do, I just might get chewed up. Bones sucked clean until there's nothing left.

A smile tugs at my mouth, and it's a bitter sting. At least I'm not holding little girl fantasies. I never did, but I also never pictured a world like this. One filled with wild beasts. Carnal, ravenous creatures that want to own and destroy. And... And even if I had, I'd have never believed I'd like it.

That's the biggest problem, isn't it? I like their touch, their violence, the sexual edge and the sweetest words that hide control and sexual desire.

It doesn't matter if they're honest or full of lies.

If I stay, there'll be nothing left.

If?

Once they find a way to solve this problem, they'll get rid of me. I don't fit into their picture.

Any thoughts I might have harbored of finding a place here are dashed.

No, I need to go.

My hand goes to my throat and I touch where Knight marked me, and it sets off waves of desire, storms of need that spin out from that sensitive place.

Shit. I'm— I take a breath.

The bite will fade, I think. And hopefully with it, my insane awareness and attraction of the three pack alphas.

I touch one of the bottles, running a finger over the smooth, cool glass and paper label. Looking at the rum, I make an instant resolve, a promise.

I'm going to work hard, earn money, put it with the rest I have hidden away. And when I've got enough, when the danger is past, I'm leaving.

Trick is to leave on my own terms and in one piece.

I might need to stay a little longer, so if I can keep working, make myself needed, then they might do that.

Instead of getting rid of me at the first chance.

Closing my eyes, I take a deep and slow breath. "Keep this in your head, Liz. No matter how they make you waver, keep it in your head. Leave when you can. When you have enough. Fuck them, enjoy them, but don't let them touch you."

Not the inner most part of me.

If I can keep that separate, I'm golden. Safe.

A lovely thought.

And way easier to say, I suspect from how I react to them all, than to do.

I'm overwrought. I'm upset. Horny. Dante didn't let me come, didn't give me that big, beautiful orgasm I could almost touch.

God, I hate Dante.

I drop my hand to the shelf below the rum and grab the nearest bottle of something to forget what happened.

Because inside, the need is throbbing. I'm turned on and more than a little dirty and pathetic inside.

"That's gross."

Almost dropping the bottle, I whirl around, eyes burning.

Knight's there, smiling softly. He leans against the door frame, arms crossed. His fine cashmere sweater in moss green brings out the green in his eyes, the copper and gold in the caramel of his hair.

I wobble.

Thing is, he's everything I need at this moment. An oasis in the storm. Everything good. He's so many firsts. And he... Oh, he's the antithesis of Dante. He's light to the other man's dark depravity.

I want to go to him, throw myself in his arms and breathe in that honey and lavender, the leather. I want his big hands to hold me, his lips against my skin, his heart beating with mine.

But I don't move.

How can I do that when I'm nothing more than a...a...an oversexed girl? One practicing her resolve, one plotting her escape. And one who was just getting finger fucked by the world's worst man, one who gave that man a blow job, a man who's my enemy. An enemy I want as much as I want Knight and Reaper.

The gentle humor on Knight's face is inviting, soft, welcoming and the resolve starts to slip, fast.

Because now, it doesn't matter what I was thinking, it doesn't matter that I sucked another man's cock and he came deep in my throat. What matters is the need and want for him. For Knight.

How can this be normal?

It can't be.

Because if he asked, I'd go to him, play the sweet submissive girl to his loving and stern Daddy Dom and let him teach me about sex. If he asked, I'd lay down and spread my legs and let him have that stupid virginity.

It's depraved, wrong. Pathetic.

Another version of pathetic. I'm collecting them all, apparently.

"Whatever you're thinking, Liz, stop. For one, you look like you're beating yourself up, and for another, if it's driving you to drink that shit, you're in trouble."

"I don't care."

He straightens and crosses to me pulling me into his arms, his lips brushing my forehead. "Oh, Liz, you do."

"Thing is, I still feel like a prisoner."

It's true, in a way. But I'm channeling the lessons my father taught me. Thinking and cooling the emotion, pushing an agenda in a way that reaps the most for me.

Right now, that's keeping a job, finding a way to be invaluable, or at least needed as staff.

"I think..." I swallow. "I think Dante's not going to let me wait tables anymore."

Knight doesn't say a word, just strokes a calming hand down along my spine.

Dante did say that, and I continue with my mild manipulations. "A job means something to me, it helps me feel less useless, like I'm giving back." I look up, smile. "And money is good."

"You don't need to worry about that. Not with us. Right now, you're in the Unholy Trinity pack's fold. You won't be wanting for anything. No rent, no groceries, no Council trying to set you up with an old fucker."

He makes it all seem so good, a dream I never knew I wanted.

"Yes, but I don't mean that," I say. "I mean..." I let my words trail, making space.

"You mean it gives you the feeling of autonomy?" Knight asks.

I nod against him. "It's just if I'm not out there, then I really am a prisoner. I want...I want to be seen. Even in that controlled part of the world."

It hits me. I'm not just saying these things in hopes I get

back the job that has the potential to make me money, I mean it.

The little note of anguish in my voice blindsides.

I didn't know I had it in me.

"And I get that I can keep doing the bussing," I say, "or... that I could start...cleaning for you all—not that I want to clean—but I'm not above it. All my life I've been hidden away. Even when I had a job, it was all cleaning or in the kitchen. It's away from people. With Dad, it was because I didn't have papers."

"Ah, shit, Liz, I'm betting he told you to stay out of the light, because that'd call attention on you. And it's not fair." Knight brushes the strands of hair that've come out of my ponytail back from my face as he tips it up to him. "I'd be proud to walk in public with you. Call you mine. But right now...there's the whole fucking Council bullshit and we don't know why they're so interested in you, and who else might be. I think your dad was someone."

"Of course he was—"

"I mean *someone*. Of interest, importance. But I was born to betas, and I didn't grow up in a pack, just a house, with parents who were, and are, complete fuck ups." He brushes my lips with his. "Reaper and Dante seem to know who he is. I can't find anything about Connor Roth. And only a name, date of birth and not much else for Elias Enver. The stuff'll be there, but so hidden I'm going to have to carefully track it down."

"He was just...Dad."

"Yeah, I know. C'mon, Liz." He looks past me, and grabs a bottle. It's wine, something fancy by the label. "I'm going to walk you to your room. I want to kiss you, maybe just hold you." There are hidden words there, ones that echo in me.

He wants to fuck me. I want to fuck him.

But he's being a gentleman.

Unlike Dante.

He laughs, gesturing to the door. "And yeah, that means fucking you, but not tonight."

I drop my gaze and move out of the room, and we take the stairs down.

We pass Dante's suite. But we don't stop, instead Knight turns left and to my room.

"I..." I clutch the wine as he hands it to me. "I guess you don't want to come in."

Knight's eyes glitter. "If I go in, I'll have my way with you, and you definitely deserve a spanking for all the self-abuse going on. I don't care if Dante pissed his claim in cum over you, or if he had every hole you own. I don't care that you smell like him and sex."

I can't move, I'm riveted to the spot.

"Actually, I lied. I want your virginity. For me, it's special and Daddy likes a good girl, and you're the most perfectly perfect good girl I've met." He leans in, his smile there, a stern light mixing with the sparkle of mischief in his eyes. "Want to know what Daddy likes even more?"

"What?" I push the word out, needing an anchor because I'm falling fast, but this isn't like with Dante. This is into a warm satin-lined place.

"Daddy likes a baby girl who knows her damn worth. Who knows her power. Who is bad by testing limits and earning her punishment. Or doing good and earning a sweet fucking reward."

My stomach flips and dances.

"Daddy fucking loves his girl to fall apart when I praise her, and have my praise send her to the brink."

"Da-Knight—"

"I don't give a shit what you do with the other two. Will I feel a twinge of jealousy?" His dimples bloom as he smiles. "Maybe, a little, just to keep it fun. But Liz, we both know I'm the prettiest, and the best."

"You don't care?"

He laughs, shakes his head, then turns serious. "If it's them, no. But if you fucking touch anyone else, or if anyone else tries it on with you, I'll destroy them. I'll go a different route than either Dante or Reaper, but trust me, I'll destroy them and make them wish they were dead. Ruin their lives, their pack, their businesses. I'll drain their accounts and burn their reputations. I'll deep fake shit so well, they'll cut their own balls off and bleed to fucking death rather than face what their lives become."

I stare at him.

Now...now I see why he's one of the three alphas of the Unholy Trinity. He's sweet, charming, self-aggrandizing enough to make me laugh, but there's the same deadly, ruthless streak in him, too.

He just also happens to possess a heart and softness. "I... I get it."

"No, you don't. It isn't a threat or a warning. It just is."

I suck in a breath. "I still feel..." I flounder, trying to find the right word.

"In need of punishment." He meets my gaze. "Yeah, you do deserve it. But not over Dante doing things with you. If he fucked you, took your virginity, well...that's between me and fucking Dante, not you. I wouldn't punish you over that."

"How does it all feel right when it's wrong?"

Knight drops his forehead against mine. "You are so innocent."

Shame burns.

He traces my hot skin. "That's one spanking, Liz."

"But I'm not innocent. Not since I stepped foot in this place. I'm... I've fooled around with all of you and there's only one time that I can blame it on heat."

Knight smiles and I melt slowly inside. "The spanking's for the red in your cheeks. Don't feel regret, or shame. You're perfect."

I moan, trying to twist away, his words doing things,

making it almost like my clit's oversensitive. I'm not perfect. And the thrumming inside, low and perfectly pitched is just as effective as if he stroked my intimate parts. My pussy, breasts, ass.

"We're a pack. Three alphas. And you seem to fit," he whispers, kissing my cheek. "And yeah, okay. Wanna know a secret? I'm fucking jealous of Dante, of that room. I thought... well, it doesn't matter."

"He didn't." I stop. "I'm still a virgin."

His eyes narrow, then he rubs a thumb over the corner of my mouth, and he dips in, kissing me. "He fucked your mouth."

Knight steps back.

"I'm not going into your room tonight, and I'm not taking you to mine. You need to unwind, sleep. We'll talk tomorrow." He takes my hand, kisses it. "Who knows? I just might have a surprise for you."

I stare.

"Fuck." He comes back in. "Don't look so stricken, the only reason I don't have you under me, or on my knee spanking you, is you've reached your limit tonight. Go to bed, lock the door."

He turns and walks away.

CHAPTER
TWENTY-EIGHT

Knight

O ver the next few hours, the number of times I curse Dante, then her, then myself, is either amazing in its excessiveness or its moderation. I'm honestly not sure which.

Cursing Liz is different to cursing the prick known as Dante. I flick to another screen and look at the code, then lean back, keyboard on my thigh. I curse her because her shame and guilt brings out the urge to punish her like a caring Daddy Dom would.

Except I don't really like punishment over that kind of shame and guilt. The kind she shouldn't have.

The kind I'm betting was put there by King fucking Dante himself.

I curse myself for both denying myself the sweet, easy spoils of the moment tonight—what is this noble fucking thing in me all of a sudden? —and actually wanting her when I knew, and still know, she's easy pickings.

If I went and knocked and announced it was me?

She'd open the door.

She'd open her pretty thighs.

She'd give herself over to me and pleasure and I'd willingly take that virginity.

It's mine, anyway. I know it. Can feel it. Taste it in the air.

I used to collect them when I was going through a phase. Not for a while now, but I remember the thrill of being the first inside a virgin, the first dick penetrating her, owning her, the thrill of teaching, honing, and creating a girl for me.

Of course, when a woman was molded for me, by me, into the perfect plaything, I lost interest.

Now I prefer the game, the play, the woman who can pretend to be the virgin by being my dirty, filthy whore, giving her fantasies to me to explore with her. I like it when they act out so I can customize a punishment.

I still like virgins. I still love being first.

And Liz...

She's different. She's all the things I crave and more. And I don't think she'd ever bore me.

Fuck. I put down the keyboard and log out. I'll work tomorrow. It's the early hours of the morning now and Pandora's is closed for business. It's not a night for the afterhours crowd. We change that up, partly to keep it interesting and partly to keep the cops on their toes.

I stretch, pick up the bottle of wine I got and take a slug from the neck. I need something stronger, I think, so I head on up to the club. It's easier than raiding the wet bar that's down here in the living room where impromptu meetings are held.

Not with outsiders; they don't know about this part of Pandora's.

Which makes me falter over Liz.

I know why I'd have her here, even without the mark. But Dante?

Shit, I trust the man, but sometimes the dude is complicated. And probably takes his denial bullshit into areas

269

that have nothing to do with sex and everything to do with feelings, if you ask me.

No one does, of course, but in all the time I've known him, this is the closest to emotional I've seen him. Dante holds his shit close to the bone. Some might say under lock and key. I don't know about that. He's complicated, just not stone-cold like Reaper.

Reaper might have layers of ice that keeps his deadly nature in place, but the man's deep. Untapped. He doesn't give much away.

He doesn't do what Dante did tonight.

Reaper kills. Brutally. Sadistically. With intent. But not with his control switch off.

Dante...fuck, I'm so mad at him I can barely see straight. He didn't need to treat her like a whore. Like one of his kinky-ass, fucked up women who like the hurt, the treatment, who crave his punishments and denial jive.

Liz is...

Liz. Shit. She's the other reason I'm going upstairs.

Less fucking temptation.

I'm halfway down the hall when voices from the club's floor make my step falter.

Dante. And Reaper?

I push into the room, setting the bottle down on the end of the bar as I go behind it, shooting Dante a filthy look as I do. Smoke hangs in the air as Reaper stubs out his cigarette, his crumpled pack on the bar.

I look at it, and then at him, then I walk along the bar, searching for hard liquor, something I'm in the mood for.

If Reaper lights up again, something's going on.

He talks more when he's got things to say. And he smokes more when things sit in him. Since he's not one for inner contemplation that I can see, I'm betting something's going on.

"Make it rum." Reaper fixes me with his stare.

I bow and pour us both a drink.

After setting his down, I lean on the back bar and gulp mine, refill it, then cross my arms, glaring at fucking Dante who is sprawled in the nearest booth.

There's a bottle of whiskey on the table, and one foot's on the long seat, his back against where it curves into the wall. He's got on a T-shirt—black, of course—and jeans, very casual wear for him, and I focus on the tattoo that spills down his exposed arm. Because I'm not ready to look the fucker in the eye.

If I do, one of us might end up dead, and I've got an uncomfortable feeling that might be me. Fucker fights way dirtier than I do.

"It's cute," he says, in that goading way he has when it's just us and he's pissed off. At least I'm not alone in the sentiment.

"What is?" I take a sip of the rum, only now remembering it's not really my drink. It's Reaper's. Then again, it'll do. What the fuck ever.

Dante's eyes narrow, and it's a sleazy, mean smile he wears. "You all sweet on your first nibble of an omega?"

Reaper turns, blowing out smoke and I can almost hear him say, *what the actual fuck is this?*

"Asshole, I say. "Nibble? You say that like it's a thing."

"It is." Dante's look is savage. "It got us in this mess, Knight."

I throw back the rest of the drink and pour another. Reaper's gaze is now back on me. "I bit her, but that's it."

"And all the rest." Dante's dark blue eyes sear into me as he picks up the bottle and takes a slug.

"All the…" I stop, shake my head and I surge forward, hitting the bar with my fist as Reaper picks up his glass as if we're having some kind of fucking afternoon tea. "Dude, she's fucking irresistible. And you—"

"Careful."

"No, you prick," I say, adrenaline shooting through me, making the world vibrate a moment as my temper comes apart at the seams, ready to explode everywhere. It's a wild experience. I don't tend to explode. I let it out, bit by bit. But fuck.

This damn guy.

I suck in a breath, slosh some more rum in my half full glass and though Reaper's barely touched his, he stubs out the cigarette in the ashtray and grabs the bottle, moving it out of my way. Smoke curls out from his nostrils like he's a fucking dragon.

I look past him to Dante who's doing an impression of the world's biggest asshole with a sore paw.

I'm mixing metaphors, I think. But I don't care. I'm not in the mood.

I should be downstairs, introducing Liz to the sublime side of sex, taking her virginity, worshiping her, getting our rocks off. I should definitely be there and not here with these two ugly dicks.

"You be careful. Glass fucking houses, man. Glass fucking houses. And yours is shattered around you. By you. Fuck, Dante, I didn't kill someone because he put a hand on Liz."

His eyes narrow. He takes a swallow from the bottle.

Reaper's looking at him now. He takes the cigarette, ashes it and studies Dante. "You killed someone?"

"He deserved torture first."

"And then," I say, before Dante says more, "he dragged pretty Liz off and fucked with her."

He doesn't say a word.

Neither does Reaper.

They should start a podcast. It'd be great. *Strong, Silent, and Dante.* Fuck. I down my drink.

The reason it tastes so damn good now is I think it's hitting me hard. Because the sharp edges are going, the explosion deflating a little.

272

"What I do, and when I do it, is none of your fucking business, Knight. This is my business, my pack. I invited you."

His voice is a snarl.

And the back of my head starts to burn as I grab the rum and fill my glass. Reaper's eyes flicker. I think that's his version of a wince.

This time, Reaper picks up his drink. "Dante."

One word. Quiet, low. Measured.

But Dante's attention's hooked and he lifts his eyes to Reaper. Narrows them.

"Back the fuck down." Reaper reaches for another cigarette from the crumpled pack but doesn't light it. "You too, Knight."

"Keep the fuck out of it, Reap." Dante lifts his bottle in the air.

"You invited us, set it up with Ghost," Reaper says.

Dante goes still.

"And," Reaper continues, "I don't give a fuck who you recruited, strong armed or sent an engraved invite to. We are the Unholy Trinity. The three of us. We have our places, but it's ours. Not yours. If I'm wrong?" He shrugs. "I walk."

Dante stares at him a long time, then finally he nods and looks at me.

"That prick deserved to die." He holds my gaze. "He touched her. Douche would have tried to fuck her and you know it. As for the rest? Lizette was fucking panting for it."

"Panting?" I say to him. "You're a cocksucker."

His smirk is nasty. "No. She is." He lifts the bottle to his lips and knocks back a mouthful. "Not very good. Yet. But still a revelation."

"Guess you couldn't keep it up to fuck her properly," I snarl.

"It's all fucking, Knight. Every hole. Matter of perspective."

"Matter of manners," I say, skating close to wafer-thin ice. No matter what I say, he's the Dante of the alphas in here. And I don't give a fuck. The difference in standing is miniscule, but

273

present. And...yeah. Right now, I don't care. "You're talking about Liz."

"She's a commodity," he says, a bitter note in his voice. "And she's not your little girlfriend. Fucker."

I know what I want to say. Cross all the lines. I want to pin him to the wall and pound my fist into his smug face. Pound some sense into him.

The bite mark's keeping her here, I'm aware of that. But he's not immune to her. None of us are.

If he truly believed all the shitty things he said about her, she'd be locked away somewhere. Unholy Trinity prison style. Locked up, kept away, and then released into the arms of her ugly, old council-chosen alpha mate to be.

"I should beat you," I snap.

He swings his foot to the ground, sliding out of his seat, and stands. He picks up the bottle, gripping it by the neck. "Like to see you fucking try."

Before I can take a step, fucking Reaper enters the fray.

"If you two are finished measuring dicks and pissing on imaginary walls," Reaper finally says, "I have something to say."

"The job went well, I know." Dante's not done, as Reaper says, pissing. I'm not sure I am, either.

We're not fighting, exactly, over her. Liz's worth a fight, and she's also, young as she is, able to choose for herself. If that's what this was about.

But it isn't.

We all chose each other. If she wants one, she apparently wants all. I've been reading up on the old, dark days, before the Council, religion, and the internet. Fuck, before TV. Packs used to have two or more head alphas. They shared the role of rule over their pack. They *were* the fucking religion.

Inside that rule, a hierarchy was always in place. God's fucking right hand, with Michael to the right, Gabriel to the left and Uriel to the front. Raphael was a turtle, I think, but I'm losing the point. He might have been behind that God.

My point, and I have one, is that in the old pack rules, there was a group of strong alphas who ruled their people and had their places in the top tier.

They all shared one omega. A special one.

I read that, too.

Dante's the God in this fucking situation. We all know that. He's the most alpha-alpha I've ever met in my life. He takes the name he chose seriously.

And, when I think about it. The Unholy Trinity?

Yeah. I'm meant to be the one who thinks and keeps us on the narrow. It might be a dark, twisted and morally gray narrow, but a narrow it is. I lead that way. I'm the consciousness. One in a metaphorical armor.

And Reaper? He's a no brainer. It's in the name. And he fucking looks like a warrior angel. The type that puts demons to shame and makes most of them shake in their snazzy demon boots.

But a reaper isn't just about killing and being a dedicated psycho who'll stop at nothing to protect what's his—though he will—it's about the sorting of souls. Culling those who need it, and letting those who don't go.

I don't think I've seen him ever kill an innocent.

But I'm digressing. I have a sip of the cheap rum that's not that bad. Maybe the whole rum thing's growing on me, or possibly it just seems that way because it's making me soft-edged.

"Yes, it went well." Reaper's tone is mild, but holds something.

I wouldn't mind getting stinking drunk, but I'm not going to. I haven't finished.

"Wait." That something filters into my brain.

Dante's frowning at Reaper and I look at him too. I point at him.

"You," I say, slowly because I'm sure I'll slur if I speak normally, "said something."

"Fucking save me from baby alphas who think they can hold their liquor," Dante mutters.

I swing my gaze at him. "Jealous she wants me?"

"She wants all of us, moron," Dante says. "And know your place."

"I do. Extremely well. And you need to—"

I stop.

Because Reaper's shouting at us. It's so loud it shuts me down flat.

Yet he hasn't uttered a word. Not really.

He stands there, still. Then he shifts his gaze from Dante to me. And when we listen to that silent noise, he studies his unlit cigarette.

"The job went well, mission accomplished. Message received by those who needed to hear it. I also won back the money." He pauses. "It was very high stakes."

"You play poker?" I ask.

Dante looks at the heavens. "He's one of the best. Rarely plays."

"After the game and the job, I sent Julien home with the winnings. It'll be in the safe. Then I went to an after-hours titty bar."

"Thanks for sharing your quirks, but—"

Again, I shut up. He doesn't look at me this time.

"You learn things at those kinds of places. People also come to talk. Drinks are cheap. Ghost's definitely back in town."

There's a beat.

"Way to bury the lede," I say, picking up the rum and sloshing a little more in my glass.

"You sure?" asks Dante.

Reaper nods, just a slight movement of his head. "I saw him."

I'm so intrigued and uneasy I pick up my glass and put it down, forgetting to take a sip. "What did he say?"

"Nothing. We didn't speak."

"Did he see you?" Dante asks.

There's something in his tone that makes me sober up a little.

Liz—she's safe. And Ghost doesn't know about her. Even if he did, why would he care?

"I caught a glimpse. So, yes."

"Maybe he didn't know you were there," I say.

"Ghost is like me. He's only seen if he wants to be. He chose the name Ghost for a reason. Me seeing him is deliberate. He wants something. Or it's a warning." Reaper stops talking.

"Or," Dante says, "he's with the Council and after Lizette."

"A little bit overkill. She's just one of many omegas," I say.

Dante snorts. "*You* think she's special."

"To us," I say. "But yeah, it's weird. I thought he was long gone, and wouldn't dare step foot in Starlight City again."

"He does what he wants," Reaper says. "As for Liz? I don't see the connection. Yet."

"We need to work out what he wants. And why. And who for. I'm going to take it as a message for us." Dante rubs his eyes and sits.

As Reaper picks up the ashtray and the purloined rum, he gives me a questioning look, but I'm not going to join them.

I'm not strategy. They are. I can do it, but my skills lie in other arenas. I like to use my gifts with tech to find secrets, paths, information. Then I can construct my own strategies or take that to the table and sit with them.

Now isn't the time. I need to sleep.

So I leave, heading downstairs, and I find my way to Liz's door.

I knock.

It creaks open a few seconds later.

Liz is a vision of post sex dreaminess, all mussed and sleepy. She's in a large shirt and girly boxers that show off her slender legs.

I don't think, I just slide my fingers in her hair and kiss her. Long. Deep. I take my time, licking paths along her tongue, delving into her, letting it rise and fall with a rhythm all its own, sex and soft, warm lust, sweet desire, all the things that make a girl sigh and melt and tremble.

Just like Liz.

She's so fucking warm. Smells so good.

Reluctantly, I break the kiss.

"You taste like rum," she whispers.

"And you taste like wet dreams."

"Why are you here?" Her voice is breathless.

I don't really know where the words come from, but the moment they hit air, I know they're right, perfect and I'm a step closer to having her virginity, that thing she desperately wants to give me.

"Wanna go on a date with me?" I ask.

TWENTY-NINE

Lizette

G*row up, Lizette. Grow up.*

The mantra beats with my heart through my head, through my veins, as I stare at the man on the other side of my door.

Dark, forbidding, black suit.

The devil himself.

He's arrived to wreak havoc on my date night.

"Hello, Angel," Dante says. "Debating whether to slam the door in my face?"

My heart beats hard and fast and out of control, the dress that arrived by Darcy delivery in my hands.

His gaze drops to it and a slow, dirty smile spreads on his face.

"Nice rags, there, Angel." He pauses. "Well?"

"I'm debating whether to kick you where it hurts."

Dante moves fast.

I'm pinned, back to the wall, inside my room and he's pressed against me. His breath is warm on my lips, his scent seeping down through my bones to my sex, the dress crushed between us.

"I'd like to see you try."

And he rocks against me, his erection pressing into me, taunting, and I somehow just manage to resist the urge to rock back against it. Inside me, the heat levels are rising to cataclysmic. My traitorous body wants him. The wetness is growing and the itch only he can scratch grows, too. I'm aching.

"Get off me, Dante," I manage.

"You want me."

"No," I whisper, "I don't. My body might. But me? I don't like you. I think you're awful and you don't even like me. I'm just a girl to taunt, torture and fuck, aren't I? Or not fuck and leave orgasmless."

Dante smooths my hair from my face, my neck, and he still rocks into me. Can a girl come from this? Because my clit is tingling and that pre-orgasmic pressure is building.

"Your mind and your body want me. You're driving yourself mad with it, aren't you? Trying to work out how someone as fucked up as you are over me can also want Reaper and his dark and still waters. Those, violent, primal and untapped depths. How you can cream your panties and swoon and want the pretty dude with the dimples and curls and soft Dom ways. At the same time."

"Go away."

Dante licks my throat, right where Knight bit. He takes his time, licking it over and over and then...oh god, then he starts to suck.

I can't help it, a cry breaks free, one that's pure need and desire.

It hurts and feels phenomenal. It's the long, slow pull of sexy urge. Of *almost* being owned.

And I push into him. I can't help it.

His teeth scrape against my skin.

I tremble. The cascade of heated excitement that showers down inside me is almost orgasmic, and I push up, harder, needing that scrape and pull, those feelings.

If he breaks the skin, then—

Dante steps back. Gaze on my throat, a glimmer coming to his blue eyes that whips hard against my senses.

He didn't break the skin, but he runs a finger over that patch, making a low moan escape. "Put your hair up on your idiotic date tonight."

Then he's gone.

I slide down the wall and hit the floor. I'm not sure how long I'm there.

My mind's fractured.

I'm back to a jumble of skittering nerve endings that Dante caused, one of the reasons I stayed in my room for a few days. I might have stayed forever, missing work, licking the emotional wounds, until Darcy stormed in. She told me to pull it all together and get out there, show Dante and the others what I'm made of.

Day one, I bussed. Same with day two. Yesterday, she told me to wait tables, and for fuck's sake, not to go into private rooms or let anyone touch me. And Dante watched. Sometimes Reaper, sometimes Knight, too.

I put a cold fingered hand to my face. I get it. They have to rotate, and I noticed before when I did the menial jobs that's what they do, keep an eye on this place, on what happens.

On me.

Pandora's Box must be their most important business place.

And I coped, dealt with every wrong thought, every urge, every whisper to run. All of it. I dealt. Stuck myself together again.

Because in the back of my head was that one thing I could

cling to. The early hours rum-soaked kiss from Knight. His asking me out. He didn't say where or when. Not until the dress arrived today with a note. One word in slanted letters. *Tonight.*

And now?

Dante's undone...everything.

"Grow up, Liz, and keep it together," I mutter.

My heart squeezes and I know I'm not alone. I look up. Into the flat, dark eyes of Reaper, that beautiful scarred face making things in me lurch.

"You're going to fuck Knight."

The breath in my body freezes. "He asked me out on a date."

Reaper steps in, crouches down. "And then he'll fuck the virgin right out of you."

"I might not. He might not," I say.

"That's a lie." A phantom of a smile appears. "And you want to."

"Reaper—"

"Don't. Just have fun. It's how this needs to be."

He picks up my hand and I think he's going to kiss it, but he doesn't. Instead, he sucks my four fingers into his mouth. It's so unexpected, my clit throbs hard.

Unexpected. Intimate. Hot.

Then, looking at me, he runs his tongue over them and bites hard on them, once, twice three times.

"Reaper." I want to touch him, reach out and trace the scars he wears like medals, like armor. I want to slide under his long-sleeved T-shirt and stroke his tattooed skin, learn all the pathways of scars and knotted skin from injuries, the places that tell silent tales of how he's survived. I want to touch and kiss and lick them all. "Reaper..."

He lets me go. "I'm sure Dante told you to wear your hair up. Show off your mark. That..." he drops his gaze to my hand a moment, "helps enhance it, as do those fresh bruises."

And with that, he leaves too.

If I live to a hundred, I won't ever understand them and that's why I'll always be an outsider. Why I need to go. Because me leaving is still on my personal agenda.

One day.

Knight takes my breath away. He's the epitome of class and dash, of modern Daddy Dom, and a charming, fun date. My first date.

He's moneyed and doesn't care and yeah, I can't breathe.

He grins, spinning for me on the pavement outside, Julien having collected and escorted me out. In the soft, early evening air, Knight's dimples flash and that caramel hair's all copper highlights with touches of gold.

His green eyes are on me, and more than appreciative.

"What do you think, Liz?"

His suit isn't black. Rather, it's the deepest, darkest violet that's almost black, with pinstripes of lavender, as is his waistcoat. The suit's modern, cutting edge, and the colors daring in their own subdued ways. But the green-gold silk tie that matches his eyes makes it.

"A dashing Daddy," I whisper.

His grin widens, catches on a little filthy intent, and he goes from charmer to filth in an instant.

"And you look like just the kind of present I love to unwrap." He leans in, his scent unadorned by perfumes or cloaks. It's just him, heady and soft and sharp, spice and sweet, masculine and mine.

And my insides go haywire.

Two hours ago, when Dante and then Reaper came to my room, seems like a lifetime ago. I showered, dressed, spent a little time applying a touch of matte red lipstick in a dark, deep rose of sunset, one redolent with rust like this all that's left when the orange burns away and the blues are ready to descend. I also put on some mascara and a little eyeshadow. Not much; I'm not really skilled in this arena.

But even the little there seems to transform me into someone else, someone more experienced, exotic. And I pinned my hair. It cascades down in tendrils, my throat bare and the mark glowing, on display, enhanced by Dante and somehow Reaper's bite on my fingers that now tingle with memory.

And the bite itself.

It's somehow *more*.

A deeper felt thrum.

Knight strokes it. His eyes glint but he doesn't say a word, just opens the sleek black car's door and pulls me to him. "The dress looks fantastic, and you, Liz, are beyond perfection."

He helps me into the car.

The dress *is* stunning. I strap myself in and he leans forward, saying something to the driver I don't catch. The fabric is the darkest chocolate, the bitter kind that's almost too much to enjoy, and it's cut low in the front, showing off my cleavage. It skims my body to my waist and hips where it ends mid-thigh.

I feel naked. Sophisticated. Naughty. The heels are high and spiked, and the stockings are sheer. He didn't provide me with a bra but the panties are things I've never worn in my life. I'm not even sure I can call them actual underwear. They're wispy, lace. See through and barely there. Just scraps.

With them on, I'm wanton, aware of every brush against my sex, and how they cling as I moisten under his gaze.

"Fuck," he says, leaning in, licking up my throat and sliding a hand over my breasts. My nipples turn hard. "I'm tempted to skip the dinner and the seduction and just take you."

My nervous system swoops and spins and I stutter out a breath. "Would you do that?"

He slips a hand along my thigh and my legs open for him. He brushes against my slit. "Hot, wet and ready."

"Knight—"

"Daddy," he corrects.

"Daddy, touch me, please..."

"You're such a good, perfect girl and with a soft, sweet kitty. Daddy likes to pet it. Open more for me."

I swallow as my eyes flutter shut and I do as asked. Knight slides a finger beneath the sodden lace and runs it along my lips, sending fiery sparks through me. He dips inside and I shudder, pleasure surging.

But he's as cruel as Dante. He takes his finger away and sucks it clean, leaning right in. "After. If you're a good girl. And call me Daddy during dinner."

Everything snaps back to reality and I shove him from me. "I'm not calling you that in public."

Knight laughs. "Now that, Liz, is a punishable offense."

"You're horrible."

"No, I'm fantastically wicked."

I press my nose to the window as the different worlds of Starlight City flash by. We go from grunge to poor to industrial to business. And then we're in the heart of it all. Bright lights and beautiful people move at a fast pace to get to wherever they're going. We pass fancy shops and theaters and I remember being here once, as a kid, when Dad and I went to see a show.

I think he snuck us in, because we were in the back, me on his lap, and we only entered when the lights were down.

It was an otherworldly, magical experience.

Like this one.

Soon we're past that part and drive into where tall buildings and multi-story dwellings with tiny gardens stand near a park that twinkles with lights. It's still busy, but the beautiful are better dressed, moving slower, like they're where they need to be and pace won't matter.

The car pulls up at a gate that leads into the park, it's lit with fairy lights and the path, when we alight the vehicle, takes us down a glittery paved trail to a gorgeous restaurant.

I'm gaping. I know I am.

I turn to Knight. "I can't go in there."

"Sure you can."

"I don't belong."

"You fucking do."

I shake my head. "I'm a fraud."

He takes my chin and guides me to look at him and he brushes my mouth with his. "Wrong kind of punishable offense. You're as much of a fraud as anyone inside. Less, really, since you don't ever pretend to be something you're not. Tonight, you're out with a powerful alpha, and as my mate, my omega, with my mark."

Knight doesn't wait, he takes my hand and leads us in, and the maître d' doesn't even blink at the sight of me.

Of course, he's all simpering eyes for the glorious Knight.

When we sit, I don't know how I'm going to be able to enjoy myself. The menu is foreboding, and the wine list short and eye-wateringly expensive. But he just closes the menu and orders wine without looking.

"Baby, Liz, you're here with me, relax," he says and puts his hand on my thigh, instantly centering me on his touch, on him.

He's wonderful company, full of jokes, and he draws me out, gets me to talk about Dad and my life, hopes, and dreams. And I find myself telling him the one thing I haven't told anyone.

"I used to sing for my dad. Never publicly. But Dante's threatened me with doing something on the stage, said it was a rule, even though there's a part of me that does want to sing again."

"Of course he made it a rule. But Liz? Dante could be right. Maybe you should sing for us."

"I didn't—"

"You know, I've heard you sing, and you have the voice of an angel." He tastes the wine when it arrives and nods approval. "Maybe we can do something about that. Try the wine."

"But I'm not angling for a job or being on a stage. I wouldn't know how to sing in front of others. I just meant..."

"I know what you meant." He nudges the glass. "Try it."

I do, and it tastes good. I wrinkle my nose. "I don't think I have a palate to tell you anything beyond if I like it or not. And I like it."

He grins, leans in and kisses me on the lips as his hand slides higher. "That's okay, it's all about if you like it or you don't. The rest is noise."

Knight orders dinner, and I don't mind. He likes that kind of control and in a place like this, I wouldn't know where to start with what to eat so I let him.

As we talk and eat, I'm aware of eyes on me, and from more than one female. At first, I think it's because of him and how he looks. And then I realize it *is* because of him and who he is. To them.

Knight's fucked them.

My stomach churns as I put down my fork on the chocolate whatever it is that melts and makes love to my mouth. "I need the bathroom."

"Liz, anyone looking is just jealous."

"I know."

"Of you," he adds.

"I know. They've slept with you and want another round."

He frowns then grins. "Some. But I was talking about the guys looking. Bathroom... In the back past the palm trees."

I wobble in my heels, feeling five-years-old as I make my

way to the back, past the palm trees and into a very low-lit hall.

"You didn't heed my warning."

The smooth, low voice almost makes me jump. The stranger's scent is there, not as strong as before, but now the man makes himself known I can smell the rum, dark chocolate, coffee and smoke.

I whip around.

And he's there. Blond, tall, good looking.

Dangerous.

That beats hard in my veins.

"Who are you?" I ask.

"Just remember what I said. And hold on, little omega, things are going to start getting jumpy."

I step towards him as someone growls behind me, and in the time it takes for me to glance at no one at all and back, the mysterious ghost of a man's gone.

Heart thumping wild and unease spreading cold through me, I find the bathroom and freshen up.

Calmer, I step out and run into a man whose fingers bite hard in my arms. "Watch it."

I look up, my heart clenching painfully. "You."

"*You.*" Jake. The one from Pandora's, the one who got me in all this. The one who wanted to rape me. "Bitch."

He shoves me hard into the door of the bathroom and it swings open. I stagger back, just managing to keep hold of my footing as I grab for the knob.

"You stupid cunt. You almost got me killed. Keep the fuck away from me."

And then he runs off.

My head spins, everything surreal.

I step out, staring in the direction he went.

And then I smell lavender, honey, leather and my knees go weak.

Knight. I turn and he slides an arm around me, pulling me

in against him and he kisses me, hard. It's pure ownership. It's comfort, and my head spins, this time in an entirely different way.

"Are you alright?"

I nod.

And he grins. "There's someone from the Council here, high up. Feel like a show?"

THIRTY

Lizette

L aughter bubbles up as we roll out of the restaurant. And I cling to him, arm around Knight's waist and hand on his vest as he holds me close.

"When you said make a show," I say, "I thought..."

He stops, spins me, right outside the door. "That I'd have my way with you in there?"

Heat floods my skin. "Well, yeah."

"Now, that's a punishable offense, little girl," he says, kissing me, bending me back so I'm overwhelmed and swept up by him in the best way. His mouth is a wonder and his kisses sublime.

He breaks the kiss and says, "Tell Daddy to take you home."

"Take me home, Daddy."

He grins, dimples flashing, and he swings me up in his arms and carries me to the car.

It's wild, insane, and I'm lost in him. I don't even know where we go, because he keeps distracting me by stealing kisses, teasing touches up my thigh, and never quite giving me anything than more throbbing needs. But the trip is short and we're at one of those little fancy houses with the tiny yards. This time, I think it's on the other side of the park.

This one is two floors of painted cream brickwork with black finishes and Knight drags me out and carries me up the stairs, punching his finger against a pad at the door.

It opens and lights bloom into buttery, welcoming light.

Then, he carries me over the threshold.

"Do you want to make small talk or just take this to the bedroom?"

I open my mouth and he steals a kiss, my arms around his neck, fingers in his soft curls and I can't think of a thing to say.

"You want to go to the bedroom, don't you?"

I nod again.

He grins and sets me down, then stalks me slowly so I back away and hit a wall, and he pins me in, kissing me, nibbling an erotic path over my lips, down my throat, to my cleavage, and back up again.

Knight looks at me. "You're all wet and hot and wanting. And I bet you're so fucking pretty naked. Wine?"

He spins away and it takes all I am not to sink down to the floor.

Instead, I follow him.

The living room is comfortable with a wet bar and muted autumn colors. He opens a bottle and pours two glasses as I wander around, touching the fabric of the sofa, running my fingers along the framed photos in black and white, things of beauty. Ugly parts of Starlight City made beautiful, otherworldly, through the lens.

Soft music plays. I don't recognize the artist, but I know it's been on the radio. It's one of the songs that would come on in the kitchen where I used to work.

This is a seducer's paradise and I hate all the women who've been here, every last one.

"You're so fucking beautiful, Liz. You steal souls and

291

hearts."

His words make me squirm and my chest tight and I don't know where to look. "I'm not."

"Take off your shoes, leave on the stockings, and loosen the zip of the dress, just a little. Just so Daddy can see little glimpses of that perfect body."

Everything's on fire, and I slide off the high heeled shoes, glad to be out of them and I unzip a little. He nods, and I unzip a little more, then another few zipper teeth.

"Enough."

Knight holds out the drink to me and sits on his sofa. I stand, not sure what to do, but he touches the seat next to him and I sit. Holding the drink, feeling...I don't know. Alive, so full of zinging nerves that don't know what to do.

But he's calm, that controlling air wrapping around me, showing he's in charge, and I find myself giving over to it. He asks how homeschooling was, and as he does, he slips one arm strap off my shoulder, followed by the other. Then he observes his handiwork and pushes up my skirt until it's obscenely high on my thighs.

"Knees together like a good, sweet girl." He strokes my thigh, and talks to me, just about my life, growing up, my likes and dislikes, what I thought of dinner.

And he listens intently to every word. Nodding here and there, inserting questions when he wants clarifications.

I know he's older than me and he looks young, he's got to be thirty at least, but he can somehow pull off the air of being older. Way older, like he's a father-like figure, my master, the man who'll provide for and love me, and take care of me.

This is a side of his kink I never really expected. I just thought it would all be sex talk and actual sex. But Knight doesn't do that. He embodies it and makes it about more than sex, something bigger, deeper, more profound. Oh, it's soaked in erotic intentions, but it's real intentions that are born out of the need to dominate, to protect.

He praises me for my perfect nipples, touching them when the air kisses one. "Lovely."

"Oh." I got to adjust the top but his hand stops me.

"You're perfect, stunning. You should always be admired, worshiped, loved."

And I melt.

He lets me ask things and he answers and my head's a mess as we continue. He tells me how Dante saved him from prison, recruited him. How he found his calling in the Unholy Trinity.

He tells me harrowing tales that twist into hilarity of his hacking days, selling drugs and the rest, of skipping school, getting into trouble from the father of the first girl he slept with—not an omega—because he accidentally knotted her and her scream brought her father running.

It's all designed to be breezy, and it feels like glossing over the ugly parts of his life.

It's designed to be hot and controlling and benevolent.

"Stand up, Liz."

I do, my legs wobbling. He stands too, and takes my drink, setting it down with his. He walks around me and unzips the dress the rest of the way. It falls to the floor in a heap.

"Even without the dress, you're fucking beyond stunning."

He touches me softly, all over, never resting. He tastes my pussy that's covered in lace, the small of my back, my nipples, nape of my neck, my waist. He then tastes my lips and cheeks. His fingers move all over, touching me everywhere.

It's the only way I can explain it. *Tasting*. Because each touch is a lick. Each touch is a bite, a mark on me.

"Fuck, Liz. You're a vision, and I think I'm back to the idea of the bedroom. But first..."

Knight strips off his jacket and undoes his waistcoat, then he pulls off his belt. He sits. Pats his lap. "Lay down, stomach to the floor, ass up."

My heart beats wild and I do just that.

He snicks the leather strap, the sound reverberating through my every cell.

"You've been bad. You doubted me. You talked back, you talked yourself into shame of your own making. You don't think you're beautiful. So, I'm going to punish you. Ten, I think..."

Without warning, he brings the belt down on my ass and I scream, more from shock than the sting that turns to a pleasant throb.

"That's one," he says.

It comes down again. And it hurts a little more, the pleasure aftermath a little more intense.

"Two." He rubs a hand over my ass. Then he brings the belt down again. And again. "Three. Four."

I moan.

He does it again. "Five." Then he leans in. "I bet you're wet. I bet you're aching and in need of alpha cock to ride. Missionary? I don't think so. You're not a missionary girl unless it's legs up and back. Unless you're spread open for the taking." He hits me again and again and again. "Six. Seven. Eight."

I'm hot, squirming, throbbing with need, my pussy wet, dripping. And I want to come, his blows holding the promise of an orgasm in with the deliverance of pain.

He hits me again, and I shriek and moan. "Nine. Usually, I like to follow up the wine and dine with drinks and kinks, I sprinkle on a little seduction and I'm there."

He holds off on the final blow.

"Please!"

"But this is you, Liz, and we've already done the wine and dine and I think I know your kinks," he says, rubbing my hot ass. "You're a versatile girl, and I like that. But I'm never, ever going to be Dante."

"I don't want you to be."

"Or Reaper."

I try and picture this man chasing me down with deadly, erotic intent. But I can't. He likes the chase, he likes his kinks, but he's Daddy over his domain. He's the master and he'll care for me.

Praise me.

Watch me squirm.

And he'll dole out measured of punishment aimed to please, and then...

I swallow. "Never, and that's a good thing."

"Good," he says. "Good girl. But you need to know Daddy means what Daddy says."

And he brings the belt down one last time, making me come. I jump and buck and moan. His fingers are in me fast, and he almost pulls out then slams them back into me, pounding me, pushing the orgasm higher and higher until I'm in tears, a mess.

"Sit up, baby."

He pulls out and I sit up and he frees himself. I stare hungrily at his cock. The curve to it. The mushroom head. The girth. I'm not sure if he's as big as Dante, but he looks it, and I stare at him.

"Come here, swing your leg over and raise your ass...good girl." Using his hand to guide my hip, I'm there, he's there, pressing at the opening of my pussy. And he looks at me and leans forward, kissing me. "Slowly lower yourself."

With his guidance, I do that and he's huge. Bigger than he looked, just like Dante and the tight fit with my mouth.

Knight stretches my pussy and it would be uncomfortable if I wasn't so wet, still recovering from that orgasm.

He stops me rushing it, fingers digging into my skin and holding me in place as he pushes deeper and deeper. Until...Oh. God.

He's in.

I'm sitting on him.

We're joined.

My body starts to pulsate, my pussy contracting, and waves of euphoria hit.

He hisses, rocking me on his thick pole. "Liz."

"I can't help it." I grasp him. "I can't help coming. It's too good."

"You're no longer a virgin and you're all fucking mine."

He draws me back in for a kiss, long and deep and slow as he starts to work my hips.

When I get the hang of it, I'm lost in a sea of pleasure and I come through that, too. But I'm still turned on, primed, and I realize this is just the first plateau. There are more, and I want to experience them all.

I find my rhythm, riding him in long, deep, undulating strokes.

It gets harder, faster, and soon I'm holding on to him as I'm slamming myself up and down, bouncing on his thick cock, wanting more.

I need more.

The kiss is over, we're staring at each other, caught in this world of stormy passion, of the constant climb for more.

Every time a fluttery orgasm hits me, I'm out of my mind, lost and needing more. And each time he grits his teeth like he's having a hard time controlling himself.

He picks me up and I wrap around him. Knight pulls out and flips us, so my ass is on the edge of the sofa and he goes to his knees. He spreads me wide and slams back in.

I cry out. He's so deep and his cock's pistoning in and out, a lewd and gorgeous sight.

It's so fucking deep, his balls slapping my ass and he's hitting all the right places.

I start to come again and his movements get wilder, the control gone. He's going at me like I'm meat he needs to pound and I dig my nails into him, trying to drag him deeper, my hips angling for optimum entry.

"Oh, fuck," he says, grunting. "Fuck."

"Harder, Daddy, harder. Punish me with your cock."

"I'm going to destroy your pretty fucking pussy. And then your ass. They're mine."

He starts to come and something happens because although I'm coming too, he's not there, something's missing and then he swells, knotting...oh, fuck, I think he's knotting in me, and it's fucking perfection.

It makes me come harder.

We both slam into each other a frantic, frenzied coupling, and his knot is so big, it's pure pleasure and I could live on this. And Knight's coming again and again. Even when we're done, the pleasure flows with tremors of orgasm as he kisses me in intense, romantic, sexual kisses. I kiss him back. We can't get enough.

The room's filled with noises from us, the intense scent of the two of us. He's damp and my skin's slick. I rock on him, on the knot, milking it for all I'm worth and when he deflates, he remains in me, still hard.

Moments, hours, later, he withdraws and tucks himself away, before picking me up and carrying me up the stairs. "We'll do it again, later, if you're not too sore."

"I feel wonderful," I admit.

"Tell me that when you wake up." He puts me down, strips off and gets into bed too, pulling me into his arms.

"I think...I think...I might love you, Knight."

"I'm a man who's shown you kindness and a fucking great time in bed. Plus, I'm fucking amazing, Of course you do." He brushes kisses on me. "I might love you, too."

And it's not until I'm almost asleep I wonder what the ramifications of the knotting will be.

Shit.

CHAPTER

THIRTY-ONE

Reaper

L iz is no longer a virgin. Her smell has changed, deepened. It's still full-on innocent and a light that fills dark places, and dark where it soothes. It's just richer now.

The change pisses Dante off, even though he didn't want a virgin. It's the *idea*. He's in this as deep as Knight with his screwed-up emotions for her.

Me? I have emotions. I've just learned to shut them down. Keep them in the limbic range. Low level, except with sex. And even then... I haven't found a woman to call home.

Fuck that. I don't want one to call home.

Too many strings and traps. Too many things that aren't me.

Yet Liz...

She is someone who bleeds through. I don't know how. I don't know why.

I swallow a sigh. I meant it when I said I'd walk. I don't need the fucking bullshit of Dante when he gets like this. I've seen it once. A long time ago. We were young and he was

298

puffed up, protecting me, blustering through something I don't really remember.

We'd had a club of sorts, a precursor that pack kids make, I guess. The other one—someone playing at alpha—didn't want me in said club. My scars scared him. But Dante knew what would happen if he let me go.

I'd do something.

Or something bad would happen.

Even then, even skinny and weaker, I'd have put money on me. Not because I was good, but because I was smart. A survivor. A quick learner who knew how to fight dirty. Even then, I'd kill.

Maybe Dante knew it, and didn't want me to lose parts of myself, more than I already had, and so he puffed up and called it his pack, not ours, and got that kid out and appointed me as his equal.

Haven't thought of that in years, not since it happened.

But we're no longer kids and while we understand the inner workings of our version of equal footing, it's Dante's pack and mine as much as it is Knight's. I personally don't care for politics. Even if Dante thinks he's the king.

A king needs his cohorts who have more powers than him in certain areas.

It's what makes us powerful.

Almost unstoppable.

It's what makes us the Unholy Trinity.

Pissing contests and ego attending are not going to be on my agenda.

I'll kill or walk. I'll agree and leave. I'll do whatever I fucking want but at the end of the day, I'll walk the fuck away if he, or Knight for that matter, start being utter fuckwits.

The clock in my head ticks.

That was four days ago.

Liz hasn't had her virtue since then, possibly before. Maybe not since I ate her out. Or when Knight finger fucked her in the alley. But apart from the lost virtue, Liz is no longer a virgin. I know deep in my bones she's now all of ours in deeper ways, more meaningful ways.

I misdirected her when I found her on the floor in her room. I didn't really bite and suck and lick her fingers to enhance the bite, to help protect her and paint her as taken. Though that is a truthful side effect.

I didn't do it because she tastes so fucking good. Though that's a perk.

I did it to solidify she's mine. Ours. It's a step closer, and one of the only times I've stepped out on pack law. If it's law. I'm not sure. It's up there.

I refocus on my job.

Candice Helmont is still home. I look up at the building where she lives from the shadows of a doorway across the street. The small binoculars are an app that Knight rigged up on my phone.

I don't pretend to know how it works, only it does, and I can hold my phone up like I'm talking or taking a photo. It's less conspicuous than binoculars.

She's the reason I'm neck deep in thoughts. I can't smoke standing here. Not often, anyway. It's a matter of position and moving about when you're surveilling. And right now, this works.

Other times, I'm in a car. Or walking. Or yes, smoking.

Candice is head alpha of the Council. And not much is known about her.

I've read her dossier and I think there might be five things in there that are true, including her sex.

She's a closed book. A secret. And too clean.

She also works from home about half the time, the rest in the main office in the city center.

Which should give me an open window to get into her place and search it.

But apart from staff, she has a rotating stream of

companions. I don't know if it's sexual or companionship or for show. After all, she's a single and powerful alpha. She should be fucking up and down the damn world.

I don't think she is.

Two things stand out.

She's a woman of extreme routine.

And there's no sign of Ghost.

That bothers me, I decide, as I pack up, and light a cigarette.

She's a lone wolf who's embedded herself high up in the Council but I know she's somehow involved with Ghost.

It's not sexual.

This woman seems closed. Anything she has in regards to relationships is planned.

I know people like that and they're usually easier to tail—as in they lead to things. Easier to pin. To work out.

I don't like them.

I don't like her.

And Ghost is enough like me for me to know he won't like her, either.

Business?

Blackmail?

An arrangement of convenience where two goals converge?

Something like that.

But one thing's for certain—he's not going to turn up any time soon.

He'd do it after dark, or drop in out of nowhere, but he has a style.

And I'm not going to get anything by standing here.

I take a drag and shake my head, moving off. I've got other things to do and I don't think we're getting to Candice this way. Short of getting arrested or kidnapping her, I'm not sure how to get information from her.

I don't like her extreme routine. It speaks of someone with

OCD or similar, something that takes routine to another dimension. She isn't that. Her time to work does vary. She goes out. But it's all...planned. And when she goes out, it's never one on one.

Maybe her extreme routine's a cover.

If Ghost shows, I'm not getting in. I'll just have a visual on what I know.

Because Ghost is Ghost.

He's involved.

I feel that, down to my sinew. But if he was going to work for someone, it would be at the top. And he'd go through her, not an underling.

They're meeting but I don't know how or where.

She wouldn't tell me if I took her, and I don't think she'd tell me even if I tortured her. As to leading me places? I'd have to follow her nonstop and have a small army doing the same.

Him? He's the smarter bet. I find him, bring him the fuck in, and then we can get somewhere.

My project isn't Candice Helmont.

It's Ghost.

I walk back to the car and drive to Pandora's.

And I smell Liz before I see her. She's somewhere she shouldn't be. Outside, a pissed off Julien standing at a distance, staring at her as she tilts her face to the evening sky like it's the sun.

"Knight told me to watch her while he's downstairs with Dante. Should I drag her in?" He crosses mighty, tattooed arms. "It's not safe out here. Not when it gets busy."

It's not safe for her at all.

She knows I'm here. Her language changes, going from relaxed to vibrating.

I wave Julien back to work and I motion to Liz to go inside.

For a moment I think she's going to complain but instead she just sighs and goes in. I follow, keeping at just the right distance to make her uncomfortable and to keep her moving.

On the club floor she turns. "I'm...I'm not sorry I went outside. I'm...trapped."

"No, you're not."

I reach behind the bar to collect any outstanding debt slips. There's one. Easy enough.

"It's fine for you," Liz says, coming at me like she's just wanting to start a fight. "You leave whenever you want."

I recognize it, that need to push to make something happen because of what's inside her. She's frustrated over something and I just slide a look at her.

"Get changed. Loose dress, combat boots and jacket. A hat. Steal one from Knight's room."

The fight rushes from her. "Why?"

"We're going hunting."

I don't go where I'm heading straight away. We have time. Our quarry is out there, and he'll be at other haunts.

Besides, even for all her chatter, Liz is a lick against dry skin.

She's not hunched into herself. And she's not the girl I chased that time. There's another reason her mouth doesn't stop talking. Finally, I take her shoulders in the bar and spin her to face me.

The place is dark, mostly empty and seemingly neglected, but come eleven p.m., it'll be full.

Still, I drag her to a quiet and dark corner, my voice pitched low. "I know you're not a virgin."

Her eyes widen. "Did Knight—"

"Didn't fucking have to. It's all over you. We don't care."

"Because you're alphas."

"And it's our pack, yeah."

303

But the nerves don't leave and her gaze jumps around. Finally, she says, "He knotted in me."

Oh, shit.

Not that he did, but she doesn't know. Fuck, maybe the little cocky bastard doesn't know either. "That only really matters if he's in rut, or if you're in heat. Besides, you're on the drugs. It stops anything catching."

Now she relaxes and I almost hug her to me, almost touch her, kiss her, bite her.

She shouldn't be out in the fucking world. She's too naive.

What I should do is take her back. Instead, I tip her very expensive hat she grabbed from Knight's room into the right position, and I just say, "Come on."

"Where?"

"To the bar."

Her hand slides over mine and it takes all I am not to turn my hand to take hers. Later, I promise myself. When the job's done.

I don't care about image, but if I'm to shake someone down, holding a girl's hand won't help.

At the bar, I get two rums, handing her one and sipping the other. As I pay, I ask the bartender, "Seen Eastman?"

Her eyes narrow. "That fuck? He owes me money. But yeah, he's hiding out at Lyle's Ladies."

"Thanks, Flo."

"Any time." I slide more money to her for the information. I take care of those who provide for me, and I drink my drink, as pretty Liz struggles with hers. "Having fun?"

"Yes." She looks up, eyes big and soft and shining. "You are a beautiful man, Reaper."

"Liz, I don't need compliments or sentiments. We're part of a unit. You're working out your place."

A funny expression comes over her, but all she says is, "I'm not sure if I actually belong."

"You do, if you want to."

"But Dante—"

"He's got his ways. But he values honesty and loyalty. And he gives it, too." The fight between Dante and Knight comes to my mind. "Look past how he says shit to the words. And don't think you're anything cheap or however you might put it. You're not. It's okay to want us equally. We all bring something to the table that works. Take that if you're to take anything." My monthly word limit's running out so I say, "Let's go."

The strip club's a sad place, and Eastman's easy to spot. Sheer panic hits his face when our eyes lock. But the idiot relaxes when he sees I'm not alone.

I motion for him to come over which he does. "I need the money."

"I...I have most."

"I'll take that," I say.

"It's in the back. Come with me."

I can't leave Lizette here. Without looking over at Flo, I know I can entrust her with such a weight. But if something happened to Liz, I'd have to take her out, and I like Flo. This isn't her fight.

It's not Liz's either.

But then again, she's ours.

I know the way omegas are viewed. Weak, protected. Fucking coddled.

She deserves the protection, not the rest. She wasn't, I suspect, brought up for the rest. It's just that Roth, which I'll call him for now, didn't expect to die.

And he was a cautious man.

There are questions, one I haven't got the answer to, ones I should have, but those can wait.

My idea of protection is to be eyes open and aware.

Staying with me is the safest of all options.

Eastman looks over his shoulder. "I said come on. I'll take you."

We've been standing here for a few seconds. My thoughts are lightning speed, but I flicker a glance at him and he stops speaking. And then I glance at Liz.

I don't know if she can read me, my blank face is the only one I use. "Stay with me," I mutter.

It's a trap, but she's safe with me.

Anyone's safe with me. Right up until I decide they're not.

She nods, half reaches for me, and stops. I turn back to Eastman. "Lead the way."

We follow him through the bar and past a bouncer, into the girl's changing rooms. There are only two girls on the stage, showing their stuff, and they must be middle shift. No one else has arrived. He goes to the black duffle on a table near the door marked *exit*.

He unzips the top. "Damn, I must have brought the wrong bag."

Before I can stop her, Liz darts out, and takes it. "I'll carry it for you, so I don't feel so useless. Do you know where... where..." She frowns, looking puzzled, at him then at me. "Is it a surprise for me, baby bear?"

The man sputters and the corner of my mouth lifts. "Yeah, honey pot. It is," I tell her.

Then I look at him, and he stops. "You can carry it. This way."

He opens the exit door. No alarm sounds, not that I expect it to. And we follow him out.

He turns and stupidly pulls a knife.

I push Liz behind me, getting nicked in the arm.

"Woohoo! Reaper boy ain't so tough!" Eastman crows.

I look at her, aware of his movements. He's showing off, but he's no threat. And shortly he won't be breathing.

The bag looked empty and he made a show of letting me see that when he opened it. False bottom, I'm betting.

"He's not going to be so alive in a minute, Liz." I say softly.

And I turn just as he swoops in, coming at me like a crazed bird.

It's a simple matter of plucking his hand mid-flight, and his neck. I smash his hand into the wall opposite and then his head, hooking his legs from him with one of mine. I smash him into the wall again, before letting him go.

Then I stand over him, one foot on his hand, crushing it. He cries out, which is a pain in the ass, so I slam my other foot down on his windpipe and neck, effectively crushing it.

He gurgles, trying to breath, neck broken, limbs useless. But he can't, and for her, so she doesn't need to witness his suffering, I smash down again.

This time, he doesn't move.

Liz's eyes are wide. She swallows. "Is he...?"

"Yes."

I stare at her, to make sure she's okay, but she's looking at me, eyes hungry, and in her hands, money. What the dead man fucking owes.

I take the cash and shove it in my boots, and then she does the same, even putting some in the inner pockets of her jacket.

"Baby's got game." I look her up and down. It's *more* money than he owes, even with the interest I wasn't expecting to collect.

She offers a fleeting smile. "Baby's got some moves," Liz says. "Dad was..."

"A good teacher."

Liz nods. Dumps the bag and skirts the body. She fusses with my arm and I completely forgot he managed to cut me. "Are you okay, Reaper?"

"Fine."

She swallows, looking at me. The light in the alley's coming from other buildings, the moon above. This alley's dark and not really used. Now I can see why there's a sign but no alarm. It looks landlocked, but I'm betting it isn't. I'm also betting no one comes out here too often, not even to smoke, judging by the ground.

"I'll take you back," I say.

She looks up at me. "If I don't want to?"

"Tough shit, Liz. You could've got hurt."

"Not," she says, "with you."

That makes me smile. Inside.

I reach for her, and search for the exit.

I start dragging her into the darkness, to the back. There's going to be a—

Something small and sweet smelling hits me in the solar plexus and the surprise sends me reeling. Allowing her to push me back into the wall.

It's blood lust, the primal sexual kind that glints in her pretty dark eyes. "What if I don't want to go back? What if I've got a taste?" She slides in close and I let her. "What if I want to hunt you?"

My dick twitches, instantly hard. "Not how it works."

"That," she whispers, trailing her hand over my cock, eyes lighting up at the size and steel of my erection, "seems convenient. But we'll play it your way."

I wait. How she touches, explores, is fucking heaven.

"What if I bargain instead?" she presses.

"Bargain with what? That's Unholy Trinity money on you."

"My life."

"Too priceless, Liz," I mutter.

"My virtue."

I laugh softly. "Knight got that."

"The rest of it."

Heat moves through me, sexual, alive, and the hunter within rears into life. "Rest of it? Your mouth and cunt's first times have been claimed."

She doesn't pick up on my meaning, so I let that slide. But it's alive in me. And in that moment, I know two things. I'm chasing her down, right after I let the prey chase me.

And then? I'm claiming her ass.

I almost groan.

"You can have both. And I'll give you a taste."

Hand still on my dick, she sinks to her knees and undoes my jeans, freeing me. The heaviness of my thick, long cock hits the air, and her, as she's a little too close, but her scent blooms big with her delight, and she starts to stroke and touch and taste me with her tongue and lips.

"You're so big. Are all alphas like this?"

She wants to fucking talk? I've talked more tonight than I have in the past month. Shit.

"I don't measure. I don't need to. And you won't either. Dante will kill you, and I'll help. Knight'll probably try and save you but when he hears what you're planning to do, or did do, he'll come to our side."

I shut the fuck up the moment my cock hits the back of her throat.

She's stretched tight around me and she's gagging. The involuntary motion is sublime on my cock.

I can't help it. I'm not really one to let someone have the time to explore. I grab her hair, knocking the hat to the dirt. My head hits the brick and every single nerve ending rushes right to my cock that gets bigger. The urge to fucking knot, here and now, is insane.

She's delightful. Her mouth stretchy and tight, the unavoidable scrape of her teeth delicious. And her tongue? Fuck. It wiggles against me.

I'm absolutely using her face as a fuck hole, so I grip her hair harder as I let her set her pace.

She's all over the place, exploring and coming almost all the way off to lick and suck and then going down slow, then fast.

Something snaps.

I take over and slam my cock into her, setting the pace I like, going as deep as I want, letting her know my needs, and she's so hot and wet and tight. She's like a combination of pussy and asshole, but with more room to do stuff. The stretch of assholes is something I fucking love. But dear lord is her mouth taking over that love.

Dante's right, this is the best experience and a terrible blowjob, but I think she's a quick learner, because I force myself to loosen my hold and she gags herself, keeping my pace, going deeper, taking my cock into her throat, pulling back at the right time before surging forward.

I could love a mouth like this. I could love her.

My cock's aching even as pleasure shoots in streaks through it to all parts of me. My balls rise and I grab her and pull her right in, loving the deepness then I push her almost off, gripping her with one hand and my cock with the other.

"Keep it open."

She does.

And I come. Hard. Shooting rope after rope of cum into her mouth.

When I'm done, I pant, leaning back against the wall. "Show me, Liz."

She does and it's a sight, her pretty face with gobs on it, her mouth open, and a pool of white on her tongue.

"Fucking spectacular," I say. "You can swallow."

She does and I wipe off the gobs that landed on her. I go to help her to her feet when she surges forward, licking me, sucking, lapping at me to clean my cock and oh, fuck, is it good.

When she's done, she runs a finger along the side of my still erect cock, along the tattoo there. "What does it say."

"Latin. *I am death.*"

"Not to me."

My eyes burn, and I tuck myself away. I help her up.

She's unfocused, smiling, and crying. I draw her in, lick her tears and I kiss her long, slow, deep, making my claim.

I smooth back her hair. "I was probably seventeen when I

got that tattoo done. And yeah, it hurt like a fucking bitch. You're the only one to ever ask what it says. Women just want to fuck me, not find out who I am. They don't like what they know beyond the fucking."

"Then they're idiots."

"No," I say, being fair. "You're the only one I've let in Liz. It's a gift to you, or a curse." Then I walk to the end wall, where it's pooling black shadows, but it doesn't take me long to find the hidden door. It opens with a click.

Light floods in weakly as I hold it open.

"Tell you what, Liz. You want to play? I'm going to run."

"So, I catch you?"

"No. That's not the game. The game is whoever catches can choose."

Her hands clench and she picks up the hat and puts it on, then takes a few steps to me. "Choose what?"

"Whatever they want to do with the other one."

"So why are you running?"

"To give you a chance to hide."

And I'm gone.

THIRTY-TWO

Lizette

This is crazy. I follow my nose, but this part of the Hollows is waking up and people are out and about.

I can't trail his scent, only catching whiffs, but other things bombard me.

Being out after just seeing him kill someone, after blowing him not far from the body, is insane.

Worse, if there's a worse, I'm out in the world when these alphas think it's best to lock me up to protect me from it. So I don't get given to some horrible old man, or raped, or—

Why else have I only been allowed to work on the "members only" floor? I'm sure it's not members only, I don't think it's that kind of place, but no one gets in without being vetted. And I haven't even seen their real pack house. Or mansion or whatever it is. I've seen a couple of places which they own or use and—

I gasp, to the right, I catch a glimpse of Reaper. A blur of black. A scarred angel disappearing into a bar that spills loud rock into the night.

Making a beeline, I talk my way past a bored bouncer. It's

early enough that they want bodies, but I'm a girl and I'm fast learning that being female and moderately attractive is a superpower.

It's dark inside and I look around as lights sweep the bar.

I don't see him, but there are little pools of people and big open spaces. Dark corners in which to hide, and everyone has a drink. They're happy hour drinks, and this must be happy hour. I peel off one of the notes in my pocket, horrified it's a fifty, but I put it down as I order a drink. The bartender's eyes almost pop out, but he reaches for the top shelf and shoves the whiskey at me.

Taking it, I pretend to relax, nodding in time to the music from the band on the stage. I don't like it, the beat's too heavy and the rest too thrashy and chaotic.

A couple of men come up but I sidestep them. I don't even have time to tell them to go away as I search for Reaper.

I know he came in here. I know it.

I saw him.

Right?

He's a hard man to miss. So why the hell can't I see him now?

Eyes follow me, burning into me, and I catch his scent, the tobacco, rum and oak moss, the smoke and roses. The sex of him, dark, deadly.

But every time I turn, he isn't there.

He's as much of a ghost as that man I met for the second time on my date with Knight.

A helplessness comes over me, but I shake it off.

Maybe Reaper came in here and left.

Or—

I stop.

I'm being felt up. Not by touch, there's no one near me, but everywhere the watcher looks, I can feel on my skin, and it sends my body into overload.

This time when I turn, I do it slowly. Because I know who it is.

Reaper's leaning against the wall just behind me, a feral smile in place and my heart beats hard.

I don't know who just caught who.

He gestures to me, an arrogant little motion that's all gloating hunter, and I throw the contents of the drink at him, missing completely. Then I turn on my heel and run, right to the exit sign on the far side. The door's open for smokers and I race out, almost knocking a man down but I dart around him and towards the shut gate at the end. It's chained, but I manage to squeeze through the sizable gap, and when I turn left, racing toward the street in the alley, a strong hand grabs me.

It's not Reaper. The man slams a hand over my mouth as I start to scream, and I kick back, trying to hurt him as I wriggle and vie for freedom.

I bite his hand. Hard.

"Cunt." At first I think it's Jake. He throws me down where I skitter on the ground, skinning my hands and knees. The burn races up my legs and arms. "Don't get up."

"Fuck you."

But it isn't Jake. I don't know this man. I barely get a chance to look before he kicks me and I tumble. "No, that's what's going to happen to you, bitch."

"Let me go and you can live."

He laughs at me, but only I know that if Reaper or Dante or Knight got hold of him, my words would be a lie. They'd kill him regardless. This man touched me. Hurt me.

That's a death sentence to them.

"You," the man says, "hurt my friend, you cunt. Had him beaten. So guess what? Since the heavens decided to land you with me, it's got to be you. Pretty, small, omega—" He says the last word like it's filth. "And stinking of the Unholy Trinity. Well, I figure those heavens want me to teach you a lesson."

I stagger up to my feet as he comes forward.

He lunges.

And topples, crumpling into a heap. Dead.

In his place is Reaper with a knife. He looks at me, and, holding my gaze, licks the blood from the blade of the knife. Then he flicks it shut and slides it away.

I stare at him. Speechless.

"Think I just won, Liz. And I'm going to collect."

I keep staring as he approaches.

"Collect?"

"Yes," he says.

"Me? You're collecting me?"

Reaper tilts his head. "Who was that?"

"I don't know." I swallow. "H-He said I got his friend beaten up so…"

I don't finish, but Reaper nods. "Knew the rapist then."

"I don't know," I whisper. "I guess."

"Good riddance. And now, I have you."

"What are you going to collect?"

Reaper's eyes glint with dangerous intent. "You know."

He stops speaking and takes my hand in an iron grip. He leads me away from the second body of the night, weaving us through the Hollows like he knows it intimately. There's a small bar up ahead. He doesn't say a word to the giantess guarding the door, or to anyone inside. He moves through the people and past the bar itself, through a door labeled *private*.

We pass an office, and he takes me up a set of stairs. At the top of the landing, he pushes open a door and drags me in, shutting it and locking it behind him.

Only then does he let me go.

"Where are we?"

"Unholy Trinity property. Time to give up the goods, Liz."

There's a feral, elemental note to his deep voice and it skitters over my skin, driving my senses into a frenzy.

"What goods?" I whisper.

He closes in on me with deadly, erotic intent. "Your ass."

A thrill rides through me, followed by cold fear and I can't move. I don't want to.

Reaper walks up, like he has all the time in the world, and he tosses the hat down, peels off my jacket and kisses me, taking me down to the floor.

The burn in my hands and knees fade to the background as every part of me focuses on him, on what's happening, on what he's going to do.

His mouth is hot and hungry, tongue demanding, and I can't help but comply to those delicious demands. Reaper pushes a hand between my thighs, and slides up to the side of my cotton panties. He keeps kissing me, mouth, chin, throat, and then along the bite. His kisses are drugs and I need more and more.

It's not until metal slides against my skin and my panties go loose that I realize he just cut them with the same knife he used to kill the man.

I shiver.

It's wrong to get turned on by that, yet I am. It's so elemental.

Then I stop thinking as his fingers stroke my clit, sliding down, way down, two pushing into my pussy, the other two into my ass. He works me, thumb on my clit, fingers in me, a slow and steady pace where he stretches my hole, using fingers in my ass and pussy to move together, stroking spots through the thin membrane that separate them until I'm half mindless with pleasure and need.

He pulls out, ripping off his shirt, and his chest is revealed as a work of art in ink and scars. I want to lick and kiss all of them but he doesn't let me near him. He is focused, hair mussed, eyelids low, as he takes me in.

His lips are swollen a little, like mine feel from those hungry, deep, pagan kisses. He looks ageless, weary, alive. And my heart throbs. How can I feel something like love for him when I feel that for Knight? It's like different parts of love that fit together, pieces of the puzzle.

Then there's Dante, who I lust for. But love? I don't even know if I like him.

Reaper flips my skirt and pulls my ruined panties to the side, and then he goes down on me, licking and sucking and fingering me, plunging into both holes again. Pleasure floods me. I come. Strong waves crash and pulsate on his fingers.

He lifts his head and bites my thigh softly, then pushes me to roll to my stomach. He lifts me by the hips so my ass is high, dress around my shoulders, and as I try to rise to my hands, he pushes down on my upper back so I can't.

I'm scared, excited. I'm spun in circles.

Reaper doesn't speak as he strokes me and the hiss of his zipper is the only sound other than our breathing and the booming beat from the floor below.

He pushes three fingers into my pussy and then he paints my asshole with my own slick, pushing some of it into me, and then...

Oh.

My.

God.

His cock presses against my ass and he pushes, one hand on my hip to hold me steady, and as he pushes, I open, stretching. I don't know if I can take him, he's so big and it's uncomfortable and strange, an invasion. Soon, he's in. And he doesn't stop. He keeps pushing until his balls slap my pussy.

I shudder.

He waits a beat, then he starts to move. He rocks in me, small motions that grow bigger and bigger until soon, he's pulling almost all the way out before slamming, balls deep, inside.

He's not gentle after that. He's rough, animalistic. It's an assault of the good kind because somewhere along the way, it stopped being strange and morphed into great, and then into delicious.

Soon I'm rocking back, caught in the wild rhythm, wanting more, needing more. I lay my cheek on the floor, reaching under me to touch my clit.

It's like a switch and I explode into an orgasm that gives way to more pleasure, I rock harder against him as he grabs both hips and hammers my ass in sweeping, punishing thrusts that push me a little along the floor, it's only his grip and strength that stop me sliding wild.

His cock is magic; it touches places I didn't know existed, makes a deep throb start inside, and it radiates in dark, body-shaking waves.

This time when I start to come, it takes my whole body and Reaper isn't immune. He starts to thrust with abandon, which only kicks up my enjoyment, and I burst into wild, orgasmic pleasure and he shouts, a guttural, wordless sound. I feel him come, and he keeps coming. So do I.

It's a wild thing, something so natural I just become it. His cock expands as he comes, right at the base, and he's knotting in me, and oh, fuck, it's insanely good. Like with Knight, it changes things, tilts the world on its axis and I'm just coming and coming. I'm mindless, boneless, just pure pleasure.

And it doesn't stop.

Finally, when he crashes down on me, the knot fading, he stays in me until he can pull out. When he does, I'm bereft. I want more. I need more.

And I know, no matter what happens in my life after this, my time with the Unholy Trinity, which has to be coming to an end, will remain the epoch of everything.

I roll over and I'm rewarded with something that pierces heart and soul.

His naked smile.

"Next time," he says, stroking my cheek, "I'm taking your cunt."

I hope there's a next time with Reaper because I get the feeling, even if I wanted to stay, that decision is Dante's, and he...he doesn't like me.

At all.

CHAPTER
THIRTY-THREE

Dante

"You wanted me?"

Angel stands there in front of me in my office, a vision. Sullied, the way she should be.

She doesn't need fucking bites for me to know she's been taken. Not just by Knight, who got her virginity, but also by Reaper.

Knight doesn't bother to hide it.

She can't, either. She wears everything on her sleeve, including her longing for and loathing of me, things that turn me the fuck on. The filthy, disgusting things I want to do to her that'll have her crawling back for more are depraved and divine. But I'm not going to.

And fucking Reaper... the only reason I know he touched her, had sex with her, is because of her. She looks at him like he's her personal savior, like she wants to nurture his soul by fucking him senseless. I've seen the look before.

I'd dismiss it, but there's a depth to the expression, like maybe she *can* see into him.

We're meant to work on finding out how to rid her of the

fucking mark or turn it to our advantage, and yes, we're also trying to find out why the Council is so interested in this particular omega.

There are others.

So, why her?

Beyond her evident attributes.

And obviously, we want to know what the fuck Ghost has to do with any of this.

"Dante?"

I flick my gaze at her. She's so fucking gorgeous. All that dark hair, those big eyes, perfect lips, banging fucking body. And she doesn't even know it.

It's a powerful mix.

Add in that angelic voice...

She's a commodity.

A potent one.

And while she's here, I want her to earn money, for us. For her. A win-win, as they say.

I stand by her obeying us—me—or she's out. She knows we'll protect her. I'm just going to pull her fucking strings.

Up on the stage is perfect. Patrons can look at her, but they can't touch. They'll want to.

They'll pay to see her in skimpy outfits, maybe do a G-rated strip tease. I like that idea, titillate and never give them what they want with Lizette.

They get the other girls, but not my Angel and certainly not her wares, nothing but a glimpse.

Except they get the gift of her voice.

The more I think about it, the better it is.

Fuck, since the first time she walked into the club, the male patrons couldn't stop staring. I knew she was a goldmine. Now that I know she can sing, truly sing, that makes her absolutely priceless.

As long as no one fucking touches her.

"Dante?" she presses again with a touch of anger.

I don't bother answering. She'll wait.

I haven't touched her since that kiss before her deflowering. And her pull is just as strong. Stronger.

Part of the magic of my Angel.

If it works on me, and I'm not sure I like her, it'll work on the customers.

I don't need to understand my wanting her beyond knowing her gifts will earn us money. Money, I get.

"Sing."

Angel frowns. "I can't—" She stops. "I'm supposed to be cleaning the bar."

Now I frown. "Who the fuck told you to do that?"

"Me. You won't let me work that often on the floor."

"I won't let you be a fuck toy for customers. Not the same. Your punishment is done. *Sing*."

"I don't. I-I don't sing in public, I mean."

I smile, and she draws back a little.

"You will," I say. "You're a shit waitress, so you'll get up and sing. Or strip. But if you strip, I'll have to blind all the customers, and that's just bad business. So...singing it is."

"H-How often?"

I think about it. "As many nights as your greedy black heart desires. But I'm thinking at least three times a week."

She nods and half-looks around, like she might find an escape hatch and make a run for it. She's out of luck there. "If I have to sing, I can do *one* night."

This fucking girl. If she keeps it up, I might like her, and then the world will probably end.

I tap my foot and ask, "Let me guess, that one night will be the quietist one?"

"Yes," she says eagerly. "Then I can just wait tables, bus, whatever the other nights—"

"Oh, sweet little Angel." I pause. "You'll be on the stage. Performing. All the nights that I command it so. You're going to be up here."

"No."

"Isn't there a rule about obeying me without fucking question?" My words are quiet. Deadly.

"Dante, please...I've never sung in public before."

"You need to pay your keep, to pay for your protection. You won't sing? Then you'll strip."

"No." She heads to the door.

I'm on my feet fast and I slam it shut, keeping my hand on it. "The answer's yes."

"I'm not stripping," she says, looking up as unwanted desire sparks in her eyes.

I feel it too. Cock hardening and the nasty thoughts coming in fast. Fuck.

"Good. Because I'm telling you to sing."

"And strip."

"No, I'm not actually asking you to fucking strip, Angel." I stop. "Not much."

"Let me out."

I grab her hand and open the door, dragging her up the stairs and into the club. Darcy's doing inventory and two deltas are cleaning.

"Everyone out," I snarl.

The two deltas scram, but Darcy just looks at me.

"You too."

She crosses her arms. "Leave the kid alone."

"Liz is fine. Aren't you, Angel?" I give her hand a squeeze.

She takes a beat, then says, "Yes."

"Now, go, Darcy. I need the space." I turn my back on her, knowing she'll go and motion to the stage. "Get the fuck up there and sing."

"N-No." Lizette trembles but she stands her ground. "I need music. And what's this about stripping, even a little?"

"G-rated." I pick up the tablet and go to the karaoke music site. "Do you know Queen of Pain?"

"No."

I hand her the device. "Get up there, press play, and sing along. And G-rated is taking off some pieces. Maybe down to silk, boy-cut shorts and a balconette. You'd be covered. Nothing showing. I don't want men ogling you."

"Just you?"

She's gotten some balls since I fucked her face. "No," I drawl, going around the bar to get a drink. She looks at the bottle so I pour her one. "I'm fair. Reaper and Knight can ogle you, too."

"Gee, thanks."

I ignore the fucking sarcasm. Instead, I cross the floor and hand her a drink. "Courage from a bottle."

She downs it, and grimaces.

I nod to the stage. "Go. And you can keep your clothes on. This is your chance to make money, prove you can be the hidden gem, the star attraction."

Settling back at one of the tables, I set my drink down as she presses play. There's a microphone that isn't used, but more for show. This time it's on and I've got it and the tablet tapped into the sound system.

She starts to sing, really sing, and her voice is utterly perfect, each note. But as she gets into it, her voice changes, loosens, becomes a soaring thing that's alive. Even without moving, she's mesmerizing. The music takes her, and soon she's moving, her hips swaying, and I'm lost in her.

When the song ends, I can't breathe.

I'm about to say something when she picks something else. It's sexy, guitar and string heavy, and she adjusts the volume and then starts to sing.

The song is fucking hot. About sex, rejection, denial, lust, and love out of reach. A woman crying, losing her mind, getting revenge.

I pick all that up in the first verse.

Lizette jumps off the stage and the power of her voice, her presence, floors me. She's full of angst and madness, heat and sex. The sound she produces wells from every part of her, it's velvet in sound, and dynamite in strength.

As Angel sings, she sashays up to me, crooning of things she hasn't experienced but she makes me believe she has. And then she pushes me back, straddles me and gives me a low, undulating lap dance that almost has me coming in my fucking trousers.

Her ass brushes my thighs, and she dips in, breasts whispering against me as the damp heat of her cunt rubs over my cock.

And I'm fucking powerless.

If she fucking does this to anyone else, I'll rip their heart and entrails out.

And I want her to do this to me over and over again.

The music ends and she's still on me. The air vibrates, she vibrates, and all I can smell is her rich gardenia scent, intertwined with mine, making it even more compelling.

She runs her hand over my beard and it snaps me out of it. I snatch her wrist. Our eyes meet. Fire cascades and her pulse's beat is mine.

Then I move, hauling her up and we stumble over table and chairs, knocking them aside, and I drag her to the area near the bar, dark, private, leading to the locked office.

It's a silence so full of noise and awareness that drowns us as I push her against the wall.

"And here we fucking are again," I say, gripping her throat, squeezing so she struggles. "You're all full of dangerous ideas."

She smacks at me, and I hold her a little longer until I see it, something that changes from panic to lust, and then I let her go.

Lizette starts to melt forward, but I shake my head, stepping back. "You fucking touched without permission."

"I—"

"If you want to touch, you ask. If you want to come, you ask." I tilt my head, observing all the changes, the wild beat to her pulse in her throat, the way the mark flares darker, how her tits rise and fall, and her thighs press together.

She's wet. Soaked from how she felt as she rubbed on my cock. And the thought makes my dick jerk and leak a little precum. Fuck me. I don't think I've ever been this turned on.

That's a lie.

Outside of *Angel*, I don't think I've ever been this turned on. She's a fucking one-stop fun ride of erotic intent.

We don't make it to even the office door.

"Now I think of it, I need to punish you. Chain you up, get out my whips."

I don't keep them here. They're at one of the places we use for sex, and at our pack building. The women I bring there are ones I tend to fuck on a regular basis. I don't fuck in this place.

Until her.

What is it about this pretty piece of omega?

She's got powers.

She's dangerous.

And I fucking want her.

I trace a line between her tits and down under her skirt to touch the cotton panties. I like her in them. There's something perverse about her wearing something so plain, so *fuck you* about them. I think I'll buy her more. Just plain Jane panties that border on ugly. They'll make peeling them off her hotter than hell.

Or pulling them down to beat her fucking ass blue. "I've got paddles with holes in it. One in hard leather, the other in wood. The holes help bring the pain home. I think since you've been fucking the other two alphas, coming all over them, that I'll beat you with those."

"No."

I smile nastily. "Yes." I lean in and breathe out, "Hard."

And the little perfect slut moans.

"But since I don't have them, I'm going to punish you this way."

I unbuckle and pull off my belt, dragging her arms behind her and binding them, down to the wrists.

That moan washes over me, another fucking song. X-rated, siren hot, and dangerous.

I spin her so she's facing the wall and I pull her hips to me. She pushes the side of her face into the plaster, and I just release myself and push her panties to the side. Then I plunge into her tight, hot, velvet depths.

It's like coming fucking home, and I know I'm going to end up knotting in her. I've been fantasizing about it. About rutting her. Knotting is dangerous for me because it unleashes the feral. I don't need her heat to go into rut. I just need to fucking want her like it's the only thing in the world. Like I need to implant my seed in her to state my ownership.

And it scares me.

But she's on the pills she needs, pills to stop accidents, to stop her heat, to let her be normal and not a slave to her physiology.

I pound into her, going deep, holding her ass cheeks, and I know I want that next. I push a finger in and she moans, whispering, "*Yes.*"

"Did Reaper get this?"

"Yes."

"Did you like it?" I slam into her, balls slapping her, and it's so fucking good, holding back's getting harder and harder.

Her body sucks at me, the tight fit, wrapping me up, not wanting to let me go, and welcoming me with each thrust. She's fucking so hot. I want it to hurt so good, feel so good. I need to own her, every inch, make her into mine.

"Yes."

"Did you fucking come?"

"Yes."

I slam in harder and then I lean over her and bring my hands down on hers, thrusting all the way in. Then deep, small thrusts that make her gasp with every motion.

327

"Tell me you want me more, Angel. That you crave this depravity. Do it," I say.

She half sobs as I slam in.

"Do it."

"I need it. I crave it," she says with a gasp. "Are you happy?"

"No. Do you want to come?"

"Yesss..." Her hiss wraps around me as I grab her bound wrists and thrust in again. "Yesss."

"Just like you came for Knight?" I push my mouth to her ear. "You know you can't come now, don't you? I'm not going to fucking stop. I'm going to come in you hard, flood you and then feed you my cum, scoop it out with my fingers and stick it down your throat, make you suck my fucking fingers clean. And then? I'll fuck you again and again and again until you beg to be whipped and paddled."

"S-Stop..." Her voice wobbles. "You have to stop."

I suck her ear. "Why?"

"B-Because I'm not strong like you, I can't stop myself from coming. I can't."

"You can. You just don't want to because you want that paddle, you want to feel the burn, own the pain and you'll come then, too."

She's moaning, crying, her ass rising up to meet me, grinding into me, and I pull back, slam into her once more as I reach around and twist her clit with a vicious, well-timed tweak, one that breaks her, and she shatters, coming all over my cock.

I pull out and she falls to the floor.

"Just where you fucking should be, Angel." I unstrap her. "Hands and fucking knees." I look at her, pumping my cock slowly in my hand, not to keep my erection, but to offset the urge to come. To slow down the roll to the inevitable.

I wasn't planning this, but now? Yeah, I'm going to make it last.

I fucking love denial, but I'm not going to force it on her. It would be a losing battle and besides, there's a time to withhold orgasm, and a time to threaten and yet give them what they crave. This is the latter.

"Suck my cock, Angel."

She comes up on her knees fast, hunger bright in her eyes, almost feral, and I'm pushed to the edge. I see something on her hands but her mouth is on me too fast to speak. And I'm lost in the pleasure of her mouth, her lack of skill is morphing *into* skill as she remembers what I like. And she goes at me, in sucking forceful thrusts with her head.

Oh, fuck. She's fucking me with her mouth. It's insane. It's more than I can bear, and I grab her and hold her, hammering deep and coming down her throat.

Then I haul her up, and turn her hands, palms up, when I see them properly. The scrapes.

Fury sears through every fiber of my being. "What the fuck, Angel? Who did this to you?"

THIRTY-FOUR

Lizette

"What?" It takes me a moment.

I'm still flying from the bone shaking orgasm I stole from him. I can still taste him in my mouth, feel him in my throat.

He likes things different from Knight and Reaper.

Last night I spent time with Knight and blew him. He's softer with it, he likes to go slow, enjoy every moment in my mouth. He likes to coach, coax me down, make me lick him all over. And he loves me sucking his nipples as I sit in his lap in nothing but lacy panties and one of his dress shirts, unbuttoned.

Reaper is closer to how Dante likes his blowjobs. Rough. But Reaper is more primal, enjoying it as part of a ritual of the taking of me.

Dante is... All consuming. He devours. Demands. Steals.

I like it all. They all speak to a part of me. Dante to my need of being really punished, treated like a filthy thing, like a fuck doll. I love his dirty talk, his nasty, filthy ways. And I like how hard he fucks me, how he twists it up into me and coming is up to him. And if I do come when he hasn't commanded it or he's told me not to, a punishment awaits.

Part of the punishment is not going near me. I'm not sure if he gets that, but for me it is. Him barely talking to me or treating me as an employee is as painful as what I imagine his whip or paddle would be like.

That part of punishment, of denial, is both horrible and a turn on and I'm in circles about whether this makes me a fuck up or it's just that it's one of the things I like.

"Lizette."

I snap out of it as he does up his pants and pulls my dress back in place. "They'll be down here to clean soon."

He sighs, opens the office and pushes me in and shuts the door, locking it. He leans against it. "Now tell me. What the fuck happened?"

"One of that Jake guy's friends attacked me. It wasn't Jake. Last time I saw him he screamed at me to keep away from him."

His eyes narrow and the stark, violent fury on his face is frightening, thrilling. "Where is this man who dared touch you, dared hurt you? Because—"

"Reaper killed him."

"Oh."

I frown. "You don't look pleased."

"Yeah?" He picks up my hands gently and sees my knees. The scabs are healing but I look a mess. I also feel like I'm ten-years-old and I fell in the playground.

Dante kisses each heel of my palms and lets go as he moves to rummage in a drawer. He's back with some salve that smells like honey, and he rubs it on my hands.

"Maybe I'm not pleased. Maybe I wanted him to let me kill the fucker. Of course, I'm also glad Reaper was there and handled the bastard. Knight would have beaten him up." He stops. Shrugs. "Actually, we're talking you. He'd have fucking killed him, too."

He crouches down and rubs the salve on my knees.

"You're so weird, Dante."

"Why?" He puts the tube down and starts clearing the desk. "Because I just looked after the merchandise?"

My mouth twitches and I don't think I hate or dislike him. I think I like him. A lot. Maybe too much, maybe too close to other things and feelings I don't want to think about.

What's that thing about love and hate?

They're so close they're pretty much the same, just move a needle a notch...

"You're also an asshole," I mutter.

He looks at me, and he smiles. It's a genuine one and my legs give way. He catches me, pulling me against him. "You just figured it out?"

"No, I always knew it."

"I'm worse than an asshole. I'm not any kind of hero. That's Knight. And he's a dubious one at best."

I take a risk, slide my palms up along his chest. He doesn't forbid it. "I didn't ask for a hero."

Dante doesn't say a word and time stands still. There's a moment, a real one that pulsates through us and the room, and then it's gone and he lets me go. "Ever had a fantasy you never really thought of acting out until you were in the fucking moment?" He looks me up and down, gaze lingering at my breasts where my nipples poke out, and says, "Of course you haven't. Take off your fucking dress."

I do. I'm not wearing a bra. I didn't bother putting one on this morning, figuring I'd wait until the cleaning was done and I grabbed a second shower. And I stand in front of him, panties slightly twisted.

I look down, my breasts are swollen, nipples hard and jutting, and my pussy is half showing, red and glistening, as are my thighs. And I shiver.

"Lucky you look good like that. Fuckable."

"You just fucked me."

"You also came when I didn't allow it. I did not."

I swallow, take a step back as panic laced with desire licks at my insides. "What are you going to do?"

He keeps clearing the desk. There's not a lot on there but he's meticulous and I think it's to stretch out my agony. "Live out my fantasy and fuck you on the desk."

"That's a pretty tame fantasy."

"It's not my only fantasy."

He doesn't wait. He picks me up and deposits me, and he dives down between my legs. It's a show case study in denial because he starts slow. The licks are soft, rhythmic, designed to make a woman disintegrate. And the stroke of his tongue starts at my clit and goes down to my tunnel, licking inside and then up. A measured pace, a thing of beauty that leads me up towards nirvana.

I start panting, I can feel the pressure building, and the orgasm there, just there.

I reach for it and start to shake.

Dante bites me, high, right on my clit and I scream out.

He clamps a hand over my mouth and starts to suck and pull and scrape me with his teeth. It's too much. It's a brutal onslaught I need to escape and I twitch, trying to get away. But his other hand holds my right hip, and his body traps my left leg. I'm caught, pinned, and spread out for his mercy.

Only he doesn't have any.

He keeps going and the hypersensitivity turns painful, and I moan into his hand, whimpering.

He doesn't stop. Dante keeps going, until I can't take it, until it's so unbearable it could turn—

Dante stops, and starts to nibble on my inner and outer lips and alternates the soft licking alternates between that. The endorphins flood me and I'm rolling high on them, building and building but I can't reach it. I can't get there. I need more. I need his tongue, fingers, cock in me, and I start trying to buck my hips up, to tell him with my body.

When he stops, I'm mindless. A mass of nerve endings that crave him. Hate him. Need him.

He lifts his hand from my mouth and smiles. "That's a fun punishment. And a reward for me. You taste like dessert. Did you know that? What kind? Today, it's salted caramel. Tomorrow, who knows? Any which way, you're a fucking tasty treat."

I want to respond, I do. Tell him no one tastes like dessert, tell him his degrading comment of tasty treat won't work. But I can't.

I like being told I'm tasty, I'm dessert. I like the degrading things he says in play. But right now, I hate it. I'm quivering with need and outrage. With shame because I'm not ashamed.

I'm so fucked up I want him to ride me, call me names, take me hard, hurt me in a way that feels good. The hard, deep, pounding fuck kind of good.

A part of my brain wants to scream to get it together, but I have. I think I have.

These three alphas feed into parts of me I never knew existed and make me feel more than the sum of those parts, more than I have before and a wave of heated goodness comes over me.

I look at Dante.

He's a dirty, cruel, and hard master. He's wicked and has the charm of the devil, and a deadly bite. He's filthy and dark and savage. And he's always, always hungry. It's there. In his eyes. In the way he looks at me. Like I'm every fucking meal.

I moan as I look down. He's rubbing me gently, spreading my slick over my pussy and it feels good. "Time for a fucking ride, Angel. Hold on."

He pulls me to the edge of the table and slams into me, balls deep. I come hard; I can't help it. No amount of him telling me not to come can stop me.

Dante growls low, and he starts to slam into me so brutally I have to lock my legs around him as the desk slides.

He grabs my face, fingers biting. "You don't fucking come again. Not until I tell you. Or this is it. The last time I ever fuck you. Look me in the eye, Angel."

I do and my stomach flips as he surges into me again. I believe him. Oh god, he feels unbelievable. How can I stop coming when he feels this good?

It's like my body's made to come for him, for all three of them. And if I've any chance of obeying his no come policy, I have to stop myself thinking of them taking me together.

I groan, angling my hips to him as he pounds into me. He lifts me, still fucking me, and takes me to the desk's chair where he sinks down, me on him. "Work me. Make me come, Angel and then, maybe I'll let you come."

He plays with my nipples as he does this and I start to ride him. Soon he's biting them, sucking them, making me half mad with desire. I rock on him. I need all I can get, and it's not enough. And I don't think it's enough for him, either.

Dante bares his teeth as he lifts his head, eyes glittering with savage intent and he grabs my hips and bounces me hard on him. It doesn't matter to him I'm cramped up in the chair, legs bent and caught either side.

I can go up and down, and he can control me, and he's merciless with it.

I'm shaking from trying not to come, whimpering, begging him. All I get is that nasty, feral grin, the one that owns me. The one that tells me this man does whatever he wants to get what he wants and right now, he wants me.

The orgasm is there, so big and just in reach. I'm tingling, aching, needing it. I want to reach out but only the look in his eye stops me.

He keeps going, working me, and my eyes roll back. All I can do is cling to him and help him with the bouncing on his cock. Harder. Wilder, more brutal. It's growing into a thing that's too much and I'm going to explode.

That's when I feel it, the swell of his cock. It's happened twice now so I know what it is, and the feeling's hot pleasure, relief. Desire. It's a different sort of thing. An orgasm for the orgasm. Pleasure's entryway.

As he knots, he slams me down, coming in me. Then he bounces me hard and fast as he growls, almost howling out his pleasure and I lose it. I'm swept up with him. And I swear I black out.

It's that good.

I'm shuddering and shaking, contracting around his cock, and I'm coming from the tip of my toes to my hair. Everything is pure, pulsating pleasure. And it doesn't stop.

It's one continuous orgasm that rolls through us and he's kissing me hard. They're nasty kisses. Violent bites of kisses. He sucks my tongue, my lips. He demands the same violence back and I'm so gone, I give it. I can't get enough. We mate with our mouths as we're joined and coming.

And as it all ebbs, I'm locked to him and I slump, his arms around me. I don't want to move. And, I realize I can't. He's gone down some, but not all the way, and I have almost no experience of this. Reaper and Knight don't count. They care. They're mindful. This man... I shiver. This man is an entity unto himself, as they say.

"So. You came."

His words hang in the air and I go still. "How could I not?"

"I told you not to."

"No, you said to hold off." I hate myself for how my voice wavers.

"What I said was if you came without permission, this was the last time," he says, "and maybe I'd let you if you made me come. I never said you could."

"Fuck you, Dante."

"Stacking up the punishments."

Fear hits me. There's no light or play to his tone. It's flat, serious. Foreboding. But then I think about it. Would he, really? Even if he doesn't like me, he wants me.

"What's the punishment?" I ask.

"Well—"

He stops, and goes still. I can't hear anything much, just voices. And then a shout goes up. "Peabody!"

I stare at him. "What?"

"Fuck, I'm so sorry, Angel." He pulls me off him and he's still big, and it pulls. A flash of pain hits. He tucks himself away and he's on his feet, moving the desk and racing to the other side to throw my clothes at me.

He comes back and lifts up the rug on the floor. And he pulls open a trapdoor. A dark maw stares at me.

I back away, clutching my clothes as he lunges for me. "If that's your idea of punishment, I'm not going down there."

"Peabody is code for raid, Angel. It won't be the cops on their own as we have too many on payroll. We'd have gotten word. This is something else. FBI? Council? Something like that."

He opens a drawer and hands me a flashlight and grabs his phone, punching in a message.

"Where the fuck's Reaper?" He turns on me. "Have you seen him?"

"Not today."

"Take the fucking flashlight, go down there, and follow the tunnel. There's a safe room at the end. Go in there and close the door. It'll lock."

Panic beats fast. "What about you? Knight? Reaper? The others. What—"

"Just fucking go. Now." he shoves me, naked except my shoes and panties to the open trapdoor and I fumble with my dress. "No time. Put it on down there. Go."

I take a gulp of air and turn on the flashlight, holding it between my teeth and start climbing down the rungs.

I'm a few rungs down when the door above slams shut, scaring me and I drop the light. It goes out.

"Fuck," I whisper.

I try and find it when I reach the floor, but it takes too long and then I feel around on the walls. Two each side. Dead end behind the ladder. One exit only. One tunnel. I pull on the dress and shuffle down, keeping a hand on the wall until I finally reach the end. There's a door. Steel by the feel. I touch it and a panel lights up.

I start to cry. He didn't tell me the code.

In frustration I press down on the handle and my heart jumps. The door opens.

I go inside and as I pull it shut, lights come on and the door locks. I'm in a room with no way out. There's a sofa that looks like it folds out, a second space with some kind of futuristic bathroom, and a pantry with a hot plate. There's food and drink in sealed packets with insane use by dates. It looks disgusting. And I hurt.

Going back to the door, I try and open it, but it's locked. I try to get it to open but it doesn't work. Who has a room that only locks from the inside?

I close my eyes. It's a safe room. That's what they're for. To stop others getting in.

"At least there was a panel on the front. So there must be a way to open it from in here."

Feeling very slightly mollified, I lay down and hug myself and hope against hope everyone is going to be okay. Because otherwise...how the hell will I get out?

I don't want to die down here.

THIRTY-FIVE

Knight

"Fuck." I wipe the history and shut my computers down, unplugging them and taking the hard drives.

I hide the drives in a hidden lockbox safe. They won't come down here, but it's protocol.

Any raid or attempt to get in here is treated like the end of the world. Everything's shut down.

When that's done, I open my trash laptop and turn on porn. Everyone loves to judge people who watch the amount and type of porn I've filled this thing with. It's very handy. Not in a spank bank way, this shit doesn't do it for me, but it paints a picture of the dude who watches it. And this amount. I leave it running. Add some lotion and tissues.

Overkill, but hey. Whatever.

I take off at a run and burst into Liz's room but she's not there. Next, I go to Reaper's suite, a goth king's pride and joy. Not really. It's plain and simple with the basics. Prison chic with some extras. Like weapons. And workout equipment. And books. Dude likes what dude likes, I guess. I grab a notebook and pen and tear out a page, scrawl a note and leave it on Liz's door in case she's here and...I don't fucking know. Maybe she's with Reaper.

Maybe she's with Dante. Or she's just walked off into the morning.

No, that's one thing she wouldn't do. Just go off. And my heart clenches in my chest because some worst case scenarios are in my head and won't go away.

I text Reaper **Peabody**, and add the word **Angel?** He'll get both references. The first tells him not to come in here until further notice.

The second? If anyone can find her, it'll be him. It needs to be him because if the Council gets their hands on her and tries to register her even with our mark—it's the Council, who knows with them? Our protection should be enough—then they won't put her on any system until she's way out of reach.

Though their version of out of reach and ours are two different things.

Still, last thing I want is her in their clutches.

And it would have to be the Council. They're powerful, more so than law and order. They're an arm of government and they can cross lines where the ones in blue can't.

I'm getting ahead of myself.

I go back and quietly go into Dante's domain. His office is empty. We both keep our offices clean and any info locked away when we're not down here. It means we can vanish our activities in second, like taking a breath. But I'm not here for his office, I'm here for his personal space.

He's a stubborn motherfucker, one whose proclivity for denial takes him all the way into the stratosphere, especially when it comes to certain dark-haired beauties, but he might have her in his bed.

I push open his bedroom door. The dark colors are strong with him, but I don't see Angel.

More importantly, like with Reaper's room, I don't smell her. In fact, apart from the faint scent embedded in her room, I don't smell her here at all.

Which is fucking odd.

My heart clenches again and with that sensation, coldness spreads, rising up the back of my neck, like fear for her.

Liz should be here. End of fucking story. Not traipsing away somewhere, or off with Reaper. And she isn't. She *was* here, he was out, and...and I heard her singing. I think a man would give anything to keep hearing her voice when she sings.

Maybe I just imagined it, or maybe it was more that I could feel it, since there's soundproofing. But she was here, so how can she—

I stop, looking down, then up.

Would fucking Dante shove her in one of the safe rooms?

Fuck, I don't know. But I'll find out.

I head up to the second floor, press the hidden button that effectively hides the floor below so it looks like it's just more wall. I then go into the storeroom and grab some bottles, and head on up.

It's overkill, what I did, but I prefer that to being caught with our dicks out.

I shove the door open, and carry the bottles out, putting them down. The look Darcy shoots is all I need.

In the office, I hear Dante reaming someone out in pure Dante-style.

"You heard me," he says. "This is private fucking property. A legit business with all the paperwork. Liquor licenses paid and up to date. On display. And I'm happy to show you our books, if you have a warrant." He pauses. "That's right, Trevor, they need just cause and a warrant."

Our lawyer's one of the top alpha lawyers in the city, possibly the east coast. He's a criminal lawyer who's schooled in Council ways and reach and politics.

There's a man in a suit who's definitely upper law enforcement, and the Council woman who looks like she'd rather be anywhere but on Unholy Trinity ground, and a boy in blue who is poking around near the stage. The little shit's on our payroll.

He's lucky it's me and not Reaper.

Reaper would mark him for death. Not for coming here—chances are the cop had no say in that—but for what he's doing, touching the dancers' belongings, and edging out the tablet, one that Sierra uses with the girl's numbers and schedules on it.

That, in Reaper's eyes, is worthy of death. The girls work for us, fall under our protection and he takes that job seriously.

I stare at the cop until he feels the prick of my gaze and looks up.

He flushes brick red and turns, looking at the curtains.

Creeper asshole.

"These bottles don't put away themselves," Darcy says.

I go over to her. "Looking to be fired?"

Her voice drops like mine. "Maybe I'm saving your ass."

"Or you covet my ass. What do you think? Better than Julien?" I turn slowly, showing her.

She laughs. "Hardly."

"A word like that gets you unemployed, quick," I say.

We start putting the bottles away. And I start chatting to her about the boring shit, inventories, what's selling.

She answers but I can hear the concern in her voice, and as I pull out the paper version to go against the one on the device, she asks, "Reaper?"

"I don't know. Not here. I texted but he's smart enough to keep away." I pause. "Liz?"

She doesn't respond, but her mouth tightens.

"What?" I ask.

"Dante."

"With him?"

"No idea."

But I do. I don't hear her and since the raiding party, such as it is, hasn't left, but hasn't done much, it means they're here for her and any dirt on us they can find. Good luck on the latter, but the former? If she's in the safe room, then she's okay.

But it's a game of chess in the manager's office, one that Dante's playing very carefully.

Both sides want to see who gives up information first.

I've seen him do this thousands of times. For someone with a hot temper, he can be fucking carved ice, heartless.

My money's on him.

Then a thought comes to me. We've been making the bite known.

Maybe they think it's a fake or...shit. I hold that thought. The man in the suit makes a line for downstairs. Darcy moves to block his way as do I.

"I think," I say, as pleasantly as I can, "that you need a warrant to go any further."

"It might help if you cooperate," the man I dub Goon says.

I smile broadly. "It might help if you have just cause. Move."

"Oh, fucking show him, Knight," Dante says.

I sigh, leading the way. The only thing back there, apart from the storeroom, is the security room with the monitors showing the store room, the bars, the floors, the front of house, and outside. I see Julien give up his post of keeping the invaders upstairs away from anything, and he goes back to what he was doing, which was setting up for tonight. The bartender, Mason, doesn't turn from his inventory and Dante herds the others to the foyer.

"Your friends are going," Goon says.

He reaches out to touch one of the monitors but I slap his hand away. "Don't, you'll turn it off and this system's touchy. She's frigid, doesn't like men playing with her. Goes cold and plays dead when they do."

Goon frowns.

"You'll fuck it up and it'll take me half the day figuring out how to turn it on. We need it working in case there's trouble." I pause. "You know. Bar trouble? A patron acting out? You have been out for a drink, right?"

He grunts.

I take that as a yes.

"So let's not cause any issues by knocking out the feeds," I say.

I march him out and the tall woman, an alpha, gives the place a visual once over.

She's older, beautiful, with ice blonde hair and the kind of regal expression that can castrate a man at twenty paces.

The woman turns to Dante.

"Dante?" Her nose wrinkles as she says his name. She clearly doesn't hold with the old school adoption of a one name moniker for pack members.

There's a familiar air about her, but I can't place it. She's on some kind of blockers, something sophisticated because there's not even a whiff of scent about her, and usually she'd give off something, even if it was subtle.

"You're busy. I won't keep you." He meets her gaze. "We're busy, too."

Did he just use his voice? On another alpha?

"We'll be in touch, Dante," she says. "Soon."

He nods to Julien who opens the door. "Only if it's on neutral ground, in court, or at your grave. If it's here, you'll need an invitation or a warrant, and this doesn't seem your kind of place, Councilwoman."

"President."

"Candice," he says.

She looks around. "Where's the third?"

He just raises a brow.

"The third," the Councilwoman, Candice, says. "You're the Unholy Trinity. It's in the name."

"Goodbye," he bites out. The merest hint of his alpha voice infusing the words. A little stronger. I pick it up for sure, and only because I know him. But yeah, it's just so she obeys, not enough for her to notice. "Our lawyer will be filing an official complaint."

That's the interesting thing we three have in common.

We rarely use the *voice.*

I would use it in sex games a little, before I found it didn't make it as fun anymore.

I don't think Reaper uses it. And Dante?

He'll do what it takes for the results he wants. The voice can bring attention when it's used full force.

This subtle use of it is pure and unadulterated control.

Candice nods, a small frown forming, like she's suddenly got things to do. "You do that." She turns and sweeps out, her entourage following.

The moment they're gone, Julien locks the doors.

Dante motions around the place and everyone starts searching in case a bug was planted.

But we come up clean.

"Didn't think they had enough time. This wasn't planned. It felt...desperate," Dante says.

"You need me, Dante?" Trevor, our lawyer, asks.

"No, have whatever you want, on the house. You did good."

"Yeah, well, no warrant means they were looking for information, getting a lay of the land. Of you. This girl, why do they want her?" Trevor wants to know.

"To marry her off." Dante pauses. "Actually, stay for a few drinks. I have some things to run past you. Client-lawyer privilege."

Darcy turns in a circle. "We've lost money today. We had to shut down all illegal operations. I don't think we should open tonight, not downstairs. Keep it up here, small crowd."

It's going to cost us more but she's right, and honestly, at this moment, I don't care.

Dante's gaze hits her. "We can use the time to set Lizette up right for her act." He turns. "Trev?"

"I'll take one drink." Trevor sits, and Dante goes behind the bar, fetching a bottle and glasses and coming back to sit with the lawyer while Mason helps with putting things back.

"Get her and work out the act," Dante says to Darcy. "There can be stripping but nothing exposed. Just a tease. Run it past me when you're done."

"Want to wait for Sienna?" Darcy asks.

He shrugs. "She can check it when she gets in."

I put my hand on Dante's shoulder before he turns his attention back to Trevor. "Where is she?"

"Safe room leading from the office on the club floor."

I stare at him. "Jesus, that one locks on the inside automatically."

"They all do."

"That one, Dante," I say, "needs a code to get out. Did you give it to her?"

"It's in there." The asshole doesn't look the least bit concerned.

My hands coil tight. "Does she know?"

He pours two drinks and spins to look at me. "She can get out. You know how it works. She's not fucking stupid and as much as you like your games, she's not a fucking child." He pauses as he takes me in. "She's ours, for all intents and purposes, so I'm not putting her in there to leave her for fucking dead."

Trevor doesn't look. Neither does anyone else. And I glare at fucking Dante. "Just how is she ours if we don't want to keep her, like you insist on saying?"

"And you're sickeningly in love with her. You want to keep her."

"And you?"

Dante doesn't answer. Not for a long time. He leans back, sips his drink, only the tight hold he has on the glass gives me any indication of his turmoil, whatever the fuck's going on with him.

"Like I told you, she's going to perform, do an act. You can help Darcy. Get Angel, and go help pick the song and outfits. Tonight, we'll perfect the act. After that, I'm going to headline her here. Down in the club. She'll sing, make us money, make her money, and they won't be able to touch her. She'll drive men crazy, knowing they can't touch our omega."

"And the fucking Council?" I ask.

"Do they have a leg to stand on?" he asks Trevor.

The man sighs. "It's more a matter of what they think they can do. Even if she's marked and you've essentially made a life bond with her, they can make that life fucked."

"Even for us?"

"That's Candice for you. She's ruthless. If you have leverage, that changes things." He shrugs. "That's all I know."

"What kind of leverage?" Dante leans forward.

Trevor clutches his drink. "Depends on the circumstances."

I look at Dante. I don't like the sound of that.

"So, we got nothing?" he asks. "Fucking Knight here marked her but didn't claim her. The mark should be enough to protect her."

"You told me they have her slated for another alpha?" Trevor asks. Dante nods. "But she's not claimed, just marked?"

"Yeah." Dante refills his glass. "Just marked." He pauses. "Even marked they can take her?"

"No, but they could use that against you. And marks wear off. If she's on their system, their radar..." Trevor takes a swallow of his drink.

"Put her in a wig to perform." Dante glances my way. "*They* got nothing."

"They do." I swallow. "What if we claim her?" I rub a hand through my hair.

Dante goes still and it's the last thing he wants, would ever want. But if it's a way...

Trevor glances at Dante, then at me and sighs. "Normal circumstances, yes. You'd be fine. This—you—aren't normal. I don't know what they'll do. Marking her might allow them to watch over their omega and use that excuse to come down on you or your business partners. Claiming her is different."

"Can they do that?" I frown.

"You are criminals they can't pin anything on. If you mark an omega, as in mark her again and she's seen with you here or you claim her, then they can maybe use it. Or maybe it makes you all safe. I don't know. We're poking in the dark here."

"Not if we don't get leverage." Safe or not safe. Know or don't know. We need leverage like in any good operation. I run a finger along the edge of the bar. "We need to—"

"We'll work it out." Dante dismisses me, turning to Trevor. "What do you know about Hover Valley?"

With that, I just fucking turn and stalk off.

"Baby? Liz?"

There's a small whisper of sound, like a foot on the floor, and the only light is from my phone. I shine it on the intercom button. I press it and hold it down. "It's me, Knight."

"Knight?" Relief drenches her voice. "Where are you?"

"Outside. Are the lights on in there?"

She sighs softly, pressed up, I imagine, against the other side of the door. "Yes, but I can't get out."

The relief fades and fear's a high note in her voice.

"You need to listen to me, okay?"

Silence spreads.

"The keypad my side won't open it without you punching in a different code that only Dante has."

"What do you mean?"

"That any code on this side needs a code *your* side for the door to open."

"What? No!"

"Liz..."

She whimpers. Fuck, I went the wrong way there. "It's okay. You can open it on your side. All you need is to put in the regular door code."

"I don't have one," she snaps. "I'm sorry, I'm just...alone, scared, sore. I don't...I don't know what's happening."

Why the fuck is she sore? But one issue at a time. "You're not alone. Look in the corner to the...right? There's a vase with fake flowers." This works as a temporary prison, too. But I keep that to myself. "See it?"

"Y-Yes."

"Pick it up. There's a barcode on it. The middle six numbers? Punch those in and then hit enter."

I can hear her through the little intercom, the beep of numbers. And then..."

"Hit enter a second time."

She does, the button beeping.

A few seconds later, the door hisses with the release of the lock, and I pull the heavy thing open, sweeping her in my arms. Since it's closed off, private, I pull it shut with me inside with her, and she screams.

"No!"

"We've got the code, Liz. It's all good, baby girl."

And because I can, I kiss her into submission. Soon she's clinging, kissing me back, and they're the bone melting kind, the boner raising kind. Boner and bone melting with her are one and the same.

She tastes of worry and sweet Liz, of desperation and happiness.

Desperate from being alone and locked up.

Happy I'm here.

"Fuck, Liz, I love you."

She buries her face in my chest and breathes in as I do the same thing. We're taking each other's scents deep, like it grounds and strengthens our bond.

I hold her for a long time as she centers herself and then she lifts her head, kissing me again, before suddenly stopping and I smell why.

Fucking Dante.

"He's a prick," I say, "and I know you were with him, but I really don't care." I amend myself, "Actually, I do care, but only because he can't get out of his way around you."

"I...I know you don't. I do, and..." She swallows. "He hurt me."

Rage sweeps me, hot and wild.

"Knight, no. It wasn't deliberate," Liz says, reading me perfectly. "He... The raid happened and..."

"Oh. Shit."

He knotted and pulled out before he was down. She doesn't have to say it. I hear it in her voice. I remember an old girlfriend of mine, who wasn't an omega. She sounded like that. A sort of not-your-fault but bewildered and hurting sound.

That time, I felt bad. I mean, I did it. I didn't know what I was then, but...yeah. This time, even though it wasn't me, I hurt for her.

"Hold on."

I pull the sofa out, turning it into a bed, and search the built-in cupboard, taking out a big, fluffy blanket and pillows and throwing them on the bed. Then I kick off my shoes. She looks at me, then bends, wincing, and takes off hers.

"Dress and panties, too."

"But—"

"We have everything we need and no one's getting in. We're alone. And don't worry. I'm not going to have my way with you. Trust me."

She gives me a doubtful look, but she does as I ask, and we slide under the covers. I'm dressed, she's naked, and I pull her in against me. I put one hand on her burning stomach, the other cupping her between her legs and she spoons into me.

My touch seems to soothe her, and she goes weak.

"Oh, that feels so good."

"I'm glad, Liz."

She rubs her cheek against me, no idea how difficult this is, how much I want to feel her up, take it further. But she needs to heal, and this is the only way I know how.

And then she says, voice sleep heavy, "I'm in love with you, too."

It makes everything better.

I must have passed out at some point, because I awake to sweet kisses and her on top of me. I want nothing more than to slide into her, but we need to get upstairs. "Liz, don't be a minx."

"I'm not. I just woke up with you everywhere. Funny, that he warned me off all of you."

I go still. "Did I miss something?"

"No, I was just thinking of that guy who warned me the night I met you. The one who was also at the restaurant. He moves like Reaper."

I go utterly still. "Is he blonde?"

She frowns and nods. "Yes."

"And he moves like...like a ghost?"

"Yes, like Reaper."

I gently push her off me. "Fuck, Liz. Get dressed. We need to find Dante now. That's Ghost. Ex-Unholy Trinity. Our enemy."

THIRTY-SIX

Reaper

"And that's what I think, you fucking asshole," Knight snaps.

I walk into the joint five days later, take one look, and light a cigarette.

This scene is one for the books. I usually run through most things in my head, all the scenarios, but Dante on the floor of the main office downstairs, with Knight standing over him, breathing like he's just discovered oxygen isn't one of those in my mental roll.

Not even once has it played out in the internal scenario playbook.

Probably because it's rare for Dante to get blindsided.

Even rarer that he's staying down. Not fighting back.

Dante allowed this.

Interesting.

I take a drag on my cigarette and catch sight of the cause of this little act of defiance and violence.

Pretty fucking Liz.

Her hair's damp, and her cheeks are pink from both water and shock, and she's in jeans and a sweater and her feet are bare.

We make eye contact right as Dante speaks.

"One. You got one shot. And that's only because I fucking let you. That shot? The one you took? It's done and fucking dusted now. So cut the dramatics and keep your fucking holy thoughts to yourself." He rubs his chin and shakes his head. "We're the Unholy Trinity, not *Holy*. Fuck."

I wait as she drifts over to me. "It's my fault," she whispers.

"Everything's your fault," snarls Dante, and she flinches. Then he takes the clearly begrudging hand offered by Knight, and lets the kid haul him up.

Me?

I wouldn't give any chances to a punk ass kid like Knight.

What there would be is blood.

But that's me.

They exchange a look. Then Dante takes one step toward us. Toward her.

"Everything's your fault," Dante repeats. "Except that. I am sorry, Angel. Like I said at the time. It was that or get caught and risk the Council..."

Liz's cheeks flare red. "I'm fine."

Knight—fucking Knight—growls.

"No, you're not. He fucking—" Knight stops, shakes his head. "Not cool, man. Totally not fucking cool."

Now Dante turns to him, grabs his shirt, and walks him back, slamming Knight against the wall. The man's out of patience, and Knight's lucky he's a member of the Trinity, one of us, otherwise...

The Trinity would be looking for a new member.

The kid's lucky.

I know that look from Dante.

It's *the* look, the one from when we did anything to

survive, before we had to part ways as our paths separated. I had things to do, things I wasn't risking the only person I'd call a friend to accomplish. The only person who'd probably get killed for me.

Some missions need to be done alone.

That was one.

We can sometimes be very similar.

We're extremely dangerous, just in our own way. He's the yang to my yin.

It's still there, this savage and dark version of him. Mine's a cooler, deeper black where, when I reach it, emotion doesn't exist.

Except maybe around this dark-eyed girl.

The one who looks and sees the me that Dante once saw.

Maybe she sees more. And I...I feel. With her, I feel. Deep.

It's overwhelming.

Maybe that's why she's standing near me now, like I'm some fucked up savior.

I'm not.

At least, not so most would recognize. Or see.

I'm a killer.

And for her, triply so.

The black humor of the word *triply* isn't lost.

I still feel the fury, that dark, viscous and sickeningly violent fury that swamped me when I saw that man push her, threaten her.

I killed him.

I killed him because I needed to, because I wanted to, because no fuck who did that should be allowed another breath.

When he fucking touched her, passion boiled and spat. So the man died.

Here she is, choosing to fucking stand near me like I'm not a demon conjured from Hell.

I'm at the point where I can even say that if Dante did

something to actually hurt her, deliberately, I'd kill him, too. And I'd never thought I'd get to that point, especially for an omega.

The way she's looking at him, how she shifts, even now, reveals to me what happened. And how she blames herself for it.

The only crime I see here is from Dante who's snarling blame at her.

Sometimes, he's a real cunt.

"You had your chance, *Griffin*," he says, using Knight's real name. "Do not make me put you down. You know me."

I blow out smoke.

"It's my fault," she whispers again.

I cut a long look at her. "Stop, Liz. It's not you." Then I look at them. "He lashed out. He didn't mean it."

Liz makes a small sound. "But..."

She shifts a little closer to me. Maybe she likes warming herself in the heat from Hell that rolls off me. Maybe I need a drink.

"You're fine, Liz." There's one thing she does that I pick up on, and I don't even think she notices. She does it when needing comfort. "Hum or sing."

"Reaper?"

"It makes you feel better. Calms you." More than I do, and I don't have to talk. Though I don't mind talking with her.

She does, it's a soft sound, no words, haunting in a way, like it's barely formed, like it came before speech, and I understand it.

Liz starts to settle a little more as she hums her feelings and it's good against my psyche. I let it flow undisturbed for a few beats.

Then I take another drag on my cigarette. Their bards are getting boring. Besides, time to end their bullshit. "I have information."

They don't listen.

I wait again.

The raid happened five days ago, and I've only been back briefly. The tensions when I did return were thick.

Thick and all about Liz. Dante's ice and anger, Knight's protective and growling over her. And Liz?

The hum twists into something else, like when I saw her last. The vibrations I picked up. Pent up energy, nerves.

Because after the fucking raid Dante made her get up on stage. And I was there. Every fucking time. In the dark at the back and under the potent spell her singing creates.

Fuck, she was a vision.

One night blonde bombshell, other nights with long, curling red hair. And the slink of her outfits were alluring on their own. Men sat forward for the girl who came on that stage, a little lost, pure innocence, the sex its own hum of sound around her. And Liz?

She would dance a little, and all the fucking punters thought they were in for hot nakedness, a sex show, something new.

They got something new.

Liz stripped off gloves, a top. A skirt, what the fuck ever, down to rivers of soft satin and silk lingerie that showed nothing and lit imaginations on fire.

Little girl lost in too much make up, the wig that changed her.

And then she started to sing.

Her voice is worthy of the name Dante has for her; Angel.

But there are so many angels.

The soft fluffy ones so fucking pure they hurt somewhere in the back of the throat. The ones who cut down the disbelievers and unworthy with a bloody and just sword.

And the ones who fell, and have seen the wrongness of the world, tasted it. Those who've looked the devil in the face and walked to tell the tale.

They all have voices.

They all cast spells.

They all come from her.

And when she sings, each and every time I came in over the last five days, including when the club was shut down and Knight got her to work out the moves, helped pick some songs, she controlled every single man.

Every. Single. One.

No one speaks when she sings.

They follow her every movement. Every note.

And while she's performed the four nights we've been open down here, business thrives and grows each night. The crowds who want in are bigger than the night before.

The angel who sings and doesn't show so much as a nipple.

Thing is, I prefer the wordless song. The power of her hum.

Her elemental magic she has in those notes.

I get a bottle of whiskey that's sitting on the edge of Dante's desk and two glasses that are sitting near it. Both clean. I pour a finger in each and hand one to Liz.

I down mine.

She holds hers, and she stops humming, thank fuck. There's only so much undoing a man can take, and she takes a swallow. Her previously unadorned nails are vixen red. They match the slinky dress and flame red wig from last night.

I wouldn't recognize her here as that woman up on the stage, which is the point.

Dante and Knight haven't stopped snarling at each other, and I'm fucking done. I don't need this and neither does Liz.

Their altercation has been festering since the raid. And since then, she's filled the place with her scent, and I'm betting she's fucked Knight exactly once during those five days as the place once smelled like them both.

She hasn't fucked me. I haven't been here more than to grab some sleep and her shows. And she hasn't fucked Dante. Or perhaps he hasn't fucked her.

It doesn't matter. What matters is that Ghost is definitely here in Starlight City.

Liz has seen him. Just one of the reasons I'm hardly around. I'm the only one who can track him, apart from, perhaps, Dante, but those two...their history.

The man betrayed Dante and Dante isn't New Testament. He isn't turn your fucking cheek. He's fire. Brimstone. The circles of hell. He's all the stories of vengeful gods and dark warriors.

Ghost is slippery. He'll play on that.

It's better if I try and find him.

I have all the players in a row. The ones I think are relevant.

There are people I've eliminated. Rival packs who rule other parts of the city, those from other cities. I contemplated them.

There are some who'd swoop in to pick over our carcasses.

And maybe others who'd want our power enough to try and join with another power to take over. Though that seems farfetched to me. We run the city. We rule crime.

Besides, the Council's somewhere in the mix and none of them would throw down with those fucks.

And without the might of an organization as strong as the Council, none of them would take us on, not even if they thought they had a small chance of winning. Because networks exist for a reason. Somehow manage to take us down and the network would eat the intruders alive. We might be gone, but someone who knows our ways will step in to protect it all.

It's convoluted and the kind of shit that bores me, but it's there, and I get it. I just leave it to the Dantes of the world.

Besides, our enemies would join us before having a thing to do with the Council.

I keep coming back to that.

It's right, it fits.

Someone like Ghost fits.

The Council and some outside power I don't know about fits.

Council and Ghost? Fits.

He knows how we work, and he knows how this world works. Ghost's now an outsider, operating like he's always preferred, even when he was one of us, alone.

He wouldn't be above using the Council to get what he wanted and then just disappearing.

If he's going against us, forming unsavory alliances, then it's not our power, our money, or our connections he wants.

It's revenge.

Destroying us.

That's a double fit for him.

And the Council?

I keep coming back to the President, Candice.

Because it isn't enough they want a little omega who escaped their grasp until her father died. Not even for that weird ass arranged Council coupling they've apparently planned. Hover's small potatoes. The pack's small. If there's an importance to this that I'm missing, I don't know what it has to do with Liz. There are plenty of pretty omegas who are loyal to the Council that they could offer up.

There is something else.

Something personal or some kind of knowledge she has and doesn't know.

That's something I'm looking for, too.

I flicker my gaze around the room once more.

"Get past whatever this is, now." I don't raise my voice, but I've had enough, and Knight stalks up, pulling Liz to him. "The asshole fucked her."

He glares.

"You've fucked her," I say.

"He knotted," Knight grinds out. "He pulled out before he was done. As in before his fucking knot was down."

Yeah, just as I thought.

I glance at her. Liz's face is flame and she's studying the floor. The misery sharpens her scent, and she starts to talk.

"I'm okay, I told him. I'm fine."

"Of course she is. And I said sorry," Dante mutters. "I had to, or they would've found us otherwise."

Knight shoves a finger at him. "Then you shouldn't have knotted. Don't you lecture me about shit and do...well, *that*."

"I didn't mark her," Dante snarls.

I pour another fucking drink and down it.

Fuck me for having to play mediator.

"Knight," I say, "she's an omega. That can happen, but she heals, and it sounds like it wasn't carnage."

"I didn't...bleed, it just..." She lifts her gaze. "Can we not have this conversation? It's my body."

She pulls away from him, from all of us, and stomps off.

It's just us. Dante and Knight continue to glare at each other.

"You told her my name, man," says Knight, clearly settling on the less of the evils in the room.

"You've been mooning over her like an idiot," Dante snaps, "so I figured she already knew."

Knight throws himself into a chair that's ended up pushed against the sofa. "Sorry if one of us cares."

"Stop, both of you." They look at me. "The Council is trying to smoke her out and I'd like to know why."

"Well, Trevor says Hover Valley's inconsequential in terms of power, but it's an important cog in getting a whole lot of scattered packs to come into line. And those packs are on land that's worth a lot of money in terms of farming, mining and the rest. The wilds, some call it," Dante mutters.

"Wilds?" I ask.

Dante pushes back his hair. "If Hover Valley was in the hands of the Council then the pack would soon be, too. This Craig hasn't wanted to play ball. He gets women, he has kids.

A mate from the Council is...stable. That's never floated or inflated any part of him."

"Except a young beauty like Liz." Knight says. "She would."

"So would others." I frown. "Why's she so important?"

"She's on the most wanted list," Knight says. "Elias's kid."

I glance at Dante.

When he doesn't say anything, I'm forced to add more. "She's the most wanted man's daughter, sure. Let's go there. She belongs to Elias. A rebel back in the day when she was a baby. But she really has nothing to do with that. So why her?"

"No fucking idea," he says. "But I'll play with Knight's theory. Hot girl, rebel's kid... Maybe the Council wants to stick it to outliers? Make an example out of her? Then..."

"It's all conjecture." I still think the Ghost thing fits. Somehow. "But we have pieces and no connector."

Except maybe Angel—I mean, Liz—but I can't see how yet.

"We can go out and bait the hook, see if anyone's biting," Dante says, peering at me. "You said you have information. Anything on Ghost?"

"It's Ghost. He's definitely in town, in some dark haunts. Seen talking to old school rebels, new ones, and Council, but beyond that? Nothing really, just he's here, he's making rounds," I say. "And he just might fit."

I need my hands on him.

I concisely outline my thoughts.

"You can find him," Knight says. "Bring him down, Reaper."

Knight's on his feet now. and this time, I approach him. "We've done this before. There are fires everywhere. I think they're distractions. Raids and arrests on small places, people canceling orders. It's part of a smoke out. Get working on that, find out everything you can. And when we open tonight, be upstairs for some of it. We need you here, Knight."

"She's not fucking bait."

"Tonight, she is. And do me a favor? Get me everything you can on her father, from way back. He was part of a pack. Something happened," I say, my cigarette down to nothing. I find an old whisky glass and dump it in there. It hisses.

"I've looked into Connor Roth."

"Look into his real name, Elias Enver," I say.

"I have—"

"Do it again, Knight. And start with the Alberto pack, where the misfits went. And look for a man and a baby."

We're both in black. Dante's in a three-piece suit. I have trousers on and a long-sleeved sweater.

In between us in the back of the car is a gorgeous redhead.

Liz looks exotic, older, prime material for wet dreams everywhere.

And the tension pulsates with sexual awareness.

Dante runs his fingers along her thigh, parting her thin cloak to take in her dress. It's a dark, shimmery gold and gives the illusion of nakedness as it paints her body, but shows nothing except expanses of flesh.

I'm fucking hard, and I'm betting he is, too.

"Ready, Angel?" he asks softly.

She looks at him, leaning towards him, her body language full of emotions I don't think she knows she's showing, and his is speaking to her right back.

Not that I'll tell him. He's not just into denial, he's actively *in* denial.

She hums before she speaks and fuck it's electric, hot. Pagan, and that wordless sound grabs me by the balls. Him too, from the power emanating from him.

She stops but the wordless song still vibrates through bones, heating blood.

"I don't know what we're doing. Are either of you going to tell me?" she asks.

"Playing cat and mouse." Dante's under her fucking spell and doesn't see it. He traces the line of her lip with his finger. "Someone's trying to pull our house down and you're helping us smoke them out. Knight's shut the club for a private event. So you're supposedly performing."

Her tits rise and fall in uneven, rapid breaths and I can smell that extra bloom of her sweet gardenia scent where it rolls into a more potent and sexual air, announcing her arousal.

Her hum also strengthened it.

She's dangerous in the way she wraps rooms of men, even women, around her finger when she sings. And the thing I noted is, she doesn't know it, either. She's so lost in the song. Once she warms up and once she's over the hump of self-awareness, the sweet awkwardness of her strip tease that shouldn't work actually does. The moment her song starts, and she doesn't have to open her mouth for it to be felt, she's lost in it, and she flourishes.

It's like peeping in on something you shouldn't.

A titillation you don't expect.

Power.

And I've never, ever seen anything like it, like her.

Back in the day, we would go to filthy sex clubs, get our fill of the omegas, gammas, and deltas selling their wares. But the betas? Oh, shit, now that was fucking beyond. There was nothing like screwing the ones who wanted their mettle tested, who liked size and pain, and we cut our kinky teeth on those girls.

The betas were the most fun. Because the omegas there were always so beyond submissive. Even if they weren't in life, they played it, played at that little wife bullshit some alphas get off on. Or the betas who wanted a taste of that style of pure submission.

But we discovered something as we moved through the lowest clubs to the most exclusive.

It didn't matter how expensive they were—all those sex clubs had that layer of filth, the air of need and desire, of secrets sold and traded. We learned, tweaked the idea of submission, and of what men want.

But first? We built our trade on places like the one we're going to.

It's a higher class, a place where those in power go. Criminal and Council, and everyone in between. If they can afford it, they come here.

For the experience, they'd get in the lowest of brothels.

This is just done up in velvet and cash. Nothing more.

We have five on our list tonight, and this is the one I've got down as the hub.

I look at Dante but he just gives me a raised brow. So I explain.

"We think the raid was meant to get to you and put pressure on us. It didn't, but someone's fucking with our shit. Someone wants their hands on you. I've been putting out fires, dealing with problems, since then. So we think it's time to go where people talk." I look at her. "We used to go to places like this, with a woman or to pick up women. And information. It's a sex club."

"And you're our party favor," Dante says.

I shoot him a mild look that he ignores, and his little twist of the knife in her works.

"Well, you can pick up a girl easily," she snaps. "Or take one of a million women who'd love to do this and have the experience."

Dante wraps his hand around her throat and squeezes and

she makes a sound, another wordless note, one that makes my cock twitch. This is hot. And she's ours. To do with what we want.

And her little protector isn't here.

If I'm thinking this, so is Dante.

Dante and I push things to the edge. Always have, always will.

It's still yin and yang, but we push things, sex, foreplay to the edges, sometimes beyond.

She needs Knight's soft ways with her.

And she needs the rough primal shit from me, the hardcore treatment from Dante.

She's turned all the way on. Fucking dialed up and ready to come.

He brings her in, kissing her deep, smearing her lipstick, and then he shoves her at me.

Before she can do anything, I push a hand under her short skirt and shove a finger into her hot, wet cunt, take hold of her nape beneath the wig and drag her in, kissing her hard.

While I do that, fingering her, Dante pulls her thighs apart and shoves two of his fingers in her as well. We work her together, stretching her. Now he takes her mouth, tugging one of her tits free.

"Tell me how I make you fucking feel," he says. "Tell me you're not ready to crawl over glass for a taste of my cock."

She moans, and my blood is hot and thrumming as I lean in, angling her with my free hand while we finger fuck her. He ravishes her mouth and I close mine around her exposed, turgid nipple, biting and sucking her.

"And," Dante goes on, "tell him you don't want him to chase you down, make you bleed, wreck your ass. Go on, I fucking dare you."

Liz comes. And holy fuck, the way her cunt crushes at our fingers is almost fucking religious.

He pushes her at me again, freeing her other tit, and I take her mouth in a deep kiss, licking and dueling with her tongue, running mine over her teeth, plundering her mouth deep, as Dante maneuvers her his way.

Liz is gasping, panting, moaning into me. She's hot and getting hotter, her skin velvet, her body electric.

She starts to come again but Dante releases her, pulling out and dragging my hand from her, too.

"No!" Liz tries to make us touch her again but I know what he's doing. It's not my jam, but I like it when she's so fucking open like this. "Please! I want it. All of it. And you know it... you...you fuck, Dante. I hate you. I need you. Please... Knight would tell you not to be mean."

Shit. Wrong words.

But I don't interfere because she's a fucking vision of depravity right now.

Spread out, everything on display, a woman who's just been fucked.

"Oh, Angel," Dante says against her ear, his fingers dancing over her folds. "Your little get out of jail card's not here. Guess what? He's to blame for me cutting you off from more pleasure."

She tries to focus, to sit up. "What—"

"Your boyfriend's to blame for hitting me."

Her eyes snap to focus. "Griffin?"

I laugh. Oh man.

"Don't call him that." I pull her top up, aware the car's stopped. Time to end the fun and games.

"Keep out of it," Dante says.

I motion my head to the tinted window. "We're here."

"So?"

"We've got shit to do." I sigh before making sure Liz is covered. I give her time to pull herself together. "Dante did bad there by revealing Knight's name. It isn't his to tell you."

"Fuck that little prick," Dante mutters, tugging her skirt

down a little more. "Come on. You look like you just got fucked. It's perfect. So play along in there."

"And if I don't want to?" she asks.

"Still play along," he says. "Angel, we're here to catch a ghost if we can."

THIRTY-SEVEN

Lizette

I don't recognize myself when I catch a glimpse in the dark sex club's mirrored walls. It's over the top sensuality in the body of a sexy, wanton stranger, and I hate the three alphas.

Just like I want more of what Dante and Reaper did in the back of the car.

Dante pulls me to him, a hand wrapping around my thigh, as Reaper orders drinks. Dante glances lazily around and then kisses me as his fingers roam up, under my skirt.

I'm quivering, on the brink of coming in front of all these people. Just from the thought of what he might do, and the way I'm at his mercy to be degraded and exalted, to be the pleasure bringer. The receiver, whether I say I want it or not.

And then he actually touches me, a finger that slides along the crease where my inner thigh stops near my pussy lips.

My heart thumps and he pulls back and smiles a dirty, sleazy smile, like he can feel that thump, and I know he can feel the new layer of wetness, of need. I shift, meaning to move away because I know I should, but instead I go to him, anxious for more.

"Angel, you're such a fucking filthy girl under the innocence, aren't you?" He strokes that spot, leans in. "Admit it, you got hot with two alphas fighting over your little cunt."

"No."

"Yes." The gloat's almost too much and anger surges, loathing too, mixing with the lust. And he laughs. "Hate me, Angel, but you want me to fuck you here and now, don't you?"

I want to say *no* again, I do, but it refuses to come.

He nudges the hair from the wig away from my ear and presses his magic mouth against it. "You want it, I know. But, Liz, when you sing, tell me, do you want those men who pant and watch your every move, all with hard and aching dicks in their pants to touch you? Have you? Taste you?"

I turn my head, and our lips are almost touching, and I'm infused with him. His smell, his presence, his heat. "And if I do?"

"You don't."

"I fantasize about them all."

His growl runs through my veins, and I shiver with desire, wanting to rub up against him. We might be alone in here except for Reaper, because no one else exists. Not one person other than them.

"Thank fuck your honest streak appeals because lying isn't your forte. There are exactly three men you want and two of them are in this room. And you want me no matter how often you wish you didn't."

Then he kisses me again.

I expect the onslaught but this time it's light, slow, the kind of kiss designed to slay with stealth. When he lifts his head, his hand's moving again.

Dante goes slow, parting my folds, running his fingers along my inner lips down to my ass and then up to my clit.

There's a part of me that's screaming, wanting to know if

everyone can see, and another part that doesn't care, that likes this wild exhibitionism.

And as he slowly begins to tease by pushing his finger in and out, deeper and deeper each time, and he looks past me, right as Reaper presses against me and his mouth finds mine.

It's heaven.

Hell.

Wild.

Perfection.

I'm already melting, and I lose form completely under the administrations of Reaper's magic tongue. I'm falling apart, coming together, falling apart, and each time it's different, like when I rebuild, another piece of me is exposed for their pleasure.

Reaper thumbs my mouth open and strokes in with his tongue and every part of me wants to stretch in opposite directions all at once. I want to reach up and meld with him, and also sink down on Dante's hand, rocking until I come.

"Liz," Reaper says, breaking the kiss, "I have to make some rounds. Stay with Dante."

And with that, he's gone and I'm bereft.

Then Dante pulls me down, on his hand and on his lap. He's thrumming my clit, pounding his fingers into me, and I roll back into him. "Don't come, Angel. Don't. Fight it. I'm going to take you to the edge and then I'm stopping. I'll do it a few times."

"And then I can come?" I'm panting.

He keeps the rhythm and I'm melting into pools of hot desire, of need, my body aching for the thing he's telling me to deny myself.

"I don't know," he murmurs, picking up his drink and feeding some to me. "Can you?"

It's getting hard to focus. And I'm trying to remember this is for show. But I keep losing track of that, the battle to not come is taking over fast.

Dante puts down his drink and skims a hand down over me, and cool air touches my upper thighs, and around my open pussy.

Oh hell, he's lifted my skirt and everyone can see what he's doing and I almost come. His fingers keep up that rhythm in me.

I need to come. It's not a want anymore, it's a need. I'm tingling, aching, so hot and liquid that I can feel the fever pitch rise higher, unspooling my thoughts until I'm just sensations.

"Liz? Angel? Focus, look around. Anyone you see?"

I'm breathing fast, heavy. "I...I can't."

He stops. I look down; the top of his hand keeps moving, but he's pulled his fingers out, and I nearly scream in frustration. "Angel, do it."

I blink, trying to focus and pretend he's still got me on that brink. I'm there, but it's the side of horrible frustration, the one that tells me I'm not coming, and I hide that response as I loll my head and see a man, glaring. He's half focused on my pussy, the rest is on Dante. And it's hate I see.

I know who it is.

He recognizes me, too.

Somehow, I shimmy down my skirt, pull free of Dante, and turn. I flip the script and kiss him hard. And then hands on his face as his grips my ass, I say, "In the far corner, past the stage with the dancer, the corner near the bathrooms. Jake."

He goes stiff, and I'm holding him down. Not that I'm that strong, but the pressure I can exude is enough to stop him storming off and spilling blood.

I'm relieved when familiar hands catch my hips.

"That asshole is here." Reapers fingers bite into me. "We can't kill him, Dante."

"Fuck," Dante says.

The asshole starts our way. He could cause trouble and before anyone can do anything, I whisper, "I can fix this."

"Nothing to fix. We ignore him," Dante says in a way that says *ignore him while he lays bleeding on the ground.*

Reaper cuts him a look. "Lizette?"

One of the topless waitresses walks by and I grab her and ask the one thing I never have before.

"Hi," I say, "Can we speak to the manager? I want to know if I can sing."

The lights are too bright and I'm glad but also frightened because they're slightly lower at Pandora's.

The crowd murmurs, restless, annoyed, probably because they aren't getting to see the girl get naked and writhe up here. And I'm not taking anything off.

But the name Unholy Trinity, the names Dante and Reaper, have clout. And...I did my job because the immediate crowd of important management around us has effectively cut Jake off from coming near.

And me up here? He can't touch me.

They have a small band that plays when the girls strip and dance and tease with their burlesque.

I feel so big and exposed, so tiny and weak at the same time. They know the song I want to sing. It's an old sexy song, slowed, all about fever. One dad used to play on his phone when he wanted to liven the place, so I know it.

More importantly, it fits here.

I clutch the microphone. "H-hi. I'm Persephone, on loan from Pandora's. I'm going to sing."

"Take it all off!" someone yells.

But I turn, nod at the band, and it starts. It would be about now at the club that I'd take off small pieces, and it's always, always awkward.

This is awkward, just standing like a lump. But then the

magic happens. The music seeps into every part of me. The notes of the double bass are the beats of my heart. When the words come, I am the song.

The words of love and sex and longing fill me, the room, and all I can pick up is Reaper and Dante's scents. I imagine Knight's aroma there, too.

I move with the words and rhythm, slinking down, off the stage, the spotlight moving with me, to slip along the front of the first tables, avoiding them until I reach my quarry.

Dante.

I sing, writhing down him and then I shift to my next, Reaper. I slip my arm up his chest to stroke his face, along the scars, then I release him, going back to the stage, Dante close, helping me up. There I sing until the song swells in the entire room and steals breath for itself.

When it's done the music stops and there's utter silence.

Not even a chair shifts. Not a whisper.

I lower the microphone and look out, my eyes used to the light a little more. Through the haloes of glare, I see Reaper and Dante, and all the men in the audience with their attention pinned to me, mine to use.

The room explodes into applause and Dante picks me up, taking me down and handing me to Reaper.

I can hear Dante's low voice talking in the microphone. Then feedback hits and I look. The damned man literally dropped the mic.

Of course, another round of applause bursts free and I see Jake try to get across to us, but too many people are in the way as the girl comes back on to dance.

There are people, though, men, who are surrounding us. Wanting to meet me. Reaper stands, an arm around my front.

He's enough to make them keep a distance.

Dante glares. "Fuck, Liz."

"You can't kill someone in here," I say. "What was I meant to do?"

"Let me kill the prick."

"As I said," Reaper says, "you can't fucking kill him. Lizette was smart by singing, got us attention, but he can't do a thing so don't kill him."

"Watch me."

"Not going to help things," Reaper mutters.

I clutch at Dante. "Please don't..."

"Listen to your Angel. Besides, our room is ready." Reaper downs the drink he's still holding.

I look at them. "Room?"

"We can't come here without going to a private room," Dante says. "Lead the way, Reap."

It's a room of brass and dark reds. Velvets and cushions and a vast bed. I look around, insanely curious. Plus, it gives my body a moment or two to cool down.

There's a couch and a table and some kind of weird bench. And a wall that's got chains, leather straps, and ropes.

I stop, swallowing, moving closer to touch as I take in another wall with shelves. In it are whips and small cages, and feathers. More ropes. There are masks and balls with straps, claw things with straps, and paddles and—

"If I'd know you really wanted in on this shit, Angel, I'd have taken you to the house. Or one of my play rooms I keep." Dante unbuttons his vest and strips his coat.

"W-What?" I look at Reaper, then at him.

Dante grins. "Those things you're currently touching are dildos and vibrators. New, for the room, if you're wondering. We pay premium. The rest of those are...well, you get the paddles and whips. That's a cock cage, and that...it's a spider gag, to keep your pretty mouth open while we fuck it. The one next to it, it's a ball gag so we can stop you screaming if we decide to double team your ass or shove a giant dildo up you."

I snatch my hand back.

Oh. God. I'm getting turned on.

He picks up something that looks like rubber pants in hot pink. "Piss pants? Your color, don't you think, Angel?"

I almost scream and slam back into the toys, leaping away.

"You want the dildos, then?" He closes in. "Eager..."

"Leave her be, Dante," Reaper says. "If you want to play with her, that's not the way to do it. And this isn't the time."

"We're using the room," he says, turning from me, leaving me breathing hard and weak kneed. "We can't go without using it, but just waiting it out won't do the trick. There's a look to just being fucked, and there are alphas out there who smell her. She has to be soaked in us."

Reaper looks past Dante and comes up to me. He breathes me in and my heart goes haywire. "He's right."

He takes my shoulders and drops a kiss on my mouth. Then he lets me go and leads me to the bed, sitting me down. He stands as Dante strips down to his trousers.

My mouth goes dry. Last time I saw him shirtless, we were fucking and I registered the ink, but now...

I go to him, tracing the four horsemen tattoo that covers his broad shoulder and arm, spilling up from his back and onto his chest.

It's intricate, as beautiful as the art on Reaper, but less violent and more exalted. He sits, motioning to Reaper. "Well?"

"I want to know why Ghost's back," Reaper says.

"We'll ask when we find him."

Reaper shoots him a hard look. "The trap to catch ghosts takes time."

"Ghost." Dante says. I just listen to them. "He's not going to be here, is he?"

"I'm not sure why, but I know he's been behind some of

the threats and fires I've been putting out, and dealing with." Reaper takes a breath. "I'm sure some of this has been done on behalf of the Council."

Dante frowns. "Why? He's got no love of the Council."

"He's got some kind of skin in the game." Reaper pauses. "He's been paying some, threatening pack members, and with the betas, their families."

"He's got backing." Dante considers Reaper. "And he's been here?"

"Often."

"Anything?" Dante asks.

Reaper doesn't say anything, but I feel the cogs in him turn. Finally he says, "Talk. Nothing more."

"You know, Reap, I get it," says Dante. "Tonight was about making noise and seeing what comes of it over the next few days. And killing that wannabe rapist is still a goal, I think. And Angel? Singing was a good idea. You control men with that voice."

A smile brushes Dante's mouth as he motions me to him, then like a god, he gestures for me to kneel. I know, in the back of my mind, I don't have to, but I do it anyway, sitting between his thighs.

"Sing again," he tells me.

"I don't want to."

"Too fucking bad. Turn on that magic for us. A private show."

Reaper takes us in and moves closer.

I don't know where it comes from but the song flows, sex and lust and need and love. That's in there, too, hidden deep beneath the seeming purity of the words. As I sing, Dante takes my hands, puts one on Reaper's cock, the other on his. I let their dicks fill my hands, the cloth nothing, their flesh so vital and warm, getting bigger and harder with each note.

When I'm done, Dante guides me in and kisses me. Reaper sinks to his knees. He peels off my hand and kisses it, and then he pulls me from Dante and his mouth claims mine in a wordless song as full as mine was.

When he's done, he hands me to Dante, who watches me. He doesn't speak.

He doesn't have to.

I know exactly what he wants.

I know.

It's like I'm mesmerized. He doesn't need to say a thing to me. But I make him wait a few beats, humming a little to stop myself devouring both of them, and finally I can't help it. Reaper stands back. Watching.

I rub my hand on Dante's hard on, over his underwear, and I kiss along his hard length, trapped in the material.

It's dirty. Erotic. Perfect.

I lean into Dante, pushing my top down, liking the pleased male light in his eyes, and then I unzip him, sucking his cock into my mouth.

"Oh, fuck, yes..." He hisses. I'm peering up, and he glances at Reaper. "How many people did you fucking kill?"

"None. Money, not violence. Ghost, spies, the Council, they'll all know we were here with a mystery guest, one we use to pull in punters. We'll hear something soon." He pauses. "But fuck that. This is way more interesting. Go on, Liz. You look amazing like that. A new pagan goddess. Both of hell and heaven."

"Fuck, you're talkative when you're horny, Reap." Dante groans as I go deep on him, needing the taste of him in the back of my throat, and though the wig's hot, I can feel the stroke of Reaper's fingers, and I pull off Dante with a pop and take out Reaper's tattooed cock.

Dante takes advantage, turning me so I'm in his lap, legs spread, and he dips into me, and he paints my ass with my slick juices.

I suck Reaper down so he's in the back of my throat, mouth stretched about him as Dante eases inside me. He starts fucking me, the pull and push something I know now, and I bounce down on him, trying to get him deeper as I urge Reaper to fuck my face.

"Oh, fuck, is she tight. Get in there, Reap, take her cunt." He pulls me off Reaper, and draws me back on him, holding me, my legs wide and back, his mouth at my ear. "We're going to fuck you up the way you like. You're a dirty, filthy girl, Angel. My kind of cunt. Perfect, pretty, willing."

I'm shaking, back up to the explosion point, all nerve ends wild and insane and ready to soak themselves in pleasure.

Reaper's still, his cock huge, erect, heavy, his gaze intent on me. My face, tits and then pussy.

Finally, he strokes his fingers through my wetness, lines up, and pushes in.

I scream, clinging to him. I've never been so full in my life, so perfectly violated and all I need to complete this is Knight. In my mouth.

I come. I can't help it. I come and come, my body going haywire, bouncing on its own on them, squeezing them.

They start to move.

Dante rises so they can use me as their fuck toy, slamming me up and down on them in hard, violent strokes that set me off all over again. My brain's melted, utter goo and I'm just a vessel for pleasure, theirs and mine.

Suddenly, I'm swept with another wild orgasm and as I fly, they do too, and we all come together.

Reaper isn't done when they pull out and Dante sits.

He puts me on the bed and spreads my legs, eating me out, pushing me to another orgasm. I try to push him away. I'm done. I'm too sensitive, but he's relentless and it turns from me writhing to get free to me pushing into him.

And someone, somewhere, is talking.

Dante.

"That's it, Angel, let him make you fly, you pretty whore. Let him show you what you are. Perfect, filthy, mine to give.

His to take. We'll get others in. Knight. Roomfuls of men, all of who can fuck you senseless, help us ruin that perfect fucking pussy. And then I'll kill every last motherfucker, let the room run red with their blood and the three of us? We'll fuck you in it, anoint you..."

I come, shaking, my body undulating and wild with the soaring pleasure.

When we're done, I'm gone.

I don't know anything. Where I am, who I am.

I'm just a mass of satiated desire, shot full of electricity, and left twitching. Boneless.

Someone dresses me, soothes me and then I'm carried out, through darkness pulsating with light and sound and smells, and then there's the bump and hum of the car and two sets of gentle hands on me.

When I come to my senses, I'm in Dante's space. He's got me wrapped in a blanket, feeding me water.

"You're back, Angel. Too much?"

The wig's gone, I note as I touch my head. And I'm in a big shirt. I look around, but it's just me and Dante and...Knight?

"Where's...Reaper?" My voice is thick, my tongue too big, and I'm sore and still needing.

They're a drug.

"He had to chase some shit down for us. Go with Knight," Dante says. "I don't need you here."

His words slap me, and I try to snap back, but by the time I sit up, he's gone.

I stare at Knight, who scoops me up, kissing me. "He's an ass."

I cling to him, needing his sweet, soft solace—the velvet-lined domination.

He takes me to my room, and when he puts me down on my bed, I'm still weak, still fevered, and it takes me a moment to know why.

"Knight?"

"Yeah?"

"I-Is Griffin your name? Your real name?"

He sits next to me on the bed and cups my cheek. "Yeah. But I'm more Knight now. I was going to tell you. It's not really a secret, I just don't use it. You can call me whatever you like." He pauses. "If you stay."

"You mean if he doesn't kick me out?"

He comes in close, arms either side of me. "No, Liz, I mean you. Don't think I don't know you've been planning to run for a while. But the world can be us, for you."

"How did you know?"

"I've been you, Liz." He brushes his lips with mine. "Go to sleep."

"No. I'm not...I'm restless, I'm not fulfilled."

Knight goes still. "You're not?"

"I had them, but I belong to you all. And tonight...I want to belong to all three. If you'll have me."

He grins. "Daddy says you bet your sweet little ass."

Knight strips off and dives under the covers, so un-Daddy like it makes me giggle. He's not being the Dom he is. He's just being him and when he pushes into me, my legs up on his shoulders, he kisses me.

"Oh, fuck, Baby Doll, you're fucking perfect." He starts to thrust, and he kisses me, hard, and soon, I'm lost in him, in the magic he weaves, and I never, ever want to leave.

Ever.

THIRTY-EIGHT

Dante

The giggling haunts me. And I want to fucking smash shit to pieces.

It doesn't matter that I had her in the most carnal, wild and dirty way with Reaper. It doesn't matter that she'd have stayed with me and let me share her with Knight.

I kicked them out and then I had to hear the fucking giggling. The fucking love talk.

Kill me now.

I head upstairs, where Julien's on day duty, keeping an eye on things and at the ready in case of trouble. Reaper's out getting dirt and Knight's meant to be doing the same. Once he finishes his fuck fest with our Lizette.

"Thoughts?" I ask.

Julien spares me a glance as he sits with a computer that has the monitor feeds. He's also at the door in case any shit comes barreling through with any shipments. We've got people on the back door, too. But Julien—along with Darcy—as my most trusted outside the inner circle, is watching those watchdogs.

"I don't fucking like it, boss."

"Me either."

There's something wrong. Reaper's spot on about it, but it's like the focus is skewed and I'm not sure how to translate that into action.

The players he's lined up are important. I just don't know who it is we need to bring down.

The Council. That fuck who tried to rape Angel—which just might be personal on my behalf. Ghost.

"When Ghost tried to betray us, take us down and strip us for parts so he could walk away the rich victor, what odds did you have of him setting foot in this fucking city again?"

Julien frowns, runs his fingers through his beard as he rests a book on the table he's at. "After what we did to him? Zero, or under that."

"My thoughts, too. And the Council? Something isn't right."

I need to draw Ghost out. Or, if Reaper succeeds in finding him, ambush him. That's assuming Reaper's after him right now. He's got other agendas, other feathers to chase.

He's obsessed with the Council and Liz's father. And I trust his instincts. He goes deep into simplicity. Over-convoluted is my game.

Just like deep dive hidden nuggets that turn out to be keys are Knight's.

Big question is, who's on the right path here? Especially when they overlap.

Because the sooner we work out who's after Liz and trying to take us down with it, then the sooner we can try to rid her of the mark and let her go.

I need to.

She's a liability.

She just is.

"It's some kind of coincidence he seemed to turn up when she did," Julien says.

I send him a sharp look. "You think she's involved?"

The irritation is so like his girlfriend's, I almost laugh. "No. I mean... It's odd and you never look away from odd. She turns up, the Council starts sniffing and there are raids and sightings of Ghost."

I start to pace. "Raids that are pure theatrics. They would have gotten a warrant if they thought they'd get anything. They were looking for her." I pause. "So how the fuck does Ghost play into that? What possible reason has he got for such low ball stakes? It's not the Trinity. Fuck."

I smell gardenias mixed with leather and honey. A touch of lavender.

Turning, it's not Angel. It's the ugly mug of Knight.

I turn back. "Go away, I'm busy."

Giggling, happy sex sounds and now him smelling like he had her sit on his face and come until she squirted? I need none of that. And it really doesn't matter—I pushed her to him, ejecting her from my room.

"If you want her to be with you, stop fucking pushing her away. She wants all of us, but," Knight says, hissing the words low, "she's better off without you. Liz deserves better."

"I just don't need you shoving your happiness at me."

"You know, Dante, I look up to you. If there's one person who I can truly call family, it's you—"

"Not Reap?"

"He's a sibling, I guess, but I look up to you. Like I said. You fucking saved me. I'll never forget it. I love you, man. But fuck. When I say you're a grade A fuckwit with a hard on for stupidity, I say it from a place of caring. You don't deserve her. There's kink and playing at edging and denial, and then there's straight up holes in the sand you like to bury your head in."

He stops, then he shakes his head, curls bouncing. "I love her," he says. "And I'm betting that Reaper does, too. She fits. She belongs and she's part of us. In ways that have

384

nothing to do with the bite. And you? You push her the fuck away."

The muscle in my jaw ticks hard.

I want her.

With a desperation I've never felt. I've fucking knotted in her. A big, fucking mistake, and one I'm obsessing over. Because I want to do it again. I want to knot her, and in the most depraved of my fantasies, have her catch my seed, grow my babies. I want to see her glow and grow big. I want her to fucking waddle and need her feet rubbed.

I don't even like fucking kids.

And the only pregnant woman I remember knowing was a full-on drug user who birthed out a poor addicted kid.

But this fucked up fantasy that's so utterly depraved it even disturbs me is there, in my head, like I want to try and knock her up. I want to bite and mark her over and over. I want to fuck her from behind while her swollen stomach sways, I want her to cry over anything and everything and crave weird shit. And I don't even know where this comes from. TV? Movies? My twisted mind?

Fuck.

"She's not mine." I keep my tone hard. "Desire is just that. Desire. And, I don't fucking like her."

It's a lie. Somewhere along the line I went from dislike to like, to something big and uncomfortable and what the fuck am I meant to do with that? It's as twisted and depraved as the rutting fantasy, the pregnancy fantasy.

I'm losing my fucking mind.

In another universe, I could, I suppose, learn to tolerate these feelings that keep bursting up into life inside me. But I'm here, and I don't have to.

"Leave it be, Knight."

He mutters something, pushing his curls back from his face and I start to turn. But he comes around in front of me, shoving a tablet at me. I swat it away.

"Look." Knight waves the tablet under my nose once more. "Look at that photo."

"To make you stop, I will." I snatch the device and my breath catches as I take in the photo.

It's grainy, not from here, but I know Ghost. "Why are you showing me a photo from some bar in Chicago?"

"Not Ghost," he says. "Who he's with."

I sigh, look again. "So?"

"Look."

"I am."

He's with a woman. Gorgeous, long curling hair, wide smile and an almost wholesome look. Not really his type.

I hand the device back. "He got himself a girlfriend at some point?" Knight shoved it to me. "I'm not really sure why this is important."

I start to give it back.

Knight pushes the tablet to me once more. "Fuck, you're obtuse sometimes. Look at her. Now picture her in a suit."

He flicks pages. It's a Council website, showing all the people who work there.

I take the device, stopping on one of the pages.

And my vision wavers a moment.

The woman from the photo with Ghost. What the fuck is her name?

Susan?

Susan Pegg... No Pem...something.

Her name doesn't matter. What matters is that she's with fucking Ghost. And she's not just Council. No. She's liaison between the excommunicated and unregistered and the Council. She works here and in an area that includes Hover Valley. I look up. "Hover—"

"Dante, not Hover fucking Valley, you dick. The woman, the Council woman? Gorgeous? Weak alpha? The one who came by. I think her name was Susan Pem or something. That's her."

"I get that. And she's working with people in Hover."

He rolls his eyes. "She's Council, of course she does, but what we need to ask is why is she dressed to the fucking nines and out with Ghost?"

"She listed playing in the mud with criminals as a hobby on her CV?" I should have pegged her as somehow off when she came in.

To be in the Council and with Ghost—the photo fucking screams with Ghost—she would have known who we all are in regards to darker history. Right? Ghost isn't a talker, but he's not someone who fucks Council, either. He's up to something.

I want my hands on him and I want him dead.

Knight taps the screen with a finger. "I'll bet you a million bucks Ghost's doing this *Susan*. And our problems, everything, is connected that way."

"Yeah, okay." I nod, and don't dismiss it. "But why is she wanting Liz?"

My heart's thudding dull and heavy as my stomach churns.

I should've known. I should have read her. I can read people. Fuck.

"How did I miss this?"

But Knight shrugs. "We all did. I don't know. Maybe that Candice Helmont wants her and this Susan—maybe she wants a promotion? She looks ambitious."

"Brings me right back to Angel. What the fuck's Liz got to do with it?" Exasperation starts creeping in because sure, Ghost might be doing this Susan or done her, but she's lower down on the rungs of real power.

She was sent into our lair because she looks higher up. She's pretty, but has some questionable taste in men, judging from the photo. She's middle management, a no one. Some power but not enough. And unless Ghost's in it for the long haul of her reaching the upper levels, I don't get what's in it for him.

Love? I almost laugh.

"Short of kidnapping her, I'm betting Ghost knows." Knight grins, getting cocky. "I know you're going to ask how we get that from him. We do that by taking him. Right, Liz?"

I glance about and frown. "Angel isn't here." Christ, he loves her. Does love warp minds?

"She isn't." He glances, too, then shoots me a glare. "You probably scared her. But she's strong. She'll be here."

I pinch the bridge of my nose. "And how do we take him?"

"We sent a message to this Susan, from Liz."

I narrow my eyes. "How's that going to work, exactly, Griffin?"

He flinches, just a little.

"Knight?" I prod.

"By offering her as bait."

I grab him and the tablet clatters. "Are you fucking crazy?"

"Supervised." He stares at me. "And it was her idea."

"Are you fucking crazy and stupid?" I shake him.

Before he can answer, Julien speaks up. "Boss? We have a problem."

Liz is outside, in the tiny alley, the one that's seemingly a dead end. Unless you're Reaper. Or Ghost. Or you know how to get in through the tunnel.

I run, bursting outside just as Ghost reaches for her. My fist connects with his face and he goes reeling.

Then he's up, and coming at me, fists flying hard, fast, dirty. He knows where my weak spots are. And I know his.

He sends me spinning to the ground and I grab his leg, twisting it so he falls. I'm on him, landing blow after blow on him. I shake him. "Why the fuck are you after her? And the fucking Council?"

"You're a fucking dinosaur," he grunts. "Stuck in your ways. I have big plans—"

I slam my fist into his face as he grabs me by the throat, he turns us, punches me.

"You always have big plans while only seeing a tiny part of the fucking picture. You're a traitor. Always have been, always will. Right up until I end your fucking life."

Ghost tries to choke me, but I knee him hard in the kidneys, right as I grab his head and give him the good old Glasgow kiss, cracking my head into his.

I shove him off me and go to grab my knife when he kicks me in the ribs, and I scuttle up to my feet. He does, too.

"Bring it on, fucker," I say.

"You think in black and white. Never seeing the nuance." He grins, laughing. "You'll never understand. I'm going to destroy you, take what you covet and destroy you by destroying her."

I drag him up, pinning him to the wall. I catch sight of Liz behind me, to my left. "Go inside, Liz. Now."

I turn and she doesn't move, so I push him away and fucking shove her even as she reaches for me, clutching at me.

"Dante—"

"Fuck, Liz, now!" I try to get her to the door and keep one eye on Ghost.

Ghost sees this, and he does what I'd do, roles reversed. He tries to take advantage, lunges at me and the door.

I whirl around and shoulder him out of the way. He comes back, swinging. He's not looking at me. His gaze is on the door and the girl on the other side.

"Close and lock that fucking door, Lizette." I grab him, holding him back and he hits my leg. It's hot and sharp. Pain lances through me. "Now."

The fucker used his knife.

The door slams, and I hold him as he plunges that fucking knife into my thigh again and again. I ignore it all the pain, his pull to get free, I just cling to the motherfucker until I hear the lock click. Then, I let him go, stepping back. I ignore the urge to buckle because of the agony and weakness that slices up through me and I gather my strength and slam my fist into his stomach.

I snarl and do it again. "Why the fuck are you here? You won't make it out alive."

"You underestimate me, Dante." His soft laughter grates against my senses and I want him dead. Gone.

Once, he meant something, his friendship, kinship. But that's fucking gone.

Nothing but dust and old memories and never-ending regret.

Nothing but fury born anew.

"Who's the Council girl?"

His smirk is too ready, his gaze too fast to glance off the locked door. "Candice won't appreciate being called girl."

"Not her, fucker. The other one." I stop, take a swing and connect with his chin, he swings at me.

The punch misses, but it's a feint and he kicks me in the thigh. I go down, rolling as he goes to punch and he hits the ground.

I'm on my feet in seconds, and if it took longer than usual and more effort, I bury it deep. I turn and face him.

"Other one?" he asks, his filthy smirk still in place.

"The one in the fucking picture." The smirk melts to nothing but hate and we both breathe heavily. I push it. "The one you've been banging."

We circle each other, ready to rip the other's throat out barehanded if we have to. I know I'm armed and I'm betting he is, too—beyond the knife I already know about.

The blood's warm and flowing, growing cool as it spreads its damp stain down my pants and my head swims.

I'm not about to staunch the flow. I'm not going to give him what he wants. Weakness. My eye off the ball. I can push through. Fuck, if he thinks he can get to Liz, he'll have to do it over my corpse.

Because it doesn't matter what he does. If there's breath left, an iota of strength, it's going toward bringing him down. It'll go to stopping the fucker in his ghostly tracks.

"Maybe it's your songbird."

"No. I know her. She's ours. Of her own volition. She's loyal, sweet, and isn't interested in you."

"Holy fuck," he says. "You have feelings for her. And you're happy to share."

"And what about you with your Council girl?" I ask. "Susan."

He takes a swing.

I dodge it. I need to conserve every scrap of energy I can. "I could kill her."

He growls and darts in, an uppercut hits that I don't have time to move away from.

"Keep away from her," he snarls. "She's got nothing to do with this."

He cares.

"You in bed with the Council?" I ask. "Or just her?"

"She's a means to an end," Ghost says. "They want your omega. I couldn't give a fuck except it's a perfect way to get my revenge. Not to mention if you've got the Hover Valley area, you're beyond rich and powerful. The little girl's perfect, and she just fell into my lap." His head tilts with realization. Then, he laughs. "Wait, you love her, the omega, don't you? That's a shame, since I'm taking her."

My chest tightens at the word *love*. "Touch her and I'll kill you, rip you apart."

"You couldn't when I was a part of your little wannabe club, and you can't now. I'll cut out your omega's fucking heart," he says. "Consider her gone. You could have saved her, marked her, had her mark you, but it's too late now. The President wants her, and I'll pick up the pieces of this place and take Hover Valley when she's done." He grins.

"How's that gonna go with you and your girl, Susan, dead?" I say. "Sounds like a more fitting end to me."

He ignores me.

"Of course I'll be the one secretly in charge...or in control of the Council through Susan. People underestimate the ones who drift through life, like me. Like Susan. I'll take everything from you and let that fat fuck, Craig, do the horrible things he's planning for his omega wife. What he and his vile sons are planning."

"They won't touch her."

"You'll be dead, Dante. By my hand. Call it payback. Call her my reward."

"And Susan? When I kill her?"

"You won't." He laughs. "As I said. You'll be dead and she'll also be mine. I might start a harem. Your omega could birth me an army. Or just be there to release tension when I'm feeling particularly cruel."

I stare. He's never been that level of vile with women. But he said it, true or not, and they're words that seal his fate.

I pull out my knife and flick it open and come at him. His knife is at the ready. He keeps circling me as I do him, neither of us coming too close or staying too far for me or even him to move. To strike.

We know each other, how we fight, the way our instincts work. There's only one way he'll go down. It's something I'd chance, too. So I go at him on my strong side, and he lashes out.

I subvert it and lean into that slash, so the knife cuts into me. The clarity of pain and its adrenaline rush allows me to come up, the weapon in my hand going in for his guts and slicing up.

I push. Hard.
Then I kick him off my knife and let him go.
He looks at me in shock.
Ghost crumples. Dead.

THIRTY-NINE

Lizette

The words that Ghost said to me play in my head as I listen to the fight, the grunts, the horrible words and what he wants to do to me. The terrible thump of a body hitting the ground.

My eyes itch and burn, and I can't move.

I don't...I don't know what happened, who went down.

There's silence, even as my ears ring.

In my hand's a note.

I crumple it and let it fall.

This is a diversion. I can see it.

And I know what I have to do. To save my men. To save their pack. He lied about the bites. He told me it was too late, that the Council would come for me no matter what. They had been trying since Dad took me.

He told me Hover Valley's a punishment for the sins of my father.

There are truth and lies in his words. And I don't like the man, no matter how appealing his scent.

He is, I think, the evil to Dante's good. They're both devils,

394

but Dante's still in the light. Ghost got twisted up and he sank.

And if I stay, that'll happen to the Unholy Trinity.

I slip into the bar, past where Julien and Knight are searching for Ghost and me, and I grab a hoodie that Mason left on the bar, and pull it on. Then I duck behind the bar, grabbing the garbage and a few things.

Those things I shove in my pockets. I'm out the door at the dumpsters with the garbage and then, I duck down and go out through the back alley.

Just like the note said.

If Dad took me, it was to protect me. I'm his daughter and no lies can say otherwise. I look like him. And he showed me nothing but love, did nothing but protect, try and give me the tools to not only survive, but live.

But the Council being after me? That I believe.

They found me too quickly after Dad died. Not immediately, but too soon. Like they were searching and the chance capture by the police pushed that over the edge.

That or this Ghost turned me in.

I flip up the hood of the jacket as I head to the Hollows, looking for the address I burned into my brain.

Along with the words, *If you want to save them...*

The Council woman Ghost mentioned, someone named Susan, he said, was waiting, risking her life. I'm not sure I believe that, but I do believe him about the Council coming for me because of my birth. And he and Dante talked about a Council girl.

Ghost said when he grabbed me, heading through the club, that the girl would help me avoid my fate.

If she's going to help.

But while I'm doing something foolhardy, my eyes are open and I run my fingers along the tools in my pocket.

3016 Denmark Street. Apartment number one. I go to ring the bell, but in the quiet of the daytime street, when this part of town sleeps, it's open.

My heart starts to thud as my senses scream. Every horror movie I've ever seen runs a similar scene through my head.

But there's nothing else to do.

If I tell Dante, they'll kill him, Knight too. And Reaper? He'll be back in prison, or dead. I can't risk it.

I take a calming breath and push the building door open and step inside.

Upstairs, I hear a TV blaring. The sweet heavy scent of weed floats from further along this floor.

Number one's to my right. I grip the corkscrew and knock.

No one answers.

My nerves jump and skitter and it takes everything I have to knock again.

This time the door opens and a man smiles at me.

It's cruel, greedy. And I gasp.

I know him.

It's Jake.

I scream and go to run, but he lunges and grabs my arm, hauling me in, tossing me to the floor. When I try to get up, he backhands me. Pain explodes as I fall back.

"Stay down, bitch."

"If I do, if I stay, will you take me to Susan?" My voice sounds slurred.

He frowns. "Who? That blonde alpha asshole's friend? No, I don't think so. The rules changed. I sent her elsewhere, but that doesn't matter. I've got you now and you, little cunt, have caused enough problems. The fact you ruined my enterprise is enough to get you dead, but I might keep you. Start it up again."

"What?"

"Girls. I sell the wares of sweet omegas to men who'll never get them. You've been used, but you still look fresh and innocent."

I'm gaping at him.

"So you aren't working with the Council?" I ask.

He snarls. "They shut us down, didn't catch me, or maybe they really want my father's land." He frowns. "You being his new mate wouldn't work for me. They'd notice you working the clubs and streets. And Liz, one look and taste of you and it'd be hands off."

I don't hide my shudder of revulsion.

"Where's Susan?"

"I told you. Off somewhere, servicing men now. Weak fucking alpha bitch. Not so uppity now." He laughs. "I turned you over to the Council, figuring with a little help, you'd end up on the streets or begging, so...I followed you. To Pandora's, and the planets fucking aligned."

My head spins, and I feel like I'm going to be sick.

"Then, when I found out who you were...I just let things fall into place. The Council had too many questions about you the moment I identified you."

He pulls up a chair, one of the only pieces of furniture in the place. I stay down. Because if I move too soon, he could get the upper hand. And...I want to know what he does.

I breathe.

I practice the mind over emotion thing Dad taught me. I'm not that good at it, my emotions are always leaking out and taking over, but this time, I need to keep it together. For Susan. All those women. And... My alphas' lives might rely on it.

If I get out alive.

But I'm going to give it my best try.

I despise this weak man and I use that too. The anger has strength. So I soak that up, steadying myself, and I make myself cower as I look at him.

He grins. Cruel men like him love the weak.

"I...I thought you were with them."

"Could have been. But," he says, "but when I went to the cops to report you and those fucks, they sent me to the Council, so I used the Council and their connections to get to you."

"When I saw you at the restaurant—"

"I followed you. Saw that blond asshole. Turned it into you thinking I wasn't a threat. Pretty fucking good, huh?"

I nod, not trusting myself with words.

"The Council and the blonde were good at supplying info. Just feed them some bullshit. He wants to bring down your fuck buddies and get his hands on Dad's region. The Council wants you for Dad. I'm going to take you and tell them that the Unholy Trinity killed you and watch them all rip each other apart. And me? I'll get a taste of you and make money off you. Win-win. For me."

I hate him. It's poison in my blood, a dark strength that feeds my anger. And I make myself crawl to him and then I sit, kneeling, and put my hands in my pockets.

"Jake?"

"Yes."

It'd be easy to think he's insane. But he isn't crazy. He's sane. Just the wrong kind of greed and lusty evil that my dad warned me about.

He never warned me about men like Knight or Reaper or even Dante.

And I don't think it's because he never thought they existed. It's because if I chose them, it would be me choosing men who I loved or wanted me; who wanted me as a part of their world, who'd fight for me. I don't think he cared or wanted to know what we did behind closed doors. He kept his love life away from me.

He had to have had one.

It would break me if he didn't.

That man deserved happiness beyond our family unit. We were very much happy. He just deserved the other part, too.

And this asshole? He doesn't deserve anything at all.

Not even air.

"I wish you'd given me the chance to know you without the lies, Jake." I'm lying now. "Without the drugs."

I open the corkscrew with my right hand and flick out the little knife that cuts through metal or plastic, that locks in the cork in wine. Then I fist it. Like keys in self-defense.

In my other hand, I fist a cocktail stirrer.

I sit up, looking at him, leaning into him. "I'd have chosen you." And I stab him in the face with the corkscrew.

He screams, staggering up, kicking at me, landing blows, and I have to curl on myself until he staggers off. Then I'm on my feet.

The corkscrew clatters to the ground in a spray of blood and I grip the stirrer tight, pick up the chair and slam it into him. It shatters. I scramble for the corkscrew, managing to grab it.

He's stronger than he looks. He picks up a chair leg and starts beating me with it.

I launch myself at him but he laughs and bats me to the ground, kicking me.

"Fucking stupid cunt," he yells, bringing his foot down to crush my ribs.

I roll out of the way but he kicks me in the back.

I roll again, grabbing his leg with one hand and topping him. Then I stab him hard in the balls.

He shrieks and I launch myself on him, pulling out the metal stirrer and with all my might, I bring it down on him, over and over again.

When he tosses me off him, he crawls, grabbing some wood, just as I connect with the stirrer.

He brings the wood down hard, and the world swims sickeningly.

I hold on as long as I can, and as he goes to hit me again, he comes down with it. And with the last piece of strength and consciousness, I drive the corkscrew into his eye. As my other hand flops, it hits metal; the stirrer is in his chest.

Then something thumps down on my head, making pain flare briefly, before the world goes black and still.

CHAPTER
FORTY

Reaper

Her note's clutched in Knight's hand as we run through the streets, something thready and wild and hot in my veins. It makes me sick.

Normally, I thrive on this, running for my life—for a life.

But this time...this time it makes me want to puke.

"We need to find her."

Knight looks at me as we run. "We will."

I don't know if I believe him. I push harder, legs burning, and I'm veering, out of control. And I almost fall.

Knight speeds up, grabs me. "Reap?"

"Something's fucking wrong. In me." There nothing around, except the streets, a few people I dismiss immediately. "I can't smell her. I should be able to fucking smell her."

His hand comes down on me, pulling me to a stop, and I almost take him out.

He knows it.

Eyes me.

"Reap, we don't need to. We know where she is. This is panic talking. Panic."

"How the fuck do you know?"

He glances around, then at me. "I know panic. I feel it too." He points. "Here, a fucking short cut."

Knight takes off running and swings left, and I do too.

"Another," he says. We take it. Trying to reach her.

Knowing it's too late.

I know. I feel it, like I'm being stabbed rapidly, like I want to throw the fuck up, like I want to smash things to pieces.

I've gotten through life not really needing anyone. But fuck.

I need her.

She sees me.

And I think I finally want to be seen.

Liz is in my veins, burning me, warming me. Cooling fires and making others spring up. She's cohesive, a cog. And right now, the old blackness that's full of nothing but death and cold destruction is sucking at me.

I fucking need to get there.

What if it's too late?

We keep going and Lizette permeates me.

It's not just being seen. It's by who.

Knight and Dante see me, but it's her, she's the one I want.

Because she's special.

She has an unsullied heart, a soul that doesn't judge or feel sorry for me. One that sees me and likes me and wants me.

The way I see her.

But it's easy to see her that way. She's easy to love.

And now it's too late.

She's been gone too long.

It's my fault. If I'd moved faster, got back earlier. Been the one to confront Ghost.

What does it fucking matter that I've got the information I

need? Information I know Knight will now be able to verify once he goes in the right direction.

What does it matter if she's dead?

It's my fucking fault.

I can't get that out of my head. I saw her on the feed out by the dumpsters in a hoodie. Mason's hoodie, so my fleeting glance filled in the wrong blanks.

I didn't put it together, didn't look again because when I came in and saw that, Dante staggered in, bleeding, and collapsed.

Ghost... Ghost's gone. And whether the fuck's gone off to die or found another life in him, now Liz is lost, he knows we'll destroy him. I don't think he'll be back.

"Here."

We look at the building. I don't usually carry a gun, but I do now, and we both pull our weapons and race in.

I can't fucking smell her, and I lose my mind.

I can't hear whatever Knight's saying, there's a roaring in my ears, and I slam into the door, splintering it.

I look at the carnage. The blood. And I fall to my knees.

Knight drops his knife, takes my gun, and shoots the prick that's dead on the ground. I can smell the death in the room.

I'm paralyzed. Lost. And I have no one to rip apart and kill.

"Snap the fuck out of it," Knight says. "See this is why you two need sensitivity classes. Get over here and help me."

My head snaps up.

I smell death but I also smell gardenias and relief floods me. She's alive.

So much for being a big bad. Love fucking sucks. If it brings a man like me to my knees then—

Then I'll take it.

Knight's checking her over, murmuring to her. "It's okay, Liz, baby, it's okay. I'm here and I'll protect you and I have your hunter, too. You brought him to his knees. You're a badass. No one brings Reap to his knees, just you. Wake up."

The thing that beats in my chest clenches. It isn't a heart. It's something else, a ball of little used emotions, a ball awakened by her. It clenches and I think I might die if she doesn't open her fucking eyes.

"Liz," I whisper. "Angel... Come on."

She moans and struggles to sit up. I look at him. The knight in his pretty armor's got glittering, shimmering eyes, and a tear slides down a cheek.

He doesn't bother dashing it away, just smiles and helps her sit straighter. She almost falls into his arms, but not from weakness or injury. From emotion. She's falling into him.

Liz touches his tear and licks her finger.

I get up and move around the place methodically, collecting the casings, and find a bag and a heeled shoe. Inside the bag is an ID belonging to Susan Pemberton —interesting —but I make quick work of wiping down everything that we touched. Then I search the dead fuck's pockets and strip him of his personal items.

When I'm done, I go to Liz, and help Knight get her up. I swing her up in my arms as he goes to call us a car. I can hear shouting from his phone and grin down into her hair.

I can't help it.

Relief floods me, and holding her is like holding the essence of life itself.

"Dante's losing his mind. I can hear him from here," I tell her.

She holds me, her arms weak.

"You did something no one's done. Made me lose my shit, Liz. Never, fucking never, get into trouble like this again. What were you thinking?"

"I wanted to save my alphas. I thought...thought the Council would destroy you. They were meant to be here. He— Jake—he told them where I was. H-He's that guy's son— Craig. He fed information to the Council, and Ghost... I guess... I guess Jake thought he would cause confusion and get his revenge on me. For rejecting him and for Knight and Julien beating him up."

I kiss her forehead. She looks like she was beaten to a pulp. Fuck. In a way I wish she hadn't killed him.

Because if life still sparked in him, I'd take absolute satisfaction of snuffing it out.

He fucking hurt her.

And if I'm feeling like this, what the fuck would Dante do if he lived?

However bad it might be, however cruel, twisted and long the torture, I know I'd be with him. Helping.

Fuck. Liz got hurt.

And there's no one I can kill.

Thank Christ we heal fast.

"Car's here in five." Knight looks at us and I give her to him because he's all puppy dog eyes for her.

And he's the best at this. She needs the best. He holds her like she's the most precious thing ever and I know how he feels.

And, as he holds her, soothes her, she passes out or falls asleep. All I know is there's a contentment to her, one I don't have.

Because now the rush of relief's past, the unfinished tendrils are still there. The reason the Council's interested in her hasn't changed.

They want her, and it's something we all have to face.

Knight shakes his head as we start to walk to where we can go for the car the moment it arrives. "Thank fuck we can go home now."

I choose my words carefully. "This isn't done."

"Of course it is. Dead asshole one and two." Then he pauses. "What do you mean it's not done?"

"We need to work this out." I take a breath. "The Council won't stop."

He doesn't still, but his head rises. And whatever he's

about to say, the platitudes or words of reassurance don't form.

Instead, he takes me in. Nods.

"What did you find, Reap? I have some pieces, but—"

"When we're back," I say, "look up Candy Enver."

"That's..." He doesn't finish.

"Her mother."

"She's dead." He looks at me. "Isn't she?"

I nod. "On paper." I know how easy it is to die and keep living. I know how to invent yourself in plain sight. Thing is, I never have had to. "We'll get her back and then you, me, and Dante will have a talk."

It's not going to be pretty.

It took Julien and four others to restrain the wounded Dante. And Dante isn't a forgiving soul. He's going to be hell for the next, oh, hundred years.

Lizette's passed out when we get back in and Darcy takes over. Everyone's down in the living area on our private third floor in Pandora's, where if we're honest, we live a lot of the time.

Dante's patched up, halfway healed and growling at her when Darcy stands him down. Stands us all down.

"No. I'm going to bathe her, dress her wounds, and then you can beat your chests. But she's going to sleep." Darcy pauses, looks each of us hard in the eye. "Properly sleep. It'll help her heal."

"She's the boss, bosses," Julien says, drinking his whiskey.

He's still got his feed up, and upstairs each entrance is watched. We're open for deliveries, which won't arrive until later, and then Julien will head up and handle it with Mason. Maybe some back up under the guise of extra helping hands.

We exchange a look as Darcy leads away a groggy, weak Liz.

I've moved on from all those emotions. And what I should be, where I should be, is cold. Dark. Perfect clarity calm.

I'm not.

Things are alive inside and won't go down.

Fury is moving through me, it's out now, and I don't know how to get it back in.

There's blood on the black t-shirt Dante wears. I can smell it. The thigh of his jeans is also stained dark brown.

But beneath the rips, cut clean by a knife, a knife I know Ghost carries—carried—because I have one the same, that cuts like everything's butter, goes in clean and deep and nasty, the flesh is already healing. It looks right now like a nasty scrape. By tonight it'll be a scar. Tomorrow? Probably gone.

He heals fast.

And it's not a knife designed to bring about slow healing. It's a knife made to kill.

Fast. Deep. Surgical.

Dante's fucking lucky he's standing.

Lucky he's alive to tell the tale.

He strums his fingers on the wall, then takes off to his office. I follow, along with Knight. But I stop him before he goes in. "Grab everything on Candy and the Council president. And Lizette's father, both under Connor and Elias."

He frowns. "Why—"

"When you see it, you'll see it. If I'm wrong, you won't."

He nods and starts to go. "Nice to see the human under the cracks."

"Fuck you."

"Yeah, I love her, too." His gaze drifts to Dante's door, and he shakes his head. "The thing with the girls?"

I don't knock, just walk in.

Dante's got a giant motherfucker hand cannon that he's

loading a clip into. I lean against the wall and pull out my cigarettes, lighting up.

"He's dead, Dar—"

"I know that, Seb," he snaps, hating that I almost used his real name.

We never do. But I think this moment calls for it.

I ignore that he used mine. "And that's for?"

"The next fucker who even dares to think he can touch her. Did you see her fucking face? Motherfucker!"

I nod and drag in smoke. I study the glowing tip as it fades to ash, and I blow out a ring of smoke. "I get it."

"Nothing to fucking get."

I nod again. "Lost my shit when I saw her. The kid was epic, though. You and I, we're a different breed. She can undo us. Destruction. It's her appeal, and also why we might feel we want to push her away."

"I don't know what the fuck you're talking about."

"Sure you do, Dante." I straighten. "You like your sex a certain way."

"Just because I like rough control, her on her knees and spitting venom in passion form, doesn't mean a thing. Just like if I want to blow apart a pile of motherfuckers who think they can take our money maker from us when we took her in doesn't mean a thing."

"Really?" I push.

"What are you fucking trying to say?" He aims the gun at me, and I just raise a brow back. "That I love her? That I care?"

"I don't know, do you?"

"She makes us fucking money. We put energy into keeping her safe. She scratches an itch and has a body made to fuck. That's not love."

Dante needs to cling to his control. But the thing is, I don't think he has it. I think he's dangling and he's wrapped up in his own brand of denial.

"If you say so," I reply.

His eyes narrow, glittering and he lowers the gun. "I do."

"Don't...don't fuck it up."

"I'm not. Nothing to fuck up."

I let that slide.

Instead, I shift gears.

"You missed out on a show earlier." I pause, blow out smoke. "You should have seen what she did to the guy."

He smiles, looks at me. "Yeah?"

"Fucking brutal."

"Good."

He's making me do a lot of talking which I don't like, but I need to get my point across. And for a man who can be verbose and also concise, I think he's stuck. I think the stubborn asshole's a little lost, like me.

Not Knight.

That prick's in touch with all his feels. Go figure.

But Dante and I, we grew up both in and out of the Council system. We always knew what we were and in our own ways, rejected it. Our paths parted and converged, over and over. Mine had a lot more death and jail time. His...

I wonder if Dante's control needs are a different sort of prison.

But I can see it all where he's too close. Blind.

I won't say scared, but there's a fear there. It's in me, too. And it's so unlike anything I've felt—me, a man who can walk into any situation without a drop of dread or fear. I see things clearly.

Emotionless, yes.

But our Lizette is something neither of us have encountered.

And the fear of losing her is strong.

So yeah, I have to keep talking, get the point across.

"She scared the fucking life from me, Dante."

"Sebastian?" He looks at me, then picks up another round

and puts that in his pocket. "I get it, you lost your mind over her and I'm going to—"

"You know, when we were young and we ran?" I interrupt. "We were out there wild, fighting our way, and we made it here. Nothing's got to me. I get it that I'm wired differently, maybe wrong. But it serves. I can get things done. I don't even fucking mind prison.

"But this fucking girl with the big dark eyes and long dark hair and voice that could crack and melt diamonds? She gets to me. And it makes it worse or better...something, anyway... that she not only sees me but she gets me. She likes me."

He pushes papers aside. A sign of his disordered thoughts. Dante's control reaches all the aspects of his life. This slight mess...it's telling.

"You're sharing this why? I'm not a touchy-feely guy. Knight's out there, I'm sure he'll give you a hug."

He finds the glass and he's about to pour another drink when I just reach over and take the bottle, drinking from it. I don't even care it's not my drop. It's got alcohol. It works. "Fuck you, Dante."

"She doesn't affect me other than I want to fuck her into all levels of submission."

"That's a lie. You want her. You like her and you take it out on her and everyone else because you wish you didn't. She's either strength or weakness, you decide, not her. The weakness for her makes me strong."

"I'm going to shoot the fuck out of people, how's that for a decision?"

I take another swallow right before he comes around his desk to snatch the bottle back. And the pain from his healing wound's etched deep in the grooves of his face. A different kind of pain's in his eyes.

It's like, I realize, a song.

Fuck, do all of us have one for her?

I know I didn't have anything like a song in me before I

met her, but now? The emptiness has a fullness, like life. Those areas that allow me to kill without compunction, the quiet and steady things now have a beat to them.

They're still there, but...

It's like an elemental beat. Drums and wild, unfettered voices.

Like she awakened something, gave it a voice, that well inside me that's always been dark now teems.

And the song in my veins is everything at once. It's emotion. Drums and flares and wildness set fee from earthly tethers. It just is. And in there is her. A center of a thing so calm it's like my emptiness except it's life.

His is a softer song that can hurt. It's the violent urges and the need to control through degradation turned into something else, something delicate. For her.

The rest of it is between them, but I see that.

And Knight's is her surface song, her quiet moments where she sings alone without an audience. He's comfort and a thing I can't give. I'm not capable. I'm not that.

The comfort of a beta upbringing.

Her father was a weak alpha, but he took her and raised her, teaching her what she was, but that she could also be so much more, and her decisions were never preordained. Because isn't that the beta way? Able to choose who and what they want from the whole world of betas?

We're different, the whole control and the reasons we left the Council ruled world—just like her father—is to escape that whole bullshit of decisions made because you were born a certain fucking way.

But Knight came from that world.

And he offers her something like home.

I rub my eyes.

Does it even matter?

We fit. With her.

Just like the three of us can rule as equal alphas of our pack.

But first I need Dante to get it together.

We need to save our omega and stop Council interference. Because that's a major disaster.

"I'm going to take them out. All of them, Seb. Every last one, and when I'm finished here, I'll burn the fucking Council down."

"Nice chest thumping, Dante, but no."

He pours himself a glass and sets the bottle down reaching for the gun once more. With his other hand he pats his pocket then his ankle, clearly checking his weapons.

Not because he's checking that he put them in place, but because he's reminding himself just how armed he is and what he wants to do.

"The Council isn't some cheap one man show, Dante. It has branches. It's all over. And yeah, there's a real HQ, but they also have octopus arms so take out one and it just fucking keeps going. You're not doing anything but getting yourself dead and our operation blown the fuck up. We keep it local, and you don't head out like some idiotic vigilante and fucking murder anyone. And that's coming from me. If I thought we could, I'd have fucking done it already."

"So I'll kill this lot. Blame it on the full moon."

I rub my head. When he's in deep denial, he's hard work, and he makes me fucking talk way too much.

"Today goes on as normal. Same as tonight. They're not making a move yet." I outline what Lizette told me the dead fucker said. "Right now, things are in holding. The Council thinks Ghost has either double crossed them or done his job and the dead fuck got in the way."

He looks at me. "The body was gone."

I know but I nod. "If he's alive, he's disappeared."

"I want to make sure."

"You're not going on a hunting expedition. His part's

finished." He opens his mouth but I keep going. "How the fuck do I know? I know him and so do you. If someone didn't take the body and he's alive, he's gone. His part is done, he knows how to cut losses, and make an exit."

"Losses?"

"Ghost, if he survived, is heading back out of town and thinks his job is done. If he lives, a loss to him is not seeing your guts spilled. But he'd take such a loss. Man like that will figure another day another chance."

He closes his eyes. "If he survived."

"We need to deal with the bigger threat and by my thinking we have..." I think about it. "We have a day or two. We let her heal and run the business as usual."

"And then?" Dante grips his hand cannon. "They won't give up. They want her for a reason and fucked if I know."

"I know."

He looks at me.

"I think I know," I amend. "If I'm right we can stop it and get things back to the status quo." Then I drop the good bomb. "And give ourselves guaranteed future protection."

Like providence, Knight bursts in with his laptop. Not his porn one, his real one. I still can't believe he went to that level on the off chance he'd need to throw someone off the scent. Then again, it is dubious genius.

And I admire it. I pay that much attention to detail on my kills. Just in a different way.

Griffin's a cocky little bastard, so I keep my praise to myself. I just smoke my cigarette and go back to silence as he talks.

As each word falls, he gets more and more excited about it all.

Dante slowly puts down the gun and takes the computer and we go over it, everything that the smug genius Knight put together in minutes. Once he got the right trail to sniff along.

"Now what?" Knight says, looking at us both.

But it's clear what we need to do.

We just have to be in agreement. Because once we do it, we can't reverse it.

I take a final drag on the cigarette and put it out.

"Now we make a decision. The three of us," I say. "And then she has to agree. More, she needs to understand what it means."

"Staying," Dante mutters.

"If she doesn't want to stay?" Knight asks, anxious.

He doesn't look at Dante, he doesn't need to. It's obvious Knight means because of him.

"That's her decision," Dante says. "She needs to be sure."

"We need to be sure, too. And now."

"I've been sure since day one, Reap." Knight takes his computer.

"Well?" I ask, turning to Dante. "I'm in."

"It's up to you, Dante," says Knight. "This can't be majority. It has to be unanimous." He looks at me. "Along with the other stuff."

Dante finally nods. "We do this."

It takes two days for her to heal, with us all visiting. I know because I catch Dante curled around her early hours of that morning.

I don't say anything to him. But while she looks worse for wear that afternoon, we're cutting it close, as the Council wants a meeting with Dante in a few days.

Liz doesn't heal like Dante or me or even Knight. But she's omega, so she's faster than a gamma or delta. She still looks rough. Gorgeous, but you can see what she's been through, she healed inside.

Heart. Mind. Psyche.

As Knight takes her through things, she frowns. "I don't..."

"Keep reading," Knights says.

Liz stares at what we're showing her. "No."

"It's true." I move closer. "Your mother's alive."

She shakes her hair and the air is filled with a rage born from lament. "No, she's dead, she...how could she leave Dad?"

"Leave you?" Dante clarified. "Very fucking easily. People are the worst."

"Not you, though, Liz. You're the best of us all." Knight touches her hand.

But she sucks in a breath. "She's dead." Then her mouth sets. "Dead."

"And if she isn't?" I ask.

"I don't care. She's dead to me." Liz rises. "If that's all, I'll pack and go to the Council. It's time. Even if I killed Jake, they still want me and want to marry me to that...that alpha. And I need to know you three will be safe."

"What if we said we know how to stop that happening?" Dante asks. "It goes back to an old fairytale that Reap told me about. And it echoes what Ghost said."

Liz goes still, but the air quivers, this time with something like hope. "Whatever it is," she whispers, "I'm in. Do it."

CHAPTER
FORTY-ONE

Dante

For Angel, we make it a ritual. Slowly, we strip her down, touching her, kissing her. She's satin soft, perfect, even with her war wounds.

Knight kisses her first, easy and romantic with an edge of gentle control. Next is Reaper.

He looks her in the eye, then kisses her in a carnal claiming, bringing it to the gentlest edge I've seen from him.

When it's my tun, she shivers, nipples hard, her body pliant. And those bruises and collected marks? They make her perfect in a different way. They make her perfect for us. They make her fit.

None of us are pristine. Reaper and I never have been. Knight might have been in his younger years, but he's one of us, and that paints us all.

And now Angel...

She killed. She fits into our world.

Do I wish she didn't?

Fuck yes, but not because I don't have...feelings. I just— "I wish we didn't have to do this," I admit.

"Fuck you, Dante."

I ignore Knight.

And Angel lifts her face. "I can still go."

"No." I don't want her gone. It's not what I mean, but I can't say the words I need to. "Just, the circumstances."

I slip my hands under the heavy warm fall of her hair and kiss her, light because if I go deep, I might never be able to climb out. And I end it by biting on her lips, making her moan.

Then I step back and she's once more in the circle of us.

"We need to bite you in the throes of passion, and you have to bite us—that's vital. We also need to tell you our real names. You know mine." Knight's gaze darts to me as my chest tightens. "I read it."

"We have to do it now, Angel," Reaper says, using my name for her. "Time's running out."

"And this President," Knight says, "you know she's going to surprise us."

"A-And Susan? And the other girls?" she asks.

"That operation will take time to close down," I say. "That's a different conversation. We need to do this now."

"Ready?" Knight asks.

This should feel artificial, odd. We don't have time to have sex because he's right. The Councilwoman will arrive early. She thinks we have her prize—Liz—the thing that'll get Candice Helmont, aka Candy, fucking mother of the year, running here, right into our grasp.

Only we're turning the tables.

She won't think we'd do this, claim Liz, have Angel claim us right back.

And we don't have time for sex, but we can all get her off and we can get off over that.

Throes of passion doesn't mean penetration.

And there's so fucking much to get passionate about with Angel.

Lizette is fucking gorgeous, and she looks better naked

with us around her. It's hot. She's free use to us, ours to have. They love her, and me—it doesn't fucking matter what I feel. I don't do emotion.

Like with the kisses, Knight moves in first.

She responds to him before he touches her. Anticipation is thick around us.

This is erotic and hot, and I watch as Knight takes her, sliding his hand between her thighs, fingering her in a way that makes her writhe and shake and come in seconds flat. To me, he misses the opportunities to make her hotter, make her beg. And I carefully avoid telling him, because this is what she wants and craves.

She's three different omegas. Each with specific appetites, and we fit her bill, and she ours.

I've never met an omega like her.

She's moaning, her thighs wet, his fingers glistening as they slide in and out of her. She's all over him, rubbing, and I'm feeling a little weird inside, like there's a hot hook in my heart.

Oh, fuck, am I jealous of fucking Knight's fingers? He's getting what I crave, and though I'm getting some eventually, I'm fucking greedy.

She starts to come and he rubs her clit, his fingers hooked as they come almost all the way out before pistoning back in. He skillfully spins out her orgasm and sinks his teeth into her, telling her his real name. "Griffin."

But then I get the sight I need.

"Lizette. Angel." She whispers as she bites Knight. He jerks, like he's fucking coming in his pants.

The moment they're done, Reaper growls, the full predator baring his teeth. He drags her into him, slamming his fingers into her, dragging her head back by her hair and kissing her with the kind of elemental and dirty passion that's at his core. She starts to come immediately and he rides her through it, bouncing her right into the next.

Then he bites down, growling out his name, "Sebastian."

She howls and bites down on him so hard blood runs, and I know exactly where he's getting his next tattoo. "Angel. Lizette."

I glance at her once they're done and grab her, hauling her to me. "You think you can just fucking come?"

"Yes." Her eyes glitter, the need in her completely unbound.

"Wrong fucking answer." And I finger fuck her hard, spearing her perfect pussy and her ass, and she pushes back on me, convulsing and coming.

I lick her throat, finding the right spot to bite. She's hot. Furnace hot, and perfectly tight, little ripples working against my fingers. I know exactly how I feel in this moment. I know how I'll always feel when it comes to her, and it infuriates me.

I don't want it.

I want her even more because of it.

How dare she rip me down into shreds of naked emotion?

How fucking dare she make me so damn vulnerable I'd worship at her altar?

"Darian." I stare at her. "You fucking say my name as I brand you."

I sink my teeth into that perfect spot, biting deep, drawing blood as she cries out, "Darian!"

I release her as I whisper, "Come as you bite me, Lizette. Angel. Come."

She bites me and it's utter euphoria. She shudders, crushing my fingers with her contractions and her heat seeps in, branding me as I brand her, and the pain and pleasure are beautiful fucking things. I can feel her breathe in my veins, feel her blood move through my bones. She's mine. And I'm hers and I fucking come.

"Lizette." Her voice is a hoarse sound. "Angel. *Your*...Angel."

She half collapses, and I hold her before handing her to the other two.

"Get showered, get changed, and get upstairs," I tell them, ignoring the wild emotions spinning inside my chest. Especially at her last words. "I've got a feeling the shit's going to go down in the next few hours."

I don't feel any different. At least, I tell myself that. Sure, my neck both hurts and feels unbelievably good and her scent ticks up notches. But no. No different.

I dress in a suit and go upstairs to the main floor. Only Julien is at the door and Darcy is behind the bar. Knight's in one of his slightly flamboyant suits and he's draped around Liz like he fucking won her at a fair. And she loves it.

She's in a pretty dress, one I suspect Darcy got for her. Because Angel tends to favor those big, boxy dresses I've grown to have an affinity for.

They're very easy access.

Reaper's in his black jeans and long T-shirt. He's smoking a cigarette and goes off to talk with Julien.

I toy with my drink, staring at it.

Fuck. I hate this.

If I had my way, I'd walk into the Council building and kill them all. Or at least, see how many of them I could get. I'm pretty fucking sure Reaper would be with me and Knight would be on his computer, shutting down the cops at every turn.

But it's a fantasy, a futile dream. The Council's too big, an octopus as Reap said. This gamble is the best we can hope for.

I don't tell the others, but it is a gamble.

And I find I don't like gambling with Angel.

Not at all.

She deserves the good.

She deserves... Not me.

I fucking wish I smoked. Because I'd be giving Reaper a run for his money. Instead, I placate myself with the whiskey and the moderate fantasy of killing her mother.

I go still as a car door slams.

They're here early enough to miss opening hours, but on time for us to be getting ready. There's commotion at the door, and I sit back in my seat and wait as Julien stops her entourage from entering, even though the main doors are open, and Reaper leads in the queen bitch herself.

Candice looks at each of us.

And I can see it. The resemblance. It's not huge. Liz looks more like her father, but it's there.

Now I know.

I wait, observing her, looking at her beneath the layer of glamor and fierce competence. Beneath the aura of power.

And I realize something.

She's fucking nervous.

Her gaze locks on mine and she looks away first. Darcy slams a bottle down, making her jump. Finally, Candice lays eyes on her daughter.

And wrinkles her fucking nose.

Knight growls.

She's seeing the fading bruises, the untamed beauty. Her youth. And she's seeing the marks on her throat. All of them.

"That can be ignored," she says, aiming her words in her alpha voice at me. "I know. I escaped the mark."

"Probably because you're a stone-cold fucking bitch," I say pleasantly. "Her father was nice. Still, can't win them all."

"Shut your mouth or I'll shut down this place and throw you in prison with this...scarred beast."

This time, the growl comes from Lizette. "Where he escaped from," she says.

Reaper locks eyes with Liz and fucking smiles.

"Quit with your alpha voice. It's like a gnat. An annoying buzz." I could use mine. We all could and she and her entourage would be commanded to leave. Or dive face first into traffic.

Point is, Candice has nothing on my voice, and combine mine with Knight and Reaper? Utterly dangerous.

"You do not want to play a game of voice with me. I'd win." I offer a smile. "But I won't say no."

"You have something that isn't yours," she says, normal-voiced.

Even if she doesn't believe me about my voice, she's smart enough not to take on three alphas with her game. Besides, she has more important things up her sleeve, things I'm looking forward to destroying.

"She's ours. And you know what, Candy? I hold pure gold in my hands."

It's time to play the card Angel doesn't know about, and I fucking hope Knight's got a strong grip on our girl.

"Fucking gold." I lay the folder on the table and slide it over. It's old school, I think she'll appreciate it. I nod at it. "The truth's in there, Candy. And it could put you down, should you pursue trying to bring us down. All of it. The bodies you stepped on. Those you buried, and the ones you blackmailed. Every last nasty deed you've done."

"You don't know shit. Lizette, come." Candice snaps her fingers.

"Liz, stay." I nod at the folder and continue. "The baby you abandoned doesn't have to go with you. The man you had killed? You know damn well he was her father."

"What?" Angel balks, her gaze whipping to everyone's face. When she lands on Candice, she lunges, but Knight is quick to grab her. "Liz, no."

The woman snatches up the folder and scans the contents, snapping it shut. "You can't prove it."

"Actually, we can. That's how we got it. Dug up all your digital and not so digital graves."

Candice presses her lips together. "So I'll just take you all out and walk with my prize girl."

"No, Candy. We didn't get to be the kings of the fucking criminal world without learning a trick or two, like scattering and copying everything and having it ready to drop if we don't report in. Plus, I'll fucking turn you inside out. Me and the rest of the Unholy Trinity," I say. "Just one more thing..."

"If it's about Elias, you can save it. Nothing's gonna take me down. Not some has-been's rebellious temper tantrum or even *family*." She glances at Liz.

"How about a sex slave ring?" I ask.

Her gaze snaps my way. I have her full attention now.

"Excuse me?"

"Well, I'm sure your involvement in an underground sex trafficking operation wouldn't be a good look for the head of the Council. Especially since you're funding it." I pause as Knight hands me another folder. I open it and push it in front of her. "It's all there. Your deal with Jake Edmonton, his death, your Council employee, Susan Pemberton. We rescued her along with the others. So try anything, and we will fucking end you." I take a swallow of my drink and nod at the folders in her hands. "You can keep those. As a gift."

I stand.

"And as I said before—Lizette is ours. We've all bonded, all bitten each other, marked each other, know each other's true names, and we've all knotted in her. You can take the readings to verify. We'll do the tests. She is, by Council definitions, ours. And selling your daughter for power and votes?" I say. "Not a good look."

She glares. "I did not sell Susan."

"Knight?" I call him into the conversation.

"According to the documents I found, that's exactly what you did," he chimes in. "Surprise."

I smile. "See? I can *destroy* you. Happily."

Candy's eyes narrow. "I know, courtesy of Ghost, where many of your bodies are buried. I have you cornered, too."

Oh, I'm sure she does know some of our crimes because that's something Ghost would do, but I don't care. What we have on her is far more damning, especially for a woman running the fucking Council.

"So? Try it," I say, "But if you double cross us, we will act. It's mutual destruction or mutual salvation. If I were you, I'd pick the latter."

The woman's cockiness disappears, and she looks like she wants to strangle me.

"I think in chess it's called stalemate?" I ask.

It's clear she's clinging. There has to be more to this, I know it, but Candy's smart. She'll work it out and leave us be. More importantly, leave her daughter the fuck alone.

She doesn't want the full wrath of the Unholy Trinity. And she doesn't want to be on Reaper's radar.

Finally, she says, "I need the Hover Valley region. That's why I sweetened the deal with the next in line. Craig is expecting a woman."

I shrug. "Get him one. We leave each other alone. Do your job and find someone else for that region. You're an alpha, strong, and there are plenty who'd want the role and be loyal. Liz isn't. She's a handful." I hold out my hand. "Do we have a deal?"

CHAPTER

FORTY-TWO

Lizette

I t's late, and I sit at the bar downstairs, numb.

One, Knight used his voice on me to keep me still and silent.

Two, I hate Candice.

She's gone. The woman who gave birth to me—she's no mother—is gone and a hand delivered contract was delivered. An NDA, apparently, where everything that happened officially never did and we don't talk about it.

Their lawyer, who's name I've forgotten, a handsome shark in a suit, came and went and said it's all airtight. Susan and the other girls the Unholy Trinity saved are a long way from here and now have a life of their choosing to live, because of... Trenton? Trevor?

It doesn't matter, I guess. I just...

I don't know.

I should be happy, except how can I be when Dad would be here, now, with me, if it wasn't for that woman?

A hand comes over mine and a drink appears. I look up and Darcy smiles at me, the friendliest I've seen her. It's like her guard's gone. I don't know if it's because I've been marked now by the alphas of the pack, or if it's because she helped me shower and clean up after Jake tried to kill me a lifetime ago, or if it's because she feels sorry for me.

"Why did she kill Dad?" I ask rhetorically.

Darcy shrugs and picks up her drink. "Why do fuckwads do anything? But from what I know, I'm guessing because your father took you."

"He said she died. He said his name was different." I shake my head, hand clenching on the bar. "Why—"

"That wasn't a maternal creature, and I know your father loved you, raised you in his protection. I know, because you're here. And strong, brave, real. Trust me, it'd take someone special to take on those three." Darcy smiles. "Whatever the reasons, it was love, to protect you, and she's the type to tie up loose ends unless she's caught like what the Trinity did. And she's the type for revenge."

"What's to stop her coming after you all?"

"Us. She wouldn't fucking dare. Your father was a visionary…I know the name, his real one, heard it, because he didn't believe in structure put in place to control people." She looks over as Julien passes by. "I don't, either."

"Thank you for that, Darcy."

"It was the truth. Drink up." She leans forward. "You wear every expression on your face and you're looking at me like you're my latest pity project. I don't have those. Maybe I like you, kid. Ever think of that?"

Heat flames in my cheeks. "I've never had a friend."

She laughs. "Heaven help you if I'm your first."

"Darcy's okay," Knight says, coming up, his dimples flashing as he kisses me long and slow and sweet. "Darcy's brilliant in a fight. Always have her in your corner."

He heads upstairs to join Dante.

"He's trying to ask you if you're staying. He wants you to stay. Men, kid, are easy. They're pathetic."

"Even Julien?" I say, teasing.

"Especially Julien." She sighs. "Don't tell him. But I think he's fucking great."

"I think he knows." I pause. "And I can't leave."

"There are different ways of leaving. You could be with them here and never have them touch you again, you know?"

"I'm not leaving in any way."

Reaper's in the corner, unlit cigarette in hand, watching the small crowd. He narrows his eyes as one man goes to touch a waitress, but she handles it, giving him a look to let him know and he relaxes. It's all microscopic, those reactions, and it makes me think about what he told me when I was half out of it, about bringing him to his knees.

I love them, and earlier, before Candice arrived, Reaper kissed me hard and whispered his words of love. Just simple, no moon and stars and whatever Knight feels like saying. I love it all, the quiet, the flowery.

The only one who hasn't said anything is Dante.

I look at Darcy and sip my drink. It's sweet and doesn't have too much alcohol, and I think I prefer it to the hard liquor and even the wine they drink.

"Do you think," I begin, "that Dante—"

But she cuts in. "Dante's a hard man. I think you unhinge him in ways he can't deal with, or isn't sure how to deal with," she mutters. "But I don't think you'd be here if he didn't want you to be. He's set in his ways."

I blink hard, my eyes burning. "I know, but I have less confidence than you with him. And I deserve... I deserve more than crumbs."

I wait for her to say I'm being greedy, wanting the three of them to love me back. But she doesn't. I sigh as the music starts for the first dancer.

"You deserve your world." She looks at the stage.

I don't push. I've said enough on that, and the only people who can work this out is me and the alphas. Me and Dante.

"But I was going to ask," I say. "Do you think, honestly, I'm to blame for Dad's death? She killed him because of me. She—"

"I once heard Dante and Reaper talking, mostly Dante, because Reaper's a man of few words. Majority of the time," she says. "But they were talking about the man who risked everything to save them. The man who got them out of the pack they were in. Reaper was drowning in trouble, and I think Dante was set to be mated to some girl from another pack. Not his thing—it was that, or they'd take down Reaper.

"Their lives would have been locked away in an old-fashioned pack life. No out. The man, he was escaping. But he took them. Got them a long way away, hid them, and when they had to go separate ways, gave them money, as much as he could spare. They've talked about him a lot."

I listen intently, wondering where Darcy's story is going.

"And always with reverence because the things he told them, how life didn't have to be this way just because they were alpha or delta or gamma or omega. They could do and be anything. And I think he was their inspiration. He had a kid, real little, a baby or toddler. The guy's name was Elias. Elias Enver. And that baby was his life. His reason for living. He saved them for his kid. Because she deserved to be in a better world than the one she'd been born in.

"You, kid. That's your dad." She takes a breath. "And those two are where I first heard the name."

"But—"

"As to why she killed your dad? You're not to blame, I know that. She is. Revenge, spite... The list goes on, so take your pick. And I get the feeling he'd be pissed the fuck off if you blamed yourself. So stop. You made him happy, end of story."

I look at her, and to my horror, I burst into tears.

Later, like the next day, they finally take me to the complex they live in. All of them. When the Trinity isn't bunking down at their nerve center, Pandora's Folly, this is where they live.

The only good thing about the tears last night is that Darcy saw and she took me to a corner and made me pull myself together before anyone else noticed.

Her no-nonsense style combined with her complete loss at what to do cleared the tears to a watery giggle.

Thank goodness, because later it was business as usual and I sang.

Not so good? The alphas let me sleep alone.

And now...

Here I am in a beautiful building that's a modern, airy dream inside.

The top floors are built to code on top of the existing building and those smaller floors, each with terraces, all belong to the three alphas.

The rest of the staff live in the other floors. And not just staff from Pandora's Folly, but from their other places, other businesses.

I know because Knight wouldn't shut up, telling me who lives where and what they do for the Unholy Trinity.

It's completely endearing.

Right now he's getting some wine for us and I move about on a shared living floor, where they could, if they were the type, entertain. The open plan great room is gorgeous and I'm...

I'm restless.

It isn't fair to be so jumpy because this place is stunning. All of it.

"So what do you think? Modern as all get out inside,

428

heritage on the shell. A home in the sky. Away from the shitty part of Starlight City." Knight grins like he built it himself.

"This building is glorious."

He hands me a white wine. "And...there's a floor for you. It took a bit to get ready, but it's there."

Then he peers at me as the elevator dings and my senses spike up again. It's Dante.

I slide him a look but he moves past and into the kitchen area.

"Took us some fast talking, but it's there." Knight sips his wine. "You want something changed, just tell Daddy."

And my libido ticks up, momentarily squashing down the emptiness that's settled since yesterday, like something's missing. That something's just...wrong.

From the corner of the shared floor of their three-story part of the building, Dante glares. "Maybe she likes it."

Cigarette smoke drifts in from the open balcony doors where Reaper stands, looking out at the city.

No doubt he can hear every word and he's just keeping out of it. This is between me and Dante. He knows it.

Why couldn't it be just Reaper and Knight?

And why the hell do I have to be in love with the complex and cruel Dante as well?

I can't be here without all of them.

I deserve everything, and Dante doesn't get to play with me when he feels like it and have his walls up, too.

Crumbs are for birds.

I'm not that.

"I do like it, Knight."

"But?" he asks, taking the wine and setting it down.

"I don't belong," I say.

The words bubble up from nowhere, from the depths of me.

On the floor near the elevator doors in in the antique white open foyer that takes up half the level, are my bags. Ratty and pitifully small.

I look like I'm on the way out.

"No." Knight looks at me as Reaper comes in. "No, we love you, we want you to stay."

"All except Dante."

"He loves you too, he's just the problem child," Knight says.

Dante and Reaper don't say a word.

Words and emotions press at me, threaten to drown me in a deluge I can't escape. It's only when Knight takes my face and kisses me that things settle.

Maybe this can work here with them, I don't need Dante.

So I try.

Lifting my face, I kiss Knight's soft lips, then all along his jaw where he needs a shave. It's all soft and I wonder what a beard would be like on him, but then I reconsider. Scruff yes, but he's the kind of Daddy who needs a smoother face, he's a Daddy with a hard shell filled with caramel and I want to sink to my knees and take him in my mouth.

"Do Daddy a favor," he says, "pay Mr. Reaper attention while I fuck your pretty pussy." Before I can move, he puts his mouth to my ear. "Give the fucker a show. He loves you, he just needs sensitivity training. Do it." He says this louder. "For Daddy."

Knight goes back to those soft, seductive little kisses, moving me backwards until hands take hold of my hips.

Reaper.

He's standing and his gaze flickers once to where Dante must be, and then his attention goes to me. For a moment there's a warming flash of bemusement, but it sinks into the Reaper mask, and there's love there, I see it, feel it.

Reaper grips my hair as Daddy Knight flips my skirt.

His fingers are magic on my hot pussy, he slides them over my panties, bringing me to a throbbing, needing ache, the kind that promises untold pleasures if he just tugs them out of the way, if he goes the distance.

"Suck."

Reaper's thick cock is out, and I don't think, I open my mouth, stretching to take him and I suck him right in, just as Knight pulls my panties to the side and sinks into my pussy.

An orgasm hits me.

"Fuuuck," Knight says. He strokes into me, deep, fingers digging into my hips. "When you come like that it's fucking amazing."

Reaper doesn't say a word, but he has me trapped in the vortex of his eyes, the depths, where so many things are speaking to me, showing secret places within. And I know what he wants, how he wants it. Not through that connection but how he guides me.

They're rougher hands than Knight's, and I like that command, the elemental level of it. And I take him in as far as I can.

I'm losing myself in their ministrations, in the way every part of me is engaged. I'm a vessel for giving and receiving pleasure and it's almost perfect. Almost.

When they come, deep down my throat and in my pussy, I fly.

This is what life here with them will be.

I clean Reaper's cock, and then move, on my hands and knees, to Knight, and clean his cock, sucking and licking our juices from it.

Not because they expect it. But because I want to.

They'd do the same, and they have.

And...it's almost perfect.

Almost.

I look up.

Dante's watching. No expression on his face. "Eight out of ten, Angel, for that performance."

"You're an ass." I get to my feet, straighten my clothes.

Knight goes to say something, but Reaper moves past me and puts a hand on his shoulder, effectively restraining him.

"Tell me something new."

Does Dante feel left out? Or is this his way of showing emotion? My gaze drops to his trousers. He's hard. So maybe it's both. And I can deal with his ways. Can't I?

But maybe I deserve more.

I wobble. "I know Knight and Reaper love me, and I know that you marked me to save me. That everything you did with Candice—you did it for me. But is that it?"

"What do you mean, is that it? That sounds like a lot to me, Angel," Dante says.

I take a shaking breath.

"The reason you haven't said *it*."

He stays quiet.

"Am I just a thing to slake your lust and a project as a way to thank the man who helped you? My father?"

Dante's gaze just holds mine and I can't read his face.

"Is that what I am to you?" I lick my lips. "You know I love Knight, and I love Reaper. And you know I love you."

Still he doesn't speak.

"Do you love me?"

Not one word.

Even Knight stays silent, and half turns to look at Dante.

It hits me. Dante's silent for a reason.

We both know, him and I, that I've committed the worst crime of all. Worse. I spoke it out loud.

I've fallen for him, too. He's the final piece of the love puzzle.

For this to work, I'd need all of them. I'd need all of it. All of them like they'd get all of me.

I look at him, and he's staring at me, like I'm the devil and not him, like I'm ripping his heart out and not the other way.

And I get it. Suddenly, horribly, I get it.

Everything Darcy said. All the things he'd said. He's Dante, but he's holding back.

He's holding back the words.

Some might say they're just words so why does it matter if he says it or not. They're just words.

But for him, they're not.

They're real. They're him.

What he doesn't say is as important as what he does. And if he doesn't say them, he's holding back, and I'm not enough for him to say them.

If he loves me, he needs to find a way, invite me in. With words.

It's not enough for him to get away with just feeling. He has to admit it. I want the opposite of denial. I know his language. But does he know mine? Reaper does. Knight knew it immediately.

And Dante?

He needs to try.

"I'm bored with this. I don't need to spell anything out. You're here. It's enough." He shifts, but doesn't actually move.

"No," I say, "it isn't."

"Sure it is. C'mon. it's just Dante. He'll come around." Knight shakes off Reaper and steps to me.

But I don't want someone to come around.

Yet I give it another go. One last leap. I know how he likes things. He needs the fight. The denial.

"I don't want to stay," I say. "Because of him. *Dante*."

He doesn't say a word. No one does.

"I don't want him."

I wait. I'm speaking his language. Denial. And with it, I'm offering him an easy ride. An easy path.

I'm giving him the chance to push me to the ground to take out his cock, to force me into admitting once more I love him, the chance to order me to stay so I know he feels love for me, too. To ease him into telling me after I told him.

Sure I said it, but I'll say it again in his language, his way.

I'm fucking speaking denial to him. Denial of him, my needs, wants, my love.

And he should get it.

He should see.

Or... maybe he does.

And he just doesn't want me.

Worse, maybe he thinks it's enough I'm here to just scratch his itches, accept whatever he feels like giving me.

And maybe he doesn't care at all.

Because he doesn't say a damn word.

I gulp down air and look at my stuff.

No, I need it all, I realize. If he can't even meet me half way, he has to go the entire distance, or not at all.

"Fuck you, Dante. This doesn't work without you."

I sweep up a bag.

And I turn.

I walk.

Out the door.

FORTY-THREE

Lizette

"God fucking damn it, Angel."

That's the first thing I hear when the elevator doors ding open.

Dante's breathing hard, there's sweat on his brow and his suit is not made for running downstairs.

Good. I hope it's ruined.

"Too late, Dante. Have a nice life." I only have one bag. It has my important things in it and I try to push past him but he grabs me. I shake him off, stalk across the foyer, and head out the door.

"Fuck." He races after me. "Where the absolute fuck do you think you're going, Angel?" He nabs my arm and I shake him off.

He clearly lets me go but moves between me and the door.

My breath pushes hard at my throat as I struggle to get the anger, the hurt, in check. "Where do you think?"

"I don't know." His eyes narrow as he sneers. "To sell your fucking wares?"

I snarl and hit him.

Almost.

He catches my hand.

"Be very fucking careful, Angel."

"Or what?" I glare. I want to pull free; I need to. But the sear of his fingers is too good, too right, to ignore. "You'll beat me up?"

"I'll tie you the fuck up and take out my nastiest whip and brand your ass so hard you'll think about getting it tattooed."

A jolt of desire shoots through me. "I hate you."

And he smiles very slow, very dirty.

Another jolt hits me and he's grasping my wrist, his thumb rubbing slowly over the sensitive spot that makes me want to moan.

"Oh, I know you fucking do," he says, shifting closer, looking down at me.

No one's in the foyer and even though I can see people passing through the glass paneled front door, I don't think they can see in. And if they could, if this foyer teemed with people, I think he'd keep on doing whatever he wanted.

"And you want me. Too bad you belong to us."

"No."

"Yes."

"I mean, there are different belongings and I'm choosing to say no. To this. To you in this place. I'll earn my keep by singing. I'll make extra waitressing. And I'll live in my room at Pandora's."

"That place is beyond expensive."

"Then I'll work for your competition." I don't know their competition and that club I did sing at was pure sleaze beneath the expensive layer. I wouldn't work there, but I don't care what he thinks. I need to lash out. "That place we went to?"

"Not happening and stop testing me."

"I'm not. I'm leaving and we will never be a thing again, fuck the bites and fuck you."

Dante nods slowly. "That is the idea, Angel."

This time, he grabs me and throws me over his shoulders, drags me back and into the elevator. He savagely punches the button as he dumps me on the floor.

"I should fucking skip straight to chaining you up and forget the whip, getting out the nastiest paddle I own out instead."

"Stop it. You don't have a paddle."

"I fucking do. Jesus. Isn't it enough I fucking bit you, licked your blood? Isn't it enough I told you my goddamn name? And you walk. I put my life on the line with that evil bitch who birthed you. And you fucking walk?"

"You put jack shit on the line, Dante." I manage to kick him.

Suddenly he slams his hand on an elevator button, and it jerks to a stop. He grabs me, shoving me against the wood paneling and he turns me, so I'm facing the wall. He rips up my skirt, pulling my ass to him as desire whips to a frenzy inside.

He shoves a finger into my pussy and fucks me with it. "You let them fucking take you in front of me? What kind of whore are you?"

"One that doesn't want or need you. One whose nice feelings really are hate."

"For them?" he asks against my ear. "Or me."

"You."

He pulls out and shoves his finger in my ass, fucking me hard.

I whimper.

"What the fuck do you want from me, Angel?" The hiss of his zipper is electric and my blood pounds as he pulls out his finger and slowly stretches me open. He sinks into me with his cock.

Then he starts to take me hard and everything's on fire, like this is right, like we belong, and I can barely breathe.

"What do you want from *me*?" I snarl. "Because I tried, but I don't want you anymore."

"Liar."

"You bore me."

"Lies."

"I...hate...you!"

"Fuck, yes!" He slams into me deep, coming, his pulsing orgasm sets off mine, and I almost cry out when he pulls out and turns me.

I'm all dancing pleasure centers, and he knows he got away with the same thing of just using sex over words, sex instead of giving his heart.

Crumbs.

I shove him away as he goes to kiss me.

"Fuck, Angel." He tucks himself away. "What do you want from me? Answer me."

I think about it. If he truly doesn't know...

The anger drains, and I lift my chin, a heaviness in my chest. "Nothing."

"Nothing? We're not playing sex games so—"

"I don't hate you; I just no longer want you. Not...not like this. We made that pact, and I'll live at the bar, down in my room. I'll sleep with the others. I'd love to say I won't with you, but I'll probably give in." I wrap my arms around my middle. "But wanting you? No, I don't want you like that. Not in a happily ever after ending kind of way."

He glares, then stabs the button on the elevator. Neither of us says a thing.

The ride up is only a few minutes. It feels like a few hours.

The elevator pings, and when the doors slide open, we're greeted by both Knight and Reaper exchanging money.

Did... Did they bet on me coming back?

Assholes.

Dante picks me up, marches me into the living room, and dumps me on the sofa.

"Let's get a few things straight," he says. "I do the denial, not you."

"That wasn't denial. I'm not playing your game. I tried and you didn't step up." I lick my lips. "I gave all of you my heart, equally, but you just trod on it, Dante. And maybe you think all this..."

I look around, put my hand to my throat where their bites have sunk down into me.

"Maybe you think all this equates love. It doesn't. It's a poor substitute. I have Reaper and Knight and I'm keeping them. But without you, me here doesn't work. And I think you like that. So you win, Dante. You win."

He closes his eyes and rubs them, and I want to cry.

Dante nods, and then he sinks down to one knee.

Suddenly, I can't breathe.

"I've been fighting how I feel for way too long, Angel. And denial in sex is good, but like this...it doesn't work. But you're wrong. This isn't a substitute I hoped—Fuck. I hoped you'd see it. How I feel."

"You have to tell me."

We stare at each other.

"I doesn't work if you don't tell me," I whisper. I...I need to hear it. From you."

"Lizette... Angel..." He takes my face in his hands and kisses me so sweet and gentle, I give a sob. "Don't cry, don't cry. I know I'm a fucking asshole. I'm sorry I hurt you, I'm sorry you felt the need to walk. I'm a coward with you because you undo me. I'm weak around you. Because I can't lock you up. I can't stop life from happening. All I can do is worry. You make me feel things I've never felt. Good and bad. I could fly with you. I could withstand the worst torture. What I couldn't stand is losing you. And that scares me. I love you, Angel. With all I am. I don't pretend to know much, but I know the three of us love you like we've never loved. You make us stronger. You *saved* us, Angel. I love you."

And then he kisses me.

Knight takes my hand and leads me away once Dante breaks the kiss. "We'll show you. I told you he loved you, by the way. You're ours, and you belong here with us."

They take me upstairs to a room on my floor. It's beautiful, delicate whites and mauves that turn buttery with the late afternoon sun. The bed is some huge custom job and there's a door that's open, leading to stairs.

"Our room, Liz. All of ours. For when we all want to fuck," Knight says. "You get to control it. You can sleep alone in your room, or with one of us, or here, with one, two or three of us. Up to you."

"I'll hunt you down inside and outdoors, but in here..." The soft, sinuous words from Reaper wrap around me and his meaning touches my heart.

"Earlier," Knight says, "was an appetizer. Let's have the real meal now. The feast. All of us."

They both start to strip me.

I look at Dante, the familiar heat rising in me, my body throbbing and growing wet for them. He sits, watching as the other two strip me down and Knight goes down on me, and Reaper feeds me his tattooed cock once more. I'm in heaven.

Dante watches.

I lose myself in the stroke of Reaper's cock in my mouth, and the hot slide of Knight's tongue and fingers in me and on my clit. Inside, the pressure builds, my body aching in that wonderful way that whispers release is coming.

Reaper starts to skull fuck me as Knight slides another finger into me and thrusts, his mouth sucking and licking my clit. He curls his fingers, hitting my G-spot with every stroke.

And then like the devil himself, Dante speaks.

"Don't come yet, Angel. I want you to come on me. I want us all to come together."

Reaper and Knight stop, pull free. Dante tosses Reaper something, and my eyes widen. It's rope.

Reaper turns me to my stomach, and ties my hands, then turns me back, so I'm vulnerable, open, unable to move my arms that are trapped by rope, trapped by my back and the bed.

Knight whispers, "Be a good girl for Daddy."

Reaper just locks eyes, and I can see his world in them, and it's a place I love, a place with room for me.

Then they move aside as Dante joins us, naked as he climbs up on the bed, over me, his cock at my entrance.

He looks down at me. "I fucking love you with everything I am, Angel."

And he thrusts into me, deep.

I cry out, a spasm of an orgasm hitting me.

"Naughty girl," he says, and bites my neck. "Hold off. I know you can do it."

"I hate you."

Delight lights up his face. "I know."

The language of denial, our language of love.

Like flowers and pretty games of gentle domination are Daddy-Dom Knight's. And rough, no frills, earthy honest talk is Reaper's.

They all speak to parts of my soul. And together we make one unit of love and sex and filth and sweet honesty.

Dante starts to thrust into me, whispering, "I love you."

I grit my teeth, holding on tenuously to my control, trying not to come. It's hard, there's an edge of pain to it where I hurt with the need for release as it builds and builds and builds. And he's getting close.

Oh, fuck, he's going to knot. He flips me and the next thing I know Reaper's behind me, thrusting into my ass and stroking my face, tilting me up to him. Knight sinks balls deep in my mouth. I'm stretched to the limit, and I can feel the strain from Dante as he tries not to come.

Denial, I think hysterically, is beautifully ugly and perfect.

Everyone's slipping, groaning and they're all knotting. A moment of panic hits me as I wonder how the hell I can have a knot in my mouth, but Knight pulls back a little so it's outside, and his cock—I swear to fucking god—gets bigger, longer, along with the knot.

It's like a gorgeous explosion as they all come, setting off the wildest, hottest orgasm in me. I transcend reality. I *am* the orgasm. I'm all of them and they're me. I can feel their seed. I can feel the euphoria in each of them as we all come hard. And it never ends. It's a wild, four-way, rolling, multiple orgasm.

That's how it feels for me. I'm not just one person. We're all each other.

And I never, ever want it to end.

Later, I sit, looking at our place, my new home, where we rule. "Do we change the name?"

Reaper's having a post-sex cigarette. I think we had three separate rounds. Maybe four. I lost count. The positions changed, and with them, the new pleasures to be found.

With three men and so many different arrangements, I'm eager to get back to exploring the possibilities sooner rather than later.

"Where's Knight?" I ask, a hand on Dante's thigh.

"Getting drinks," Dante mutters. "What do you mean with the name change? You mean Pandora's?"

"No," I say. "That's perfect."

"Which name?" Dante leans against the wall, pants on but not done up and I follow the line of hair heading straight to one of my happy towns.

"The Unholy Trinity."

"Because there are four of us?"

I nod.

"Fuck no," he says. "You sit on the throne. The three of us are the Unholy Trinity, bound by the ancient fucking marks on you, and yours on us, to complete the circle. But we are the Unholy Trinity, sworn to protect you."

"Do you believe that?"

"That we'd protect you? Fuck yes."

"And then what am I?"

"The Goddess we worship," Reaper says.

"That—" Knight says, coming back in and handing out drinks. He drops a kiss on my head. "—is the truth. This man speaks the truth, Angel."

"You're our Goddess, the Unholy Trinity's reason for being," Dante says.

"And what about my name?" I ask.

"What about it?"

"I've been through so much with you three... I don't really feel much like a Lizette anymore."

Something sparks in his dark eyes. "Oh?"

"I think I'll be Angel from now on. Permanently."

"I always thought it fit you." His gaze searches my face, and a smile lifts his lips. "All this time, I thought I would be the one to corrupt you, to bring you down to my level of Hell, but really, you became our saving grace. You saved us from total damnation, Angel."

"We're not divine by any means," Knight is quick to add. "But he's right. Now, we're complete."

Reaper nods.

I look at the three of them, full of so much love for each of them, it must be spilling everywhere.

The three of them lean in closer, surrounding me in their warmth and intoxicating alpha scents.

This is what Dad had meant about mating for love. This is the happiness he wanted for me. I just know it.

Darian, Sebastian, and Griffin—they are my pack.

My heart.

My home.

My *Heaven*.

EPILOGUE

Six Months Later

Angel

"What the fuck do you mean," Dante says, voice low, dangerous, "you're in the middle of changing your blockers?"

A thrill spirals up through me as through the pain it becomes hard to breathe.

His eyes glitter, his cock is hard, pushing at his pants as he starts to stalk me.

The bed I share with them is soft, full of blankets that caress me, make me safe. It's where I've been spending a lot of my time recently, nesting, and getting ready for my heat to hit in full bloom.

This time, with my heat, I know what's coming, the need, the way my body coils in, aching already for him.

For Knight.

For Reaper.

I raise my chin. "Knight found better, safer ones, and we

can adjust the dosage, let me go through heat on my terms, as intense or as mild as I want."

Dante's mouth turns in a smile, one that's full of sex.

I know he can smell me, my scent filling the air tangles with his...and it sends all thoughts spinning, making them hard to grab.

"As you want?"

I nod, fear and need and longing filling every cell.

"So you're telling me you're fucking potent? Unprotected?"

I scoot back to my pillows, body crying out in protest at my running from him.

He lunges, grabs a fist of my hair, the pain a relief, sexual, and I cry out as I slam against him, a fever burning as we touch.

Dante's mouth crashes down on mine, his tongue sliding in, warring with mine, conquering. The kiss relieves some of the fast-coming heat. It's only the fact he's kissing me, fucking me with his tongue, the wet heat of him in my veins that stops me from freaking out.

That and the state he's in.

He lifts his head.

The glitter in his gaze is feverish.

Oh, he's so damn hard, and I rub against him, earning a guttural groan.

"I'm going to fucking rut your brains out. And we're alone. No one else. It's been a while since I've had you to myself," he says, which is true. The other two alphas and the mate bond between us makes feelings and intentions known to all of us, so getting alone time with only one of the alphas has become basically nonexistent. "With Knight trying to put the pieces of the Council back together and Reaper out there stalking Candy, it's just you and me."

He's right about one thing—not too long ago, someone dropped an anonymous tip about Candice and her corruption, specifically her involvement in sex trafficking rings, bribery, blackmailing, and the embezzlement of Council money. Whoever revealed her had a lot of evidence to provide to authorities, so naturally, I assumed it was the Trinity who ousted her.

Of course, Dante denied it, but I'm not sure he'd tell me the truth either way.

After that, things happened really fast. The Council crumbled and Candice went missing. She ran for it, like the coward she is, and Knight moved in to try to rebuild the Council from the ground up. He's making some major adjustments in the department that oversees the omega-mate assignments, for obvious reasons.

"Fuck, you're turning me on," Dante growls, staring at me like a hungry wolf. "Like you flipped a switch. And guess what? I think rutting is the only way out of this. You won't be able to fucking move."

To my surprise, he leaves. The lock clicks.

I sit up, breathing fast. Everything in me is happening all at once, and fear laps against my skin for a moment until I look around.

The blankets are soft and silky and everything in here smells like me. Almost. There's a hint of Knight. The dark of Reaper. And the feral elemental scent of Dante that's all over me.

My body...I never expected it to ramp up into heat so fast, but maybe it's because I'm getting rid of the other blockers and I'm actually free. But my body, it pulsates with needs I know only mates can fulfil. They do it all the time, sometimes all at once.

But the room is low golden light, and gentle music starts, old melodies they know I love; they know me now.

A mixtape? Is that what this is? Something to soothe during my heat. But I just told—

I sob. It gets free and I slide down, wrapping the sweet-smelling blankets around me. I read they shouldn't smell like anything but me. Maybe there's something wrong with me because that heady subtle infusion of my mates makes it better.

So does the realization that Dante put on an act. He knew this was happening.

Of course he did. They don't keep secrets.

I think I drift in a haze of misery and happiness, a strange dichotomy. Part biology, part me knowing I'm part of something special. But while I'm drifting, I know it's not enough, my nest they made for me with love and tenderness in our room isn't enough.

Not when my body beats and aches with need.

The door opens, and he slides in, the fever still in his gaze. He has a hot water bottle, and he's not wearing shoes or a shirt. Just his trousers.

"You're fucking potent, Angel. Your heat puts us into rut."

And suddenly my insides cramp, and I need...I need...

Him.

Like he can hear me, he narrows his eyes, and he tosses the hot water bottle down.

Then he pulls the blankets off.

"Strip."

Shaking, I pull my dress up and off, and he leans in, biting one bare nipple and then the other as he peels my panties off, sending the heat inside skyrocketing. The ache pulsates, pushing at me deep inside and I devour him as he stands back, drops his trousers and boxers and pumps his huge cock.

My world is swimming, swirling, down to him and me and the wild drive. I reach for him but he's already there, on me, shoving my legs apart, and his cock pushes in, past my lips, splitting my pussy and wiping out that ache with pleasure.

It's instantaneous.

Like nothing I've ever experienced. I go from one to a hundred immediately and it's hot and wild. Dante grips my hair and fucks into me. Savage and deep.

I need more. Him deeper, harder and like he can read my thoughts he pounds into me, his cock swelling as I come. There's no build, it just happens, my entire body pulsating and radiating waves of wild pleasure, and I scream out. How can I not?

Because he's doing this for him. He's in rut, jackhammering harder and harder, and every deep slam is a thrill and another note of searing pleasure sings.

He comes hard, his cock expanding in me, bigger than that last time he knotted, and he keeps fucking me, and I cum again. It's hotter, better, deeper, pure body ecstasy from head to toe.

I can't stop and neither can Dante. I rock hard on his knot that's in me as he comes and comes, shaking, convulsing, savage words of carnage and love on his lips.

"Couldn't wait for me?"

I think I come even as Dante stops, and I don't know if it's from Knight being there, or from the knot that's slowly going down.

When Dante pulls out, finally, I'm both placated and unfulfilled.

"Out of the way, Dante," Knight says, already naked.

My head is swimming now as he rolls me on the bed, and pulls me on top, him below, thrusting up.

I lock eyes with Dante who's still there, naked, watching, on the far side of the bed, and then I close mine as Knight fucks up into me. Slower, softer and scratching my second itch of need.

He kisses me and I lose myself in that.

"Daddy," I whisper when we come up for air.

"Hold on, baby girl," he says, gripping my hips as I start to come yet again. It's a slower orgasm that takes its time spreading out, undulating, and as I shudder, rocking on him, rubbing my clit to get maximum relief, maximum pleasure, he groans.

"You've set us all in rut, Angel," Dante says. "So hang on tight."

I do.

"He's fucking right, Angel."

Knight changes from his softer ways to dark and hard and he knots, too. I scream out, arching my back as he flips us so he can hammer in, and I'm in a constant state of pleasure.

He swells, his big cock swollen, the knot stretching me to the limits, giving me something to get off on yet again.

I'm getting lost in sensation, and I don't even know how long it takes. He comes, and I shudder as he does so, needing more.

It's when he slows, fucking the knot in me leisurely that I'm aware someone's stroking my hair.

Reaper.

I smile at him, and then close my eyes, lifting my hips to Knight, and we slowly fuck, everything right inside again, until his knot goes down and he pulls out.

When I manage to focus, I open my eyes and look up, the soothing fingers still there. His wordlessness is something I need, and I don't know why.

I'm never at a loss around him, and he soothes her.

Even as the need starts up again.

But there's one thing I notice.

Reaper has the same fever expression in his dark eyes as Dante, as Knight, and it floors me.

Because it's for me.

I've made them all strong and vulnerable at the same time. The fever, the fierceness. The protectiveness is for me and I try to get up but I can't.

"Now," I say to him.

His offers me his private smile as the other two sit back on the bed and I can smell the sharpness of alcohol, sweet, too.

"*Now*." Reaper doesn't question, he just offers me that

syllable, and strips, clothes hitting the floor as I take in his inked skin.

My feverish need rises once more and he's there before I even reach for him, between my thighs, pushing up into me, splitting me for his pleasure. And mine.

Oh, God. I can see why some people want their heat natural. There's nothing like a cock inside to make pleasure burst like flame everywhere. There's nothing better than your mate or mates holding you.

This is pleasure on a different scale. It's out past the stratosphere.

He fucks me hard, rough, fingers rounding under me, pushing into my ass as he ruts up into me.

And I'm flying. I'm all elemental bliss and thrills as my orgasm pulsates out. Yet another one, this one rough, biting, and what I need.

It's hard and fast this fuck, this rut. My heat and his rut are a collision of sensations and he orgasms hard, knotting into me and using it to fuck me even harder as his finger thrusts into my ass, bringing a special extra to the violent pulse of my orgasm.

He fucks me hard through his knot until it's down, and when he pulls out, Dante slides over, giving me a drink. "It'll help, Angel."

I grasp the cup and swallow the burning liquid down, aware of the moisture beneath me, seeping from me and right now I'm satiated, but I can feel the edges stir.

Reaper lifts me into his arms as Knight lays down more blankets and when Reaper puts me back down on the bed, the three of them tuck me up, wrap around me.

"If it's too much, we can go," Knight says.

But Dante laughs and pulls me up against him, covers and all, as he bites my ear. "Fuck that. I'm not going anywhere. I'm here. I'll be taking you again, and protecting you."

"Agreed," says Reaper, on my other side.

Knight kisses my nose and lies at my head. "Yeah, I was just saying that to soothe her."

As my eyes get heavy, my heart swells, this is right. Perfect.

I don't think I've ever felt more loved, or safer in my life.

As I drift off, they fuss about me, keeping me warm, stroking my skin, and murmuring about how much they love me.

Sometimes it's hard to believe that I went from being an outsider, undocumented, and not really belonging anywhere, to now being the center of the Unholy Trinity.

And the luckiest omega in the world.

THE END

PRETTY LITTLE THINGS

They say there are two sides to every story...
Now both sides want to own me, claim me as theirs.

I'm a professional thief. High security to picking pockets, doesn't matter. I'm an expert.

So when I'm hired to steal a priceless necklace by a wealthy stranger, I don't hesitate to take the job. Little do I know, the seemingly normal task will put me in the middle of two of the deadliest gangs in The Quinate.

And their leaders might just kill me.

Hendrick Agnossio and Jac Miller are the heads of their

families—both young and handsome, but violent and brutal killers who see me as their new prize.

Their bloody rivalry is generations in the making, and I've been thrown right smack in the middle of it.

Even though I refuse to be part of their games, I can't escape them. They're everywhere, poisoning my thoughts, under my skin, heating my blood...

I may be a thief, but they've stolen my life.

Maybe even my heart.

More Books by Brooke Harper

MAFIA ROSE

Wilt

Thorn

Bloom

Wild: A Mafia Rose Novella

Root: A Mafia Rose Novel

THIEVES' HONOR

Pretty Little Things

Wicked Little Lies

CRUEL EMPIRE

All That Glitters

Fool's Gold

OMEGAS IN BLOOM

Violet

Iris

Marigold

Dahlia

Rue

STANDALONES

A Mafia Mistress for Christmas

Fallen Omega: A Dark Omegaverse

All Eyes on Me: A Short Story

About the Author

Brooke Harper creates dark and sexy worlds for her characters to play. A lover of strong coffee and old tombstones, she spins dark tales of sex and sin, pain and passion, and misery and madness that'll have you flipping the pages and begging for more.

AuthorBrookeHarper.com

Join Brooke's Reader Group

Made in the USA
Middletown, DE
12 October 2024

62525763R00276